A pair of booted feet appeared in the firebox, dangling down uncertainly, both boots as worn as harness leather. *Whumpf!* The boots crashed through the crumpled newspaper to the hearth. A pair of skinny legs in mud-fouled khaki materialized in the shadows above them. With a grunt and a muttered curse, a man in a heavy red-plaid coat kicked away the papers, ducked out of the firebox, and hobbled over to the tree, carrying what looked like a grungy World War II duffel bag.

Santa Claus? wondered Danny. Father Christmas? Kris Kringle? Saint Nick? A ghost? Or just a chimney-shinnying thief?

—From "Icicle Music"

Plus many more
spine-tingling tales
of Christmas shudders!

Tor Anthologies Edited by
David G. Hartwell

The Ascent of Wonder (with Kathryn Cramer)
The Dark Descent
Foundations of Fear
Christmas Magic
Christmas Stars
Christmas Forever
Northern Stars (with Glenn Grant)
Spirits of Christmas (with Kathryn Cramer)
The Science Fiction Century
Visions of Wonder (with Milton T. Wolf)
Centaurus (with Damien Broderick)

SPIRITS of Christmas

Edited by
DAVID G. HARTWELL and
KATHRYN CRAMER

A TOM DOHERTY ASSOCIATES BOOK
NEW YORK

This is a work of fiction. All the characters and events portrayed in this book are fictitious, and any resemblance to real people or incidents is purely coincidental.

SPIRITS OF CHRISTMAS

Copyright © 1989 by David G. Hartwell and Kathryn Cramer

Cover art by Nicholas Jainschigg

A Tor Book
Published by Tom Doherty Associates, LLC
175 Fifth Avenue
New York, NY 10010

www.tor.com

Tor® is a registered trademark of Tom Doherty Associates, LLC.

ISBN: 0-812-55159-1

First Tor edition: November 1995

Printed in the United States of America

0 9 8 7 6 5 4 3 2

To Alison and Geoffrey,
my Christmas Spirits—DGH
and
to Jim Young, who was cheerful
throughout the preparation of
this book in the hectic weeks
before our wedding. —KC

ACKNOWLEDGMENTS

The editors wish to acknowledge the help of the following people in the preparation of this book: Jessica Amanda Salmonson, L. W. Currey, Susan Ann Protter, Stephen Jones, and Richard Dalby.

The editors also wish to thank the following authors for valiantly writing to deadline: Greg Cox, Martha Soukup, Gene Wolfe, James Morrow, Michael Bishop, Chet Williamson.

Finally, we wish to thank Bill Thompson, our editor.

CONTENTS

INTRODUCTION

The tradition of Christmas ghosts—of the fears and hopes of the supernatural expressed in the form of stories at Christmas—reached its first peak of popularity in the 1840s, with the publication of the famous Christmas books of Charles Dickens. The most successful of them, *A Christmas Carol*, is a classic of the literature of our language. In these moral tales Dickens reinvented Christmas for the modern era, at least for the English-speaking world. These are stories of Christmas trees, Christmas gifts, Christmas meals, Christmas sentiments, Christmas memories, and ghosts. Although Washington Irving popularized the Christmas holiday somewhat earlier in nearly the same form, with the intent of arousing sentiments in his readers, Dickens's inspiration was to link the holiday to the secular supernatural.

And it was Dickens, the editor of such magazines as *All the Year Round* and *Household Words*, who encouraged other writers to produce ghost stories for the Christmas issues of his magazines, thus founding and building a popular tradition linking Christmas and ghosts. But as we discovered when we began to research our first volume of these tales (*Christmas Ghosts*, Arbor House, 1987; Dell, 1988), most ghost stories from the tradition are actually tales published or told *at* Christmas, but not tales *about* Christmas. Thus in recent decades, although the ghost story has remained a popular form, it has become to a large extent dissociated from Christmas. The Christmas ghost tradition, which generated such classics as Henry James's *The Turn of the Screw* and the stories of M.R. James, has become something we know of only from the one masterwork of Dickens, *A Christmas Carol*, and perhaps from films such as *It's a Wonderful Life* and *Miracle on 34th Street*, which are rerun every holiday season.

So we have gone back through the decades to find a garland of Christmas delights from this tradition that are stories of Christmas with ghosts in them, and we have in addition discovered a few contemporary pieces that carry on the tradition (even one science-fiction Christmas ghost story!) and, as a special contribution to reviving the form today, have invited several writers to create original pieces especially for this book.

Commentators in recent years on the Christmas ghost tradition have tended to emphasize the fearful and uncanny aspect of the Christmas ghost tradition. Angela Carter, for instance, has characterized the intent of the form ("to beguile our Christmas good cheer with a little, delicious shiver of unease") and concluded:

The Christmas ghost-story, the Christmas spine-chiller, horror for Christmas—somehow it's become part and parcel of the whole Dickensy seasonal myth of snow and holly and churchbells and groaning boards. At a time of goodwill to all men, we can contemplate with equanimity the idea that beings might exist that bear us positive malice ... and the titillation of fear adds a special savour to the rich diet, as if a shiver down the spine were an aid to digestion. (*Radio Times*, 1975)

Peter Haining, the anthologist and scholar, describes the tradition as "our bill of Christmas horror fare."

Yet from our reading of stories in the tradition, we find the form a great deal broader and more varied in tone and atmosphere, from the comic to the horrific, from the romantic to the sentimental to the ironic, and we have included examples from the entire range, both historic and contemporary, to represent the whole tradition. We have brought together ghosts of lovers and at least one ghost who brings lovers together, evil ghosts and angelic ghosts, two different men who haunt themselves, gaggles of ghosts, and at least one ghost who wasn't there, all at Christmas.

What is the Christmas ghost story without Dickens? So we reprint the last and one of the least known of his great Christmas novellas, *The Haunted Man*, in which the theme of memory and its beneficial effect on moral life common to all Dickens's Christmas stories is most highly developed. The idea that we need to remember sorrow, wrong, trouble, and dread in order to forgive and be forgiven is one of the great themes of the whole Christmas ghost tradition, one that we can see in many other tales throughout the nearly 150 years of stories, for instance, in both the first and the last story in this book. The conversion of the reader, as well as of a character in the story, by means of the supernatural from a negative to a positive and charitable state of mind is the point of this moral tale, a point that spread in ripples through the decades, even in parody. Robert Louis Stevenson said of Dickens's Christmas books, ". . . Oh dear God, they are *good*—and I feel so good after them—I shall do good and lose no time—I want to go out and comfort someone—I *shall* give money. Oh, what a jolly thing it is for a man to have written books like these and just filled people's hearts with pity." And in *The Haunted Man* Dickens arrived at one of his seminal insights into society and social criticism, one that formed the bedrock of his later novels: that what is nobody's fault must be everybody's fault.

Most of the stories in this book have not been reprinted in recent decades, and regardless of age or style, they all share an energy and a freshness that is timeless. And seven of the stories are brand new. For Christmas in our time remains a special holiday, a time of mystery and of the supernatural; the Spirits of the season have a power as at no other time of year to arouse in us feelings deadened by the pressures of ordinary daily life. The power of the stories in this volume is to reawaken the Christmas spirit in us.

Many of the stories found herein can be read aloud— we have read some of them that way—and we recommend that you try, perhaps, to revive that part of the Christmas ghost tradition during your holiday season. A Christmas ghost story read aloud to a group of family and friends was a thrill for generations past, and we can testify from experience that the powers of the Christmas ghost tradition have not waned. Like fine wines, the stories have aged well and, from sweet to tart, still tickle the palate.

DAVID G. HARTWELL

A ghost seeks a doctor to save a ghost's life.

THE PRESCRIPTION
———

Marjorie Bowen

John Cuming collected ghost stories; he always declared that this was the best that he knew, although it was partially secondhand and contained a mystery that had no reasonable solution, while most really good ghost stories allow of a plausible explanation, even if it is one as feeble as a dream, excusing all; or a hallucination or a crude deception. Cuming told the story rather well. The first part of it at least had come under his own observation and been carefully noted by him in the flat green book which he kept for the record of all curious cases of this sort. He was a shrewd and trained observer; he honestly restrained his love of drama from leading him into embellishing facts. Cuming told the story to us all on the most suitable occasion—Christmas Eve—and prefaced it with a little homily.

"You all know the good old saw—'The more it changes the more it is the same thing'—and I should like you to notice that this extremely up-to-date ultra-modern ghost story is really almost exactly the same as one that might have puzzled Babylonian or Assyrian sages. I can give you the first start of the tale in my own words, but the second part will have to be in the words of someone else. They were, however, most carefully and scrupulously taken down. As for the conclusion, I must leave you to draw that for yourselves—each according to your own mood, fancy, and temperament; it may be that you will all think of the same solution, it may be that you will each think of a different one, and it may be that everyone will be left wondering."

Having thus enjoyed himself by whetting our curiosity, Cumings settled himself down comfortably in his deep armchair and unfolded his tale.

"It was about five years ago. I don't wish to be exact with time, and of course I shall alter names—that's one of the first rules of the game, isn't it? Well, whenever it was, I was the guest of a—Mrs. Janey we will call her—who was, to some extent, a friend of mine; an intelligent, lively, rather bustling sort of woman who had the knack of gathering interesting people about her. She had lately taken a new house in Buckinghamshire. It stood in the grounds of one of those large estates which are now so frequently being broken up. She was very pleased with the house, which was quite new and had only been finished a year, and seemed, according to her own rather excited imagination, in every way desirable. I don't want to emphasize anything about the house except that it was new and did stand on the verge, as it were, of this large old estate, which had belonged to one of those notable English families now extinct and completely forgotten. I am no antiquarian or connoisseur in architecture, and the rather blatant modernity of the house did not offend me. I was able to appreciate its comfort and to enjoy what Mrs. Janey rather maddeningly called 'the old-world gardens,' which were really a section of the larger gardens of the vanished mansion which had once commanded this domain. Mrs. Janey, I should tell you, knew nothing about the neighborhood nor anyone who lived there, except that for the first it was very convenient for town, and for the second she believed that they were all 'nice' people, not likely to bother one. I was slightly disappointed with the crowd she had gathered together at Christmas. They were all people whom either I knew too well or whom I didn't wish to know at all, and at first the party showed signs of being extremely flat. Mrs. Janey seemed to perceive this too, and with rather nervous haste produced, on Christmas Eve, a trump card in the way of amusement—a professional medium, called Mrs. Mahogany, because that could not possibly have been her name. Some of us 'believed in,' as the saying goes, mediums, and some didn't; but we were all willing to be diverted by the experiment. Mrs. Janey continually lamented that a certain Dr. Dilke would not be present. He was going to be one of the party, but had been detained in town and would not reach Verrall, which was the name of the house, until later, and the medium, it seemed, could not stay; for she, being a personage in great demand, must go on to a further engagement. I, of course, like everyone else possessed of an intelligent curiosity and a certain amount of leisure, had been to mediums before. I had been slightly impressed, slightly disgusted, and very much bewildered, and on the whole had decided to let the matter alone, considering that I really preferred the more direct and old-fashioned method of getting in touch with what we used to call 'The Unseen.' This sitting in the great new house seemed rather banal. I could understand in some haunted old manor that a clairvoyant, or a clairaudient, or a trance-medium might have found something interesting to say, but what was she going to get out of Mrs. Janey's bright, brilliant, and comfortable dwelling?

"Mrs. Mahogany was a nondescript sort of woman—neither young nor old, neither clever nor stupid, neither dark nor fair, placid, and not in the least self-conscious. After an extremely good luncheon (it was a gloomy, stormy afternoon) we all sat down in a circle in the cheerful drawing room; the curtains were pulled across the dreary prospect of gray sky and gray landscape, and we had merely the light of the fire. We sat quite close together in order to increase the 'the power,' as Mrs. Mahogany said, and the medium sat in the middle, with no special precautions against trickery; but we all knew that trickery would have been really impossible, and we were quite prepared to be tremendously impressed and startled if any manifestations took place. I think we all felt rather foolish, as we did not know each other very well, sitting around there, staring at this very ordinary, rather common, stout little woman, who kept nervously pulling a little tippet of gray wool over her shoulders, closing her eyes and muttering, while she twisted her fingers together. When we had sat silent for about ten minutes Mrs. Janey announced in a rather raw whisper that the medium had gone into a trance. 'Beautifully,' she added. I thought that Mrs. Mahogany did not look at all beautiful. Her communication began with a lot of rambling talk which had no point at all, and a good deal of generalization under which I think we all became a little restive. There was too much of various spirits who had all sorts of ordinary names, just regular Toms, Dicks, and Harrys of the spirit world, floating round behind us, their arms full of flowers and their mouths of

good will, all rather pointless. And though, occasionally, a Tom, a Dick, or a Harry was identified by some
of us, it wasn't very convincing, and, what was worse,
not very interesting. We got, however, our surprise and
our shock, because Mrs. Mahogany began suddenly to
writhe into ugly contortions and called out in a loud
voice, quite different from the one that she had hitherto
used: 'Murder!'

"This word gave us all a little thrill, and we leaned
forward eagerly to hear what further she had to say.
With every sign of distress and horror Mrs. Mahogany
began to speak:

" 'He's murdered her. Oh, how dreadful. Look at
him! Can't somebody stop him? It's so near here, too.
He tried to save her. He was sorry, you know. Oh, how
dreadful! Look at him—he's borne it as long as he can,
and now he's murdered her! I see him mixing it in a
glass. Oh, isn't it awful that no one could have saved
her—and he was so terribly remorseful afterward. Oh,
how dreadful! How horrible!'

"She ended in a whimpering of fright and horror, and
Mrs. Janey, who seemed an adept at this sort of thing,
leaned forward and asked eagerly:

" 'Can't you get the name—can't you find out who it
is? Why do you get that here?'

" 'I don't know,' muttered the medium. 'It's somewhere near here—a house, an old dark house, and there
are curtains of mauve velvet—do you call it mauve? a
kind of blue red—at the windows. There's a garden outside with a fishpond and you go through a low doorway
and down stone steps.'

" 'It isn't near here,' said Mrs. Janey decidedly. 'All
the houses are new.'

" 'The house is near here,' persisted the medium. 'I

am walking through it now; I can see the room, I can
see that poor, poor woman, and a glass of milk—'

" 'I wish you'd get the name,' insisted Mrs. Janey,
and she cast a look, as I thought not without suspicion,
round the circle. 'You can't be getting this from my
house, you know, Mrs. Mahogany,' she added decidedly, 'it must be given out by someone here—
something they've read or seen, you know,' she said, to
reassure us that our characters were not in dispute.

"But the medium replied drowsily, 'No, it's somewhere near here. I see a light dress covered with small
roses. If he could have got help he would have gone for
it, but there was no one; so all his remorse was useless. . . .'

"No further urging would induce the medium to say
more; soon afterward she came out of the trance, and all
of us, I think, felt that she had made rather a stupid
blunder by introducing this vague piece of melodrama,
and if it was, as we suspected, a cheap attempt to give
a ghostly and mysterious atmosphere to Christmas Eve,
it was a failure.

"When Mrs. Mahogany, blinking round her, said
brightly, 'Well, here I am again! I wonder if I said anything that interested you?' we all replied rather coldly,
'Of course it has been most interesting, but there hasn't
been anything definite.' And I think that even Mrs.
Janey felt that the sitting had been rather a disappoint-
ment, and she suggested that if the weather was really
too horrible to venture out of doors we should sit round
the fire and tell old-fashioned ghost stories. 'The kind,'
she said brightly, 'that are about bones and chairs and
shrouds. I really think that is the most thrilling kind after all.' Then, with some embarrassment, and when
Mrs. Mahogany had left the room, she suggested that

not one of us should say anything about what the medium had said in her trance.

" 'It really was rather absurd,' said our hostess, 'and it would make me look a little foolish if it got about; you know some people think these mediums are absolute fakes, and anyhow, the whole thing, I am afraid, was quite stupid. She must have got her contacts mixed. There is no old house about here and never has been since the original Verrall was pulled down, and that's a good fifty years ago, I believe, from what the estate agent told me; and as for a murder, I never heard the shadow of any such story.'

"We all agreed not to mention what the medium had said, and did this with the more heartiness as we were, not any one of us, impressed. The feeling was rather that Mrs. Mahogany had been obliged to say something and had said that. . . .

"Well," said Cuming comfortably, "that is the first part of my story, and I daresay you'll think it's dull enough. Now we come to the second part.

"Latish that evening Dr. Dilke arrived. He was not in any way a remarkable man, just an ordinary successful physician, and I refuse to say that he was suffering from overwork or nervous strain; you know that is so often put into this kind of story as a sort of excuse for what happens afterward. On the contrary, Dr. Dilke seemed to be in the most robust of health and the most cheerful frame of mind, and quite prepared to make the most of his brief holiday. The car that fetched him from the station was taking Mrs. Mahogany away, and the doctor and the medium met for just a moment in the hall. Mrs. Janey did not trouble to introduce them, but without waiting for this, Mrs. Mahogany turned to the doctor, and looking at him fixedly, said, 'You're very psychic, aren't you?' And upon that Mrs. Janey was forced to say hastily: 'This is Mrs. Mahogany, Dr. Dilke, the famous medium.'

"The physician was indifferently impressed. 'I really don't know,' he answered, smiling. 'I have never gone in for that sort of thing. I shouldn't think I am what you call "psychic" really; I have had a hard, scientific training, and that rather knocks the bottom out of fantasies.'

" 'Well, you are, you know,' said Mrs. Mahogany; 'I felt it at once; I shouldn't be at all surprised if you had some strange experience one of these days.'

"Mrs. Mahogany left the house and was duly driven away to the station. I want to make the point very clear that she and Dr. Dilke did not meet again and that they held no communication except those few words in the hall spoken in the presence of Mrs. Janey. Of course Dr. Dilke got twitted a good deal about what the medium had said; it made quite a topic of conversation during dinner and after dinner, and we all had queer little ghost stories or incidents of what we considered 'psychic' experiences to trot out and discuss. Dr. Dilke remained civil, amused, but entirely unconvinced. He had what he called a material, or physical, or medical explanation for almost everything that we said, and, apart from all these explanations he added, with some justice, that human credulity was such that there was always someone who would accept and embellish anything, however wild, unlikely, or grotesque it was.

" 'I should rather like to hear what you would say if such an experience happened to you,' Mrs. Janey challenged him; 'whether you use the ancient terms of "ghost," "witches," "black magic," and so on, or whether you speak in modern terms like "medium," "clairvoyance," "psychic contacts," and all the rest of it; well, it seems one is in a bit of a tangle anyhow, and if any queer thing ever happens to you—'

"Dr. Dilke broke in pleasantly: 'Well, if it ever does I will let you all know about it, and I dare say I shall have an explanation to add at the end of the tale.'

"When we all met again the next morning we rather hoped that Dr. Dilke *would* have something to tell us— some odd experience that might have befallen him in the night, new as the house was, and banal as was his bedroom. He told us, of course, that he had passed a perfectly good night.

"We most of us went to the morning service in the small church that had once been the chapel belonging to the demolished mansion, and which had some rather curious monuments inside and in the churchyard. As I went in I noticed a mortuary chapel with niches for the coffins to be stood upright, now whitewashed and used as a sacristy. The monuments and mural tablets were mostly to the memory of members of the family of Verrall—the Verralls of Verrall Hall, who appeared to have been people of little interest or distinction. Dr. Dilke sat beside me, and I, having nothing better to do through the more familiar and monotonous portions of the service, found myself idly looking at the mural tablet beyond him. This was a large slab of black marble deeply cut with a very worn Latin inscription which I found, unconsciously, I was spelling out. The stone, it seemed, commemorated a woman who had been, of course, the possessor of all the virtues; her name was Philadelphia Carwithen, and I rather pleasantly sampled the flavor of that ancient name—Philadelphia. Then I noticed a smaller inscription at the bottom of the slab, which indicated that the lady's husband also rested in the vault; he had died suddenly about six months after her—of grief at her loss, I thought, scenting out a pretty romance.

"As we walked home across the frost-bitten fields

and icy lanes Dr. Dilke, who walked beside me, as he had sat beside me in church, began to complain of cold; he said he believed that he had caught a chill. I was rather amused to hear this old-womanish expression on the lips of so distinguished a physician, and I told him that I had been taught in my more enlightened days that there was no such thing as 'catching a chill.' To my surprise he did not laugh at this, but said:

" 'Oh, yes, there is, and I believe I've got it—I keep on shivering; I think it was that slab of black stone I was sitting next. It was as cold as ice, for I touched it, and it seemed to me exuding moisture—some of that old stone does, you know; it's always, as it were, sweating; and I felt exactly as if I were sitting next a slab of ice from which a cold wind was blowing; it was really as if it penetrated my flesh.'

"He looked pale, and I thought how disagreeable it would be for us all, and particularly for Mrs. Janey, if the good man was to be taken ill in the midst of her already not-too-successful Christmas party. Dr. Dilke seemed, too, in that ill-humor which so often presages an illness; he was quite peevish about the church and the service, and the fact that he had been asked to go there.

" 'These places are nothing but charnel houses, after all,' he said fretfully; 'one sits there among all those rotting bones, with that damp marble at one's side. . . .'

" 'It is supposed to give you atmosphere,' " I said. 'The atmosphere of an old-fashioned Christmas. . . . Did you notice who your black stone was erected "to the memory of"?' I asked, and the doctor replied that he had not.

" 'It was to a young woman—a young woman, I took it, and her husband: "Philadelphia Carwithen," I noticed that, and of course there was a long eulogy of her vir-

tues, and then underneath it just said that he had died a
few months afterward. As far as I could see it was the
only example of that name in the church—all the rest
were Verralls. I suppose they were strangers here.'

" 'What was the date?' asked the doctor, and I replied
that really I had not been able to make it out, for where
the Roman figures came the stone had been very worn.

"The day ambled along somehow, with games, diver-
sions, and plenty of good food and drink, and toward
the evening we began to feel a little more satisfied with
each other and our hostess. Only Dr. Dilke remained a
little peevish and apart, and this was remarkable in one
who was obviously of a robust temperament and an
even temper. He still continued to talk of a 'chill,' and
I did notice that he shuddered once or twice, and continually sat near the large fire which Mrs. Janey had
rather laboriously arranged in imitation of what she
would call 'the good old times.'

"That evening, the evening of Christmas Day, there
was no talk whatever of ghosts or psychic matters; our
discussions were entirely topical and of mundane matters, in which Dr. Dilke, who seemed to have recovered
his spirits, took his part with ability and agreeableness.
When it was time to break up I asked him, half in jest,
about his mysterious chill, and he looked at me with
some surprise and appeared to have forgotten that he
had ever said he had got such a thing; the impression,
whatever it was, which he had received in the church,
had evidently been effaced from his mind. I wish to
make that quite clear.

"The next morning Dr. Dilke appeared very late at
the breakfast table, and when he did so his looks were
matter for hints and comment; he was pale, distracted,
troubled, untidy in his dress, absent in his manner, and

I, at least, instantly recalled what he had said yesterday, and feared he was sickening for some illness.

"On Mrs. Janey putting to him some direct question as to his looks and manner, so strange and so troubled, he replied rather sharply, 'Well, I don't know what you can expect from a fellow who's been up all night. I thought I came down here for a rest.'

"We all looked at him as he dropped into his place and began to drink his coffee with eager gusto; I noticed that he continually shivered. There was something about this astounding statement and his curious appearance which held us all discreetly silent. We waited for further developments before committing ourselves; even Mrs. Janey, whom I had never thought of as tactful, contrived to say casually:

" 'Up all night, doctor. Couldn't you sleep, then? I'm so sorry if your bed wasn't comfortable.'

" 'The bed was all right,' he answered, 'that made me the more sorry to leave it. Haven't you got a local doctor who can take the local cases?' he added.

" 'Why, of course we have; there's Dr. Armstrong and Dr. Fraser—I made sure about that before I came here.'

" 'Well, then,' demanded Dr. Dilke angrily, 'why on earth couldn't one of them have gone last night?'

"Mrs. Janey looked at me helplessly, and I, obeying her glance, took up the matter.

" 'What do you mean, doctor? Do you mean that you were called out of your bed last night to attend a case?' I asked deliberately.

" 'Of course I was—I only got back with the dawn.'

"Here Mrs. Janey could not forbear breaking in.

" 'But whoever could it have been? I know nobody about here yet, at least, only one or two people by name, and they would not be aware that you were here.

And how did you get out of the house? It's locked every night.'

"Then the doctor gave his story in rather, I must confess, a confused fashion, and yet with an earnest conviction that he was speaking the simple truth. It was broken up a good deal by ejaculations and comments from the rest of us, but I give it you here shorn of all that and exactly as I put it down in my notebook afterward.

" 'I was awakened by a tap at the door. I was instantly wide-awake and I said, "Come in." I thought immediately that probably someone in the house was ill—a doctor, you know, is always ready for these emergencies. The door opened at once, and a man entered holding a small ordinary storm-lantern. I noticed nothing peculiar about the man. He had a dark greatcoat on, and appeared extremely anxious. "I am sorry to disturb you," he said at once, "but there is a young woman dangerously ill. I want you to come and see her." I, somehow, did not think of arguing or of suggesting that there were other medical men in the neighborhood, or of asking how it was he knew of my presence at Verrall. I dressed myself quickly and accompanied him out of the house. He opened the front door without any trouble, and it did not occur to me to ask him how it was he had obtained either admission or egress. There was a small carriage outside the door, such a one as you may still see in isolated country places, but such a one as I was certainly surprised to see here. I could not very well make out either the horse or the driver, for, though the moon was high in the heavens, it was frequently obscured by clouds. I got into the carriage and noticed, as I have often noticed before in these ancient vehicles, a most repulsive smell of decay and damp. My companion got in beside me. He did not speak a word during the whole of the journey, which was, I have the impression, extremely long. I had also the sense that he was in the greatest trouble, anguish, and almost despair; I do not know why I did not question him. I should tell you that he had drawn down the blinds of the carriage and we traveled in darkness, yet I was perfectly aware of his presence and seemed to see him in his heavy dark greatcoat turned up round the chin, his black hair low on his forehead, and his anxious, furtive dark eyes. I think I may have gone to sleep in the carriage. I was tired and cold. I was aware, however, when it stopped, and of my companion opening the door and helping me out. We went through a garden, down some steps and past a fishpond; I could see by the moonlight the silver and gold shapes of fishes slipping in and out of the black water. We entered the house by a side door—I remember that very distinctly—and went up what seemed to be some secret or seldom-used stairs, and into a bedroom. I was, by now, quite alert, as one is when one gets into the presence of the patient, and said to myself, "What a fool I've been, I've brought nothing with me," and I tried to remember, but could not quite do so, whether or not I had brought anything with me—my cases and so on—to Verrall. The room was very badly lighted, but a certain illumination—I could not say whether it came from any artificial light within the room or merely from the moonlight through the open window, draped with mauve velvet curtains—fell on the bed, and there I saw my patient. She was a young woman, who, I surmised, would have been, when in health, of considerable though coarse charm. She was now in great suffering, twisted and contorted with agony, and in her struggles of anguish had pulled and torn the bedclothes into a heap. I noticed that she wore a dress of some light material spotted with small roses, and it occurred to me at once that she had been taken ill during the daytime and must have lain thus in great pain for many hours, and I turned with some reproach to the man who had fetched me and demanded why help had not been sought sooner. For answer he wrung his hands—a gesture that I do not remember having noticed in any human being before; one hears a great deal of hands being wrung; but one does not so often see it. This man, I remember distinctly, wrung his hands, and muttered, "Do what you can for her—do what you can!" I feared that this would be very little. I endeavored to make an examination of the patient, but owing to her half-delirious struggles this was very difficult; she was, however, I thought, likely to die, and of what malady I could not determine. There was a table near by on which lay some papers—one I took to be a will—and a glass in which there had been milk. I do not remember seeing anything else in the room—the light was so bad. I endeavored to question the man, whom I took to be the husband, but without any success. He merely repeated his monotonous appeal for me to save her. Then I was aware of a sound outside the room—of a woman laughing, perpetually and shrilly laughing. "Pray stop that," I cried to the man; "who have you got in the house—a lunatic?" But he took no notice of my appeal, merely repeating his own hushed lamentations. The sick woman appeared to hear that demonical laughter outside, and raising herself on one elbow said, "You have destroyed me and you may well laugh."

" 'I sat down at the table on which were the papers and the glass half full of milk, and wrote a prescription on a sheet torn out of my notebook. The man snatched it eagerly. "I don't know when and where you can get that made up," I said, "but it's the only hope." At this he seemed wishful for me to depart, as wishful as he

had been for me to come. "That's all I want," he said.
He took me by the arm and led me out of the house by
the same back stairs. As I descended I still heard those
two dreadful sounds—the thin laughter of the woman I
had not seen, and the groans, becoming every moment
fainter, of the young woman whom I had seen. The carriage was waiting for me, and I was driven back by the
same way I had come. When I reached the house and
my room I saw the dawn just breaking. I rested till I
heard the breakfast gong. I suppose some time had gone
by since I returned to the house, but I wasn't quite
aware of it; all through the night I had rather lost the
sense of time.'

"When Dr. Dilke had finished his narrative, which I
give here badly—but, I hope, to the point—we all
glanced at each other rather uncomfortably, for who was
to tell a man like Dr. Dilke that he had been suffering
from a severe hallucination? It was, of course, quite impossible that he could have left the house and gone
through the peculiar scenes he had described, and it
seemed extraordinary that he could for a moment have
believed that he had done so. What was even more remarkable was that so many points of this story agreed
with what the medium, Mrs. Mahogany, had said in her
trance. We recognized the frock with the roses, the
mauve velvet curtains, the glass of milk, the man who
had fetched Dr. Dilke sounded like the murderer, and
the unfortunate woman writhing on the bed sounded
like the victim; but how had the doctor got hold of
these particulars? We all knew that he had not spoken to
Mrs. Mahogany, and each suspected the other of having
told him what the medium had said, and that this having
wrought on his mind he had the dream, vision, or hallucination he had just described to us. I must add that
this was found afterward to be wholly false; we were all

reliable people and there was not a shadow of doubt we
had all kept our counsel about Mrs. Mahogany. In fact,
none of us had been alone with Dr. Dilke the previous
day for more than a moment or so save myself, who
had walked with him from the church, when we had
certainly spoken of nothing except the black 'stone in
the church and the chill which he had said emanated
from it. . . . Well, to put the matter as briefly as possible, and to leave out a great deal of amazement and
wonder, explanation, and so on, we will come to the
point when Dr. Dilke was finally persuaded that he had
not left Verrall all the night. When his story was taken
to pieces and put before him, as it were, in the raw, he
himself recognized many absurdities: How could the
man have come straight to his bedroom? How could
he have left the house?—the doors were locked every
night, there was no doubt about that. Where did the carriage come from and where was the house to which he
had been taken? And who could possibly have known
of his presence in the neighborhood? Had not, too, the
scene in the house to which he was taken all the resemblance of a nightmare? Who was it laughing in the other
room? What was the mysterious illness that was de-
stroying the young woman? Who was the black-browed
man who had fetched him? And, in these days of telephone and motorcars, people didn't go out in the old-
fashioned one-horse carriages to fetch doctors from
miles away in the case of dangerous illness.

"Dr. Dilke was finally silenced, uneasy, but not convinced. I could see that he disliked intensely the idea
that he had been the victim of a hallucination and that
he equally intensely regretted the impulse which had
made him relate his extraordinary adventure of the
night. I could only conclude that he must have done so
while still, to an extent, under the influence of his delu-

sion, which had been so strong that never for a moment had he questioned the reality of it. Though he was forced at last to allow us to put the whole thing down as a most remarkable dream, I could see that he did not intend to let the matter rest there, and later in the day (out of good manners we had eventually ceased discussing the story) he asked me if I would accompany him on some investigation in the neighborhood.

" 'I think I should know the house,' he said, 'even though I saw it in the dark. I was impressed by the fishpond and the low doorway through which I had to stoop in order to pass without knocking my head.'

"I did not tell him that Mrs. Mahogany had also mentioned a fishpond and a low door.

"We made the excuse of some old brasses we wished to discover in a nearby church to take my car and go out that afternoon on an investigation of the neighborhood in the hope of discovering Dr. Dilke's dream house.

"We covered a good deal of distance and spent a good deal of time without any success at all, and the short day was already darkening when we came upon a row of almshouses in which, for no reason at all that I could discern, Dr. Dilke showed an interest and insisted on stopping before them. He pointed out an inscription cut in the center gable, which said that these had been built by a certain Richard Carwithen in memory of Philadelphia, his wife.

" 'The people whose tablet you sat next in the church,' I remarked.

" 'Yes,' murmured Dr. Dilke, 'when I felt the chill,' and he added, 'when I *first* felt the chill. You see, the date is 1830. That would be about right.'

"We stopped in the little village, which was a good many miles from Verrall, and after some tedious delays because everything was shut up for the holiday, we did discover an old man who was willing to tell us something about the almshouses, though there was nothing much to be said about them. They had been founded by a certain Mr. Richard Carwithen with his wife's fortune. He had been a poor man, a kind of adventurer, our informant thought, who had married a wealthy woman; they had not been at all happy. There had been quarrels and disputes, and a separation (at least, so the gossip went, as his father had told it to him); finally, the Carwithens had taken a house here in this village of Sunford—a large house it was and it still stood. The Carwithens weren't buried in this village, though, but at Verrall; she had been a Verrall by birth—perhaps that's why they came to this neighborhood—it was the name of a great family in those days, you know. . . . There was another woman in the old story, as it went, and she got hold of Mr. Carwithen and was for making him put his wife aside; and so, perhaps, he would have done, but the poor lady died suddenly, and there was some talk about it, having the other woman in the house at the time, and it being so convenient for both of them. . . . But he didn't marry the other woman, because he died six months after his wife. . . . By his will he left all his wife's money to found these almshouses.

"Dr. Dilke asked if he could see the house where the Carwithens had lived.

" 'It belongs to a London gentleman,' the old man said, 'who never comes here. It's going to be pulled down and the land sold in building lots; why, it's been locked up these ten years or more. I don't suppose it's been inhabited since—no, not for a hundred years.'

" 'Well, I'm looking for a house round about here. I don't mind spending a little money on repairs if that house is in the market.'

"The old man didn't know whether it was in the market or not, but kept repeating that the property was to be sold and broken up for building lots.

"I won't bother you with all our delays and arguments, but merely tell you that we did finally discover the lodgekeeper of the estate, who gave us the key. It was not such a very large estate, nothing to be compared to Verrall, but had been, in its time, of some pretension. Builders' boards had already been raised along the high road frontage. There were some fine old trees, black and bare, in a little park. As we turned in through the rusty gates and motored toward the house it was nearly dark, but we had our electric torches and the powerful head lamps of the car. Dr. Dilke made no comment on what we had found, but he reconstructed the story of the Carwithens whose names were on that black stone in Verrall church.

" 'They were quarreling over money, he was trying to get her to sign a will in his favor; she had some little sickness perhaps—brought on probably by rage—he had got the other woman in the house, remember; I expect he was no good. There was some sort of poison about—perhaps for a face wash, perhaps as a drug. He put it in the milk and gave it to her.'

"Here I interrupted: 'How do you know it was in the milk?'

"The doctor did not reply to this. I had now swung the car round to the front of the ancient mansion—a poor, pretentious place, sinister in the half-darkness.

" 'And then, when he had done it,' continued Dr. Dilke, mounting the steps of the house, 'he repented most horribly; he wanted to fly for a doctor to get some antidote for the poison with the idea in his head that if he could have got help he could have saved her himself. The other woman kept on laughing. He couldn't forgive her that—that she could laugh at a moment like that; he couldn't get help! He couldn't find a doctor. His wife died. No one suspected foul play—they seldom did in those days as long as the people were respectable; you must remember the state in which medical knowledge was in 1830. He couldn't marry the other woman, and he couldn't touch the money; he left it all to found the almshouses; then he died himself, six months afterward, leaving instructions that his name should be added to that black stone. I dare say he died by his own hand. Probably he loved her through it all, you know—it was only the money, that cursed money, a fortune just within his grasp, but which he couldn't take.'

" 'A pretty romance,' I suggested, as we entered the house; 'I am sure there is a three-volume novel in it of what Mrs. Janey would call "the good old-fashioned" sort.'

"To this Dr. Dilke answered: 'Suppose the miserable man can't rest? Supposing he is still searching for a doctor?'

"We passed from one room to another of the dismal, dusty, dismantled house. Dr. Dilke opened a damaged shutter which concealed one of the windows at the back, and pointed out in the waning light a decayed garden with stone steps and a fishpond; and a low gateway to pass through which a man of his height would have had to stoop. We could just discern this in the twilight. He made no comment. We went upstairs."

Here Cuming paused dramatically to give us the full flavor of the final part of his story. He reminded us, rather unnecessarily, for somehow he had convinced us that this was all perfectly true.

"I am not romancing; I won't answer for what Dr. Dilke said or did, or his adventure of the night before, or the story of the Carwithens as he constructed it, but *this* is actually what happened. . . .We went upstairs by the wide main stairs. Dr. Dilke searched about for and found a door which opened on to the back stairs, and then he said: 'This must be the room.' It was entirely devoid of any furniture, and stained with damp, the walls stripped of paneling and cheaply covered with decayed paper, peeling, and in parts fallen.

" 'What's this?' said Dr. Dilke.

"He picked up a scrap of paper that showed vivid on the dusty floor and handed it to me. It was a prescription. He took out his notebook and showed me the page where this fitted in.

" 'This page I tore out last night when I wrote that prescription in this room. The bed was just there, and there was the table on which were the papers and the glass of milk.'

" 'But you couldn't have been here last night,' I protested feebly, 'the locked doors—the whole thing! . . .'

"Dr. Dilke said nothing. After a while neither did I. 'Let's get out of this place,' I said. Then another thought struck me. 'What is your prescription?' I asked.

"He said: 'A very uncommon kind of prescription, a very desperate sort of prescription, one that I've never written before, nor I hope shall again—an antidote for severe arsenical poisoning.'

"I leave you," smiled Cuming, "to your various attitudes of incredulity or explanation."

Is there a clever ghost, or just a garrulous writer?

THE MYSTERY OF
MY GRANDMOTHER'S
HAIR SOFA

John Kendrick Bangs

It happened last Christmas Eve, and precisely as I am about to set it forth. It has been said by critics that I am a romancer of the wildest sort, but that is where my critics are wrong. I grant that the experiences through which I have passed, some of which have contributed to the gray matter in my hair, however little they may have augmented that within my cranium—experiences which I have from time to time set forth to the best of my poor abilities in the columns of such periodicals as I have at my mercy—have been of an order so excessively supernatural as to give my critics a basis for their aspersions; but they do not know, as I do, that that basis is as uncertain as the shifting sands of the sea, inasmuch as in the setting forth of these episodes I have narrated them as faithfully as the most conscientious realist could wish, and am therefore myself a true and faithful follower of the realistic school. I cannot be blamed because these things happen to me. If I sat down in my study to imagine the strange incidents to which I have in the past called attention, with no other object in view than to make my readers unwilling to retire for the night, to destroy the peace of mind of those who are good enough to purchase my literary wares, or to titillate till tense the nerve tissue of the timid who come to smile and who depart unstrung, then should I deserve the severest condemnation; but these things I do not do. I have a mission in life which I hold as sacred as my good friend Mr. Howells holds his. Such phases of life as I see I put down faithfully, and if the Fates in their wisdom have chosen to make of me the Balzac of the Supernatural, the Shakespeare of the Midnight Visitation, while elevating Mr. Howells to the high office of the Fielding of Massachusetts and its adjacent States, the Smollett of Boston, and the Sterne of Altruria, I can only regret that the powers have dealt more graciously with him than with me, and walk my little way as gracefully as I know how. The slings and arrows of outrageous fortune I am prepared to suffer in all meekness of spirit; I accept them because it seems to me to be nobler in the mind so to do rather than by opposing to end them. And so to my story. I have prefaced it at such length for but one reason, and that is that I am aware that there will be those who will doubt the veracity of my tale, and I am anxious at the outset to impress upon all the unquestioned fact that what I am about to tell is the plain, unvarnished truth, and, as I have already said, it happened last Christmas Eve.

I regret to have to say so, for it sounds so much like the description given to other Christmas Eves by writers with a less conscientious regard for the truth than I possess, but the facts must be told, and I must therefore state that it was a wild and stormy night. The winds howled and moaned and made all sorts of curious noises, soughing through the bare limbs of the trees, whistling through the chimneys, and, with reckless disregard of my children's need of rest, slamming doors until my house seemed to be the centre of a bombardment of no mean order. It is also necessary to state that the snow, which had been falling all day, had clothed the lawns and housetops in a dazzling drapery of white, and, not content with having done this to the satisfaction of all, was still falling, and, happily enough, as silently as usual. Were I the "wild romancer" that I have been called, I might have had the snow fall with a thunderous roar, but I cannot go to any such length. I love my fellow-beings, but there is a limit to my philanthropy, and I shall not have my snow fall noisily just to make a critic happy. I might do it to save his life, for I should hate to have a man die for the want of what I could give him with a stroke of my pen, and without any special effort, but until that emergency arises I shall not yield a jot in the manner of the falling of my snow.

Occasionally a belated home-comer would pass my house, the sleighbells strung about the ample proportions of his steed jingling loud above the roaring of the winds. My family retired, and I sat alone in the glow of the blazing log—a very satisfactory gas affair—on the hearth. The flashing jet flames cast the usual grotesque shadows about the room, and my mind had thereby been reduced to that sensitive state which had hitherto betokened the coming of a visitor from other realms—a fact which I greatly regretted, for I was in no mood to be haunted. My first impulse, when I recognized the oncoming of that mental state which is evidenced by the goosing of one's flesh, if I may be allowed the expression, was to turn out the fire and go to bed. I have always found this the easiest method of ridding myself of

unwelcome ghosts, and, conversely, I have observed
that others who have been haunted unpleasantly have
suffered in proportion to their failure to take what has
always seemed to me to be the most natural course in
the world—to hide their heads beneath the bed-
covering. Brutus, when Caesar's ghost appeared beside
his couch, before the battle of Philippi, sat up and stared
upon the horrid apparition, and suffered correspond-
ingly, when it would have been much easier and more
natural to put his head under his pillow, and so shut out
the unpleasant spectacle. That is the course I have invariably pursued, and it has never failed me. The most luminous ghost man ever saw is utterly powerless to shine
through a comfortably stuffed pillow, or the usual
Christmas-time quota of woollen blankets. But upon
this occasion I preferred to await developments. The
real truth is that I was about written out in the matter of
visitations, and needed a reinforcement of my uncanny
vein, which, far from being varicose, had become sclerotic, so dry had it been pumped by the demands to
which it had been subjected by a clamorous, mystery-
loving public. I had, I may as well confess it, run out of
ghosts, and had come down to the writing of tales full
of the horror of suggestion, leaving my readers unsatis-
fied through my failure to describe in detail just what
kind of looking thing it was that had so aroused their
apprehension; and one editor had gone so far as to re-
ject my last ghost-story because I had worked him up to
a fearful pitch of excitement, and left him there without
any reasonable way out. I was face to face with a
condition—which, briefly, was that hereafter that desirable market was closed to the products of my pen unless my contributions were accompanied by a diagram
which should make my mysteries so plain that a little
child could understand how it all came to pass. Hence

it was that, instead of following my own convenience and taking refuge in my spectre-proof couch, I stayed where I was. I had not long to wait. The dial in my fuel-meter below-stairs had hardly had time to register the consumption of three thousand feet of gas before the faint sound of a bell reached my straining ears—which, by the way, is an expression I profoundly hate, but must introduce because the public demands it, and a ghost-story without straining ears having therefore no chance of acceptance by a discriminating editor. I started from my chair and listened intently, but the ringing had stopped, and I settled back to the delights of a nervous chill, when again the deathly silence of the night—the wind had quieted in time to allow me the use of this faithful, overworked phrase—was broken by the tintinnabulation of the bell. This time I recognized it as the electric bell operated by a push-button upon the right side of my front door. To rise and rush to the door was the work of a moment. It always is. In another instant I had flung it wide. This operation was singularly easy, considering that it was but a narrow door, and width was the last thing it could ever be suspected of, however forcible the fling. However, I did as I have said, and gazed out into the inky blackness of the night. As I had suspected, there was no one there, and I was at once convinced that the dreaded moment had come. I was certain that at the instant of my turning to re-enter my library I should see something which would make my brain throb madly and my pulses start. I did not therefore instantly turn, but let the wind blow the door to with a loud clatter, while I walked quickly into my dining-room and drained a glass of cooking-sherry to the dregs. I do not introduce the cooking-sherry here for the purpose of eliciting a laugh from the reader, but in order to be faithful to life as we live it. All our other sherry had been used by the queen of the kitchen for cooking purposes, and this was all we had left for the table. It is always so in real life, let critics say what they will.

This done, I returned to the library, and sustained my first shock. The unexpected had happened. There was still no one there. Surely this ghost was an original, and I began to be interested.

"Perhaps he is a modest ghost," I thought, "and is a little shy about manifesting his presence. That, indeed, would be original, seeing how bold the spectres of commerce usually are, intruding themselves always upon the privacy of those who are not at all minded to receive them."

Confident that something would happen, and speedily at that, I sat down to wait, lighting a cigar for company; for burning gas-logs are not as sociable as their hissing, spluttering originals, the genuine logs, in a state of ignition. Several times I started up nervously, feeling as if there was something standing behind me about to place a clammy hand upon my shoulder, and as many times did I resume my attitude of comfort, disappointed. Once I seemed to see a minute spirit floating in the air before me, but investigation showed that it was nothing more than the fanciful curling of the clouds of smoke I had blown from my lips. An hour passed and nothing occurred, save that my heart from throbbing took to leaping in a fashion which filled me with concern. A few minutes later, however, I heard a strange sound at the window, and my leaping heart stood still. The strain upon my tense nerves was becoming unbearable.

"At last!" I whispered to myself, hoarsely, drawing a deep breath, and pushing with all my force into the soft upholstered back of my chair. Then I leaned forward and watched the window, momentarily expecting to see it raised by unseen hands; but it never budged. Then I watched the glass anxiously, half hoping, half fearing to see something pass through it; but nothing came, and I began to get irritable.

I looked at my watch, and saw that it was half-past one o'clock.

"Hang you!" I cried, "whatever you are, why don't you appear, and be done with it? The idea of keeping a man up until this hour of the night!"

Then I listened for a reply; but there was none.

"What do you take me for?" I continued, querulously. "Do you suppose I have nothing else to do but to wait upon your majesty's pleasure? Surely, with all the time you've taken to make your debut, you must be something of unusual horror."

Again there was no answer, and I decided that petulance was of no avail. Some other tack was necessary, and I decided to appeal to his sympathies—granting that ghosts have sympathies to appeal to, and I have met some who were so human in this respect that I have found it hard to believe that they were truly ghosts.

"I say, old chap," I said, as genially as I could, considering the situation—I was nervous, and the amount of gas consumed by the logs was beginning to bring up visions of bankruptcy before my eyes—"hurry up and begin your haunting—there's a good fellow. I'm a father—please remember that—and this is Christmas Eve. The children will be up in about three hours, and if you've ever been a parent yourself you know what that means. I must have some rest, so come along and show yourself, like the good spectre you are, and let me go to bed."

I think myself it was a very moving address, but it helped me not a jot. The thing must have had a heart of stone, for it never made answer.

"What?" said I, pretending to think it had spoken and I had not heard distinctly: but the visitant was not to be caught napping, even though I had good reason to believe that he had fallen asleep. He, she, or it, whatever it was, maintained a silence as deep as it was aggravating. I smoked furiously on to restrain my growing wrath. Then it occurred to me that the thing might have some pride, and I resolved to work on that.

"Of course I should like to write you up," I said, with a sly wink at myself. "I imagine you'd attract a good deal of attention in the literary world. Judging from the time it takes you to get ready, you ought to make a good magazine story—not one of those comic ghost-tales that can be dashed off in a minute, and ultimately get published in a book at the author's expense. You stir so little that, as things go by contraries, you'll make a stirring tale. You're long enough, I might say, for a three-volume novel—but—ah—I can't do you unless I see you. You must be seen to be appreciated. I can't imagine you, you know. Let's see, now, if I can guess what kind of a ghost you are. Um! You must be terrifying in the extreme—you'd make a man shiver in mid-August in mid-Africa. Your eyes are unfathomably green. Your smile would drive the sanest mad. Your hands are cold and clammy as a—ah—as a hot-water bag four hours after."

And so I went on for ten minutes, praising him up to the skies, and ending up with a pathetic appeal that he should manifest his presence. It may be that I puffed him up so that he burst, but, however that may be, he would not condescend to reply, and I grew angry in earnest.

"Very well," I said, savagely, jumping up from my chair and turning off the gas-log. "Don't! Nobody asked you to come in the first place, and nobody's going to complain if you sulk in your tent like Achilles. I don't want to see you. I could fake up a better ghost than you are anyhow—in fact, I fancy that's what's the matter with you. You know what a miserable specimen you are—couldn't frighten a mouse if you were ten times as horrible. You're ashamed to show yourself—and I don't blame you. I'd be that way too if I were you."

I walked half-way to the door, momentarily expecting to have him call me back; but he didn't. I had to give him a parting shot.

"You probably belong to a ghost union—don't you? That's your secret? Ordered out on strike, and won't do any haunting after sundown unless some other employer of unskilled ghosts pays his spooks skilled wages."

I had half a notion that the word "spook" would draw him out, for I have noticed that ghosts do not like to be called spooks. They consider it vulgar. He never yielded in his reserve, however, and after locking up I went to bed.

For a time I could not sleep, and I began to wonder if I had been just, after all. Possibly there was no spirit within miles of me. They symptoms were all there, but might not that have been due to my depressed condition—for it does depress a writer to have one of his best veins become sclerotic—I asked myself, and finally, as I went off to sleep, I concluded that I had been in the wrong all through, and had imagined there was something there when there really was not.

"Very likely the ringing of the bell was due to the wind," I said, as I dozed off. "Of course it would take a very heavy wind to blow the button in, but then—" and then I fell asleep, convinced that no ghost had ventured within a mile of me that night. But when morning came I was undeceived. Something must have visited us that Christmas Eve, and something very terrible; for while I was dressing for breakfast I heard my wife calling loudly from below.

"Henry!" she cried. "Please come down here at once."

"I can't. I'm only half shaved," I answered.

"Never mind that," she returned. "Come at once."

So, with the lather on one cheek and a cut on the other, I went below.

"What's the matter?" I asked.

"Look at that!" she said, pointing to my grandmother's hair sofa, which stood in the hall just outside of my library door.

It had been black when we last saw it, but as I looked I saw that a great change had come over it.

It had turned white in a single night!

Now, I can't account for this strange incident, nor can any one else, and I do not intend to try. It is too awful a mystery for me to attempt to penetrate, but the sofa is there in proof of all that I have said concerning it, and any one who desires can call and see it at any time. It is not necessary for them to see me; they need only ask to see the sofa, and it will be shown.

We have had it removed from the hall to the white-and-gold parlor, for we cannot bear to have it stand in any of the rooms we use.

A Christmas journey and a ghostly
encounter point the way.

How the Bishop Sailed
to Inniskeen

Gene Wolfe

This is the story Hogan told us as we sat before our
fire in the unroofed chapel, looking up at the
niche above the door—the niche that had held the
holy stone.

"'Twas Saint Cian's pillow," said Hogan, "an'
rough when he got it—rough as a pike's kiss. Smooth
it was when he died, for his head had smoothed it
sixty years. Couldn't a maid have done it nicer, an'
where the stone had worn away was the Virgin. Her
picture, belike, sir, in the markin's that'd been in the
stone."

It sounded as if he meant to talk no more, so I said,
"What would he want with a stone pillow, Pat?" This,
though I knew the answer, simply because the night and
the lonesome wind sweeping in off the Atlantic had
made me hungry for a human voice.

"Not for his own sins, sure, for he'd none. But for

yours, sir, an' mine. There was others, too, that come to
live on this island."

"Other hermits, you mean?"

Hogan nodded. "An' when they was gone the fisherfolk come, me own folk with them. 'Twas they that
built this chapel here, an' they set the holy stone above
the door, for he was dead an' didn't want it. When it
was stormin' they'd make a broom, an' dip it in the water, an' sprinkle the holy stone, an' the storm would
pass. But if it was stormin' bad, they'd carry the stone
to the water an' dip it in."

I nodded, thinking how hard and how lonely life
must have been for them on the Inniskeas, and of fishermen drowned. "What happened to it, Pat?"

" 'Twas sunk in the bay in me grandfather's time."
Hogan paused, but I could see that he was thinking—
still talking in himself, as he himself would have said.
"Some says it was the pirates an' some the Protestants.
They told that to the woman that come from Dublin, an'
she believed them."

I had been in Hogan's company for three days and
was too sage a hound to go haring off after the woman
from Dublin; in any event, I knew already that she was
the one who had fenced the cromlech at the summit of
the island. So I said, "But what do you think, Pat? What
really happened to it?"

"The bishop took it. Me own grandfather saw him,
him that was dead when I was born. Or me great-
grandfather it might be, one or the other don't matter.
But me father told me, an' the bishop took it Christmas
Eve."

The wind was rising. Hogan's boat was snug enough
down in the little harbor, but I could hear the breakers
crash not two hundred yards from where we sat.

"There was never a priest here, only this an' a man to take care of it. O'Dea his name was."

Because I was already thinking of writing about some of the things he told me (though in the event I have waited so long), I said, "That was your grandfather, Pat, I feel certain."

"A relative, no doubt, sir," Hogan conceded, "for they were all relations on this island, more or less. But me grandfather was only a lad. O'Dea cared for the place when he wasn't out in his boat. 'Twas the women, you see, that wetted the holy stone, when the men were away."

I said, "It's a pity we haven't got it now, but if it's in the bay it ought to be wet enough."

" 'Tis not, sir. 'Tis in Dublin, in their big museum there, an' dry as a bone. The woman from there fetched it this summer."

"I thought you said the bishop threw it into the bay."

"She had a mask for her face," Hogan continued, as though he had not heard me, "an' a rubber bathin' costume for the rest of her, an' air in a tin tied to her back, just like you see." (He meant, "as I have seen it on television.") "Three days she dove from Kilkelly's boat. Friday it was she brought it up in two pieces. Some say she broke it under the water to make the bringing up easier." Hogan paused to light his pipe.

I asked, "Did the bishop throw it into the bay?"

"In a manner of speakin', sir. It all began when he was just a young priest, do you see? The bishop that was before him had stuck close to the cathedral, as sometimes they will. In the old days it was not easy, journeyin'. Very bad, it was, in winter. 'If you'd seen the roads before they were made, you'd thank the Lord for General Wade.' "

Having had difficulties of my own in traveling

around the west of Ireland in a newish Ford Fiesta, I nodded sympathetically.

"So this one, when he got the job, he made a speech. 'The devil take me,' he says, 'if ever I say Mass Christmas Eve twice in the same church.' "

"And the devil took him," I suggested.

"That he did not, sir, for the bishop was as good as his word. As the times wore on, there was many a one that begged him to stop, but there was no holdin' him. Come the tag end of Advent, off he'd go. An' if he heard that there was one place worse than another, it's where he went. One year a priest from Ballycroy went on the pilgrimage, an' he told the bishop a bit about Inniskeen, havin' been once or twice. 'Send word,' says the bishop, 'to this good man O'Dea. Tell him to have a boat waitin' for me at Erris.'

"They settled it by a fight, an' it was me grandfather's own father that was to bring him."

"Ah," I said.

"Me grandfather wanted to come along to help with the boat, sure, but his father wouldn't allow it, it was that rough, an' he had to wait in the chapel—right here, sir—with his mother. They was all here a long time before midnight, sure, talkin' the one to the other an' waitin' on the bishop, an' me grandfather—recollect he was but a little lad, sir—he fell asleep.

"Next thing he knew, his mother was shakin' him. 'Wake up, Sean, for he's come!' He wakes an' sits up, rubbin' his eyes, an' there's the bishop. But, Lord, sir, there wasn't half there that should've been! Late as the sun rises at Christmas, it was near the time.

"It didn't matter a hair to His Excellency. He shook all the men by the hand, an' smiled at all the women, an' patted me grandfather's head, an' blessed everybody. Then he begun the Mass. You never heard the like sir. When they sang, there was angels singin' with them. Sure, they couldn't see them, but they knew that they were there an' they could hear them. An' when the bishop preached, they saw the Gates an' got the smell of Heaven. It was like cryin' for happiness, an' it was forever. Me father said the good man used to cry a bit himself when he talked of it—which he did, sir, every year about this time, until he left this world.

"When the Mass was over, the bishop blessed them all again, an' he give O'Dea a letter, an' O'Dea kissed his ring, which was an honor to him after. Me grandfather saw his father waiting to take the bishop back to Erris, an' knew he'd been in the back of them. Right back there, sir."

We were burning wreckage we had picked up on the beach earlier. Hogan paused to throw a broken timber on the fire.

"The stone, Pat," I said.

"The bishop took it, sir, sure. After he give the letter, he points at it, do you see." Hogan pointed to the empty niche. "An' he says, 'Sorry I am, O'Dea, but I must have that.'

"Then O'Dea gets up on a stool—'twas what they sat on here—an' gives it to him, an' off he goes with me grandfather's father.

"All natural, sir. But me grandfather lagged behind when the women went home, an' as soon as there wasn't one lookin', off he runs after the bishop, for he'd hopes his father'd allow him this time, it bein' not so rough as the night before. You know where the rock juts, sir? You took a picture from there."

"Of course," I said.

"Me grandfather run out onto that rock, sir, for there's a bit of a moon by then an' he's wantin' to see if they'd put out. They hadn't, sir. He sees his father there in the boat, holdin' it close in for the bishop. An' he sees the bishop, holdin' the holy stone an' steppin' into it. Up comes the sun, an' devil a boat, or bishop, or father, or holy stone there is.

"Me grandfather's father's body washed up on Duvillaun, but never the bishop's. He'd wanted the holy stone, do you see, to weight him. Or some say to sleep on, there on the bottom. 'Tis the same thing, maybe."

I nodded. In that place, with the wind moaning around the ruined stone chapel, it did not seem impossible or even strange.

"They're all dead now, sir. There's not a man alive that was born on these islands, or a woman, either. But they do say the ghosts of them that missed midnight Mass can be seen comin' over the bay Christmas Eve, for they was buried on the mainland, sir, most of 'em, or died at sea like the bishop. I never seen 'em, mind, an' don't want to."

Hogan was silent for a long time after that, and so was I.

At last I said, "You're suggesting that I come back here and have a look."

Hogan knocked out his pipe. "You've an interest in such things, sir, an' so I thought I ought to mention it. I could take you out by daylight an' leave you here with your food an' sleepin' bag, an' your camera. Christmas day, I'd come by for you again."

"I have to go to Bangor, Pat."

"I know you do, sir."

"Let me think about it. What was in the letter?"

" 'Twas after New Year's when they read it, sir, for O'Dea wouldn't let it out of his hands. Sure, there wasn't a soul on the island that could read, an' no school. It says the bishop had drowned on his way to Inniskeen to say the midnight Mass, an' asked the good people to make a novena for his soul. The priest at Erris wrote it, two days after Christmas."

Hogan lay down after that, but I could not. I went outside with a flashlight and roamed over the island for an hour or more, cold though it was.

I had come to Inniskeen, to the westernmost of Ireland's westernmost island group, in search of the remote past. For I am, among various other things, a writer of novels about that past, a chronicler of Xerxes and "King" Pausanias. And indeed the past was here in plenty. Sinking vessels from the Spanish Armada had been run aground here. Vikings had stridden the very beaches I paced, and earlier still, Neolithic people had lived here largely upon shellfish, or so their middens suggest.

And yet it seemed to me that night that I had not found the past, but the future; for they were all gone, as Hogan had said. The Neolithic people had fallen, presumably, before the modern, Celtic Irish, becoming one of the chief strands of Irish fairy lore. The last of St. Cian's hermits had died in grace, leaving no disciple. The fishermen had lived here for two hundred years or more, generation after generation, harvesting the treacherous sea and tiny gardens of potatoes; and for a few years there had actually been a whaling station on North Island.

No more.

The Norwegians sailed from their whaling station for the last time long ago. Long ago the Irish Land Commission removed the fisherfolk and resettled them; their thatched stone cottages are tumbling down, as the hermits' huts did earlier. Gray sea-geese nest upon Inniskeen again, and otters whistle above the whistling wind. A few shaggy black cattle are humanity's sole contribution; I cannot call them wild, because they do not know

human beings well enough for fear. In the Inniskeas our
race is already extinct. We stayed a hundred centuries
and are gone.

I drove to Bangor the following day, December 22.
There I sent two cables, made transatlantic calls, and
learned only that my literary agent, who might perhaps
have acted, had not the slightest intention of doing so
before the holidays, and that my publishers, who might
certainly have acted if they chose, would not.

Already all of Ireland, which delights in closing at
every opportunity, was gleefully locking its doors. I
would have to stay in Bangor over Christmas, or drive
on to Dublin (praying the while for an open petrol station), or go back to Erris. I filled my rented Ford's tank
until I could literally dabble my forefinger in gasoline
and returned to Erris.

I will not regale you here with everything that went
wrong on the twenty-fourth. Hogan had an errand that
could neither be neglected nor postponed. His usually
dependable motor would not start, so that eventually we
were forced to beg the proprietor of the only store that
carried such things to leave his dinner to sell us a spark
plug. It was nearly dark before we pushed off, and the
storm that had been brewing all day was ready to burst
upon us.

"We're mad, you know," Hogan told me. "Me as
much as you." He was at the tiller, his pipe clenched between his teeth; I was huddled in the bow in a life
jacket, my hat pulled over my ears. "How'll you make
a fire, sir? Tell me that."

Through chattering teeth, I said that I would manage
somehow.

"No, you won't, sir, for we'll never get there."

I said that if he was waiting for me to tell him to turn
back, he would have to wait until we reached Inniskeen;

and I added—bitterly—that if Hogan wanted to turn back I could not prevent him.

"I've taken your money an' given me word."

"We'll make it, Pat."

As though to give me the lie, lightning lit the bay.

"Did you see the island, then?"

"No," I said, and added that we were surely miles from it still.

"I must know if I'm steerin' right," Hogan said.

"Don't you have a compass?"

"It's no good for this, sir. We're shakin' too much." It was an ordinary pocket compass, as I should have remembered, and not a regular boat's compass in a binnacle.

After that I kept a sharp lookout forward. Low-lying North Island was invisible to my right, but from time to time I caught sight of higher, closer South Island. The land I glimpsed at times to our left might have been Duvillaun or Innisglora, or even Achill, or all three. Black Rock Light was visible only occasionally, which was somewhat reassuring. At last, when the final, sullen twilight had vanished, I caught sight of Inniskeen only slightly to our left. Pointing, I half rose in the bow as Hogan swung it around to meet a particularly dangerous comber. It lifted us so high that it seemed certain we were being flipped end for end; we raced down its back and plunged into the trough, only to be lifted again at once.

"Hang on!" Hogan shouted. At that moment lightning cut the dark bowl of the sky from one horizon to the other.

I pointed, indeed, but I pointed back toward Erris. I would have spoken if I could, but I did not need to. In two hours or less we were sitting comfortably in Hogan's parlor, over whiskey toddies. The German tradition of the Christmas tree, which we Americans now count among American customs, has not taken much root in Ireland, but there was an Advent calendar with all its postage-stamp-sized windows wide, and gifts done up in brightly colored papers. And the little crèche (we would call it a crib set) with its as-yet empty manager, cracked, ethereal Mary, and devoted Joseph, had more to say about Christmas than any tree I have ever seen.

"Perhaps you'll come back next year," Hogan suggested after we had related our adventures, "an' then we'll have another go."

I shook my head.

His wife looked up from her knitting, and with that single glance understood everything I had been at pains to hide. "What was it you saw?" she asked.

I did not tell her, then or later. Nor am I certain that I can tell you. It was no ghost, or at least there was nothing of sheet or skull or ectoplasm, none of the conventional claptrap of movies and Halloween. In appearance, it was no more than the floating corpse of a rather small man with longish white hair. He was dressed in dark clothes, and his eyes—I saw them plainly as he rolled in the wave—were open. No doubt it was the motion of the water; but as I stared at him for half a second or so in the lightning's glare, it appeared to me that he raised his arm and gestured, invitingly and with the utmost good will, in the direction of Inniskeen.

I have never returned to Ireland, and never will. And yet I have no doubt at all that the time will soon come when I, too, shall attend his midnight Mass in the ruined chapel. What will follow that service, I cannot guess.

In Christ's name, I implore mercy for my soul.

A Christmas ghost has holiday cheer
on his mind.

OLD APPLEJOY'S GHOST

Frank R. Stockton

The large and commodious apartments in the upper
part of the old Applejoy mansion were occupied
exclusively, at the time of our story, by the ghost
of the grandfather of the present owner of the estate.

For many, many years old Applejoy's ghost had been
in the habit of wandering freely about the grand old
house and the fine estate of which he had once been the
lord and master, but early in that spring a change had
come over the household of his grandson, John
Applejoy, an elderly man and a bachelor, a lover of
books, and—for the later portion of his life—almost a
recluse. A young girl, his niece Bertha, had come to
live with him, and make part of his very small family,
and it was since the arrival of this newcomer that old
Applejoy's ghost had confined himself almost exclusively to the upper portions of the house.

This secluded existence, so different from his ordinary habits, was adopted entirely on account of the kindness of his heart. During the lives of two generations of his descendants he knew that he had frequently been seen by members of the family and others, but this did not disturb him, for in life he had been a man who had liked to assert his position, and the disposition to do so had not left him now. His grandson John had seen him, and two or three times had spoken with him, but as old Applejoy's ghost had heard his skeptical descendant declare that these ghostly interviews were only dreams or hallucinations, he cared very little whether John saw him or not. As to other people, it might be a very good thing if they believed that the house was haunted. People with uneasy consciences would not care to live in such a place.

But when this fresh young girl came upon the scene the case was entirely different. She might be timorous and she might not, but old Applejoy's ghost did not want to take any risks. There was nothing the matter with her conscience, he was quite sure, but she was not twenty yet, her character was not formed, and if anything should happen which would lead her to suspect that the house was haunted she might not be willing to live there, and if that should come to pass it would be a great shock to the ghost.

For a long time the venerable mansion had been a quiet, darkened, melancholy house. A few rooms only were opened and occupied, for John Applejoy and his housekeeper, Mrs. Dipperton, who for years had composed the family, needed but little space in which to pass the monotonous days of their lives. Bertha sang, she played on the old piano; she danced by herself on the broad piazza; she wandered through the gardens and brought flowers into the house, and, sometimes, it almost might have been imagined that the days which were gone had come back again.

One winter evening, when the light of the full moon entered softly through every unshaded window of the house, old Applejoy's ghost sat in a stiff, high-backed chair, which on account of an accident to one of its legs had been banished to the garret. It was not at all necessary either for rest or comfort that this kind old ghost should seat himself in a chair, for he would have been quite as much at his ease upon a clothes-line, but in other days he had been in the habit of sitting in chairs, and it pleased him to do so now. Throwing one shadowy leg over the other, he clasped the long fingers of his hazy hand, and gazed thoughtfully out into the moonlight.

"Winter has come," he said to himself. "All is hard and cold, and soon it will be Christmas. Yes, in two days it will be Christmas!"

For a few minutes he sat reflecting, and then he suddenly started to his feet.

"Can it be!" he exclaimed. "Can it possibly be that that closed-fisted old John, that degenerate son of my noble George, does not intend to celebrate Christmas! It has been years since he has done so, but now that Bertha is in the house, since it is her home, will he dare to pass over Christmas as though it were but a common day? It is almost incredible that such a thing could happen, but so far there have been no signs of any preparations. I have seen nothing, heard nothing, smelt nothing, but this moment will I go and investigate the state of affairs.

Clapping his misty old cocked hat on his head, and tucking under his arm the shade of his faithful cane, he descended to the lower part of the house. Glancing into the great parlors dimly lighted by the streaks of moonlight which came between the cracks of the shutters, he saw that all the furniture was shrouded in ancient linen covers, and that the pictures were veiled with gauzy hangings.

"Humph!" ejaculated old Applejoy's ghost, "he expects no company here!" and forthwith he passed through the dining room—where in the middle of the wide floor was a little round table large enough for three—and entered the kitchen and pantry. There were no signs in the one that anything extraordinary in the way of cooking had been done, or was contemplated, and when he gazed upon the pantry shelves, lighted well enough from without for his keen gaze, he groaned. "Two days before Christmas," he said to himself, "and a pantry furnished thus! How widely different from the olden time when I gave orders for the holidays! Let me see what the old curmudgeon has provided for Christmas."

So saying, old Applejoy's ghost went around the spacious pantry, looking upon shelves and tables, and peering through the doors of a closed closet. "Emptiness! Emptiness! Emptiness!" he ejaculated. "A cold leg of mutton with, I should say, three slices cut out of it; a ham half gone, and the rest of it hardened by exposure to the air; a piece of steak left over from yesterday, or nobody knows when, to be made into hash, no doubt! Cold boiled potatoes—it makes me shiver to look at them!—to be cut up and fried! Pies? There ought to be rows and rows of them, and there is not one! Cake? Upon my word, there is no sign of any! And Christmas two days off!

"What is this? Is it possible? A fowl! Yes, it is a chicken not full grown, enough for three, no doubt, and the servants can pick the bones. Oh, John, John! How have you fallen! A small-sized fowl for Christmas day!

"And what more now! Cider? No trace of it! Here is

vinegar—that suits John, no doubt," and then forgetting the present condition of his organism, he said to himself, "It makes my very blood run cold to look upon a pantry furnished out like this! I must think about it! I must think about it!" And with bowed head he passed out into the great hall.

If it were possible to do anything to prevent the desecration of his old home during the sojourn therein of the young and joyous Bertha, the ghost of old Applejoy was determined to do it, but in order to do anything he must put himself into communication with some living being, and who that being should be he did not know. Still rapt in reverie he passed up the stairs and into the great chamber where his grandson slept. There lay the old man, his hard features tinged by the moonlight, his eyelids as tightly closed as if there had been money underneath them. The ghost of old Applejoy stood by his bedside.

"I can make him wake up and look at me," he thought, "for very few persons can remain asleep when anyone is standing gazing down upon them—even if the gazer be a ghost—and I might induce him to speak to me so that I might open my mind to him and tell him what I think of him, but what impression could I expect my words to make upon the soul of a one-chicken man like John? I am afraid his heart is harder than that dried-up ham. Moreover, if I should be able to speak to him and tell him his duty, he would persuade himself that he had been dreaming, and my words would be of no avail. I am afraid it would be lost time to try to do anything with John!"

Old Applejoy's ghost turned away from the bedside of his sordid descendant, crossed the hall, and passed into the room of Mrs. Dipperton, the elderly housekeeper. There she lay fast asleep, her round face glimmering like a transparent bag filled with milk, and from her slightly parted lips there came at regular intervals a feeble little snore, as if even in her hours of repose she was afraid of disturbing somebody.

The kind-hearted ghost shook his head as he looked down upon her. "It would be of no use," he said, "she hasn't any backbone, and she would never be able to induce old John to turn one inch aside from his parsimonious path. More than that, if she were to see me she would probably scream and go into a spasm—die, for all I know—and that would be a pretty preparation for Christmas!"

Out he went, and into the dreams of the good woman there came no suspicion that the ghost had been standing by her considering her character with a pitying contempt.

Now the kind ghost, getting more and more anxious in his mind, passed to the front of the house and entered the chamber occupied by young Bertha. Once inside the door, he stopped reverently and removed his cocked hat. The head of the little bed was near the uncurtained window, and the bright light of the moon shone upon a face more beautiful in slumber than in the sunny hours of day.

She was not under the influence of the sound, hard sleep which lay upon the master of the house and the mild Mrs. Dipperton. She slept lightly, her delicate lids, through which might almost be seen the deep blue of her eyes, trembled now and then as if they would open, and sometimes her lips moved, as if she would whisper something about her dreams.

Old Applejoy's ghost drew nearer to the maiden, and bent slightly over her. He knew very well that it was mean to be eavesdropping like this, but it was really necessary that he should know this young girl better than he did. If he could hear a few words from that little mouth he might find out what she thought about, where her mind wandered, what she would like him to do for her.

At last, faintly whispered, scarcely more audible than her breathing, he heard one word, and that was "Tom!"

"Oh," said old Applejoy's ghost, as he stepped back from the bedside, "she wants Tom! I like that! I do not know anything about Tom, but she ought to want him. It is natural, it is true, it is human, and it is long since there has been anything natural, true, or human in this house! But I wish she would say something else. She can't have Tom for Christmas—at least, not Tom alone. There is a great deal else necessary before this can be made a place suitable for Tom!"

Again he drew near to Bertha and listened, but instead of speaking, suddenly the maiden opened wide her eyes. The ghost of old Applejoy drew back, and made a low, respectful bow. The maiden did not move, but her lovely eyes opened wider and wider, and she fixed them upon the apparition, who trembled as he stood, for fear that she might scream, or faint, or in some ways foil his generous purpose. If she did not first address him he could not speak to her.

"Am I asleep?" she murmured, and then, after slightly turning her head from side to side, as if to assure herself that she was in her own room and surrounded by familiar objects, she looked full into the face of old Applejoy's ghost, and boldly spoke to him. "Are you a spirit?" said she.

If a flush of joy could redden the countenance of a filmy shade, the face of old Applejoy's ghost would have glowed like a sunlit rose.

"Dear child," he exclaimed, "I am a spirit! I am the ghost of your uncle's grandfather. His sister Maria, the youngest of the family, and much the most charming, I assure you, was your mother, and, of course, I was her grandfather, and just as much, of course, I am the ghost of your great-grandfather, but I declare to you I never felt prouder at any moment of my existences, previous or present!"

"Then you must be the original Applejoy," said Bertha; "and I think it very wonderful that I am not afraid of you, but I am not. You look as if you would not hurt anybody in this world, especially me!"

"There you have it," he exclaimed, bringing his cane down upon the floor with a violence which had it been the cane it used to be would have wakened everybody in the house. "There you have it, my dear! I vow to you there is not a person in this world for whom I have such an affection as I feel for you. You remind me of my dear son George. You are the picture of Maria when she was about your age. Your coming to this house has given me the greatest pleasure; you have brought into it something of the old life. I wish I could tell you how happy I have been since the bright spring day that brought you here."

"I did not suppose I would make anyone happy by coming here," said Bertha. "Uncle John does not seem to care much about me, and I suppose I ought to be satisfied with Mrs. Dipperton if she does not object to me—but now the case is different. I did not know about you."

"No, indeed," exclaimed the good ghost, "you did not know about me, but I intend you to know about me. But now we must waste no more words—we must get down to business. I came here tonight with a special object."

"Business?" said Bertha, inquiringly.

"Yes," said the ghost, "it is business, and it is important, and it is about Christmas. Your uncle does not mean to have any Christmas in this house, but I intend, if I can possibly do so, to prevent him from disgracing himself, but I cannot do anything without somebody's help, and there is nobody to help me but you. Will you do it?"

Bertha could not refrain from a smile. "It would be funny to help a ghost to do anything," she said; "but if I can assist you I shall be very glad."

"I want you to go into the lower part of the house," said he. "I have something to show you that I am sure will interest you very much. I shall now go down into the hall, where I shall wait for you, and I should like you to dress yourself as warmly and comfortably as you can. It would be well to put a shawl around your head and shoulders. Have you some warm, soft slippers that will make no noise?"

"Oh, yes," said Bertha, her eyes twinkling with delight at the idea of this novel expedition, "I shall be dressed and with you in no time."

"Do not hurry yourself," said the good ghost, as he left the room, "we have most of the night before us."

When the young girl had descended the great staircase almost as noiselessly as the ghost, who had preceded her, she found her venerable companion waiting for her.

"Do you see the lantern on the table?" said he. "John uses it when he goes his round of the house at bedtime. There are matches hanging above it. Please light it. You may be sure I would not put you to this trouble if I were able to do it myself."

She dimly perceived the brass lantern, and when she had lighted it the ghost invited her to enter the study.

"Now," said he, as he led the way to the large desk

with the cabinet above it, "will you be so good as to open that glass door? It is not locked."

Bertha hesitated a little, but she opened the door.

"Now, please put your hand into the front cover of that middle shelf. You cannot see anything, but you will feel a key hanging upon a little hook."

But Bertha did not obey. "This is my uncle's cabinet," she said, "and I have no right to meddle with his keys and things!"

Now the ghost of old Applejoy drew himself up to the six feet two inches which had been his stature in life; he slightly frowned, his expression was almost severe—but he controlled himself, and spoke calmly to the girl. "This was my cabinet," he said, "and I have never surrendered it to your Uncle John! With my own hands I screwed the little hook into that dark corner and hung the key upon it! Now I beg that you will take down that key. You have the authority of your great-grandfather."

Without a moment's hesitation Bertha put her hand into the dark corner of the shelf and took the key from the hook.

"Thank you very much," said the ghost of old Applejoy. "And now please unlock that little drawer—the one at the bottom."

Bertha unlocked and opened the drawer. "It is full of old keys!" she said.

"Yes," said the ghost, "and you will find that they are all tied together in a bunch. Those keys are what we came for! Now, my dear," said he, standing in front of her and looking down upon her very earnestly, but so kindly that she was not in the least afraid of him, "I want you to understand that what we are going to do is strictly correct and proper, without a trace of inquis-itive meanness about it. This was once my house—

everything in it I planned and arranged. I am now going to take you into the cellars of my old mansion. They are wonderful cellars; they were my pride and glory! I often used to take my visitors to see them, and wide and commodious stairs lead down to them. Are you afraid," he said, "to descend with me into these subterranean regions?"

"Not a bit of it!" exclaimed Bertha, almost too loud for prudence. "I have heard of the cellars and wanted to see them, though Mrs. Dipperton told me that my uncle never allowed anyone to enter them; but I think it will be the jolliest thing in the world to go with my great-grandfather into the cellars which he built himself, and of which he was so proud!"

This speech so charmed the ghost of old Applejoy that he would instantly have kissed his great-granddaughter had it not been that he was afraid of giving her a cold.

"You are a girl to my liking!" he exclaimed, "and I wish with all my heart that you had been living at the time I was alive and master of this house. We should have had gay times together—you may believe that!"

"I wish you were alive now, dear great-grandpapa," said she, "and that would be better than the other way! And now let us go on—I am all impatience!"

They then descended into the cellars, which, until the present owner came into possession of the estate, had been famous throughout the neighborhood. "This way," said old Applejoy's ghost. "You will find the floor perfectly dry, and if we keep moving you will not be chilled.

"Do you see that row of old casks nearly covered with cobwebs and dust? Now, my dear, those casks contain some of the choicest spirits ever brought into this country, and most of them are more than half full! The finest rum from Jamaica, brandy from France, and gin from Holland—gin with such a flavor, my dear, that if you were to take out the bung the delightful aroma would fill the whole house! There is port there, too, and if it is not too old it must be the rarest wine in the country! And Madeira, a little glass of which, my dear, is a beverage worthy even of you!

"These things were not stowed away by me, but by my dear son George, who knew their value; but as for John—he drinks water and tea! He is a one-chicken man, and if he has allowed any of these rare spirits to become worthless, simply on account of age, he ought to be sent to the county prison!

"But we must move on! Do you see all these bottles—dingy looking enough, but filled with the choicest wines? Many of these are better than ever they were, although some of them may have spoiled. John would let everything spoil. He is a dog in the manger!

"Come into this little room. Now, then, hold up your lantern, and look all around you. Notice that row of glass jars on the shelf. They are filled with the finest mincemeat ever made by mortal man—or woman! It is the same kind of mincemeat I used to eat. George had it put up so that he might have the sort of pies at Christmas which I gave him when he was a boy. That mincemeat is just as good as ever it was! John is a dyspeptic; he wouldn't eat mince-pie! But he will eat fried potatoes, and they are ten times worse for him, if he did but know it!

"There are a lot more jars and cans, all sealed up tightly. I do not know what good things are in them, but I am sure their contents are just what will be wanted to fill out a Christmas table. If Mrs. Dipperton were to come down here and open those jars and bottles she would think she was in Heaven!

"But now, my dear, I want to show you the grandest thing in these cellars, the diamond of the collection! Behold that wooden box! Inside of it is another box made of tin, soldered up tightly, so that it is perfectly airtight. Inside of that tin box is a great plum-cake! And now listen to me, Bertha! That cake was put into that box by me. I intended it to stay there for a long time, for plum-cake gets better the longer it is kept, but I did not suppose that the box would not be opened for three generations! The people who eat that cake, my dear Bertha, will be blessed above all their fellow mortals! That is to say, as far as cake-eating goes.

"And now I think you have seen enough to understand thoroughly that these cellars are the abode of many good things to eat and to drink. It is their abode, but if John could have his way it would be their sepulchre! I was fond of good living, as you may well imagine, and so was my dear son George, but John is a degenerate!"

"But why did you bring me here, great-grandpapa?" said Bertha. "Do you want me to come down here, and have my Christmas dinner with you?" And as she said this she unselfishly hoped that when the tin box should be opened it might contain the ghost of a cake, for it was quite plain that her great-grandfather had been an enthusiast in the matter of plum-cake.

"No, indeed," said old Applejoy's ghost. "Come upstairs, and let us go into the study. There are some coals left on the hearth, and you will not be chilled while we talk."

When the great cellar-door had been locked, the keys replaced in the drawer, the little key hung upon its hook, and the cabinet closed, Bertha sat down before the fireplace and warmed her fingers over the few embers it contained, while the spirit of her great-grandfather stood by her and talked to her.

"Bertha," said he, "it is wicked not to celebrate Christmas—especially when one is able to do so—in the most hospitable and generous way. For years John has taken no notice of Christmas, and it is full time that he should reform, and it is your duty and my duty to reform him if we can! You have seen what he has in the cellars; there are turkeys in the poultry-yard—for I know he has not sold them all—and if there is anything wanting for a grand Christmas celebration he has an abundance of money with which to buy it. There is not much time before Christmas Day, but there is time enough to do everything that has to be done, if you and I go to work and set other people to work."

"And how are we to do that?" asked Bertha.

"We haven't an easy task before us," said the ghost, "but I have been thinking a great deal about it, and I believe we can accomplish it. The straightforward thing to do is for me to appear to your uncle, tell him his duty, and urge him to perform it, but I know what will be the result. He would call the interview a dream, and attribute it to too much hash and fried potatoes, and the result would be that he would have a plainer table for awhile and half starve you and Mrs. Dipperton. But there is nothing dreamlike about you, my dear. If anyone hears you talking he will know he is awake."

"I think that is very true," said Bertha, smiling. "Do you want me to talk to Uncle?"

"Yes," said old Applejoy's ghost, "I do want you to talk to him. I want you to go to him immediately after breakfast to-morrow morning, and tell him exactly what has happened this night. He cannot believe dreams are fried potatoes when you tell him about the little key in the corner of the shelf, the big keys in the drawer, the casks of spirits (and you can tell him what is in each one), the jars of mincemeat, and the wooden box nailed fast and tight with the tin box inside holding the cake. John knows all about that cake, for his father told him, and he knows all about me, too, although he tried not to believe in me, and when you have told him all you have seen, and when you give him my message, I think it will make him feel that you and I are awake, and that he would better keep awake, too, if he knows what's good for him."

"And what is the message?" asked Bertha.

"It is simply this," said old Applejoy's ghost. "When you have told him all the events of this night, and when he sees that they must have happened, for you could not have imagined them, I want you to tell him that it is my wish and desire, the wish and desire of his grandfather, to whom he owes everything he possesses, that there shall be worthy festivities in this house on Christmas Day and Night—I would say something about Christmas Eve, but I am afraid there is not time enough for that. Tell him to kill his turkeys, open his cellars, and spend his money. Tell him to send for at least a dozen good friends and relatives, for they will gladly give up their own Christmas dinner when they know that the great holiday is to be celebrated in this house. There is time enough, messengers and horses can be hired, and you can attend to the invitations. Mrs. Dipperton is a good manager when she has a chance, and I know she will do herself honor this time if John will give her the range.

"Now, my dear," said old Applejoy's ghost, drawing near to the young girl, "I want to ask you a question—a private, personal question. Who is Tom?"

At these words a sudden blush rushed into the cheeks of Bertha.

"Tom?" she said, "what Tom?"

"Now, don't beat about the bush with me," said old Applejoy's ghost. "I am sure you know a young man named Tom, and I want you to tell me who he is. My name was Tom, and for the sake of my past life I am very fond of Toms. But you must tell me about your Tom—is he a nice young fellow? Do you like him very much?"

"Yes," said Bertha, meaning the answer to cover both questions.

"And does he like you?"

"I think so," said Bertha.

"That means you are in love with each other!" exclaimed old Applejoy's ghost. "And now, my dear, tell me his name? Out with it! You can't help yourself."

"Mr. Burcham," said Bertha, her cheeks now a little pale, for it seemed to her a very bold thing for her to talk in this way even in the company of only a spirit.

"Son of Thomas Burcham of the Meadows? Grandson of old General Burcham?"

"Yes, sir," said Bertha.

The ghost of old Applejoy gazed down upon his great-granddaughter with pride and admiration.

"My dear Bertha," he exclaimed, "I congratulate you! I knew the old general well, and I have seen young Tom. He is a fine-looking fellow, and if you love him I know he is a good one. Now, I'll tell you what we will do, Bertha. We will have Tom here on Christmas."

"Oh, great-grandfather," exclaimed the girl, "I can't ask Uncle to invite him."

"We will make it all right," said the beaming ghost. "We will have a bigger party than we thought we would. All the guests when they are invited will be asked to bring their families. When a big dinner is given at this house Thomas Burcham, Esq., must not be left out, and don't you see, Bertha, he is bound to bring Tom. And now you must not stay here a minute longer. Skip back to your bed, and immediately after breakfast come here to your uncle and tell him everything I have told you to tell him."

Bertha rose to obey, but she hesitated.

"Great-grandfather," she said, "if uncle does allow us to celebrate Christmas, will you be with us?"

"Yes, indeed, my dear," said he. "And you need not be afraid of my frightening anybody. When I choose I can be visible to some and invisible to others. I shall be everywhere and I shall hear everything, but I shall appear only to the loveliest woman who ever graced this mansion. And now be off to bed without another word."

"If she hadn't gone," said old Applejoy's ghost to himself, "I couldn't have helped giving her a good-night kiss."

The next morning, as Bertha told the story of her night's adventures to her uncle, the face of John Applejoy grew paler and paler. He was a hard-headed man, but a superstitious one, and when the story began he wondered if it were a family failing to have dreams about ghosts; but when he heard of the visit to the cellars, and especially when Bertha told him of his grandfather's plum-cake, the existence of which he had believed was not known to anyone but himself, he felt it was impossible for the girl to have dreamed these things. When Bertha had finished he actually believed that she had seen and talked with the ghost of her great-grandfather. With all the power of his will he opposed this belief, but it was too much for him, and he surrendered. But he was a proud man and would not admit to his niece that he put any faith in the existence of ghosts.

"My dear," said he, rising and standing before the fire, his face still pale, but his expression under good control, "you have had a very strange dream. Now, don't declare that it wasn't a dream—people always do that—but hear me out. Although there is nothing of weight in what you have told me—for traditions about my cellars have been afloat in the family—still your pretty little story suggests something to me. This is Christmas-time and I had almost overlooked it. You are young and lively and accustomed to the celebration of holidays. Therefore, I have determined, my dear, to consider your dream just as if it had been a real happening, and we will have a grand Christmas dinner, and invite our friends and their families. I know there must be good things in the cellars, although I had almost forgotten them, and they shall be brought up and spread out and enjoyed. Now go and send Mrs. Dipperton to me; and when we have finished our consultation, you and I will make out a list of guests and send off the invitations."

When she had gone, John Applejoy sat down in his big chair and looked fixedly into the fire. He would not have dared to go to bed that night if he had disregarded the message from his grandfather.

Never since the old house had begun to stand upon its foundations had there been such glorious Christmas-time within its walls. The news that old Mr. Applejoy was sending out invitations to a Christmas dinner spread like wildfire through the neighborhood, and those who were not invited were almost as much excited as those who were asked to be guests. The idea of inviting people by families was considered a grand one, worthy indeed of the times of old Mr. Tom Applejoy, the grandfather of the present owner, who had been the most hospitable man in the whole country.

For the first time in nearly a century all the leaves of the great dining-table were put into use, and chairs for the company were brought from every part of the house. All the pent-up domestic enthusiasm in the soul of Mrs. Dipperton, the existence of which no one had suspected, now burst out in one grand volcanic eruption, and the great table had as much as it could do to stand up under its burdens brought from cellar, barn, and surrounding country.

In the very middle of everything was the great and wonderful plum-cake which had been put away by the famous grandfather of the host.

But the cake was not cut. "My friends," said Mr. John Applejoy, "we may all look at this cake but we will not eat it! We will keep it just as it is until a marriage shall occur in this family. Then you are all invited to come and enjoy it!"

At the conclusion of this little speech old Applejoy's ghost patted his degenerate grandson upon the head. "You don't feel that, John," he said to himself, "but it is approbation, and this is the first time I have ever approved of you! You must know of the existence of young Tom! You may turn out to be a good fellow yet, and if you will drink some of that rare old Madeira every day, I am sure you will!"

Late in the evening there was a grand dance in the great hall, which opened with an old-fashioned minuet, and when the merry guests were forming on the floor, a young man named Tom came forward and asked the hand of Bertha.

"No," said she, "not this time. I am going to dance this first dance with—well, we will say by myself!"

At these words the most thoroughly gratified ghost in all space stepped up to the side of the lovely girl, and with his cocked hat folded flat under his left arm, he made a low bow and held out his hand. With his neatly tied cue, his wide-skirted coat, his long waistcoat trimmed with lace, his tightly drawn stockings and his buckled shoes, there was not such a gallant figure in the whole company.

Bertha put out her hand and touched the shadowy fingers of her partner, and then, side by side, she and the ghost of her great-grandfather opened the ball. Together they made the coupé, the high step, and the balance. They advanced, they retired, they came together. With all the grace of fresh young beauty and ancient courtliness they danced the minuet.

"What a strange young girl," said some of the guests, "and what a queer fancy to go through that dance all by herself, but how beautifully she did it!"

"Very eccentric, my dear!" said Mr. John Applejoy, when the dance was over. "But you danced most charmingly. I could not help thinking as I looked at you that there was nobody in this room that was worthy to be your partner."

"You are wrong there, old fellow!" was the simultaneous mental ejaculation of young Tom Burcham and of old Applejoy's ghost.

The ghosts and the moderns do not quite connect—an ironic fable of intelligence.

GREEN HOLLY

Elizabeth Bowen

Mr. Rankstock entered the room with a dragging tread: nobody looked up or took any notice. With a muted groan, he dropped into an armchair—out of which he shot with a sharp yelp. He searched the seat of the chair, and extracted something. '*Your* holly, I think, Miss Bates,' he said, holding it out to her.

Miss Bates took a second or two to look up from her magazine. 'What?' she said. 'Oh, it must have fallen down from that picture. Put it back, please; we haven't got very much.'

'I regret,' interposed Mr. Winterslow, 'that we have any: it makes scratchy noises against the walls.'

'It is seasonable,' said Miss Bates firmly.

'You didn't do this to us last Christmas.'

'Last Christmas,' she said, 'I had Christmas leave. This year there seems to be none with berries: the birds have eaten them. If there were not a draught, the leaves would not scratch the walls. I cannot control the forces of nature, can I?'

'How should I know?' said Mr. Rankstock, lighting his pipe.

These three by now felt that, like Chevalier and his Old Dutch, they had been together for forty years: and to them it did seem a year too much. Actually, their confinement dated from 1940. They were Experts—in what, the Censor would not permit me to say. They were accounted for by their friends in London as 'being somewhere off in the country, nobody knows where, doing something frightfully hush-hush, nobody knows what.' That is, they were accounted for in this manner if there were still anybody who still cared to ask; but on the whole they had dropped out of human memory. Their reappearances in their former circles were infrequent, ghostly and unsuccessful: their friends could hardly disguise their pity, and for their own part they had not a word to say. They had come to prefer to spend leaves with their families, who at least showed a flattering pleasure in their importance.

This Christmas, it so worked out that there was no question of leave for Mr. Rankstock, Mr. Winterslow or Miss Bates: with four others (now playing or watching Ping-Pong in the next room) they composed in their high-grade way a skeleton staff. It may be wondered why, after years of proximity, they should continue to address one another so formally. They did not continue; they had begun again, in the matter of appellations, as in that of intimacy, they had by now, in fact by some time ago, completed the full circle. For some months, they could not recall in which year, Miss Bates had been engaged to Mr. Winterslow; before that, she had been extremely friendly with Mr. Rankstock. Mr. Rankstock's deviation towards one Carla (now at her

Ping-Pong in the next room) had been totally uninteresting to everybody; including, apparently, himself. If the war lasted, Carla might next year be called Miss Tongue; at present, Miss Bates was foremost in keeping her in her place by going on addressing her by her Christian name.

If this felt like their fortieth Christmas in each other's society, it was their first in these particular quarters. You would not have thought, as Mr. Rankstock said, that one country house could be much worse than any other; but this had proved, and was still proving, untrue. The Army, for reasons it failed to justify, wanted the house they had been in since 1940; so they—lock, stock and barrel and files and all—had been bundled into another one, six miles away. Since the move, tentative exploration (for they were none of them walkers) had established that they were now surrounded by rather more mud but fewer trees. What they did know was, their already sufficient distance from the market town with its bars and movies had now been added to by six miles. On the other side of their new home, which was called Mopsam Grange, there appeared to be nothing; unless, as Miss Bates suggested, swineherds, keeping their swine. Mopsam village contained villagers, evacuees, a church, a public-house on whose never-open door was chalked 'No Beer, No Matches, No Teas Served,' and a vicar. The vicar had sent up a nice note, saying he was not clear whether Security regulations would allow him to call; and the doctor had been up once to lance one of Carla's boils.

Mopsam Grange was neither old nor new. It replaced—unnecessarily, they all felt—a house on this site that had been burned down. It had a Gothic porch and gables, French windows, bow windows, a conservatory, a veranda, a hall which, puce-and-buff tiled and

pitch-pine panelled, rose to a gallery: in fact, every ad-
vantage. Jackdaws fidgeted in its many chimneys—for
it had, till the war, stood empty: one had not to ask why.
The hot-water system made what Carla called rude
noises, and was capricious in its supplies to the (only)
two mahogany-rimmed baths. The electric light ran
from a plant in the yard; if the batteries were not kept
charged the light turned brown.

The three now sat in the drawing-room, on whose
walls, mirrors and fitments, long since removed, left
traces. There were, however, some pictures: General
Montgomery (who had just shed his holly) and some
Landseer engravings that had been found in an attic.
Three electric bulbs, naked, shed light manfully; and in
the grate the coal fire was doing far from badly. Miss
Bates rose and stood twiddling the bit of holly. 'Something,' she said, 'has got to be done about this.' Mr.
Winterslow and Mr. Rankstock, the latter sucking in his
pipe, sank lower, between their shoulder-blades, in their
respective arm-chairs. Miss Bates, having drawn a
breath, took a running jump at a table, which she pro-
pelled across the floor with a grating sound. '*Achtung!*'
she shouted at Mr. Rankstock, who, with an oath, withdrew his chair from her route. Having got the table
under General Montgomery, Miss Bates—with a display
of long, slender leg, clad in ribbed scarlet sports stockings, that was of interest to no one—mounted it, then
proceeded to tuck the holly back into position over the
General's frame. Meanwhile, Mr. Winterslow, choosing
his moment, stealthily reached across her empty chair
and possessed himself of her magazine.

What a hope!—Miss Bates was known to have eyes
all the way down her spine. 'Damn you, Mr. Winterslow,' she said, 'put that down! Mr. Rankstock, interfere
with Mr. Winterslow: Mr. Winterslow has taken my

magazine!' She ran up and down the table like something in a cage; Mr. Rankstock removed his pipe from
his mouth, dropped his head back, gazed up and said:
'Gad, Miss Bates; you look fine. . . .'

'It's a pretty *old* magazine,' murmured Mr. Winterslow, flicking the pages over.

'Well, *you're* pretty old,' she said. 'I hope Carla gets
you!'

'Oh, I can do better, thank you; I've got a ghost.'

This confidence, however, was cut off by Mr.
Rankstock's having burst into song. Holding his pipe at
arm's length, rocking on his bottom in his arm-chair, he
led them:

' "Heigh-ho! sing Heigh-ho! unto the green holly:
Most friendship is feigning, most loving mere folly—" '

' *"Mere folly, mere folly,"* ' contributed Mr. Winterslow, picking up, joining in. Both sang:

> Then, heigh-ho, the holly!
> This life is most jolly.

'Now—*all!*' said Mr. Rankstock, jerking his pipe at
Miss Bates. So all three went through it once more,
with degrees of passion: Miss Bates, when others desisted, being left singing 'Heigh-ho! sing heigh-ho!
sing—' all by herself. Next door, the Ping-Pong came
to an awestruck stop. 'At any rate,' said Mr. Rankstock,
'we all like Shakespeare.' Miss Bates, whose intelligence, like her singing, to-night seemed some way at
the tail of the hunt, looked blank, began to get off the
table, and said, 'But I thought that was a Christmas
carol?'

Her companions shrugged and glanced at each other.

Having taken her magazine away from Mr. Winterslow, she was once more settling down to it when she seemed struck. 'What was that you said, about you had got a ghost?'

Mr. Winterslow looked down his nose. 'At this early stage, I don't like to say very much. In fact, on the whole, forget it; if you don't mind—'

'Look,' Mr. Rankstock said, 'if you've started seeing things—'

'I am only sorry,' his colleague said, 'that I've spoke.'

'Oh no, you're not,' said Miss Bates, 'and we'd better know. Just what *is* fishy about this Grange?'

'There is nothing "fishy," ' said Mr. Winterslow in a fastidious tone. It was hard, indeed, to tell from his manner whether he did or did not regret having made a start. He had reddened—but not, perhaps, wholly painfully—his eyes, now fixed on the fire, were at once bright and vacant; with unheeding, fumbling movements he got out a cigarette, lit it and dropped the match on the floor, to slowly burn one more hole in the fibre mat. Gripping the cigarette between tense lips, he first flung his arms out, as though casting off a cloak; then pressed both hands, clasped firmly, to the nerve-centre in the nape of his neck, as though to contain the sensation there. 'She was marvellous,' he brought out—'what I could see of her.'

'Don't talk with your cigarette in your mouth,' Miss Bates said. '—Young?'

'Adorably, not so very. At the same time, quite—oh well, you know what I mean.'

'Uh-huh,' said Miss Bates. 'And wearing—?'

'I am certain she had a feather boa.'

'You mean,' Mr. Rankstock said, 'that this brushed your face?'

'And when and where did this happen?' said Miss Bates with legal coldness.

Cross-examination, clearly, became more and more repugnant to Mr. Winterslow in his present mood. He shut his eyes, sighed bitterly, heaved himself from his chair, said: 'Oh, well—' and stood indecisively looking towards the door. 'Don't let us keep you,' said Miss Bates. 'But one thing I don't see is: if you're being fed with beautiful thoughts, why you wanted to keep on taking my magazine?'

'I wanted to be distracted.'

'?'

'There *are* moments when I don't quite know where I am.'

'You surprise me,' said Mr. Rankstock.—'Good *God*, man, what is the matter?' For Mr. Winterslow, like a man being swooped around by a bat, was revolving, staring from place to place high up round the walls of the gaunt, lit room. Miss Bates observed: 'Well, now we *have* started something.' Mr. Rankstock, considerably kinder, said: 'That is only Miss Bates's holly, flittering in the wind.'

Mr. Winterslow gulped. He walked to the inch of mirror propped on the mantelpiece and, as nonchalantly as possible, straightened his tie. Having done this, he said: 'But there isn't a wind to-night.'

The ghost hesitated in the familiar corridor. Her visibleness, even on Christmas Eve, was not under her own control; and now she had fallen in love again her dependence upon it began to dissolve in patches. This was a concentration of every feeling of the woman prepared to sail downstairs *en grande tenue*. Flamboyance and agitation were both present. But between these, because of her years of death, there cut an extreme anxiety: it was not merely a matter of how was she? but of *was* she—to-night—at all? Death had left her to be her own mirror; for into no other was she able to see.

For to-night, she had discarded the feather boa; it had been dropped into the limbo that was her wardrobe now. Her shoulders, she knew, were bare. Round their bareness shimmered a thousand evenings. Her own person haunted her—above her forehead, the crisped springy weight of her pompadour; round her feet the frou-frou of her skirts on a thick carpet; in her nostrils the scent from her corsage; up and down her forearm the glittery slipping of bracelets warmed by her own blood. It is the haunted who haunt.

There were lights in the house again. She had heard laughter, and there had been singing. From those few dim lights and untrue notes her senses, after their starvation, set going the whole old grand opera. She smiled, and moved down the corridor to the gallery, where she stood looking down into the hall. The tiles of the hall floor were as pretty as ever, as cold as ever, and bore, as always on Christmas Eve, the trickling pattern of dark blood. The figure of the man with the side of his head blown out lay as always, one foot just touching the lowest step of the stairs. It was too bad. She had been silly, but it could not be helped. They should not have shut her up in the country. How could she not make hay while the sun shone? The year round, no man except her husband, his uninteresting jealousy, his dull passion. Then, at Christmas, so many men that one did not know where to turn. The ghost, leaning further over the gallery, pouted down at the suicide. She said: 'You should have let me explain.' The man made no answer: he never had.

Behind a door somewhere downstairs, a racket was going on: the house sounded funny, there were no carpets. The morning-room door was flung open and four flushed people, headed by a young woman, charged out. They clattered across the man and the trickling pattern as though there were nothing there but the tiles. In the morning-room, she saw one small white ball trembling to stillness upon the floor. As the people rushed the stairs and fought for a place in the gallery the ghost drew back—a purest act of repugnance, for this was not necessary. The young woman, to one of whose temples was strapped a cotton-wool pad, held her place and disappeared round a corner exulting: '*My* bath, *my* bath!' 'Then may you freeze in it, Carla!' returned the scrawniest of the defeated ones. The words pierced the ghost, who trembled—they did not know!

Who were they? She did not ask. She did not care. She never had been inquisitive: information had bored her. Her schooled lips had framed one set of questions, her eyes a consuming other. Now the mills of death with their catching wheels had stripped her of semblance, cast her forth on an everlasting holiday from pretense. She was left with—nay, had become—her obsession. Thus is it to be a ghost. The ghost fixed her eyes on the other, the drawing-room door. He had gone in there. He would have to come out again.

The handle turned; the door opened; Winterslow came out. He shut the door behind him, with the sedulous slowness of an uncertain man. He had been humming, and now, squaring his shoulders, began to sing, '. . . *Mere folly, mere folly*—' as he crossed the hall towards the foot of the staircase, obstinately never raising his eyes. 'So it is you,' breathed the ghost, with unheard softness. She gathered about her, with a gesture not less proud for being tormentedly uncertain, the total of her visibility—was it possible diamonds should not glitter now, on her rising-and-falling breast—and swept from the gallery to the head of the stairs.

Winterslow shivered violently, and looked up. He licked his lips. He said: 'This cannot go on.'

The ghost's eyes, with tender impartiality and mockery, from above swept Winterslow's face. The hair receding, the furrowed forehead, the tired sag of the jowl, the strain-reddened eyelids, the blue-shaved chin—nothing was lost on her, nothing broke the spell. With untroubled wonder she saw his handwoven tie, his coat pockets shapeless as saddle-bags, the bulging knees of his flannel trousers. Wonder went up in rhapsody: so much chaff in the fire. She never had had illusions: *the* illusion was all. Lovers cannot be choosers. He'd do. He would have to do. 'I know!' she agreed, with rapture, casting her hands together. 'We are mad—you and I. Oh, what is going to happen? I entreat you to leave this house to-night!'

Winterslow, in a dank, unresounding voice, said: 'And anyhow, what made you pick on me?'

'It's Kismet,' wailed the ghost zestfully. 'Why did you have to come here? Why you? I had been so peaceful, just like a little girl. People spoke of love, but I never knew what they meant. Oh, I could wish we had never met, you and I!'

Winterslow said: 'I have been here for three months; we have all of us been here, as a matter of fact. Why all this all of a sudden?'

She said: 'There's a Christmas Eve party, isn't there, going on? One Christmas Eve party, there was a terrible accident. Oh, comfort me! No one has understood. Don't stand *there*; I can't bear it—not just *there*!'

Winterslow, whether he heard or not, cast a scared glance down at his feet, which were in slippers, then shifted a pace or two to the left. 'Let me up,' he said wildly. 'I tell you, I want my spectacles! I just want to get my spectacles. Let me by!'

'*Let* you up!' the ghost marvelled. 'But, I am only waiting. . . .'

She was more than waiting: she set up a sort of suction, an icy indrawing draught. Nor was this wholly psychic, for an isolated holly leaf of Miss Bates's, dropped at a turn of the staircase, twitched. And not, you could think, by chance did the electric light choose this moment for one of its brown fade-outs: gradually, the scene—the hall, the stairs and the gallery—faded under this fog-dark but glass-clear veil of hallucination. The feet of Winterslow, under remote control, began with knocking unsureness to mount the stairs. At their turn he staggered, steadied himself, and then stamped derisively upon the holly leaf. 'Bah,' he neighed— '*spectacles!*'

By the ghost now putting out everything, not a word could be dared.

'Where are you?'

Weakly, her dress rustled, three steps down: the rings on her hand knocked weakly over the panelling. 'Here, oh here,' she sobbed. 'Where I was before. . . .'

'Hell,' said Miss Bates, who had opened the drawing-room door and was looking resentfully round the hall. 'This electric light.'

Mr. Rankstock, from inside the drawing-room, said: 'Find the man.'

'The man has gone to the village. Mr. Rankstock, if *you* were half a man—Mr. Winterslow, what are you doing, kneeling down on the stairs? Have you come over funny? Really, this is the end.'

At the other side of a baize door, one of the installations began ringing. 'Mr. Rankstock,' Miss Bates yelled implacably, 'yours, this time.' Mr. Rankstock, with an expression of hatred, whipped out a pencil and pad and shambled across the hall. Under cover of this Mr. Winterslow pushed himself upright, brushed his knees and began to descend the stairs, to confront his colleague's narrow but not unkind look. Weeks of exile from any hairdresser had driven Miss Bates to the Alice-in-Wonderland style: her snood, tied at the top, was now thrust back, adding inches to her pale, polished brow. Nicotine stained the fingers she closed upon Mr. Winterslow's elbow, propelling him back to the drawing-room. 'There is always drink,' she said. 'Come along.'

He said hopelessly: 'If you mean the bottle between the filing cabinets, I finished that when I had to work last night. Look here, Miss Bates, why should she have picked on *me*?'

'It has been broken off, then?' said Miss Bates. 'I'm sorry for you, but I don't like your tone. I resent your attitude to my sex. For that matter, why did you pick on her? Romantic, nostalgic, Blue-Danube-fixated—hein? There's Carla, an understanding girl, unselfish, getting over her boils; there are Avice and Lettice, due back on Boxing Day. There is me, as you have ceased to observe. But oh dear no; *we* do not trail feather boas—'

'—She only wore that in the afternoon.'

'Now let me tell you something,' said Miss Bates. 'When I opened the door, just now, to have a look at the lights, what do you think *I* first saw there in the hall?'

'Me,' replied Mr. Winterslow, with returning assurance.

'*O-oh* no; oh indeed no,' said Miss Bates. 'You—why should I think twice of that, if you *were* striking attitudes on the stairs? You?—no, I saw your enchanting inverse. Extended, and it is true stone dead, I saw the man of my dreams. From his attitude, it was clear he had died for love. There were three pearl studs in his boiled shirt, and his white tie must have been tied in heaven. And the hand that had dropped the pistol had dropped a white rose; it lay beside him brown and crushed from having been often kissed. The ideality of those kisses, for the last of which I arrived too late'— here Miss Bates beat her fist against the bow of her snood—'will haunt, and by haunting satisfy me. The destruction of his features, before I saw them, made their former perfection certain, where I am concerned. And here I am, left, left, left, to watch dust gather on Mr. Rankstock and you; to watch—yes, I who saw in a flash the ink-black perfection of *his* tailoring—mildew form on those clothes that you never change; to remember how both of you had in common that way of blowing your noses before you kissed me. He had been deceived—hence the shot, hence the fall. But who was *she*, your feathered friend, to deceive him? Who could have deceived him more superbly than I?—*I could be fatal,*' moaned Miss Bates, pacing the drawing-room, '*I could be fatal*—only give me a break!'

'Well, I'm sorry,' said Mr. Winterslow, 'but really, what can I do, or poor Rankstock do? We are just ourselves.'

'You put the thing in a nutshell,' said Miss Bates. 'Perhaps I could bear it if you just got your hairs cut.'

'If it comes to that, Miss Bates, you might get yours set.'

Mr. Rankstock's re-entry into the drawing-room—this time with brisker step, for a nice little lot of new trouble was brewing up—synchronized with the fall of the piece of holly, again, from the General's frame to the Rankstock chair. This time he saw it in time. '*Your* holly, I think, Miss Bates,' he said, holding it out to her.

'We must put it back,' said Miss Bates. 'We haven't got very much.'

'I cannot see,' said Mr. Winterslow, 'why we should have any. I don't see the point of holly without berries.'

'The birds have eaten them,' said Miss Bates. 'I cannot control the forces of nature, can I?'

'Then heigh-ho! sing heigh-ho!' Mr. Rankstock led off.

'Yes,' she said, 'let us have that pretty carol again.'

A young woman's salvation depends upon
the ghosts of memory.

FLOODLIGHTS

Martha Soukup

The house was cold. Someone, one of her father's
neighbors, or the lawyer who was his executor,
must have turned the heat all the way down. She
hoped so. If the furnace was off, she had no idea how
to relight it. The thermostat was a few steps away at the
foot of the stair. It took a moment to (*"Don't* touch that
thermostat!") make herself dial it from 55 up to 70.

Then with a clunk Celia heard the furnace go on in
the basement. She rubbed her chilled fingers and told
herself: *There's nothing hard about this. This is an in-
and-out operation, an evening's work. Go through the
house, get anything of importance, and drive back home
to Chicago.* Tomorrow was Christmas Eve. They would
spend it at home.

Another blast of wind made her turn. "Where do you
want these?" David held four liquor-store boxes, two in
each gloved hand.

"I don't know, just drop them. For God's sake, close that door!" Cardboard boxes tumbled across hardwood floor as he closed the door, pushing it firmly against the wind.

"Where do we start?" We. As though he knew what was important to her in this place. If anything was.

"I'm going upstairs," she said abruptly. She took the steps two at a time, the way she had when she was a teenager and speed was the next best thing to invisibility. Leaving David at the foot of the stairs.

"Take one of these," he called. He heaved a box underhanded up to her. Aerodynamics nearly caught it short, but it thumped at her feet. "Thanks," she said, more shortly than she'd meant to, and picked it up. California Chablis. (But she smelled gin.)

The first room down the hall was the twins' room. Still two twin beds in it. As a child she'd been amazed they made a bed just for twins.

Amy and Ann were four years younger than Celia. They were well grown up now, Amy in Connecticut with a husband and a baby (odd to picture her baby sister with a baby) and Ann in California, selling surfboards. When she thought of them, though, she thought of toddlers who always giggled at Celia's silly faces, bright, pretty toddlers growing up into increasingly quiet, frightened little girls.

What arrangements the twins would make to get their remaining things out of the house she didn't know. She went to the dresser and picked up a porcelain figurine. It was Ann's white horse with the gilt glazing in its blue mane; Amy's pink-maned horse wasn't there. She turned the horse over to see the lumpy, clumsy glue line that joined its foreleg to the body. There it was. Amazing what you could remember after twenty years, all the way forward to 1989.

She knew what Ann would remember about the horse, because her sister had talked about it gratefully for years: the horse was a gift from their grandmother that promised some unpredictable but terrible punishment if her mother had discovered it in two pieces. When Ann broke it and panicked, when she had no idea what to do, Celia took charge and swiftly glued it back together, matter-of-factly protecting the younger girl. As she always did.

Celia's memory, more mature, saw more completely and harshly: the broken horse, the stricken, tight-chested feeling, dread that turned quickly into a black rage of her own. She had grabbed the figurine and screamed at the frightened five-year-old, and when Ann started crying, she'd hit her hard on the arm, screaming louder. Ann started to hiccup her tears back into herself, the way she would with their mother, and Celia's rage drained instantly away, leaving nothing but the guilt. She raced down the back stairs, found some glue, and mended the horse with shaking hands; returning the same way, she took her little sister into her lap, rocking and whispering to her. Secret, it was a secret, and it was safe. Ann smiled a roomful of gratitude at her, which made the guilt bigger. Growing up to be like her mother. She could feel it already at nine. It terrified her.

"Hey, there's a back staircase!" came David's voice, hollow and distant. She heard his footsteps echoing from behind the staircase door. "Pretty neat," he said, emerging. "I thought it was a closet until I opened the door. I'll bet you kids used it all the time. The hide-and-seek possibilities are endless!"

"Yes," she said. "It's pretty narrow. I don't think my parents used it much." But she and the twins used it to conceal their movements. Several times, to see a forbidden movie, she would sneak out down the stairs after bedtime, one slow step at a time, duck down to the basement, pry open a window, and run all the way downtown to the theater. She was never caught, and she always expected to be.

"Could be," David said. "It's about the only place I've seen here that isn't full of clutter." He looked interested. "Except for this room." He nodded at it. "Hospital setup. Your mom?"

Celia glanced unwillingly at it, the hospital bed, the chrome handrails set up optimistically around the room. "I guess so." The accident had happened after she'd gone to England for her doctorate, but before she met David there, two Americans shoved together by mutual friends. By the time she came back to the States two years later, her father, sick himself, had given up and put her mother in a nursing home. Celia had visited her mother three times over the last three years. Birthday visits. They had been grueling, for two reasons. Her mother was too far gone to recognize Celia; and Celia could not help thinking every time: *You asked for it, drinking all the time. No wonder you crashed into that tree.*

And feeling the overwhelming guilt, again.

"I don't think there's anything I'm going to want here," she said to David. "I've still got presents to wrap at home. Let's leave."

"After an hour's drive to get here? I want to look around a little more, if that's okay with you." Without waiting for an answer, he went into her parents' bedroom.

She followed reluctantly. This room had been forbidden territory. Of course, that made it fascinating to a child. She sat down on the bed and felt her hand automatically steal under the mattress on her mother's side.

How old was she when she'd found the hip bottle of gin hidden between mattress and box spring? Six, perhaps. Old enough to know there was something terribly wrong with it being there, something she couldn't tell anyone about. Old enough to be frightened of her mother finding her finding the bottle, and to worry for days that some small smudge of fingerprint would be visible on the glass when her mother pulled it out.

"You've got wrapping to do?" asked David from the closet. "Then I found some paper for you." He came out with his arms full of rolls of Christmas paper. Celia took one. Santa after Santa smiled a round red smile at her. The paper was stiff with age. He dumped them onto the bed beside her. "Want it?"

"No," she said. "This junk is too old. Cheap looking." David was already back noisily rooting around in the closet. ". . . Would you stop that!" she shouted. He poked his head out, looking startled. Celia swallowed. "I'm sorry. I just don't like it here."

"Okay, okay. You really meant it when you said you didn't like this place, didn't you? Don't worry, I'll stay out of your way. I'll go see what's buried in the basement." She couldn't meet his eyes. A few moments later she heard his shoes clomping down the back staircase.

I never touch a drop of alcohol and I sound just like her anyway, she thought. *Damn me.*

She promised herself she could go home after she'd checked out her bedroom.

All her books were long gone. The closet was full of old clothes she didn't care about; she'd tell her father's lawyer to call the Goodwill. She pulled out all the drawers in the dresser. There was a thin gold bracelet she thought she might as well take. She slid it into a back pocket, wondering why she'd bothered to bring any boxes at all.

The room looked alien, its familiarity old and dreamlike. She sat on the bed and sank into its over-worn softness. Definitely her bed. She lay down on it and traced a familiar crack in the wall, an outline like a cowboy with a branching crack for a hat and a curl at the bottom that served as his lariat, curled at his feet. She used to lie on this bed and dream a cowboy would sweep her off on his horse to a place that was all rust-red horizon, distant, strange, very far away. She used to lie on this bed and listen to her mother shouting at her father, his voice never raised back. She used to lie on this bed and wonder miserably what she had done wrong today, what she'd be punished for next.

Night after night, every night the same.

And fantasizing, oh, fantasizing, when she was twelve and thirteen and in junior high school, when her friends' parents all seemed to be divorcing. Fantasizing that she would come home someday and her quiet ac-countant father would be waiting for her in front with the car, her little sisters in the back, hopping with ex-citement. "We're leaving now," her father would say in the fantasy. "Your mother gets the house and I get you." She would get in the car and sit next to her father, and he would pull it out of park into drive and say, "Where do you want to go, Celia? We can go anywhere you want," and the twins would be shouting, "Disneyland! France! China! Disneyland!" and Celia would look at her father and grin and say, "West. Drive west," and into a rust-red sunset they would drive, to the land of cowboy hats and open plains, leaving the house on Hawthorne far, far away.

She wished it so hard she knew it had to happen.

Families split up all the time, and the kids didn't need to stay with their mother. Maybe her father would just come quietly tapping at her door in the middle of the night, so her mother wouldn't know about it, and together they would gather up the twins and a few changes of clothes and they would leave. Maybe it would be tonight.

It was never tonight. Her father was nothing. A coward. Her father was worse than her mother, because he didn't have the excuse of a bottle, because every day he saw what was happening in his house and he never did a damned thing about it.

She opened her eyes, grabbed blindly at something by the bedside—an alarm clock—and hurled it at the cowboy crack on the wall. It smashed against the wall, crushing the cowboy into unrecognizability. "Damn you!" she whispered harshly. "Damn you, old man. You never gave one good goddamn about any of us! I hate you!" And the guilty part deep inside her told her in her mother's voice that it was because she'd never deserved it. She didn't deserve a father to take her away, and now she didn't even deserve a father alive at all.

Look at the mess she had made of the wall, at the clock lying by the long shards of its broken plastic face. No matter how bad things were, she was able to make things worse. She buried her face in the musty, yellowed pillowcase and sobbed the racking, silent sobs she'd learned so many years ago.

Nobody was ever going to take her away, free her, save her. However far she fled, the house was there. Filled with strangers, it would still seethe with her memories: she couldn't run away from them. She sobbed until the pillow was soaked with it.

A long time later she rolled over. It was dark. The

lights were all off. There was a quality to the darkness that suggested dawn about to break. She looked for her clock, but it wasn't by the bed, so she tiptoed out of the room. The house was very still. Her new flannel nightgown whispered crisply around her slippered feet. She crept to the head of the stairs and sat with her feet on the first step like sitting in the middle of a bench. She waited. She knew she could wait a long time.

The hallway was purple with the first light when she heard another creeping noise behind her. Annie squeezed in on Celia's left side, by the stairway wall. A minute late, Amy snuggled in on her other side, and the three of them sat there, warm, flanneled thighs pressed against each other, suppressing Christmas morning giggles.

Purple light turned pink, and then white, a special Christmas light no other morning had. Celie had one twin's hand in each of hers. The three new Christmas nightgowns all matched each other, white with red snowflakes all over. Their new Christmas slippers were different colors. Celie's red, Annie's blue, Amy's green. The slippers felt very clean. She wiggled her toes inside them.

There was a tiny sound of the back stair door opening, and a creaking from the back stairs. A few minutes later, the house smelled like bacon. There was always breakfast on Christmas, breakfast and no fights. Her stomach growled and the twins squirmed with anticipation, but she held them fast, like a good big sister. Waiting for everything to be perfect.

Then the lights went on! Flooding up the stairs, the Hollywood lights, hot on her face. The twins squealed and jumped to their feet. Celie put on her Hollywood smile and stood to begin the stately march down the stairs. She could hear the film rolling in Daddy's camera. Christmas morning, and she was a star!

Mother came from the kitchen with a spatula in her hand, and they all grinned at each other. The twins waved frantically. They burst down to the bottom of the stairs and threw themselves at Daddy's knees. He turned the camera down to their upturned faces. They dragged him toward the living room. Celie turned the corner and saw the stockings stuffed up past their tops, the tree ambushed by bright-wrapped presents. "Santa's been here!" she shouted. The twins squealed again, let loose of Daddy's knees, and ripped their stockings down from the fireplace screen. Daddy set the camera on the coffee table.

Celie had her stocking in her hand, but something made her stop and climb on her Daddy's lap. The camera rolled. "I love you, Daddy," she said. She put her arms up around his neck. "Do you know that? Do you know that, Daddy?"

"I know that," he said soberly. "I love you, Celie. I wish it was always like this." He stroked her hair. Then he picked up the camera and said, "Close-up! Smile for all the people out there!" and Celie threw her head back and shook her short hair like a movie star, like Marilyn Monroe on television. Then she ran laughing past her father and up the stairs, posing at the head like a Southern belle atop a grand spiral staircase, enthralling her admirers below. Her father turned the camera up at her. The light was very bright, and it made her eyes tear up, and she blinked the tears away. . . .

And she was standing at the top of the stairs, struck with vertigo. She grabbed for the newel post.

"Are you okay?" David asked from the foot of the stairs. "What are you doing?"

"Um," she said stupidly.

"I wanted to show you what I found in the basement."

Celia shook the dizziness away and peered down at him. David was holding a strange contraption of wood and floodlights. She recognized her father's movie camera and homebuilt light rig.

"Did—did you have that plugged in? The lights?"

"Are you kidding? This thing's such a mess I'd probably start a fire. What is it?"

Celia worked her way slowly down the stairs, as slowly as the Christmas morning procession. "My dad's movie camera." It was as she'd just seen it, a mess of two-by-twos, protruding nails, and electrical cord. "He built that light setup. He only used it for Christmas, and vacation once or twice."

"Pretty wild," said David. "Good thing he didn't try for a career in electrical engineering."

"What do you have there on the floor?"

He glanced down at a pile of flat boxes. "Bunch of videotapes. They were with the camera. I think he had your Christmas movies transferred to tape."

She bent and picked them up. *Christmas, 1963,* said the first one in her father's careful accountant's handwriting. *Christmas, 1966. Christmas 1965. Christmas 1971.* No particular order. *Christmas 1967.*

"Do you want to look at them?"

Her throat was beginning to ache. "Not now. Later." She gathered the tapes together and slid them into a champagne box, taking the camera and light rig from David's hands and putting them carefully on top of the tapes. "Let's go home."

"Have you seen everything you need to see here?"

"Yes," she said. "Yes."

* * *

They had opened the stockings they had separately snuck out of bed to stuff for each other, pretending to be Santa; and now David was rustling around in the kitchen. Celia gathered scraps of wrapping paper from around the living room, crumpling them and dropping them in one of the leftover liquor boxes. Then the champagne box caught her eye. The top videotape was just visible through the wiring of the light rig.

Christmas 1989 it said in neat blue ink.

But it must mean 1969. She pulled the tape out from under the wiring to look more closely. There was no mistaking the numbers of a man who had worked with numbers for a living.

The smell of bacon drifted from the kitchen. Celia took the tape over to the VCR and slid it into the slot. She hit Play, and held her breath as snow filled the screen.

It fluttered twice, and Amy and Ann, looking about three, danced in front of the camera, pushing each other out of center frame, giggling. There was an odd flicker to the picture. Their bright new nightgowns were white with red snowflakes.

"Santa's been here!" shouted a child's voice. The picture lurched violently into the living room. Her father was never much of a cinematographer.

She stared at the screen. The night before Christmas Eve she had had a dream, she told herself. The tape was mislabeled, and it was a coincidence that she'd dreamed the same nightgowns.

She wanted to see her father.

The picture steadied and she saw herself climb into her father's lap, throwing her arms up around his neck. "I love you, Daddy," said Celia on the screen, her voice muffled by her father's pajama top.

"I do," said Celia to the television, wishing he could hear. "I do. I don't hate you because you didn't take me away forever, Daddy, I don't. You did the best you could."

Her father embraced the child on the screen, bending forward and showing his bald spot. He looked up at the camera. "That's only part of an excuse, Celia. I could have done better. I could have done something."

Celia blinked. "You didn't know what to do," she whispered.

He inclined his head. "I didn't know what to do. But I loved you, Celie, and I wish I'd made your childhood better. It was such a mess, trying to take care of your mother, and you, and your sisters, and I never did know the right thing to do. I tried."

"I know. . . ."

"You came out okay, you know? Despite my mistakes. Maybe I never told you how proud I was of my daughter the history professor. Of the way you girls always stuck together. You and Amy and Ann. You did okay."

She put her hand up and laid it on the screen.

"I can't take you away, Celia," he said, stroking her younger self's hair. "You have to try to do that yourself. You and your David have to take each other into the future. Try not to make the same mistakes your mother and I made. She loved you, too. It may have been hard to tell, but she did. Will you do that?"

"I promise, Daddy." Tears were starting, but this time they didn't hurt coming out.

He smiled. "Merry Christmas, Celie." The picture began to snow out. Celia put her face next to it, to see the last of him fade away.

"Good-bye, Daddy. . . ."

The picture went black. She took her face from the cool, wet glass and wiped her eyes. "David," she whispered. "David!"

He appeared in the doorway, spatula in hand. "What is it? What's wrong?"

Clumsily, she hit the eject button. "My father," she said, afraid to be saying it. "My father was on this tape."

"It's one of the Christmas films, isn't it?"

"Yes, but he talked to me!" David looked blank. "Look. Look at the date."

"Nineteen eighty-nine. So it's new. What is it, one of those will videos? Is that what's upset you?"

"No—it was Christmas, and I was a kid on the film, but he was talking to me *now*—I don't know how he could do that, how could he do that?"

"You're overstressed." He took the tape from her hand. "Too much has happened lately. Why don't I put this away?"

"No, I want to see it again. You can see him. He was talking right to me. . . ."

"All right, okay." He put the tape in the rewinder next to the television. "I'm sure it's nothing." The rewind machine popped the tape out; he slid it into the VCR.

Celia leaned forward.

The picture was blank.

"You see?" said David. "He must've been planning to tape you, before the stroke. Invite us out and tape it on his video camera."

"He didn't have a video camera." The screen stayed blank.

"So he was going to get one." David ejected the tape and put it in its box. "Why don't you lie down for a while after breakfast?"

Celia looked at the rewinder, its erase button right beside the rewind button, and at David's careful, concerned face. He had erased it.

"I'll lie down." she said. It would give her time to tell David what she had to do, that she had stopped running. That evening they were going to visit her mother. She took the blank tape and held it, warm and solid, in her lap.

Jolly chills turn colder when a young man
pretends to be a ghost.

THE REAL AND THE
COUNTERFEIT

Mrs. Alfred Baldwin

Will Musgrave determined that he would neither
keep Christmas alone, nor spend it again with his
parents and sisters in the south of France. The
Musgrave family annually migrated southward from
their home in Northumberland, and Will as regularly followed them to spend a month with them in the Riviera,
till he had almost forgotten what Christmas was like in
England. He rebelled at having to leave the country at a
time when, if the weather was mild, he should be hunting, or if it was severe, skating, and he had no real or
imaginary need to winter in the south. His chest was of
iron and his lungs of brass. A raking east wind that
drove his parents into their thickest furs, and taught
them the number of their teeth by enabling them to
count a separate and well-defined ache for each, only
brought a deeper colour into the cheek, and a brighter
light into the eye of the weather-proof youth. Decidedly

he would not go to Cannes, though it was no use annoying his father and mother, and disappointing his sisters,
by telling them beforehand of his determination.

Will knew very well how to write a letter to his
mother in which his defection should appear as an event
brought about by the overmastering power of circumstances, to which the sons of Adam must submit. No
doubt that a prospect of hunting or skating, as the fates
might decree, influenced his decision. But he had also
long promised himself the pleasure of a visit from two
of his college friends, Hugh Armitage and Horace
Lawley, and he asked that they might spend a fortnight
with him at Stonecroft, as a little relaxation had been
positively ordered for him by his tutor.

"Bless him," said his mother fondly, when she had
read his letter, "I will write to the dear boy and tell him
how pleased I am with his firmness and determination."
But Mr. Musgrave muttered inarticulate sounds as he
listened to his wife, expressive of incredulity rather than
of acquiescence, and when he spoke it was to say,
"Devil of a row three young fellows will kick up alone
at Stonecroft! We shall find the stables full of broken-
kneed horses when we go home again."

Will Musgrave spent Christmas day with the Armi-
tages at their place near Ripon. And the following night
they gave a dance at which he enjoyed himself as only
a very young man can do, who has not yet had his fill
of dancing, and who would like nothing better than to
waltz through life with his arm round his pretty partner's waist. The following day, Musgrave and Armitage
left for Stonecroft, picking up Lawley on the way, and
arriving at their destination late in the evening, in the
highest spirits and with the keenest appetites. Stonecroft
was a delightful haven of refuge at the end of a long
journey across country in bitter weather, when the east

wind was driving the light dry snow into every nook
and cranny. The wide, hospitable front door opened into
an oak panelled hall with a great open fire burning
cheerily, and lighted by lamps from overhead that effec-
tually dispelled all gloomy shadows. As soon as Musgrave had entered the house he seized his friends, and
before they had time to shake the snow from their coats,
kissed them both under the mistletoe bough and set the
servants tittering in the background.

"You're miserable substitutes for your betters," he
said, laughing and pushing them from him, "but it's awfully unlucky not to use the mistletoe. Barker, I hope
supper's ready, and that it is something very hot and
plenty of it, for we've travelled on empty stomachs and
brought them with us," and he led his guests upstairs to
their rooms.

"What a jolly gallery!" said Lawley enthusiastically
as they entered a long wide corridor, with many doors
and several windows in it, and hung with pictures and
trophies of arms.

"Yes, it's our one distinguishing feature at Stonecroft," said Musgrave. "It runs the whole length of the
house, from the modern end of it to the back, which is
very old, and built on the foundations of a Cistercian
monastery which once stood on this spot. The gallery's
wide enough to drive a carriage and pair down it, and
it's the main thoroughfare of the house. My mother
takes a constitutional here in bad weather, as though it
were the open air, and does it with her bonnet on to aid
the delusion."

Armitage's attention was attracted by the pictures on
the walls, and especially by the life-size portrait of a
young man in a blue coat, with powdered hair, sitting
under a tree with a stag-hound lying at his feet.

"An ancestor of yours?" he said, pointing at the picture.

"Oh, they're all one's ancestors, and a motley crew they are, I must say for them. It may amuse you and Lawley to find from which of them I derive my good looks. That pretty youth whom you seem to admire is my great-great-grandfather. He died at twenty-two, a preposterous age for an ancestor. But come along, Armitage, you'll have plenty of time to do justice to the pictures by daylight, and I want to show you your rooms. I see everything is arranged comfortably, we are close together. Our pleasantest rooms are on the gallery, and here we are nearly at the end of it. Your rooms are opposite to mine, and open into Lawley's in case you should be nervous in the night and feel lonely so far from home, my dear children."

And Musgrave bade his friends make haste, and hurried away whistling cheerfully to his own room.

The following morning the friends rose to a white world. Six inches of fine snow, dry as salt, lay everywhere, the sky overhead a leaden lid, and all the signs of a deep fall yet to come.

"Cheerful this, very," said Lawley, as he stood with his hands in his pockets, looking out of the window after breakfast. "The snow will have spoilt the ice for skating."

"But it won't prevent wild duck shooting," said Armitage, "and I say, Musgrave, we'll rig up a toboggan out there. I see a slope that might have been made on purpose for it. If we get some tobogganing, it may snow day and night for all I care, we shall be masters of the situation any way."

"Well thought of, Armitage," said Musgrave, jumping at the idea.

"Yes, but you need two slopes and a little valley be-

tween for real good tobogganing," objected Lawley.
"Otherwise you only rush down the hillock like you do
from the Mount Church to Funchal, and then have to re-
trace your steps as you do there, carrying your car on
your back. Which lessens the fun considerably."

"Well, we can only work with the material at hand,"
said Armitage; "let's go and see if we can't find a better
place for our toboggan, and something that will do for
a car to slide in."

"That's easily found—empty wine cases are the
thing, and stout sticks to steer with," and away rushed
the young men into the open air, followed by half a
dozen dogs barking joyfully.

"By Jove! If the snow keeps firm, we'll put runners
on strong chairs and walk over to see the Harradines at
Garthside, and ask the girls to come out sledging, and
we'll push them," shouted Musgrave to Lawley and
Armitage, who had outrun him in the vain attempt to
keep up with a deer-hound that headed the party. After
a long and careful search they found a piece of land exactly suited to their purpose, and it would have amused
their friends to see how hard the young men worked
under the beguiling name of pleasure. For four hours
they worked like navvies making a toboggan slide.
They shovelled away the snow, then with pickaxe and
spade, levelled the ground, so that when a carpet of
fresh snow was spread over it, their improvised car
would run down a steep incline and be carried by the
impetus up another, till it came to a standstill in a snow
drift.

"If we can only get this bit of engineering done to-
day," said Lawley, chucking a spadeful of earth aside as
he spoke, "the slide will be in perfect order for to-
morrow."

"Yes, and when once it's done, it's done for ever,"

said Armitage, working away cheerfully with his pick where the ground was frozen hard and full of stones, and cleverly keeping his balance on the slope as he did so. "Good work lasts no end of a time, and posterity will bless us for leaving them this magnificent slide."

"Posterity may, my dear fellow, but hardly our progenitors if my father should happen to slip down it," said Musgrave.

When their task was finished, and the friends were transformed in appearance from navvies into gentlemen, they set out through thick falling snow to walk to Garthside to call on their neighbours the Harradines. They had earned their pleasant tea and lively talk, their blood was still aglow from their exhilarating work, and their spirits at the highest point. They did not return to Stonecroft till they had compelled the girls to name a time when they would come with their brothers and be launched down the scientifically prepared slide, in wine cases well padded with cushions for the occasion.

Late that night the young men sat smoking and chatting together in the library. They had played billiards till they were tired, and Lawley had sung sentimental songs, accompanying himself on the banjo, till even he was weary, to say nothing of what his listeners might be. Armitage sat leaning his light curly head back in the chair, gently puffing out a cloud of tobacco smoke. And he was the first to break the silence that had fallen on the little company.

"Musgrave," he said suddenly, "an old house is not complete unless it is haunted. You ought to have a ghost of your own at Stonecroft."

Musgrave threw done the yellow-backed novel he had just picked up, and became all attention.

"So we have, my dear fellow. Only it has not been seen by any of us since my grandfather's time. It is the desire of my life to become personally acquainted with our family ghost."

Armitage laughed. But Lawley said, "You would not. say that if you really believed in ghosts."

"I believe in them most devoutly, but I naturally wish to have my faith confirmed by sight. You believe in them too, I can see."

"Then you see what does not exist, and so far you are in a fair way to see ghosts. No, my state of mind is this," continued Lawley, "I neither believe, nor entirely disbelieve in ghosts. I am open to conviction on the subject. Many men of sound judgment believe in them, and others of equally good mental capacity don't believe in them. I merely regard the case of the bogies as not proven. They may, or may not exist, but till their existence is plainly demonstrated, I decline to add such an uncomfortable article to my creed as a belief in bogies."

Musgrave did not reply, but Armitage laughed a strident laugh.

"I'm one against two, I'm in an overwhelming minority," he said. "Musgrave frankly confesses his belief in ghosts, and you are neutral, neither believing nor disbelieving, but open to conviction. Now I'm a complete unbeliever in the supernatural, root and branch. People's nerves no doubt play them queer tricks, and will continue to do so to the end of the chapter, and if I were so fortunate as to see Musgrave's family ghost tonight, I should no more believe in it than I do now. By the way, Musgrave, is the ghost a lady or a gentleman?" he asked flippantly.

"I don't think you deserve to be told."

"Don't you know that a ghost is neither he nor she?" said Lawley. "Like a corpse, it is always *it*."

"That is a piece of very definite information from a

man who neither believes nor disbelieves in ghosts. How do you come by it, Lawley?" asked Armitage.

"Mayn't a man be well informed on a subject although he suspends his judgment about it? I think I have the only logical mind among us. Musgrave believes in ghosts though he has never seen one, you don't believe in them, and say that you would not be convinced if you saw one, which is not wise, it seems to me."

"It is not necessary to my peace of mind to have a definite opinion on the subject. After all, it is only a matter of patience, for if ghosts really exist we shall each be one in the course of time, and then, if we've nothing better to do, and are allowed to play such unworthy pranks, we may appear again on the scene, and impartially scare our credulous and incredulous surviving friends."

"Then I shall try to be beforehand with you, Lawley, and turn bogie first; it would suit me better to scare than to be scared. But, Musgrave, do tell me about your family ghost; I'm really interested in it, and I'm quite respectful now."

"Well, mind you are, and I shall have no objection to tell you what I know about it, which is briefly this: Stonecroft, as I told you, is built on the site of an old Cistercian monastery destroyed at the time of the Reformation. The back part of the house rests on the old foundations, and its walls are built with the stones that were once part and parcel of the monastery. The ghost that has been seen by members of the Musgrave family for three centuries past, is that of a Cistercian monk, dressed in the white habit of his order. Who he was, or why he has haunted the scenes of his earthly life so long, there is no tradition to enlighten us. The ghost has usually been seen once or twice in each generation. But as I said, it has not visited us since my grandfather's time, so, like a comet, it should be due again presently."

"How you must regret that was before your time," said Armitage.

"Of course I do, but I don't despair of seeing it yet. At least I know where to look for it. It has always made its appearance in the gallery, and I have my bedroom close to the spot where it was last seen, in the hope that if I open my door suddenly some moonlight night I may find the monk standing there."

"Standing where?" asked the incredulous Armitage.

"In the gallery, to be sure, midway between your two doors and mine. That is where my grandfather last saw it. He was waked in the dead of night by the sound of a heavy door shutting. He ran into the gallery where the noise came from, and, standing opposite the door of the room I occupy, was the white figure of the Cistercian monk. As he looked, it glided the length of the gallery and melted like mist into the wall. The spot where he disappeared is on the old foundations of the monastery, so that he was evidently returning to his own quarters."

"And your grandfather believed that he saw a ghost?" asked Armitage disdainfully.

"Could he doubt the evidence of his senses? He saw the thing as clearly as we see each other now, and it disappeared like a thin vapour against the wall."

"My dear fellow, don't you think that it sounds more like an anecdote of your grandmother than of your grandfather?" remarked Armitage. He did not intend to be rude, though he succeeded in being so, as he was instantly aware by the expression of cold reserve that came over Musgrave's frank face.

"Forgive me, but I never can take a ghost story seriously," he said. "But this much I will concede—they may have existed long ago in what were literally the dark ages, when rushlights and sputtering dip candles could not keep the shadows at bay. But in this latter part of the nineteenth century, when gas and the electric light have turned night into day, you have destroyed the very conditions that produced the ghost—or rather the belief in it, which is the same thing. Darkness has always been bad for human nerves. I can't explain why, but so it is. My mother was in advance of the age on the subject, and always insisted on having a good light burning in the night nursery, so that when as a child I woke from a bad dream I was never frightened by the darkness. And in consequence I have grown up a complete unbeliever in ghosts, spectres, wraiths, apparitions, dopplegängers, and the whole bogie crew of them," and Armitage looked round calmly and complacently.

"Perhaps I might have felt as you do if I had not begun life with the knowledge that our house was haunted," replied Musgrave with visible pride in the ancestral ghost. "I only wish that I could convince you of the existence of the supernatural from my own personal experience. I always feel it to be the weak point in a ghost-story, that it is never told in the first person. It is a friend, or a friend of one's friend, who was the lucky man, and actually saw the ghost." And Armitage registered a vow to himself, that within a week from that time Musgrave should see his family ghost with his own eyes, and ever after be able to speak with his enemy in the gate.

Several ingenious schemes occurred to his inventive mind for producing the desired apparition. But he had to keep them burning in his breast. Lawley was the last man to aid and abet him in playing a practical joke on their host, and he feared he should have to work without an ally. And though he would have enjoyed his help and sympathy, it struck him that it would be a double triumph achieved, if both his friends should see the Cistercian monk. Musgrave already believed in ghosts, and was prepared to meet one more than half way, and Lawley, though he pretended to a judicial and impartial mind concerning them, was not unwilling to be convinced of their existence, if it could be visibly demonstrated to him.

Armitage became more cheerful than usual as circumstances favoured his impious plot. The weather was propitious for the attempt he meditated, as the moon rose late and was approaching the full. On consulting the almanac he saw with delight that three nights hence she would rise at 2 A.M., and an hour later the end of the gallery nearest Musgrave's room would be flooded with her light. Though Armitage could not have an accomplice under the roof, he needed one within reach, who could use needle and thread, to run up a specious imitation of the white robe and hood of a Cistercian monk. And the next day, when they went to the Harradines to take the girls out in their improvised sledges, it fell to his lot to take charge of the youngest Miss Harradine. As he pushed the low chair on runners over the hard snow, nothing was easier than to bend forward and whisper to Kate, "I am going to take you as fast as I can, so that no one can hear what we are saying. I want you to be very kind, and help me to play a perfectly harmless practical joke on Musgrave. Will you promise to keep my secret for a couple of days, when we shall all enjoy a laugh over it together?"

"O yes, I'll help you with pleasure, but make haste and tell me what your practical joke is to be."

"I want to play ancestral ghost to Musgrave, and make him believe that he has seen the Cistercian monk in his white robe and cowl, that was last seen by his respected credulous grandpapa."

"What a good idea! I know he is always longing to see the ghost, and takes it as a personal affront that it has never appeared to him. But might it not startle him more than you intend?" and Kate turned her glowing face towards him, and Armitage involuntarily stopped the little sledge, "for it is one thing to wish to see a ghost, you know, and quite another to think that you see it."

"Oh, you need not fear for Musgrave! We shall be conferring a positive favour on him, in helping him to see what he's so wishful to see. I'm arranging it so that Lawley shall have the benefit of the show as well, and see the ghost at the same time with him. And if two strong men are not a match for one bogie, leave alone a home-made counterfeit one, it's a pity."

"Well, if you think it's a safe trick to play, no doubt you are right. But how can I help you? With the monk's habit, I suppose?"

"Exactly. I shall be so grateful to you if you will run up some sort of garment, that will look passably like a white Cistercian habit to a couple of men, who I don't think will be in a critical frame of mind during the short time they are allowed to see it. I really wouldn't trouble you if I were anything of a sempster (is that the masculine of sempstress?) myself, but I'm not. A thimble bothers me very much, and at college, when I have to sew on a button, I push the needle through on one side with a three-penny bit, and pull it out on the other with my teeth, and it's a laborious process."

Kate laughed merrily. "Oh, I can easily make something or other out of a white dressing gown, fit for a ghost to wear, and fasten a hood to it."

Armitage then told her the details of his deeply laid scheme, how he would go to his room when Musgrave and Lawley went to theirs on the eventful night, and sit up till he was sure that they were fast asleep. Then when the moon had risen, and if her light was obscured by clouds he would be obliged to postpone the entertainment till he could be sure of her aid, he would dress himself as the ghostly monk, put out the candles, softly open the door and look into the gallery to see that all was ready. "Then I shall slam the door with an awful bang, for that was the noise that heralded the ghost's last appearance, and it will wake Musgrave and Lawley, and bring them both out of their rooms like a shot. Lawley's door is next to mine, and Musgrave's opposite, so that each will command a magnificent view of the monk at the same instant, and they can compare notes afterwards at their leisure."

"But what shall you do if they find you out at once?"

"Oh, they won't do that! The cowl will be drawn over my face, and I shall stand with my back to the moonlight. My private belief is, that in spite of Musgrave's yearnings after a ghost, he won't like it when he thinks he sees it. Nor will Lawley, and I expect they'll dart back into their rooms and lock themselves in as soon as they catch sight of the monk. That would give me time to whip back into my room, turn the key, strip off my finery, hide it, and be roused with difficulty from a deep sleep when they come knocking at my door to tell me what a horrible thing has happened. And one more ghost story will be added to those already in circulation," and Armitage laughed aloud in anticipation of the fun.

"It is to be hoped that everything will happen just as you have planned it, and then we shall all be pleased. And now will you turn the sledge round and let us join the others, we have done conspiring for the present. If we are seen talking so exclusively to each other, they will suspect that we are brewing some mischief together. Oh, how cold the wind is! I like to hear it whistle in my hair!" said Kate as Armitage deftly swung the little sledge round and drove it quickly before him, facing the keen north wind, as she buried her chin in her warm furs.

Armitage found an opportunity to arrange with Kate, that he would meet her half way between Stonecroft and her home, on the afternoon of the next day but one, when she would give him a parcel containing the monk's habit. The Harradines and their house party were coming on Thursday afternoon to try the toboggan slide at Stonecroft. But Kate and Armitage were willing to sacrifice their pleasure to the business they had in hand.

There was no other way but for the conspirators to give their friends the slip for a couple of hours, when the important parcel would be safely given to Armitage, secretly conveyed by him to his own room, and locked up till he should want it in the small hours of the morning.

When the young people arrived at Stonecroft Miss Harradine apologised for her younger sister's absence, occasioned, she said, by a severe headache. Armitage's heart beat rapidly when he heard the excuse, and he thought how convenient it was for the inscrutable sex to be able to turn on a headache at will, as one turns on hot or cold water from a tap.

After luncheon, as there were more gentlemen than ladies, and Armitage's services were not necessary at the toboggan slide, he elected to take the dogs for a walk, and set off in the gayest spirits to keep his appointment with Kate. Much as he enjoyed maturing his ghost plot, he enjoyed still more the confidential talks with Kate that had sprung out of it, and he was sorry that this was to be the last of them. But the moon in heaven could not be stayed for the performance of his little comedy, and her light was necessary to its due performance. The ghost must be seen at three o'clock next morning, at the time and place arranged, when the proper illumination for its display would be forthcoming.

As Armitage walked swiftly over the hard snow, he caught sight of Kate at a distance. She waved her hand gaily and pointed smiling to the rather large parcel she was carrying. The red glow of the winter sun shone full upon her, bringing out the warm tints in her chestnut hair, and filling her brown eyes with soft lustre, and Armitage looked at her with undisguised admiration.

"It's awfully good of you to help me so kindly," he said as he took the parcel from her, "and I shall come round to-morrow to tell you the result of our practical joke. But how is the headache?" he asked smiling. "You look so unlike aches or pains of any kind, I was forgetting to enquire about it."

"Thank you, it is better. It was not altogether a made-up headache, though it happened opportunely. I was awake in the night, not in the least repenting that I was helping you, of course, but wishing it was all well over. One has heard of this kind of trick sometimes proving too successful, of people being frightened out of their wits by a make-believe ghost, and I should never forgive myself if Mr. Musgrave or Mr. Lawley were seriously alarmed."

"Really, Miss Harradine, I don't think that you need give yourself a moment's anxiety about the nerves of a couple of burly young men. If you are afraid for anyone, let it be for me. If they find me out, they will fall upon me and rend me limb from limb on the spot. I can assure you I am the only one for whom there is anything to fear," and the transient gravity passed like a cloud from Kate's bright face. And she admitted that it was rather absurd to be uneasy about two stalwart young men compounded more of muscle than of nerves. And they parted, Kate hastening home as the early twilight fell, and Armitage, after watching her out of sight, retracing his steps with the precious parcel under his arm.

He entered the house unobserved, and reaching the gallery by a back staircase, felt his way in the dark to his room. He deposited his treasure in the wardrobe, locked it up, and attracted by the sound of laughter, ran downstairs to the drawing-room. Will Musgrave and his friends, after a couple of hours of glowing exercise, had been driven indoors by the darkness, nothing loath to partake of tea and hot cakes, while they talked and laughed over the adventures of the afternoon.

"Wherever have you been, old fellow?" said Musgrave as Armitage entered the room. "I believe you've a private toboggan of your own somewhere that you keep quiet. If only the moon rose at a decent time, instead of at some unearthly hour in the night, when it's not of the slightest use to anyone, we would have gone out looking for you."

"You wouldn't have had far to seek, you'd have met me on the turnpike road."

"But why this subdued and chastened taste? Imagine preferring a constitutional on the high road when you might have been tobogganing with us! My poor friend, I'm afraid you are not feeling well!" said Musgrave with an affectation of sympathy that ended in boyish laughter and a wrestling match between the two young men, in the course of which Lawley more than once saved the tea table from being violently overthrown.

Presently, when the cakes and toast had disappeared before the youthful appetites, lanterns were lighted, and

Musgrave and his friends, and the Harradine brothers, set out as a bodyguard to take the young ladies home. Armitage was in riotous spirits, and finding that Musgrave and Lawley had appropriated the two prettiest girls in the company, waltzed untrammelled along the road before them lantern in hand, like a very will-o'-the-wisp.

The young people did not part till they had planned fresh pleasures for the morrow, and Musgrave, Lawley, and Armitage returned to Stonecroft to dinner, making the thin air ring to the jovial songs with which they beguiled the homeward journey.

Late in the evening, when the young men were sitting in the library, Musgrave suddenly exclaimed, as he reached down a book from an upper shelf, "Hallo! I've come on my grandfather's diary! Here's his own account of how he saw the white monk in the gallery. Lawley, you may read it if you like, but it shan't be wasted on an unbeliever like Armitage. By Jove! What an odd coincidence! Its forty years this very night, the thirtieth of December, since he saw the ghost," and he handed the book to Lawley, who read Mr. Musgrave's narrative with close attention.

"Is it a case of 'almost thou persuadest me'?" asked Armitage, looking at his intent and knitted brow.

"I hardly know what I think. Nothing positive either way at any rate." And he dropped the subject, for he saw Musgrave did not wish to discuss the family ghost in Armitage's unsympathetic presence.

They retired late, and the hour that Armitage had so gleefully anticipated drew near. "Good-night, both of you," said Musgrave as he entered his room. "I shall be asleep in five minutes. All this exercise in the open air makes a man absurdly sleepy at night," and the young men closed their doors, and silence settled down upon

Stonecroft Hall. Armitage and Lawley's rooms were next to each other, and in less than a quarter of an hour Lawley shouted a cheery good-night, which was loudly returned by his friend. Then Armitage felt somewhat mean and stealthy. Musgrave and Lawley were both confidingly asleep, while he sat up alert and vigilant maturing a mischievous plot that had for its object the awakening and scaring of both the innocent sleepers. He dared not smoke to pass the tedious time, lest the tell-tale fumes should penetrate into the next room through the keyhole, and inform Lawley if he woke for an instant that his friend was awake too, and behaving as though it were high noon.

Armitage spread the monk's white habit on the bed, and smiled as he touched it to think that Kate's pretty fingers had been so recently at work upon it. He need not put it on for a couple of hours yet, and to occupy the time he sat down to write. He would have liked to take a nap. But he knew that if he once yielded to sleep, nothing would wake him till he was called at eight o'clock in the morning. As he bent over his desk the big clock in the hall struck one, so suddenly and sharply it was like a blow on the head, and he started violently. "What a swinish sleep Lawley must be in that he can't hear a noise like that!" he thought, as snoring became audible from the next room. Then he drew the candles nearer to him, and settled once more to his writing, and a pile of letters testified to his industry, when again the clock struck. But this time he expected it, and it did not startle him, only the cold made him shiver. "If I hadn't made up my mind to go through with this confounded piece of folly, I'd go to bed now," he thought, "but I can't break faith with Kate. She's made the robe and I've got to wear it, worse luck," and with a great yawn he threw down his pen, and rose to look out of the window. It was a clear frosty night. At the edge of the dark sky, sprinkled with stars, a faint band of cold light heralded the rising moon. How different from the grey light of dawn, that ushers in the cheerful day, is the solemn rising of the moon in the depth of a winter night. Her light is not to rouse a sleeping world and lead men forth to their labor; it falls on the closed eyes of the weary, and silvers the graves of those whose rest shall be broken no more. Armitage was not easily impressed by the sombre aspect of nature, though he was quick to feel her gay and cheerful influence, but he would be glad when the farce was over, and he was no longer obliged to watch the rise and spread of the pale light, solemn as the dawn of the last day.

He turned from the window, and proceeded to make himself into the best imitation of a Cistercian monk that he could contrive. He slipt the white habit over all his clothing, that he might seem of portly size, and marked dark circles round his eyes, and thickly powdered his face a ghastly white.

Armitage silently laughed at his reflection in the glass, and wished that Kate could see him now. Then he softly opened the door and looked into the gallery. The moonlight was shimmering duskily on the end window to the right of his door and Lawley's. It would soon be where he wanted it, and neither too light nor too dark for the success of his plan. He stepped silently back again to wait, and a feeling as much akin to nervousness as he had ever known came over him. His heart beat rapidly; he started like a timid girl when the silence was suddenly broken by the hooting of an owl. He no longer cared to look at himself in the glass. He had taken fright at the mortal pallor of his powdered face. "Hang it all! I wish Lawley hadn't left off snoring. It was quite companionable to hear him." And again he looked into the gallery, and now the moon shed her cold beams where he intended to stand. He put out the light and opened the door wide, and stepping into the gallery threw it to with an echoing slam that only caused Musgrave and Lawley to start and turn on their pillows. Armitage stood dressed as the ghostly monk of Stonecroft, in the pale moonlight in the middle of the gallery, waiting for the door on either side to fly open and reveal the terrified faces of his friends.

He had time to curse the ill-luck that made them sleep so heavily that night of all nights, and to fear lest the servants had heard the noise their master had been deaf to, and would come hurrying to the spot and spoil the sport. But no one came, and as Armitage stood, the objects in the long gallery became clearer every moment, as his sight accommodated itself to the dim light. "I never noticed before that there was a mirror at the end of the gallery! I should not have believed the moonlight was bright enough for me to see my own reflection so far off, only white stands out so in the dark. But is it my own reflection? Confound it all, the thing's moving and I'm standing still! I know what it is! It's Musgrave dressed up to try to give me a fright, and Lawley's helping him. They've forestalled me, that's why they didn't come out of their rooms when I made a noise fit to wake the dead. Odd we're both playing the same practical joke at the same moment! Come on, my counterfeit bogie, and we'll see which of us turns white-livered first!"

But to Armitage's surprise, that rapidly became terror, the white figure that he believed to be Musgrave disguised, and like himself playing ghost, advanced towards him, slowly gliding over the floor which its feet did not touch. Armitage's courage was high, and he determined to hold his ground against the something ingeniously contrived by Musgrave and Lawley to terrify him into belief in the supernatural. But a feeling was creeping over the strong young man that he had never known before. He opened his dry mouth as the thing floated towards him, and there issued a hoarse inarticulate cry, that woke Musgrave and Lawley and brought them to their doors in a moment, not knowing by what strange fright they had been startled out of their sleep. Do not think them cowards that they shrank back appalled from the ghostly forms the moonlight revealed to them in the gallery. But as Armitage vehemently repelled the horror that drifted nearer and nearer to him, the cowl slipped from his head, and his friends recognised his white face, distorted by fear, and, springing towards him as he staggered, supported him in their arms. The Cistercian monk passed them like a white mist that sank into the wall, and Musgrave and Lawley were alone with the dead body of their friend, whose masquerading dress had become his shroud.

A ghost haunts his own past at Christmas.

SNOW GHOSTS

—

Richard A. Lupoff

He pushed at the heavy door with all the strength of his frail frame. He couldn't budge it. From inside the Garnet Saloon he could hear the music, something by Mozart, a relief from the jinglelike Christmas carols and canned cheer that went with the season. And he could see the decorative lights within, a few annoying red and green bulbs but mostly the Garnet's traditional pleasant amber and ruby.

It was cold, and the snow sifted down the collar of his mackinaw. He looked around to see if anyone was approaching, but there was only the occasional pair of headlights moving cautiously through the center of town. Not many people out on December 24. They were home with their families or celebrating with friends.

He felt in his pockets and found a coin. He rapped with it against the small pane in the Garnet's door. Inside, the bartender moved around the end of the bar, headed for the door, and pulled it open for him. He gathered his strength to step across the threshold, but the bartender had already taken him by the arm and was half lifting and half pulling him inside.

"You shouldn't be out, Old Timer." She smiled at him, but her face showed concern. "You'll catch your death!"

He mumbled something, thanking her for letting him in. He tried to climb onto a barstool.

"Come on, Old Timer. Can you make it? Rather sit in a chair?"

"I was balancing on one of these things before you were born, Jen."

"I know, Old Timer. I know you can handle it. But you might be comfier by the fireplace."

He let her lead him to a captain's chair near the hearth. A wood fire was burning, and its warmth felt good on his face.

"Coming down pretty hard, is it?" Jennifer asked.

"Little bit."

She didn't wait for his order but poured hot water into a glass and then dumped it out again. She lifted a bottle of Bushmills and poured some of its contents into the glass. She filled it the rest of the way with coffee and then spooned whipped cream on top. She brought it to him. "This will warm your insides, Old Timer."

He took the glass and studied it without speaking. After a little while he sipped. They were making the drinks weak nowadays. In his heyday he would have swallowed his Irish without the coffee, but everyone thought he was feeble now and had to take care of him. Well, maybe they were right. Not everybody made it to ninety. In a small town like this, on the edge of the lake, hardly anybody. The winters were too cold, the air too thin, life too demanding. But he'd made it through nine decades. And now he was alone.

Jennifer looked into his face, patted him on the shoulder, and started away. "Let me know how you're doing."

He nodded.

The Garnet wasn't as empty as he'd expected. Two or three tables were occupied by couples. They looked amazingly young, eyes shining, skins glowing. They touched hands, exchanged glances. Occasionally one of them would look at him surreptitiously. He smiled and they looked away.

The Mozart was pleasant. Time was when the Garnet wouldn't have played anything more classical than Hank Williams, but they'd gone upscale and put in a CD player and concealed speakers to make the big-spending skiers from San Francisco happy. He couldn't place the piece, but it was familiar, peaceful. Maybe one of the German dances. At the far end of the bar, he could see a huge TV screen and on it a colorized version of *It's a Wonderful Life*, happily sans soundtrack. Jimmy Stewart and Donna Reed were dancing at the high school gym, and he knew that they would shortly fall into the swimming pool. How many times had he seen them do that?

There were a few drinkers at the bar. They were hunched over; unlike the couples at the tables, they were serious about their alcohol.

Jennifer looked at him, came out from behind the bar again, and squatted beside his chair. She was a full-figured woman, her generous bosom filling the button-down shirt that she wore whenever she was on duty. "Are you okay, Old Timer?"

He nodded, ignoring the TV images, peering instead into the dancing oranges and reds in the fireplace.

Christmas Eve, alone in a saloon. Ninety years old, and all alone on Christmas Eve. He looked up at Jennifer, tried to nod reassuringly to her. She was a good woman, a kind woman. If he were a few years younger, he thought . . . then almost laughed. Some few years! Fifty or sixty would be more like it.

"I'm okay," he managed.

"Want me to freshen that up a little?" She took his glass without waiting for an answer. Had he finished his drink already? Or was she just taking it away from him, afraid that he'd drop it on his lap?

He looked at her and she seemed blurred. He had good eyes, he was proud of that. But they were watering a little. The cold and wind outside, the heavy flakes of falling snow, and then the warmth inside the Garnet, and the drink, and the fire—that must be it.

Jennifer could almost be her granddad, Jack McGyver, wearing the same white shirt and the same black bow tie. Of course, Jack didn't have the bosom that Jen did, but he'd been a hearty, beefy man all the same. And beyond Jennifer, seated at the bar, a tall, gray-haired fellow swung about and held his glass high in a friendly gesture, almost a Christmas toast.

Seated in his chair by the fire, he tried to return the toast but discovered that he didn't have his glass any longer. He looked around for Jennifer. She'd gone to re-fill his glass, hadn't she? He could use another Irish coffee.

Seated at the bar, the gray-haired man saw the bartender returning. "The old fellow all right?" he asked.

"He'll be okay," Jack said. "Ninety years old, and alone at Christmas. Christ, I feel for the old man. I hope I never get that old."

"Beats the alternative," Shelton said.

"I'm not so sure."

"Doesn't he have anybody? Not anybody?"

"Old Timer's wife died years ago. They had a daughter, career army nurse. Served in Vietnam, working in a field hospital. Vietcong smuggled a porcupine mine into the place and—*wham!*—that was that. Didn't think the old fellow was going to navigate for a while after that, but he came out of it all right."

Shelton shook his head pityingly.

Jack McGyver took a few steps, reached up, and turned the knobs on the 17-inch Magnavox. Even though it was Christmas Eve, the local station was showing an old Humphrey Bogart–Lauren Bacall movie. There were a few Christmas decorations scattered through the Garnet, but the atmosphere was gloomy. The dominant feature was a huge black wreath framing a hand-tinted portrait of John F. Kennedy.

"Sure don't feel like Christmas," Jack said.

"No." Shelton looked into his shot glass. He shoved it across the mahogany. McGyver reached for the Bushmills and refilled the glass. "You're the only Scotsman I've ever met who'd rather drink Irish."

"To you, Jack." Shelton hoisted his shot glass and saluted first his living friend and then the portrait of the dead president.

"You think Johnson can do the job?" McGyver asked.

Shelton sipped thoughtfully at his drink. "I don't know, Jack. He's a smart one, but I don't know."

"He wouldn't have pulled that boner at the Bay of Pigs, you can bet on that."

"Maybe not."

"Neither would Nixon. They're two of a kind, Nixon and Johnson. Don't know how Johnson got mixed up with Kennedy, but things work out funny sometimes."

"They do that."

"You think he'll bring the troops back from Asia?"

Shelton shook his head. He'd had a blurry moment. Not exactly as if his eyes were blurry, and not exactly dizziness, either. But one moment he'd been looking at the old fellow near the fire, and the old fellow was ninety, he knew that, and the female bartender was bringing him a drink—there *was* a female bartender, wasn't there?

But—he peered up at the Magnavox. There was a Buick commercial ending, the camera lingering on the chrome-rimmed decorative portholes above the front fender, and then it was replaced by a jingle and a pack of dancing Old Golds.

"Kennedy said something about pulling out by Christmas," he said.

"Sure, he did," Jack McGyver said. "And said we're going to the moon, too."

They shared a bitter laugh.

The door of the Garnet swung open, and a draft of cold air brought a flurry of snowflakes with it. Shelton swung around on his barstool, catching a glimpse of the codger still warming himself at the fireplace.

The man who entered the Garnet wore a fedora pulled down over his forehead and a tweed overcoat with its collar turned up. A woolen scarf swathed his features and thick gloves covered his hands, so that only his eyes were visible.

"Close it!" a chorus rang out.

Scotty Shelton shoved the door shut and crossed the barroom to the coat tree beside the fireplace.

Young Jack McGyver, the bartender, said, "You manage to park okay, Scotty?"

"Slipped a little bit, but it's okay."

"You going to keep running that old Hupmobile?"

"Don't have much choice, do I? Won't be any new cars, now we're in the war."

"Won't be much chance to buy gas or tires, either."

"Well, I don't suppose I'll be here very long, anyhow. Going to get back in my old outfit."

"Come on, Scotty. They don't want duffers like you. War's a young man's game! Why, they put you up against one of Adolf's storm troopers or a squad of those little Jap monkeys, they'd take you to pieces."

"I haven't seen you rushing to enlist, Jack."

"I know better. You must love getting up at five o'clock in the morning and marching around with a rifle on your shoulder. Heck, Scotty, rifles are for deer-hunting, that's my motto!"

Behind McGyver, a Philco radio was playing a transcription of the Andrews Sisters singing "The Pennsylvania Polka." The song ended and the announcer said, "It's 10:30 P.M. Pacific War Time. That's 22:30, you GIs on leave. And in a minute we'll have Der Bingle to lend a little Christmas cheer, but first, have you thought about your teeth lately? You know, in wartime, we can't afford to neglect our health. Uncle Sam needs our doctors and nurses in his armed forces—and, yes, the dentists, too! So the makers of Ipana tooth powder and paste urge you. . . ."

"Turn that thing off, will you, Jack?"

Instead, McGyver turned the volume down.

"You really want to go back in, don't you?" the bartender asked.

Scott looked around the Garnet. An aged man sat huddled near the fireplace. Another aging citizen with silver-gray hair had apparently left his place at the bar and was walking slowly toward the oldster, drink in hand. Scott Shelton swung back to face the waiting Jack McGyver. Again he pushed his shot glass toward the barkeep. "Want to? No, I don't want to. But this one, well. . . ."

"But you served in the last one."

"I know. That time they drafted me. What did I know? I was just a young kid."

The bartender snorted. "Don't flimflam me, Scotty. I remember how you went jumping up and down when you got your notice. Just 'cause I was too young to go, you acted like lord high-muck-a-muck. But you did your share, Scotty. Let the kids go this time, too."

"The kids don't know anything. They don't know why they're fighting. Put 'em in a uniform, hand 'em a gun, and they'll go anyplace, fight anybody. They think a set of khakis and some polished brass and they can get drunk, get laid, go off on a great adventure, and come home heroes. It isn't like that, Jack. I've been watching this Hitler character for a long time."

"I read the papers, too. Is he any better than Stalin? What's the difference between a Nazi and a Bolshie? Or that man in the White House, for that matter?"

"Don't say that, Jack."

"Don't say what?"

"About FDR."

"Aah, you Democrats are all alike." McGyver reached behind him and picked up a day-old *San Francisco Call*. He spread it on the bar between himself and Scott Shelton. There was a war situation map on the front page, and the two men put their heads together over it.

"God, it looks bad there in the Philippines." McGyver rubbed his heavily stubbled cheeks. "Those poor bastards don't stand a chance. If I could just get my hands on that slant-eyed Tojo and his buck-toothed boss Hirohito. . . ."

"You can join up, Jack. You didn't go last time, go now."

"Can't do it, Scott. I've got a wife and baby to think of."

"Me too, in case you haven't noticed."

The Philco was playing Bing Crosby's record of "White Christmas." The front windows of the Garnet were draped with thick blackout curtains to prevent any Jap bomber flying over the Tahoe region from zeroing in on the landmark.

"Well, I'm just an in-betweener," McGyver said. "I was too young for the last war, too old for this one. I think you're a fool to go, Scott, but I can't stop you."

"That you can't, Jack." Scott Shelton lifted his glass. "Well, to Christmas, anyway." He turned from the bar toward the crackling fire. He took his glass with him and climbed from his stool.

The elderly, gray-haired man was standing behind the ancient character, and they both seemed hypnotized by the dancing flames. Scotty moved toward them.

There was a rapping at the door, in a complex pattern. McGyver came out from behind the bar, stood by the door, and yelled, "Who's there?"

"It's me. Open up, Jack."

"Who sent you? What's the governor's middle name?"

"Will you cut that out and open the door! I'm freezing my hind end off out here."

McGyver slid the latch-bolt back. The door swung open and a rattle of hailstones clattered across the hardwood floor. A young man, hardly into his thirties, stood in the doorway.

"Well, close the damned door before we all freeze," the bartender commanded. He was even younger than the newcomer, his hair slicked down and his cheeks smooth.

"Sorry, Jack." The man in the doorway took another step into the Garnet and shoved the door closed behind him. A few hailstones that had somehow clung to his long coat and battered fedora bounced on the floor and then lay still, beginning to melt.

The newcomer surveyed the bar, his eye passing over the old man at the fireplace and the two younger ones standing near him. "Let me have a double, will you, Jack?"

"A double what?"

"Irish."

"Scott, you know we don't serve illegal booze here. You can have a mug of coffee, a glass of fruit juice. How about a nice hot cup of tea on a cold, dark Christmas Eve?"

"Come on, Jack, cut it out. You've been paying off the sheriff ever since prohibition came in, and you're not about to start worrying about it now. Besides, Roosevelt's going to repeal it. The country's going wet. At least that will be something to cheer about."

"Okay, okay. You have any luck yet, Scott?"

Scott shook his head.

"You want this on your tab, then."

"What do you think?"

"I think you're into us for a lot of money, old son."

"Is that my fault?"

"I'm working, Scott."

"Your father owns a saloon, Jack. How many people you know have jobs today?"

McGyver dropped the conversation, placed a glass on the mahogany, and poured a double Irish for Shelton.

Shelton downed half the drink and then lowered the glass. "Thanks, Jack. You know I'm good for it."

"I know you're no deadbeat, Scott. But if you don't have it, you can't pay me, can you? What are you going to do, rob a bank?"

Shelton laughed. The line about robbing a bank was a standing joke. The banks were broke, too. "Maybe Roosevelt will do something."

"I doubt it."

Behind Jack McGyver the amber dials of an Atwater-Kent radio glowed warmly. In some distant studio a pair of musicians were playing "Adeste Fidelis" on a scratchy violin and an off-key cornet. The Atwater-Kent's reception was uneven, and the music was barely louder than the superhet hum, but it was remarkable that they could hear the station at all, up here at the lake.

"Well, Hoover's had three years to work on the Depression, and things just keep getting worse."

"Give the man time, Scott. He didn't cause the crash, you know."

"Who did, then?"

"That's easy. Red agitators. Open your eyes, man. Don't you see, there's a bunch of Rooshians running around this country, stirring things up, making trouble, them and their dupes. They *wanted* the Depression. They *love* it!"

"Oh, come on, Jack."

"They did! They had to get rid of Hoover, and now they're about to put Roosevelt in the White House. You know, that isn't even his real name. His real name is Rosenfeld, and he's descended from a family of Dutch Jews. I just read it the other day in one of those little news things. *Lightning*, they call it. It's a real eye-opener."

Shelton shook his head in disgust and turned away from McGyver, moving from the bar toward the fireplace. He didn't neglect to bring his half-full glass with him.

The door swung open and a young man—hardly more than a boy—charged into the Garnet. Behind him the night was cold and the December constellations blazed like points of flame, almost as brilliant in the reflective waters of Lake Tahoe as in the black winter sky above the Sierra Nevada.

"Mr. McGyver! Is Jackie here?"

"He's cleaning out the back, Scotty. What's the excitement?"

"I got it! It came in the afternoon mail!"

"I see." The elder McGyver leaned on the bar, his white-shirted elbows rubbing on the polished mahogany. "What came in the afternoon mail, Scotty?"

"It's here, she can't stop me now!"

The barkeep laughed at the youngster's enthusiasm. He called his son from the back room. "Your friend Scotty's here, Jackie! Come on out and talk to him before the boy has a conniption fit."

Jackie emerged from the back room. He was three years younger than Scotty, but he was big for his age and the two boys were very nearly of a size.

"Look at this!" Scotty waved the letter. "My mom wouldn't let me enlist when I wanted, but she can't stop me now! It's my draft notice, Jackie! Kaiser Bill, watch out! The Yanks are coming!"

Proudly he held the letter for his friend to see. "See this? I have to go to Truckee to report, and then the train down to Sacramento. I bet I'll see San Francisco, New York, Paris—everyplace!"

"You lucky dog! I wish I could go."

"Maybe the war will last and you will, Jackie. But don't bet on it! Oh, boy, I can hardly wait!"

Behind him the door of the Garnet swung open, and

a huge man in a bowler hat entered. He kicked the door closed behind him. He held a bundle in his arms. Balancing it carefully on one elbow, he hung his bowler on the rack and smoothed his heavy mustache. "Here he is, my lads!"

He advanced across the hardwood floor and laid his bundle carefully on the bar. The bartender gazed at the tiny boy. "He's a fine one, Joseph."

The proud father beamed. There were Christmas wreaths and berries throughout the saloon, and a fire roared on the hearth. A fragile-looking, aged man, thin almost to the point of transparency, sat beside it in a captain's chair, warming himself. Several others stood at points between the old man and the mahogany bar.

"His name is Scott Shelton," the big man announced. "Scott so he'll never forget the land of his ancestors. It's a joy—having a new son to go with this new century, Mr. McGyver."

"And what does the missus think of your taking the little one out on such a night?"

"It's warm enough in here, Mr. McGyver! And besides, didn't the little Lord Jesus lie in a chilly barn on this very night?"

"He had the animals to keep him warm."

"Aah, I won't argue theology with an Irishman!"

"Nor I with a Scot! He's a lovely baby, Mr. Shelton. Long life and happiness to him! And convey my best wishes of the season to his mother, will you?"

The big man nodded, grinning still. "And aren't you and your own missus going to start adding to the population?"

The bartender reddened. "We'll get to it, Mr. Shelton, rest assured. In good time, we'll get to it." There was a brief, uncomfortable silence. Then, "Let me pour you a big one, on the house," the bartender said. "And while I take care of that, Mr. Shelton, perhaps you'd do an act of kindness."

"Eh?" The big man raised a thick eyebrow.

"You see the old gentleman sitting by the hearth?"

"I do that."

"He seems very sad, Mr. Shelton. It must be hard to be so old, and all alone on Christmas Eve. I think it might cheer him a bit to have a look at the little one. If you think the missus wouldn't mind, of course."

The big man thought about that and then nodded. He turned away from the bar and carried the baby carefully to the old man sitting beside the hearth. He stood with his back to the fire, towering over the fragile oldster. In a semicircle behind the old man, hardly moving, stood others. A man with gray-white hair, another in an odd soft-crowned hat and dark overcoat, another with a face that looked younger but seemed filled with despair, and still another, this one hardly more than a schoolboy, his face filled with an energy and excitement that the big man could remember from his own past.

They all seemed to be concentrating their gaze on the fireplace. All except for the very old man.

The man holding the baby in his arms loomed above the oldster. After a moment he knelt, slowly, and with great care he placed the infant in the old man's arms.

He thought he saw the old man look at the infant, and almost imperceptibly nod, and then for the briefest instant raise his eyes to those of the infant's father. Then the old man's eyes fell shut.

An elderly couple is rewarded at Christmas
with a ghostly fulfillment of their dreams.

UNAWARES

Hildegarde Hawthorne

"It's going to be a real, old-fashioned Christmas Eve,
Selina," said her husband, looking out into the gray
afternoon, fluttering with snowflakes. "It makes me
think of the days when I used to drag you about in the
little red sled with black horses painted on it—it's up in
the garret now, Selina, isn't it? Well, well, that was a
long while ago."

"A long while ago," answered the little white-haired
lady, knitting by the wood fire. "A long while ago,
Silas. The years between have been happy—and have
been sad, too! But I'd willingly live them all over again,
if it weren't for just one thing." And she gave a sigh,
quickly followed by a smile as her husband turned towards her.

"Yes, dear?" he said, half inquiringly, half wistfully.

"If we'd had the little child, Silas. A child to cherish,
to guide, to—Oh, Silas, a little one to play about us, to

love us, to grow up and have a little one of its own, that should gleam about our old age as the sunlight flickers and glows about the old oaks at our door. What a Christmas Eve we should have, getting the pretty toys and candy, lighting the tree, seeing the big blue eyes dance with happiness, hearing the sweet voice crying joyfully, 'Grandpapa, grandmamma.' " She stopped, with a sudden movement of her hands to her throat. "Silas, *dearie*, don't mind me—" she turned away to hide the tears in her eyes.

But Silas understood, and sitting beside her drew her close, their white hairs mingling together, while the firelight shone in kindly wise on their sweet old faces, wrinkled and worn, perhaps, but expressing in every line their gentle natures.

"We have had much, dear," he whispered. "What a life, what a world would this have been for me without you—without you? Why, it is inconceivable!"

She laughed a tearful laugh and patted his hand.

"I couldn't realize life without you any more than I could realize not being born at all," she murmured.

For a while they sat silent, looking at the fire that danced and played on the hearth, even as the child they desired might have danced and played about the chamber.

"I knew I wanted too much for Earth," went on Selina, presently, "but I have longed, dear, yes, and wept. You never knew, I would not tell even you. I know it is wrong, when the Lord has given me such happiness, such peace. But I—oh, just to clasp it close, just once to make a Christmas for it. First it was our own little child, now it is our own little grandchild I want—I wanted."

"I knew, beloved wife. I knew. I too have not spoken,

not told even you I too have longed to see you as a
mother—to bless our child."

They drew closer, with a sigh at once sad and happy.
Selina looked up at last.

"I am content, dear," she said, "we have had much—
more than many, than most. We are old—perhaps this is
our last Christmas Eve. Give me a kiss, dear husband.
The Lord knows best, and I am content."

They kissed each other, solemnly, smilingly.

"Isn't some one knocking?" replied Silas, going towards the door. Just as he reached it a decided knock
made him throw it open, crying, "Come in, neighbor,"
in his hearty old voice, full of friendly welcome.

On the threshold, blown by the wind, powdered by
the snow, stood a little girl, smiling out of big blue
eyes, her cheeks rosy as the dawn, her hair yellow as
the ripened wheat.

"Why, come in, darling," said the old man, drawing
her inside and closing the door. "Whose little girl you
are, out in such a stormy afternoon?"

The child shook off the snow laughingly, clasping
one of his fingers in her little hand.

"Where's your mother?" asked Silas, and then—
"Look here, Selina, here's a little girl come to see us."

The laughing child ran eagerly across the room,
throwing herself into Selina's lap and putting up her
rosy face for a kiss.

"Kiss me, G'anmamma," she cried, "kiss little Désirée."

Selina turned pale and clasped the little one close—
close.

"Little Désirée," she whispered. "Little Désirée. But
I'm not your grandmamma, dearie. Who are you?
Where do you belong?"

The baby drew back, shaking her head and smiling.

"Is it *nearly* Ch'istmas?" she asked, eagerly. "Shall I soon have my sled and my dolly and my candies—dear g'anpapa, is it *nearly* Ch'istmas?"

Silas and Selina exchanged a look.

"She's not one of the neighbor's children, Silas," said the old lady, presently, her eyes following the child, that had now seated itself on the hearthrug, and was holding out its little hands to the blaze. "I never saw her before—it is very strange."

"Someone visiting over Christmas," replied Silas. "I will go around among the neighbors presently and inquire. But in the meantime let us make the little creature at home—she shall have a Christmas here, too, Selina. I will get the little sled out of the garret—" Silas's eyes lighted up, and he smiled eagerly at his wife—"and perhaps they will let us keep her a while—she came here so—" he stopped, and bending over the little head, kissed the clustering hair. "So like an angel," he ended.

"Dear g'anpapa," murmured the child, putting up a hand to stroke his cheek.

"Take off Désirée's coat," she added, struggling up.

Selina began slipping off her things. Such a pretty fur-trimmed coat, so white and warm and soft.

"You look like a transfigured snowflake yourself, pet," she said, as the child, freed from her outer garments, danced in the flickering shadows thrown by the leaping flames. Her dress was as white and soft as her coat, and she fluttered back and forth like a bird, too light and free to stay on the dull earth while such a medium of pure air existed to float or fly in.

"Ch'istmas is coming, Ch'istmas is coming," she chanted, and suddenly clambered to Selina's lap. "Tell me a story," she implored, snuggling down and laying her sweet face against Selina's gentle breast. "Tell me a story, g'anmamma."

Silas stood looking at the group a moment, and then, with a smile like the singing of birds in spring, sat down beside them.

"A story, precious? G'anmother hasn't told many stories to little girls, but perhaps—perhaps—" she paused, looking dreamily into the fire.

The child lay warm against her, its fair curls spread over her arm, its soft breathing perceptible to her ear, its clasping hands on her wrists. So holding it, her mind drifted back to the golden days of her young womanhood, her young wifehood. The dreams, the fancies, the hope—never, alas, fulfilled—of that time transmuted themselves into words, and fell quietly, gently, on the listening ears of the two. As Selina sat there, talking out the long-hidden desire of her heart, her husband occasionally whispered a word of love. She seemed not to hear him. Her words came with a sort of rhythm; it was as though they moved to unheard music. All the pent-up mother love of her heart expressed itself nobly, exquisitely, self forgetting, earth forgetting, inspired by the heavenly regions of her soul. Finally she stopped, still looking at the fire, now fallen into a smoldering glow, still clasping the child to her heart. Then she bent and kissed her.

"Precious darling," she murmured, "mother's own dearest."

The child threw its little arms about her neck, in a quick, enchanting embrace. Then slipping to the floor—

"See, mamma, papa has a sled for me," she cried, clapping her hands. "A red sled for little Désirée."

Selina laughed gayly, and presently Silas joined in, and soon the three of them were shouting together, while the rafters of the unaccustomed room fairly quivered in sympathy.

"How young you look, dear Silas," observed his wife, smiling at him rather roguishly. "And why don't you bring little Désirée the pretty dolly we have for her, and the Christmas candies?"

"If I look young, you look beautiful, Selina," replied Silas, with his gentle smile—"Doesn't mother look beautiful?" he asked the baby, laughingly, catching her up in his arms. "Come, kiss papa for the red sled and the Christmas candies, that are hidden there in the cupboard all ready for our little Désirée."

And Désirée kissed him and kissed Selina, and crowed over the candy. Then Selina brought out a doll with rosy cheeks and golden hair, even like Désirée's own. And they threw fresh wood on the fire, and put apples to roast. And Désirée played on the hearthrug, while the couple sat hand in hand smiling and watching her.

"Isn't she pretty?" said Selina. "See, she seems to throw a light of her own as she moves. Silas dear, how absurd we've been, thinking we were old and worn out. *You* old, beloved!" She laid her hand over his, gazing up at him. "I never saw you look so well before."

"Old, sweetheart? The child would be enough to keep us young, even without our immortal love to safeguard us."

Again the child, tired of play, climbed into Selina's lap. The light faded outdoors, the snow still fell, whitening all the land. Inside the room the long shadows drew together, but the fire still leaped about the huge logs, cheery as a laugh.

"You must go to bed soon, baby," said Selina. "Soon mother must tuck you in, to wake up and play with your red sled in the snow on Christmas Day."

"Let her stay with us a little longer, sweetheart," pleaded Silas. "Christmas Eve comes so seldom, and we are so happy, we three."

"So happy," murmured his wife, leaning towards him, gathering the sleeping child close. "So happy."

"Hold the horse a moment, Sally," said her lover, "and I'll just run in with the basket and wish Silas and Selina a Merry Christmas—dear old people." He vanished within the house, but the next moment came back again.

"Sally," he called, gravely, "come here—something has happened."

Before the cold hearth the old couple were sitting, hand in hand, their white heads close together, a tender smile on their faces.

For a little while Sally regarded them, the tears filling her eyes, then turning to her lover, she whispered, "It must have been a happy death. See, dear, how beautiful they look."

A science-fiction tale of an alien ghost on
a distant planet at Christmas.

A MIDWINTER'S TALE

Michael Swanwick

Maybe I shouldn't tell you about that childhood
Christmas Eve in the Stone House, so long ago.
My memory is no longer reliable, not since I con-
tracted the brain fever. Soon I'll be strong enough to
be reposted offplanet, to some obscure star light-years
beyond that plangent moon rising over your father's
barn, but how much has been burned from my mind!
Perhaps none of this actually happened.

Sit on my lap and I'll tell you all. Well then, my
knee. No woman was ever ruined by a knee. You laugh,
but it's true. Would that it were so easy!

The hell of war as it's now practiced is that its purpose is not so much to gain territory as to deplete the
enemy, and thus it's always better to maim than to kill.
A corpse can be bagged, burned, and forgotten, but the
wounded need special care. Regrowth tanks, false skin,
medical personnel, a long convalescent stay on your

parents' farm. That's why they will vary their weapons,
hit you with obsolete stone axes or toxins or radiation,
to force your Command to stock the proper prophy-
laxes, specialized medicines, obscure skills. Mustard
gas is excellent for that purpose, and so was the brain
fever.

All those months I lay in the hospital, awash in pain,
sometimes hallucinating. Dreaming of ice. When I
awoke, weak and not really believing I was alive, parts
of my life were gone, randomly burned from my memory. I recall standing at the very top of the iron bridge
over the Izveltaya, laughing and throwing my books
one by one into the river, while my best friend
Fennwolf tried to coax me down. "I'll join the militia!
I'll be a soldier!" I shouted hysterically. And so I did.
I remember that clearly but just what led up to that preposterous instant is utterly beyond me. Nor can I remember the name of my second-eldest sister, though
her face is as plain to me as yours is now. There are odd
holes in my memory.

That Christmas Eve is an island of stability in my
sea-changing memories, as solid in my mind as the
Stone House itself, that Neolithic cavern in which we
led such basic lives that I was never quite sure in which
era of history we dwelt. Sometimes the men came in
from the hunt, a larl or two pacing ahead content and
sleepy-eyed, to lean bloody spears against the walls,
and it might be that we lived on Old Earth itself then.
Other times, as when they brought in projectors to fill
the common room with colored lights, scintillae nesting
in the branches of the season's tree, and cool, harmless
flames dancing atop the presents, we seemed to belong
to a much later age, in some mythologized province of
the future.

The house was abustle, the five families all together for this one time of the year, and outlying kin and even a few strangers staying over, so that we had to put bedding in places normally kept closed during the winter, moving furniture into attic lumber rooms, and even at that there were cots and thick bolsters set up in the blind ends of hallways. The women scurried through the passages, scattering uncles here and there, now settling one in an armchair and plumping him up like a cushion, now draping one over a table, cocking up a mustachio for effect. A pleasant time.

Coming back from a visit to the kitchens where a huge woman I did not know, with flour powdering her big-freckled arms up to the elbows, had shooed me away, I surprised Suki and Georg kissing in the nook behind the great hearth. They had arms about each other and I stood watching them. Suki was smiling, cheeks red and round. She brushed her hair back with one hand so Georg could nuzzle her ear, turning slightly as she did so, and saw me. She gasped and they broke apart, flushed and startled.

Suki gave me a cookie, dark with molasses and a single stingy, crystalized raisin on top, while Georg sulked. Then she pushed me away, and I heard her laugh as she took Georg's hand to lead him away to some darker forest recess of the house.

Father came in, boots all muddy, to sling a brace of game birds down on the hunt cabinet. He set his unstrung bow and quiver of arrows on their pegs, then hooked an elbow atop the cabinet to accept admiration and a hot drink from Mother. The larl padded by, quiet and heavy and content. I followed it around a corner, ancient ambitions of riding the beast rising up within. I could see myself, triumphant before my cousins, high atop the black carnivore. "Flip!" my father called sternly. "Leave Samson alone! He is a bold and noble creature, and I will not have you pestering him."

He had eyes in the back of his head, had my father.

Before I could grow angry, my cousins hurried by, on their way to hoist the straw men into the trees out front, and swept me up along with them. Uncle Chittagong, who looked like a lizard and had to stay in a glass tank for reasons of health, winked at me as I skirled past. From the corner of my eye, I saw my second-eldest sister beside him, limned in blue fire.

Forgive me. So little of my childhood remains; vast stretches were lost in the blue ice fields I wandered in my illness. My past is like a sunken continent with only mountaintops remaining unsubmerged, a scattered archipelago of events from which to guess the shape of what was lost. Those remaining fragments I treasure all the more and must pass my hands over them periodically to reassure myself that something remains.

So where was I? Ah, yes: I was in the north bell tower, my hidey-place in those days, huddled behind Old Blind Pew, the bass of our triad of bells, crying because I had been deemed too young to light one of the Yule torches. "Hallo!" cried a voice, and then, "Out here, stupid!" I ran to the window, tears forgotten in my astonishment at the sight of my brother Karl silhouetted against the yellowing sky, arms out, treading the roof gables like a tightrope walker.

"You're going to get in trouble for that!" I cried.

"Not if you don't tell!" Knowing full well how I worshiped him. "Come on down! I've emptied out one of the upper kitchen cupboards. We can crawl in from the pantry. There's a space under the door—we'll see everything!"

Karl turned and his legs tangled under him. He fell. Feet first, he slid down the roof.

I screamed. Karl caught the guttering and swung himself into an open window underneath. His sharp face rematerialized in the gloom, grinning. "Race you to the jade ibis!"

He disappeared, and then I was spinning wildly down the spiral stairs, mad to reach the goal first.

It was not my fault we were caught, for I would never have giggled if Karl hadn't been tickling me to see just how long I could keep silent. I was frightened, but not Karl. He threw his head back and laughed until he cried, even as he was being hauled off by three very angry grandmothers; he was pleased more by his own roguery than by anything he might have seen.

I myself was led away by an indulgent Katrina, who graphically described the caning I was to receive and then contrived to lose me in the crush of bodies in the common room. I hid behind the goat tapestry until I got bored—not long!—and then Chubkin, Kosmonaut, and Pew rang, and the room emptied.

I tagged along, ignored, among the moving legs, like a marsh bird scuttling through waving grasses. Voices clangoring in the east stairway, we climbed to the highest balcony to watch the solstice dance. I hooked hands over the crumbling balustrade and pulled myself up on tiptoe so I could look down on the procession as it left the house. For a long time nothing happened, and I remember being annoyed at how casually the adults were taking all this, standing about with drinks, not one in ten glancing away from themselves. Pheidre and Valerian (the younger children had been put to bed, complaining, an hour ago) began a game of tag, running through the adults, until they were chastened and ordered with angry shakes of their arms to be still.

Then the door below opened. The women who were

witches walked solemnly out, clad in hooded terry-cloth robes as if they'd just stepped from the bath. But they were so silent I was struck with fear. It seemed as if something cold had reached into the pink, giggling women I had seen preparing themselves in the kitchen and taken away some warmth or laughter from them. "Katrina!" I cried in panic, and she lifted a moon-cold face toward me. Several of the men exploded in laughter, white steam puffing from bearded mouths, and one rubbed his knuckles in my hair. My second-eldest sister drew me away from the balustrade and hissed at me that I was not to cry out to the witches, that this was important, that when I was older I would understand, and in the meantime if I did not behave myself I would be beaten. To soften her words, she offered me a sugar crystal, but I turned away stern and unappeased.

Single file the women walked out on the rocks to the east of the house, where all was barren slate swept free of snow by the wind from the sea, and at a great distance—you could not make out their faces—doffed their robes. For a moment they stood motionless in a circle, looking at one another. Then they began the dance, each wearing nothing but a red ribbon tied about one upper thigh, the long end blowing free in the breeze.

As they danced their circular dance, the families watched, largely in silence. Sometimes there was a muffled burst of laughter as one of the younger men muttered a racy comment, but mostly they watched with great respect, even a kind of fear. The gusty sky was dark and flocked with small clouds like purple-headed rams. It was chilly on the roof, and I could not imagine how the women withstood it. They danced faster and faster, and the families grew quieter, packing the edges more tightly, until I was forced away from the railing.

Cold and bored, I went downstairs, nobody turning to watch me leave, back to the main room, where a fire still smouldered in the hearth.

The room was stuffy when I'd left and cooler now. I lay down on my stomach before the fireplace. The flag-stones smelled of ashes and were gritty to the touch, staining my fingertips as I trailed them in idle little circles. The stones were cold at the edges, slowly growing warmer, and then suddenly too hot and I had to snatch my hand away. The back of the fireplace was black with soot, and I watched the fireworms crawl over the stone heart-and-hands carved there, as the carbon caught fire and burned out. The log was all embers and would burn for hours.

Something coughed.

I turned and saw something moving in the shadows, an animal. The larl was blacker than black, a hole in the darkness, and my eyes swam to look at him. Slowly, lazily, he strode out onto the stones, stretched his back, yawned a tongue-curling yawn, and then stared at me with those great green eyes.

He spoke.

I was astonished, of course, but not in the way my father would have been. So much is inexplicable to a child! "Merry Christmas, Flip," the creature said, in a quiet, breathy voice. I could not describe its accent; I have heard nothing quite like it before or since. There was a vast alien amusement in his glance.

"And to you," I said politely.

The larl sat down, curling his body heavily about me. If I had wanted to run, I could not have gotten past him, although that thought did not occur to me then. "There is an ancient legend, Flip, I wonder if you have heard of it, that on Christmas Eve the beasts can speak in human tongue. Have your elders told you that?"

I shook my head.

"They are neglecting you." Such strange humor dwelt in that voice. "There is truth to some of those old legends, if only you knew how to get at it. Though perhaps not all. Some are just stories. Perhaps this is not happening now; perhaps I am not speaking to you at all?"

I shook my head. I did not understand. I said so.

"That is the difference between your kind and mine. My kind understands everything about yours, and yours knows next to nothing abut mine. I would like to tell you a story, little one. Would you like that?"

"Yes," I said, for I was young and I liked stories very much.

He began:

"When the great ships landed. . . ."

Oh, God. When—no, no, no, wait. Excuse me. I'm shaken. I just this instant had a vision. It seemed to me that it was night and I was standing at the gates of a cemetery. And suddenly the air was full of light, planes and cones of light that burst from the ground and nested twittering in the trees. Fracturing the sky. I wanted to dance for joy. But the ground crumbled underfoot, and when I looked down the shadow of the gates touched my toes, a cold rectangle of profoundest black, deep as all eternity, and I was dizzy and about to fall and I, and I. . . .

Enough! I have had this vision before, many times. It must have been something that impressed me strongly in my youth, the moist smell of newly opened earth, the chalky whitewash on the picket fence. It must be. I do not believe in hobgoblins, ghosts, or premonitions. No, it does not bear thinking about. Foolishness! Let me get on with my story.

"When the great ships landed, I was feasting on my

grandfather's brains. All his descendants gathered respectfully about him, and I, as youngest, had first bite. His wisdom flowed through me, and the wisdom of his ancestors and the intimate knowledge of those animals he had eaten for food, and the spirit of valiant enemies who had been killed and then honored by being eaten, even as if they were family. I don't suppose you understand this, little one."

I shook my head.

"People never die, you see. Only humans die. Sometimes a minor part of a Person is lost, the doings of a few decades, but the bulk of his life is preserved, if not in this body, then in another. Or sometimes a Person will dishonor himself, and his descendants will refuse to eat him. This is a great shame, and the Person will go off to die somewhere alone.

"The ships descended bright as newborn suns. The People had never seen such a thing. We watched in inarticulate wonder, for we had no language then. You have seen the pictures, the baroque swirls of colored metal, the proud humans stepping down onto the land. But I was there, and I can tell you your people were ill. They stumbled down the gangplanks with the stench of radiation sickness about them. We could have destroyed them all then and there.

"Your people built a village at Landfall and planted crops over the bodies of their dead. We left them alone. They did not look like good game. They were too strange and too slow, and we had not yet come to savor your smell. So we went away, in baffled ignorance.

"That was in early spring.

"Half the survivors were dead by midwinter, some of disease but most because they did not have enough food. It was of no concern to us. But then the woman in the wilderness came to change our universe forever.

"When you're older, you'll be taught the woman's tale, and what desperation drove her into the wilderness. It's part of your history. But to myself, out in the mountains and winter-lean, the sight of her striding through the snows in her furs was like a vision of winter's queen herself. A gift of meat for the hungering season, life's blood for the solstice.

"I first saw the woman while I was eating her mate. He had emerged from his cabin that evening as he did every sunset, gun in hand, without looking up. I had observed him over the course of five days, and his behavior never varied. On that sixth nightfall I was crouched on his roof when he came out. I let him go a few steps from the door, then leaped. I felt his neck break on impact, tore open his throat to be sure, and ripped through his parka to taste his innards. There was no sport in it, but in winter we will take game whose brains we would never eat.

"My mouth was full and my muzzle pleasantly, warmly moist with blood when the woman appeared. I looked up, and she was topping the rise, riding one of your incomprehensible machines, what I know now to be a snowstrider. The setting sun broke through the clouds behind her, and for an instant she was embedded in glory. Her shadow stretched narrow before her and touched me, a bridge of darkness between us. We looked in one another's eyes. . . ."

Magda topped the rise with a kind of grim, joyless satisfaction. *I am now a hunter's woman,* she thought to herself. *We will always be welcome at Landfall for the meat we bring, but they will never speak civilly to me again. Good, I would choke on their sweet talk anyway.* The baby stirred and without looking down she stroked him through the furs, murmuring, "Just a little longer, my brave little boo, and we'll be at our new home. Will you like that, eh?"

The sun broke through the clouds to her back, making the snow a red dazzle. Then her eyes adjusted, and she saw the black shape crouched over her lover's body. A very great distance away, her hands throttled down the snowstrider and brought it to a halt. The shallow bowl of land before her was barren, the snow about the corpse black with blood. A last curl of smoke lazily separated from the hut's chimney. The brute lifted its bloody muzzle and looked at her.

Time froze and knotted in black agony.

The larl screamed. It ran straight at her, faster than thought. Clumsily, hampered by the infant strapped to her stomach, Magda clawed the rifle from its boot behind the saddle. She shucked her mittens, fitted hands to metal that stung like hornets, flicked off the safety, and brought the stock to her shoulder. The larl was halfway to her. She aimed and fired.

The larl went down. One shoulder shattered, slamming it to the side. It tumbled and rolled in the snow. "You sonofabitch!" Magda cried in triumph. But almost immediately the beast struggled to its feet, turned and fled.

The baby began to cry, outraged by the rifle's roar. Magda powered up the engine. "Hush, small warrior." A kind of madness filled her, a blind anesthetizing rage. "This won't take long." She flung her machine downhill, after the larl.

Even wounded, the creature was fast. She could barely keep up. As it entered the spare stand of trees to the far end of the meadow, Magda paused to fire again, burning a bullet by its head. The larl leaped away. From then on, it varied its flight with sudden changes of direction and unexpected jogs to the side. It was a fast learner. But it could not escape Magda. She had always been a hothead, and now her blood was up. She was not about to return to her lover's gutted body with his killer still alive.

The sun set and in the darkening light she lost sight of the larl. But she was able to follow its trail by two-shadowed moonlight, the deep, purple footprints, the darker spatter of blood it left, drop by drop, in the snow.

"It was the solstice, and the moons were full—a holy time. I felt it even as I fled the woman through the wilderness. The moons were bright on the snow. I felt the dread of being hunted descend on me, and in my inarticulate way I felt blessed.

"But I also felt a great fear for my kind. We had dismissed the humans as incomprehensible, not very interesting creatures, slow-moving, bad-smelling, and dull-witted. Now, pursued by this madwoman on her fast machine as she brandished a weapon that killed from afar, I felt all natural order betrayed. She was a goddess of the hunt, and I was her prey.

"The People had to be told.

"I gained distance from her, but I knew the woman would catch up. She was a hunter, and a hunter never abandons wounded prey. One way or another she would have me.

"In the winter all who are injured or too old must offer themselves to the community. The sacrifice rock was not far, by a hill riddled from time beyond memory with our burrows. My knowledge must be shared: The humans were dangerous. They would make good prey.

"I reached my goal when the moons were highest. The flat rock was bare of snow when I ran limping in. Awakened by the scent of my blood, several People emerged from their dens. I lay myself down on the sacrifice rock. A grandmother of the People came forward and licked my wound, tasting, considering. Then she nudged me away with her forehead. The wound would heal, she thought, and winter was young; my flesh was not yet needed.

"But I stayed. Again she nudged me away. I refused to go. She whined in puzzlement. I licked the rock.

"That was understood. Two of the People came forward and placed their weight on me. A third lifted a paw. He shattered my skull, and they ate."

Magda watched through power binoculars from atop a nearby ridge. She saw everything. The rock swarmed with lean black horrors. It would be dangerous to go down among them, so she waited and watched the puzzling tableau below. The larl had wanted to die, she'd swear it, and now the beasts came forward daintily, almost ritualistically, to taste, the young first and then the old. She raised her rifle, thinking to exterminate a few of the brutes from afar.

A curious thing happened then. All the larls that had eaten of her prey's brain leaped away, scattering. Those that had not eaten waited, easy targets, not understanding. Then another dipped to lap up a fragment of brain and looked up with sudden comprehension. Fear touched her.

The hunter had spoken often of the larls and had said that they were so elusive he sometimes thought them intelligent. "Come spring, when I can afford to waste ammunition on carnivores, I look forward to harvesting a few of these beauties," he'd said. He was the colony's xenobiologist, and he loved the animals he killed, treasured them even as he smoked their flesh, tanned their hides, and drew detailed pictures of their internal organs. Magda had always scoffed at his theory that larls gained insight into the habits of their prey by eating their brains, even though he'd spent much time observing the animals minutely from afar and gathering evidence. Now she wondered if he had been right.

Her baby whimpered, and she slid a hand inside her furs to give him a breast. Suddenly the night seemed cold and dangerous, and she thought: *What am I doing here?* Sanity returned to her all at once, her anger collapsing to nothing, like an ice tower shattering in the wind. Below, sleek black shapes sped toward her across the snow. They changed direction every few leaps, running evasive patterns to avoid her fire.

"Hang on, kid," she muttered, and turned her strider around. She opened up the throttle.

Magda kept to the open as much as she could, the creatures following her from a distance. Twice she stopped abruptly and turned her rifle on her pursuers. Instantly they disappeared in puffs of snow, crouching belly-down but not stopping, burrowing toward her under the surface. In the eerie night silence, she could hear the whispering sound of the brutes tunneling. She fled.

Some frantic timeless period later—the sky had still not lightened in the east—Magda was leaping a frozen stream when the strider's left ski struck a rock. The machine was knocked glancingly upward, cybernetics screaming as they fought to regain balance. With a sickening crunch, the strider slammed to earth, one ski twisted and bent. It would take extensive work before the strider could move again.

Magda dismounted. She opened her robe and looked down on her child. He smiled up at her and made a gurgling noise.

Something went dead in her.

A fool. I've been a criminal fool, she thought. Magda

was a proud woman who had always refused to regret, even privately, anything she had done. Now she regretted everything: her anger, the hunter, her entire life, all that had brought her to this point, the cumulative madness that threatened to kill her child.

A larl topped the ridge.

Magda raised her rifle; and it ducked down. She began walking down-slope, parallel to the stream. The snow was knee deep and she had to walk carefully not to slip and fall. Small pellets of snow rolled down ahead of her and were overtaken by other pellets. She strode ahead, pushing up a wake.

The hunter's cabin was not many miles distant; if she could reach it, they would live. But a mile was a long way in winter. She could hear the larls calling to each other, soft coughlike noises, to either side of the ravine. They were following the sound of her passage through the snow. Well, let them. She still had the rifle, and if it had few bullets left, they didn't know that. They were only animals.

This high in the mountains, the trees were sparse. Magda descended a good quarter mile before the ravine choked with scrub and she had to climb up and out or risk being ambushed. *Which way?* she wondered. She heard three coughs to her right and climbed the left slope, alert and wary.

"We herded her. Through the long night we gave her fleeting glimpses of our bodies whenever she started to turn to the side she must not go and let her pass unmolested the other way. We let her see us dig into the distant snow and wait motionless, undetectable. We filled the woods with our shadows. Slowly, slowly, we turned her around. She struggled to return to the cabin, but she could not. In what haze of fear and despair she walked!

We could smell it. Sometimes her baby cried, and she hushed the milky-scented creature in a voice gone flat with futility. The night deepened as the moons sank in the sky. We forced the woman back up into the mountains. Toward the end, her legs failed her several times; she lacked our strength and stamina. But her patience and guile were every bit our match. Once we approached her still form, and she killed two of us before the rest could retreat. How we loved her! We paced her, confident that sooner or later she'd drop.

"It was at night's darkest hour that the woman was forced back to the burrowed hillside, the sacred place of the People where stood the sacrifice rock. She topped the same rise for the second time that night and saw it. For a moment she stood helpless, and then she burst into tears.

"We waited, for this was the holiest moment of the hunt, the point when the prey recognizes and accepts her destiny. After a time, the woman's sobs ceased. She raised her head and straightened her back.

"Slowly, steadily she walked downhill."

She knew what to do.

Larls retreated into their burrows at the sight of her, gleaming eyes dissolving into darkness. Magda ignored them. Numb and aching, weary to death, she walked to the sacrifice rock. It had to be this way.

Magda opened her coat, unstrapped her baby. She wrapped him deep in the furs and laid the bundle down to one side of the rock. Dizzily, she opened the bundle to kiss the top of his sweet head, and he made an angry sound. "Good for you, kid," she said hoarsely. "Keep that attitude." She was so tired.

She took off her sweaters, her vest, her blouse. The raw cold nipped at her flesh with teeth of ice. She stretched slightly, body aching with motion. God it felt good. She laid down the rifle. She knelt.

The rock was black with dried blood. She lay down flat, as she had earlier seen her larl do. The stone was cold, so cold it almost blanked out the pain. Her pursuers waited nearby, curious to see what she was doing; she could hear the soft panting noise of their breathing. One padded noiselessly to her side. She could smell the brute. It whined questioningly.

She licked the rock.

"Once it was understood what the woman wanted, her sacrifice went quickly. I raised a paw, smashed her skull. Again, I was youngest. Innocent, I bent to taste.

"The neighbors were gathering, hammering at the door, climbing over one another to peer through the windows, making the walls bulge and breathe with their eagerness. I grunted and bellowed, and the clash of silver and clink of plates next door grew louder. Like peasant animals, my husband's people tried to drown out the sound of my pain with toasts and drunken jokes.

"Through the window I saw Tevin the Fool's bone-white skin gaunt on his skull, and behind him a slice of face—sharp nose, white cheeks—like a mask. The doors and walls pulsed with the weight of those outside. In the next room children fought and wrestled, and elders pulled at their long white beards, staring anxiously at the closed door.

"The midwife shook her head, red lines running from the corners of her mouth down either side of her stern chin. Her eye sockets were shadowy pools of dust. 'Now push!' she cried. 'Don't be a lazy sow!'

"I groaned and arched my back. I shoved my head back, and it grew smaller, eaten up by the pillows. The bedframe skewed as one leg slowly buckled under it.

My husband glanced over his shoulder at me, an angry look, his fingers knotted behind his back.

"All of Landfall shouted and hovered on the walls.

" 'Here it comes!' shrieked the midwife. She reached down and eased out a tiny head, purple and angry, like a goblin.

"And then all the walls glowed red and green and sprouted large flowers. The door turned orange and burst open, and the neighbors and crew flooded in. The ceiling billowed up, and aerialists tumbled through the rafters. A boy who had been hiding beneath the bed flew up laughing to where the ancient sky and stars shone through the roof.

"They held up the child, bloody on a platter."

Here the larl touched me for the first time, that heavy black paw like velvet on my knee, talons sheathed. "Can you understand?" he asked. "What it meant to me? All that, the first birth of human young on this planet, I experienced in an instant. I felt it with full human comprehension. I understood the personal tragedy and the community triumph, and the meaning of the lives and culture behind it. A second before I lived as an animal, with an animal's simple thoughts and hopes. Then I ate of your ancestor. I was lifted in an instant halfway to godhood.

"As the woman had hoped I would be. She had died with her child's birth foremost in her mind. She gave us that. She gave us more. She gave us language. We were wise animals before we ate her brain, and we were the People afterward. We owed her so much. And we knew what she wanted from us." The larl stroked my cheek with his great, velvety paw, the ivory claws sheathed but quivering slightly, as if about to awake.

I hardly dared breathe.

"That morning I entered Landfall, carrying the baby's sling in my mouth. It slept through most of the journey. At dawn I passed through the empty street as silently as I knew how. I came to the First Captain's house. I heard the murmur of voices within, the entire village assembled for worship. I tapped the door with one paw. There was sudden, astonished silence. Then slowly, fearfully, the door opened."

The larl was silent for a moment. "That was the beginning of the association of the People with humans. We were welcomed into your homes, and we helped with the hunting. It was a fair trade. Our food saved many lives that first winter. No one needed to know how the woman had perished, or how well we understood your kind.

"That child was your ancestor, Flip. Every few generations we take one of your family out hunting and taste his brains to maintain our closeness with your line. If you are a good boy and grow up to be as bold and honest, as intelligent and noble a man as your father, then perhaps it will be you we eat."

The larl presented his blunt muzzle to me in what might have been meant as a friendly smile. Perhaps not; the expression hangs unreadable, ambiguous in my mind even now. Then he stood and padded away into the friendly dark shadows of the Stone House.

I was sitting staring into the coals a few minutes later when my second-eldest sister—her face a featureless blaze of light, like an angel's—came into the room and saw me. She held out a hand, saying, "Come on, Flip, you're missing everything." And I went with her.

Did any of this actually happen? Sometimes I wonder. But it's growing late, and your parents are away. My room is small but snug, my bed warm but empty.

We can burrow deep in the blankets and scare away the cave-bears by playing the oldest winter games there are.

You're blushing! Don't tug away your hand. I'll be gone soon to some distant world to fight in a war for people who are as unknown to you as they are to me. Soldiers grow old slowly, you know. We're shipped frozen between the stars. When you are old and plump and happily surrounded by grandchildren, I'll still be young and thinking of you. You'll remember me then, and our thoughts will touch in the void. Will you have nothing to regret? Is that really what you want?

Come, don't be shy. Let's put the past aside and get on with our lives. That's better. Blow the candle out, love, and there's an end to my tale.

All this happened long ago, on a planet whose name has been burned from my memory.

A tale of a man who forgets—and
almost loses Christmas.

THE HAUNTED MAN

—

Charles Dickens

CHAPTER I

THE GIFT BESTOWED

Everybody said so.

Far be it from me to assert that what everybody says must be true. Everybody is, often, as likely to be wrong as right. In the general experience, everybody has been wrong so often, and it has taken in most instances such a weary while to find out how wrong, that authority is proved to be fallible. Everybody may sometimes be right; "but *that's* no rule," as the ghost of Giles Scroggins says in the ballad.

The dread word, GHOST, recalls me.

Everybody said he looked like a haunted man. The extent of my present claim for everybody is, that they were so far right. He did.

Who could have seen his hollow cheek, his sunken brilliant eye; his black-attired figure, indefinably grim, although well-knit and well-proportioned; his grizzled hair hanging, like tangled sea-weed, about his face,—as if he had been, through his whole life, a lonely mark for the chafing and beating of the great deep of humanity,—but might have said he looked like a haunted man?

Who could have observed his manner, taciturn, thoughtful, gloomy, shadowed by habitual reserve, retiring always and jocund never, with a distraught air of reverting to a bygone place and time, or of listening to some old echoes in his mind, but might have said it was the manner of a haunted man?

Who could have heard his voice, slow-speaking, deep, and grave, with a natural fulness and melody in it which he seemed to set himself against and stop, but might have said it was the voice of a haunted man?

Who that had seen him in his inner chamber, part library and part laboratory,—for he was, as the world knew, far and wide, a learned man in chemistry, and a teacher on whose lips and hands a crowd of aspiring ears and eyes hung daily,—who that had seen him there, upon a winter night, alone, surrounded by his drugs and instruments and books; the shadow of his shaded lamp a monstrous beetle on the wall, motionless among a crowd of spectral shapes raised there by the flickering of the fire upon the quaint objects around him; some of these phantoms (the reflection of glass vessels that held liquids), trembling at heart like things that knew his power to uncombine them, and to give back their component parts to fire and vapor;—who that had seen him then, his work done, and he pondering in his chair before the rusted grate and red flame, moving his thin mouth as if in speech, but silent as the dead, would not have said that the man seemed haunted and the chamber too.

Who might not, by a very easy flight of fancy, have believed that everything about him took this haunted tone, and that he lived on haunted ground?

His dwelling was so solitary and vault-like,—an old, retired part of an ancient endowment for students, once a brave edifice planted in an open place, but now the obsolete whim of forgotten architects; smoke-age-and-weather-darkened, squeezed on every side by the over-growing of the great city, and choked, like an old well, with stones and bricks; its small quadrangles, lying down in very pits formed by the streets and buildings, which, in course of time, had been constructed above its heavy chimney stacks; its old trees, insulted by the neighboring smoke, which deigned to droop so low when it was very feeble and the weather very moody; its grass-plots, struggling with the mildewed earth to be grass, or to win any show of compromise; its silent pavement, unaccustomed to the tread of feet, and even to the observation of eyes, except when a stray face looked down from the upper world, wondering what nook it was; its sun-dial in a little bricked-up corner, where no sun had straggled for a hundred years, but where, in compensation for the sun's neglect, the snow would lie for weeks when it lay nowhere else, and the black east wind would spin like a huge humming-top, when in all other places it was silent and still.

His dwelling, at its heart and core—within doors—at his fireside—was so lowering and old, so crazy, yet so strong, with its worm-eaten beams of wood in the ceiling and its sturdy floor shelving downward to the great oak chimney-piece; so environed and hemmed in by the pressure of the town, yet so remote in fashion, age, and custom; so quiet, yet so thundering with echoes when a distant voice was raised or a door was shut,—echoes not confined to the many low passages and empty rooms, but rumbling and grumbling till they were stifled in the heavy air of the forgotten Crypt where the Norman arches were half buried in the earth.

You should have seen him in his dwelling about twilight, in the dead winter time.

When the wind was blowing, shrill and shrewd, with the going down of the blurred sun. When it was just so dark, as that the forms of things were indistinct and big—but not wholly lost. When sitters by the fire began to see wild faces and figures, mountains and abysses, ambuscades and armies, in the coals. When people in the streets bent down their heads and ran before the weather. When those who were obliged to meet it, were stopped at angry corners, stung by wandering snow-flakes alighting on the lashes of their eyes,—which fell too sparingly, and were blown away too quickly, to leave a trace upon the frozen ground. When windows of private houses closed up tight and warm. When lighted gas began to burst forth in the busy and the quiet streets, fast blackening otherwise. When stray pedestrians, shivering along the latter, looked down at the glowing fires in kitchens, and sharpened their sharp appetites by sniffing up the fragrance of whole miles of dinners.

When travellers by land were bitter cold, and looked wearily on gloomy landscapes, rustling and shuddering in the blast. When mariners at sea, outlying upon icy yards, were tossed and swung above the howling ocean dreadfully. When light-houses, on rocks and headlands, showed solitary and watchful; and benighted sea-birds breasted on against their ponderous lanterns, and fell dead. When little readers of story-books, by the fire-light, trembled to think of Cassim Baba cut into quarters, hanging in the Robbers' Cave, or had some small misgivings that the fierce little old woman, with the crutch, who used to start out of the box in the merchant Abudah's bedroom, might, one of these nights, be found upon the stairs, in the long, cold, dusky journey up to bed.

When, in rustic places, the last glimmering of daylight died away from the ends of avenues; and the trees, arching overhead, were sullen and black. When, in parks and woods, the high wet fern and sodden moss and beds of fallen leaves, and trunks of trees, were lost to view, in masses of impenetrable shade. When mists arose from dike, and fen, and river. When lights in old halls and in cottage windows were a cheerful sight. When the mill stopped, the wheelwright and the blacksmith shut their workshops, the turnpike-gate closed, the plough and harrow were left lonely in the fields, the laborer and team went home, and the striking of the church-clock had a deeper sound than at noon, and the church-yard wicket would be swung no more that night.

When twilight everywhere released the shadows, prisoned up all day, that now closed in and gathered like mustering swarms of ghosts. When they stood lowering in corners of rooms, and frowned out from behind half-opened doors. When they had full possession of unoccupied apartments. When they danced upon the floors, and walls, and ceilings of inhabited chambers while the fire was low, and withdrew like ebbing waters when it sprung into a blaze. When they fantastically mocked the shapes of household objects, making the nurse an ogress, the rocking-horse a monster, the wondering child, half-scared and half-amused, a stranger to itself,—the very tongs upon the hearth a straddling giant with his arms a-kimbo, evidently smelling the blood of Englishmen, and wanting to grind people's bones to make his bread.

When these shadows brought into the minds of older people other thoughts, and showed them different images. When they stole from their retreats, in the likenesses of forms and faces from the past, from the grave, from the deep, deep gulf, where the things that might have been, and never were, are always wandering.

When he sat, as already mentioned, gazing at the fire. When, as it rose and fell, the shadows went and came. When he took no heed of them, with his bodily eyes; but, let them come or let them go, looked fixedly at the fire. You should have seen him, then.

When the sounds that had arisen with the shadows, and come out of their lurking-places at the twilight summons, seemed to make a deeper stillness all about him. When the wind was rumbling in the chimney, and sometimes crooning, sometimes howling, in the house. When the old trees outward were so shaken and beaten, that one querulous old rook, unable to sleep, protested now and then, in a feeble, dozy, high-up "Caw!" When, at intervals, the window trembled, the rusty vane upon the turret-top complained, the clock beneath it recorded that another quarter of an hour was gone, or the fire collapsed and fell in with a rattle.

—When a knock came at his door, in short, as he was sitting so, and roused him.

"Who's that?" said he. "Come in!"

Surely there had been no figure leaning on the back of his chair; no face looking over it. It is certain that no gliding footstep touched the floor, as he lifted up his head with a start, and spoke. And yet there was no mirror in the room on whose surface his own form could have cast its shadow for a moment: and Something had passed darkly and gone!

"I'm humbly fearful, sir," said a fresh-colored busy man, holding the door open with his foot for the admission of himself and a wooden tray he carried, and letting it go again by very gentle and careful degrees, when he and the tray had got in, lest it should close noisily, "that it's a good bit past the time to-night. But Mrs. William has been taken off her legs so often"—

"By the wind? Ay! I have heard it rising."

—"By the wind, sir—that it's a mercy she got home at all. Oh dear, yes. Yes. It was by the wind, Mr. Redlaw. By the wind."

He had, by this time, put down the tray for dinner, and was employed in lighting the lamp, and spreading a cloth on the table. From this employment he desisted in a hurry, to stir and feed the fire, and then resumed it; the lamp he had lighted, and the blaze that rose under his hand so quickly changing the appearance of the room, that it seemed as if the mere coming in of his fresh red face and active manner had made the pleasant alteration.

"Mrs. William is of course subject at any time, sir, to be taken off her balance by the elements. She is not formed superior to *that*."

"No," returned Mr. Redlaw good-naturedly, though abruptly.

"No, sir. Mrs. William may be taken off her balance by Earth; as, for example, last Sunday week, when sloppy and greasy, and she going out to tea with her newest sister-in-law, and having a pride in herself, and wishing to appear perfectly spotless though pedestrian. Mrs. William may be taken off her balance by Air; as being once over-persuaded by a friend to try a swing at Peckham Fair, which acted on her constitution instantly like a steamboat. Mrs. William may be taken off her balance by Fire; as on a false alarm of engines at her mother's, when she went two mile in her nightcap. Mrs. William may be taken off her balance by Water; as at

Battersea, when rowed into the piers by her young nephew, Charley Swidger, junior, aged twelve, which had no idea of boats whatever. But these are elements. Mrs. William must be taken out of elements for the strength of *her* character to come into play."

As he stopped for a reply, the reply was "Yes," in the same tone as before.

"Yes, sir. Oh dear, yes!" said Mr. Swidger, still proceeding with his preparations, and checking them off as he made them. "That's where it is, sir. That's what I always say myself, sir. Such a many of us Swidgers!—Pepper. Why there's my father, sir, superannuated keeper and custodian of this Institution, eighty-seven year old. He's a Swidger!—Spoon."

"True, William," was the patient and abstracted answer, when he stopped again.

"Yes, sir," said Mr. Swidger. "That's what I always say, sir. You may call him the trunk of the tree!—Bread. Then you come to his successor, my unworthy self—Salt—and Mrs. William, Swidgers both.—Knife and fork. Then you come to all my brothers and their families, Swidgers, man and woman, boy and girl. Why, what with cousins, uncles, aunts, and relationships of this, that, and t'other degree, and what-not degree, and marriages, and lyings-in, the Swidgers—Tumbler—might take hold of hands, and make a ring round England!"

Receiving no reply at all here, from the thoughtful man whom he addressed, Mr. William approached him nearer, and made a feint of accidentally knocking the table with a decanter to rouse him. The moment he succeeded, he went on, as if in great alacrity of acquiescence.

"Yes, sir! That's just what I say myself, sir. Mrs. William and me have often said so. 'There's Swidgers enough,' we say, 'without *our* voluntary contributions,'—Butter. In fact, sir, my father is a family in himself—Castors—to take care of; and it happens all for the best that we have no child of our own, though it's made Mrs. William rather quiet-like, too. Quite ready for the fowl and mashed potatoes, sir? Mrs. William said she'd dish in ten minutes when I left the Lodge?"

"I am quite ready," said the other, waking as from a dream, and walking slowly to and fro.

"Mrs. William has been at it again, sir!" said the keeper, as he stood warming a plate at the fire, and pleasantly shading his face with it. Mr. Redlaw stopped in his walking, and an expression of interest appeared in him.

"What I always say myself, sir. She *will* do it! There's a motherly feeling in Mrs. William's breast that must and will have vent."

"What has she done?"

"Why, sir, not satisfied with being a sort of mother to all the young gentlemen that come up from a variety of parts, to attend your courses of lectures at this ancient foundation—it's surprising how stone-chancy catches the heat, this frosty weather, to be sure!" Here he turned the plates and cooled his fingers.

"Well?" said Mr. Redlaw.

"That's just what I say myself, sir," returned Mr. William, speaking over his shoulder, as if in ready and delighted assent. "That's exactly where it is, sir. There a'n't one of our students but appears to regard Mrs. William in that light. Every day, right through the course, they put their heads into the Lodge, one after another, and have all got something to tell her, or something to ask her. 'Swidge' is the appellation by which they speak of Mrs. William in general, among themselves, I'm told; but that's what I say, sir. Better be called ever so far out of your name, if it's done in real liking, than have it made ever so much of, and not cared about! What's a name for? To know a person by. If Mrs. William is known by something better than her name—I allude to Mrs. William's qualities and disposition—never mind her name, though it *is* Swidger, by rights. Let 'em call her Swidge, Widge, Bridge—Lord! London Bridge, Blackfriars, Chelsea, Putney, Waterloo, or Hammersmith Suspension—if they like!"

The close of this triumphant oration brought him and the plate to the table, upon which he half laid and half dropped it, with a lively sense of its being thoroughly heated, just as the subject of his praises entered the room, bearing another tray and a lantern, and followed by a venerable old man with long gray hair.

Mrs. William, like Mr. William, was a simple, innocent-looking person, in whose smooth cheeks the cheerful red of her husband's official waistcoat was very pleasantly repeated. But whereas Mr. William's light hair stood on end all over his head, and seemed to draw his eyes up with it in an excess of bustling readiness for anything, the dark brown hair of Mrs. William was carefully smoothed down, and waved away under a trim tidy cap, in the most exact and quiet manner imaginable. Whereas Mr. William's very trousers hitched themselves up at the ankles, as if it were not in their iron-gray nature to rest without looking about them, Mrs. William's neatly-flowered skirts—red and white, like her own pretty face—were as composed and orderly, as if the very wind that blew so hard out of doors could not disturb one of their folds. Whereas his coat had something of a fly-away and half-off appearance about the collar and breast, her little bodice was so placid and neat, that there should have been protection for her, in it, had she needed any, with the roughest people. Who could have had the heart to make so calm a bosom swell with grief, or throb with fear, or flutter with a thought of shame! To whom would its repose and peace have not appealed against disturbance, like the innocent slumber of a child!

"Punctual, of course, Milly," said her husband, relieving her of the tray, "or it wouldn't be you. Here's Mrs. William, sir!—He looks lonelier than ever tonight," whispering to his wife, as he was taking the tray, "and ghostlier altogether."

Without any show of hurry or noise, or any show of herself even, she was so calm and quiet, Milly set the dishes she had brought upon the table,—Mr. William, after much clattering and running about, having only gained possession of a butter-boat of gravy, which he stood ready to serve.

"What is that the old man has in his arms?" asked Mr. Redlaw, as he sat down to his solitary meal.

"Holly, sir," replied the quiet voice of Milly.

"That's what I say myself, sir," interposed Mr. William, striking in with the butter-boat. "Berries is so seasonable to the time of year!—Brown gravy!"

"Another Christmas come, another year gone!" murmured the Chemist, with a gloomy sigh. "More figures in the lengthening sum of recollection that we work and work at to our torment, till Death idly jumbles altogether, and rubs all out. So Philip!" breaking off, and raising his voice as he addressed the old man standing apart, with his glistening burden in his arms, from which the quiet Mrs. William took small branches, which she noiselessly trimmed with her scissors, and decorated the room with, while her aged father-in-law looked on much interested in the ceremony.

"My duty to you, sir," returned the old man. "Should

have spoke before, sir, but know your ways, Mr. Redlaw—proud to say—and wait till spoke to! Merry Christmas, sir, and happy New Year, and many of 'em. Have had a pretty many of 'em myself—ha, ha!—and may take the liberty of wishing 'em. I'm eighty-seven!"

"Have you had so many that were merry and happy?" asked the other.

"Ay, sir, ever so many," returned the old man.

"Is his memory impaired with age? It is to be expected now," said Mr. Redlaw, turning to the son, and speaking lower.

"Not a morsel of it, sir," replied Mr. William. "That's exactly what I say myself, sir. There never was such a memory as my father's. He's the most wonderful man in the world. He don't know what forgetting means. It's the very observation I'm always making to Mrs. William, sir, if you'll believe me!"

Mr. Swidger, in his polite desire to seem to acquiesce at all events, delivered this as if there were no iota of contradiction in it, and it were all said in unbounded and unqualified assent.

The Chemist pushed his plate away, and, rising from the table, walked across the room to where the old man stood looking at a little sprig of holly in his hand.

"It recalls the time when many of those years were old and new, then?" he said, observing him attentively, and touching him on the shoulder. "Does it?"

"Oh, many, many!" said Philip, half awaking from his reverie. "I'm eighty-seven!"

"Merry and happy, was it?" asked the Chemist, in a low voice. "Merry and happy, old man?"

"Maybe as high as that, no higher," said the old man, holding out his hand a little way above the level of his knee, and looking retrospectively at his questioner, "when I first remember 'em! Cold, sunshiny day it was, out a-walking, when some one—it was my mother as sure as you stand there, though I don't know what her blessed face was like, for she took ill and died that Christmas time—told me they were food for birds. The pretty little fellow thought—that's me, you understand—that birds' eyes were so bright, perhaps, because the berries that they lived on in the winter were so bright. I recollect that. And I'm eighty-seven!"

"Merry and happy!" mused the other, bending his dark eyes upon the stooping figure, with a smile of compassion. "Merry and happy—and remember well?"

"Ay, ay, ay!" resumed the old man, catching the last words. "I remember 'em well in my school-time, year after year, and all the merrymaking that used to come along with them. I was a strong chap then, Mr. Redlaw; and, if you'll believe me, hadn't my match at foot-ball within ten mile. Where's my son William? Hadn't my match at foot-ball, William, within ten mile!"

"That's what I always say, father!" returned the son promptly, and with great respect. "You ARE a Swidger, if ever there was one of the family!"

"Dear!" said the old man, shaking his head as he again looked at the holly. "His mother—my son William's my youngest son—and I, have set among 'em all, boys and girls, little children and babies, many a year, when the berries like these were not shining half so bright all round us, as their bright faces. Many of 'em are gone; she's gone; and my son George (our eldest, who was her pride more than all the rest!) is fallen very low: but I can see them, when I look here, alive and healthy, as they used to be in those days; and I can see him, thank God, in his innocence. It's a blessed thing to me, at eighty-seven."

The keen look that had been fixed upon him with so much earnestness, had gradually sought the ground.

"When my circumstances got to be not so good as
formerly, through not being honestly dealt by, and I first
come here to be custodian," said the old man,—"which
was upwards of fifty years ago—where's my son, William? More than half a century ago, William!"

"That's what I say, father," replied the son, as
promptly and dutifully as before, "that's exactly where
it is. Two times ought's an ought, and twice five ten,
and there's a hundred of 'em."

"It was quite a pleasure to know that one of our
founders—or more correctly speaking," said the old
man, with a great glory in his subject and his knowledge of it, "one of the learned gentlemen that helped
endow us in Queen Elizabeth's time, for we were
founded afore her day—left in his will, among the other
bequests he made us, so much to buy holly, for garnish-
ing the walls and windows, come Christmas. There was
something homely and friendly in it. Being but strange
here, then, and coming at Christmas time, we took a liking for his very picter that hangs in what used to be, an-
ciently, afore our ten poor gentlemen commuted for an
annual stipend in money, our great Dinner Hall.—A sedate gentleman in a peaked beard, with a ruff round his
neck, and a scroll below him, in old English letters,
'Lord! keep my memory green!' You know all about
him, Mr. Redlaw?"

"I know the portrait hangs there, Philip."

"Yes, sure, it's the second on the right, above the
panelling. I was going to say—he has helped to keep
my memory green, I thank him; for, going round the
building every year, as I'm a doing now, and freshening
up the bare rooms with these branches and berries,
freshens up my bare old brain. One year brings back another, and that year another, and those others numbers!
At last, it seems to me as if the birth-time of our Lord

was the birth-time of all I have ever had affection for, or mourned for, or delighted in,—and they're a pretty many, for I'm eighty-seven!"

"Merry and happy," murmured Redlaw to himself.

The room began to darken strangely.

"So you see, sir," pursued old Philip, whose hale wintry cheek had warmed into a ruddier glow, and whose blue eyes had brightened while he spoke, "I have plenty to keep, when I keep this present season. Now where's my quiet Mouse? Chattering's the sin of my time of life, and there's half the building to do yet, if the cold don't freeze us first, or the wind don't blow us away, or the darkness don't swallow us up."

The quiet Mouse had brought her calm face to his side, and silently taken his arm, before he finished speaking.

"Come away, my dear," said the old man. "Mr. Redlaw won't settle to his dinner, otherwise, till it's cold in the winter. I hope you'll excuse me rambling on, sir, and I wish you good-night, and, once again, a merry"—

"Stay!" said Mr. Redlaw, resuming his place at the table, more, it would have seemed from his manner, to reassure the old keeper, than in any remembrance of his own appetite. "Spare me another moment, Philip. William, you were going to tell me something to your excellent wife's honor. It will not be disagreeable to her to hear you praise her. What was it?"

"Why, that's where it is, you see, sir," returned Mr. William Swidger, looking towards his wife in considerable embarrassment. "Mrs. William's got her eye upon me."

"But you're not afraid of Mrs. William's eye?"

"Why, no, sir," returned Mr. Swidger, "that's what I say myself. It wasn't made to be afraid of. It wouldn't have been made so mild, if that was the intention. But

I wouldn't like to—Milly!—him, you know. Down in the Buildings."

Mr. William, standing behind the table, and rummaging disconcertedly among the objects upon it, directed persuasive glances at Mrs. William, and secret jerks of his head and thumb at Mr. Redlaw, as alluring her towards him.

"Him, you know, my love," said Mr. William. "Down in the Buildings. Tell, my dear! You're the works of Shakespeare in comparison with myself. Down in the Buildings, you know, my love,—Student."

"Student!" repeated Mr. Redlaw, raising his head.

"That's what I say, sir!" cried Mr. William, in the utmost animation of assent. "If it wasn't the poor student down in the Buildings, why should you wish to hear it from Mrs. William's lips? Mrs. William, my dear—Buildings."

"I didn't know," said Milly, with a quiet frankness, free from any haste or confusion, "that William had said anything about it, or I wouldn't have come. I asked him not to. It's a sick young gentleman, sir—and very poor, I am afraid—who is too ill to go home this holiday-time, and lives, unknown to any one, in but a common kind of lodging for a gentleman, down in Jerusalem Buildings. That's all, sir."

"Why have I never heard of him?" said the Chemist, rising hurriedly. "Why has he not made his situation known to me? Sick!—give me my hat and cloak. Poor!—what house?—what number?"

"Oh, you mus'n't go there, sir," said Milly, leaving her father-in-law, and calmly confronting him with her collected little face and folded hands.

"Not go there?"

"Oh dear, no!" said Milly, shaking her head as at

a most manifest and self-evident impossibility. "It couldn't be thought of!"

"What do you mean? Why not?"

"Why, you see, sir," said Mr. William Swidger, persuasively and confidentially, "that's what I say. Depend upon it, the young gentleman would never have made his situation known to one of his own sex. Mrs. William has got into his confidence, but that's quite different. They all confide in Mrs. William; they all trust *her*. A man, sir, couldn't have got a whisper out of him; but woman, sir, and Mrs. William combined!"—

"There is good sense and delicacy in what you say, William," returned Mr. Redlaw, observant of the gentle and composed face at his shoulder. And laying his finger on his lip, he secretly put his purse into her hand.

"Oh dear no, sir!" cried Milly, giving it back again. "Worse and worse! Couldn't be dreamed of!"

Such a staid matter-of-fact housewife she was, and so unruffled by the momentary haste of this rejection, that, an instant afterwards, she was tidily picking up a few leaves which had strayed from between her scissors and her apron, when she had arranged the holly.

Finding, when she rose from her stooping posture, that Mr. Redlaw was still regarding her with doubt and astonishment, she quietly repeated—looking about, the while, for any other fragments that might have escaped her observation:—

"Oh dear no, sir! He said that of all the world he would not be known to you, or receive help from you— though he is a student in your class. I have made no terms of secrecy with you, but I trust to your honor completely."

"Why did he say so?"

"Indeed I can't tell, sir," said Milly, after thinking a little, "because I am not at all clever, you know; and I wanted to be useful to him in making things neat and comfortable about him, and employed myself that way. But I know he is poor, and lonely, and I think he is somehow neglected too.—How dark it is!"

The room had darkened more and more. There was a very heavy gloom and shadow gathering behind the Chemist's chair.

"What more about him?" he asked.

"He is engaged to be married when he can afford it," said Milly, "and is studying, I think, to qualify himself to earn a living. I have seen, a long time, that he has studied hard and denied himself much.—How very dark it is!"

"It's turned colder, too," said the old man, rubbing his hands. "There's a chill and dismal feeling in the room. Where's my son William? William, my boy, turn the lamp, and rouse the fire!"

Milly's voice resumed, like quiet music very softly played:—

"He muttered in his broken sleep yesterday afternoon, after talking to me" (this was to herself) "about some one dead, and some great wrong done that could never be forgotten; but whether to him or to another person, I don't know. Not *by* him, I am sure."

"And, in short, Mrs. William, you see—which she wouldn't say herself, Mr. Redlaw, if she was to stop here till the new year after this next one"—said Mr. William, coming up to him to speak in his ear, "has done him worlds of good! Bless you, worlds of good! All at home just the same as ever—my father made us snug and comfortable—not a crumb of litter to be found in the house, if you were to offer fifty pound ready money for it—Mrs. William apparently never out of the way—yet Mrs. William backwards and forwards, backwards and forwards, up and down, up and down, a mother to him!"

The room turned darker and colder, and the gloom and shadow gathering behind the chair was heavier.

"Not content with this, sir, Mrs. William goes and finds, this very night, when she was coming home (why it's not above a couple of hours ago), a creature more like a young wild beast than a young child, shivering upon a door-step. What does Mrs. William do, but brings it home to dry it, and feed it, and keep it till our old Bounty of food and flannel is given away on Christmas morning! If it ever felt a fire before, it's as much as it ever did; for it's sitting in the old Lodge chimney, staring at ours as if its ravenous eyes would never shut again. It's sitting there, at least," said Mr. William, correcting himself, on reflection, "unless it's bolted!"

"Heaven keep her happy!" said the Chemist aloud, "and you too, Philip! and you, William! I must consider what to do in this. I may desire to see this student, I'll not detain you longer now. Good-night!"

"I thankee, sir, I thankee!" said the old man, "for Mouse, and for my son William, and for myself. Where's my son William? William, you take the lantern and go on first, through them long dark passages, as you did last year and the year afore. Ha, ha! *I* remember—though I'm eighty-seven! 'Lord keep my memory green!' It's a very good prayer, Mr. Redlaw, that of the learned gentleman in the peaked beard, with a ruff round his neck—hangs up, second on the right above the panelling, in what used to be, afore our ten poor gentlemen commuted, our great Dinner Hall. 'Lord keep my memory green!' It's very good and pious, sir. Amen! Amen!"

As they passed out and shut the heavy door, which, however carefully withheld, fired a long train of thundering reverberations when it shut at last, the room turned darker.

As he fell a-musing in his chair alone, the healthy holly withered on the wall, and dropped—dead branches!

As the gloom and shadow thickened behind him, in that place where it had been gathering so darkly, it took, by slow degrees,—or out of it there came, by some unreal, unsubstantial process—not to be traced by any human sense, an awful likeness of himself.

Ghastly and cold, colorless in its leaden face and hands, but with his features, and his bright eyes, and his grizzled hair, and dressed in the gloomy shadow of his dress, it came into its terrible appearance of existence, motionless, without a sound. As *he* leaned his arm upon the elbow of his chair, ruminating before the fire, *it* leaned upon the chair-back, close above him, with its appalling copy of his face looking where his face looked, and bearing the expression his face bore.

This, then, was the Something that had passed and gone already. This was the dread companion of the haunted man!

It took, for some moments, no more apparent heed of him, than he of it. The Christmas Waits were playing somewhere in the distance, and, through his thoughtfulness, he seemed to listen to the music. It seemed to listen too.

At length he spoke; without moving or lifting up his face.

"Here again!" he said.

"Here again!" replied the Phantom.

"I see you in the fire," said the haunted man; "I hear you in music, in the wind, in the dead stillness of the night."

The Phantom moved his head, assenting.

"Why do you come, to haunt me thus?"

"I come as I am called," replied the Ghost.

"No. Unbidden," exclaimed the Chemist.

"Unbidden be it," said the Spectre. "It is enough. I am here."

Hitherto the light of the fire had shone on the two faces—if the dread lineaments behind the chair might be called a face—both addressed towards it, as at first, and neither looking at the other. But, now, the haunted man turned, suddenly, and stared upon the Ghost. The Ghost, as sudden in its motion, passed to before the chair, and stared on him.

The living man, and the animated image of himself dead, might so have looked, the one upon the other. An awful survey, in a lonely and remote part of an empty old pile of building, on a winter night, with the loud wind going by upon its journey of mystery—whence, or whither, no man knowing since the world began—and the stars, in unimaginable millions, glittering through it, from eternal space, where the world's bulk is as a grain, and its hoary age is infancy.

"Look upon me!" said the Spectre. "I am he, neglected in my youth, and miserably poor, who strove and suffered, and still strove and suffered, until I hewed out knowledge from the mine where it was buried, and made rugged steps thereof, for my worn feet to rest and rise on."

"I *am* that man," returned the Chemist.

"No mother's self-denying love," pursued the Phantom, "no father's counsel, aided *me*. A stranger came into my father's place when I was but a child, and I was easily an alien from my mother's heart. My parents, at the best, were of that sort whose care soon ends, and whose duty is soon done; who cast their offspring loose, early as birds do theirs; and, if they do well, claim the merit; and, if ill, the pity."

It paused, and seemed to tempt and goad him with its look, and with the manner of its speech, and with its smile.

"I am he," pursued the Phantom, "who, in this struggle upward, found a friend. I made him—won him—bound him to me! We worked together, side by side. All the love and confidence that in my earlier youth had had no outlet, and found no expression, I bestowed on him."

"Not all," said Redlaw, hoarsely.

"No, not all," returned the Phantom. "I had a sister."

The haunted man, with his head resting on his hands, replied, "I had!" The Phantom, with an evil smile, drew closer to the chair, and resting its chin upon its folded hands, its folded hands upon the back, and looking down into his face with searching eyes, that seemed instinct with fire, went on:—

"Such glimpses of the light of home as I had ever known, had streamed from her. How young she was, how fair, how loving! I took her to the first poor roof that I was master of, and made it rich. She came into the darkness of my life, and made it bright.—She is before me!"

"I saw her, in the fire, but now. I hear her in music, in the wind, in the dead stillness of the night," returned the haunted man.

"*Did* he love her?" said the Phantom, echoing his contemplative tone. "I think he did once. I am sure he did. Better had she loved him less—less secretly, less dearly, from the shallower depths of a more divided heart!"

"Let me forget it," said the Chemist, with an angry motion of his hand. "Let me blot it from my memory!"

The Spectre, without stirring, and with its unwinking cruel eyes still fixed upon his face, went on:—

"A dream, like hers, stole upon my own life."

"It did," said Redlaw.

"A love, as like hers," pursued the Phantom, "as my inferior nature might cherish, arose in my own heart. I was too poor to bind its object to my fortune then, by any thread of promise or entreaty. I loved her far too well, to seek to do it. But, more than ever I had striven in my life, I strove to climb! Only an inch gained, brought me something nearer to the height. I toiled up! In the late pauses of my labor at that time,—my sister (sweet companion!) still sharing with me the expiring embers and the cooling hearth,—when day was breaking, what pictures of the future did I see!"

"I saw them in the fire, but now," he murmured. "They come back to me in music, in the wind, in the dead stillness of the night, in the revolving years."

—"Pictures of my own domestic life, in after-time, with her who was the inspiration of my toil. Pictures of my sister, made the wife of my dear friend, on equal terms—for he had some inheritance, we none—pictures of our sobered age and mellowed happiness, and of the golden links, extending back so far, that should bind us, and our children, in a radiant garland," said the Phantom.

"Pictures," said the haunted man, "that were delusions. Why is it my doom to remember them too well!"

"Delusions," echoed the Phantom in its changeless voice, and glaring on him with its changeless eyes. "For my friend (in whose breast my confidence was locked as in my own), passing between me and the centre of the system of my hopes and struggles, won her to himself, and shattered my frail universe. My sister, doubly dear, doubly devoted, doubly cheerful in my home, lived on to see me famous, and my old ambition so rewarded when its spring was broken, and then"—

"Then died," he interposed. "Died, gentle as ever happy, and with no concern but for her brother. Peace!"

The Phantom watched him silently.

"Remembered!" said the haunted man, after a pause. "Yes. So well remembered, that even now, when years have passed, and nothing is more idle or more visionary to me than the boyish love so long outlived, I think of it with sympathy, as if it were a younger brother's or a son's. Sometimes I even wonder when her heart first inclined to him, and how it had been affected towards me.—Not lightly, once, I think.—But that is nothing. Early unhappiness, a wound from a hand I loved and trusted, and a loss that nothing can replace, outlive such fancies."

"Thus," said the Phantom, "I bear within me a Sorrow and a Wrong. Thus I prey upon myself. Thus, memory is my curse; and, if I could forget my sorrow and my wrong, I would!"

"Mocker!" said the Chemist, leaping up, and making, with a wrathful hand, at the throat of his other self. "Why have I always that taunt in my ears?"

"Forbear!" exclaimed the Spectre in an awful voice. "Lay a hand on me, and die!"

He stopped midway, as if its words had paralyzed him, and stood looking on it. It had glided from him; it had its arm raised high in warning; and a smile passed over its unearthly features, as it reared its dark figure in triumph.

"If I could forget my sorrow and wrong, I would," the Ghost repeated. "If I could forget my sorrow and my wrong, I would!"

"Evil spirit of myself," returned the haunted man, in a low, trembling tone, "my life is darkened by that incessant whisper."

"It is an echo," said the Phantom.

"If it be an echo of my thoughts—as now, indeed, I know it is," rejoined the haunted man, "why should I, therefore, be tormented? It is not a selfish thought. I suffer it to range beyond myself. All men and women have their sorrows,—most of them their wrongs; ingratitude, and sordid jealousy, and interest, besetting all degrees of life. Who would not forget their sorrows and their wrongs?"

"Who would not truly, and be the happier and better for it?" said the Phantom.

"These revolutions of years, which we commemorate," proceeded Redlaw, "what do *they* recall! Are there any minds in which they do not reawaken some sorrow, or some trouble? What is the remembrance of the old man who was here to-night? A tissue of sorrow and trouble."

"But common natures," said the Phantom, with its evil smile upon its glassy face, "unenlightened minds and ordinary spirits, do not feel or reason on these things like men of higher cultivation and profounder thought."

"Tempter," answered Redlaw, "whose hollow look and voice I dread more than words can express, and from whom some dim foreshadowing of greater fear is stealing over me while I speak, I hear again an echo of my own mind."

"Receive it as a proof that I am powerful," returned the Ghost. "Hear what I offer! Forget the sorrow, wrong, and trouble you have known!"

"Forget them!" he repeated.

"I have the power to cancel their remembrance—to leave but very faint, confused traces of them, that will die out soon," returned the Spectre. "Say! Is it done?"

"Stay!" cried the haunted man, arresting by a terrified gesture the uplifted hand. "I tremble with distrust and doubt of you; and the dim fear you cast upon me deepens into a nameless horror I can hardly bear.—I would not deprive myself of any kindly recollection, or any sympathy that is good for me, or others. What shall I lose, if I assent to this? What else will pass from my remembrance?"

"No knowledge; no result of study; nothing but the intertwisted chain of feelings and associations, each in its turn dependent on, and nourished by, the banished recollections. Those will go."

"Are they so many?" said the haunted man, reflecting in alarm.

"They have been wont to show themselves in the fire, in music, in the wind, in the dead stillness of the night, in the revolving years," returned the Phantom scornfully.

"In nothing else?"

The Phantom held its peace.

But, having stood before him, silent, for a little while, it moved towards the fire; then stopped.

"Decide!" it said, "before the opportunity is lost!"

"A moment! I call Heaven to witness," said the agitated man, "that I have never been a hater of my kind. —never morose, indifferent, or hard, to anything around me. If, living here alone, I have made too much of all that was and might have been, and too little of what is, the evil, I believe, has fallen on me, and not on others. But, if there were poison in my body, should I not, possessed of antidotes and knowledge how to use them, use them? If there be poison in my mind, and through this fearful shadow I can cast it out, shall I not cast it out?"

"Say," said the Spectre, "is it done?"

"A moment longer!" he answered hurriedly. "*I would forget it if I could!* Have *I* thought that, alone, or has it been the thought of thousands upon thousands, genera-

tion after generation? All human memory is fraught
with sorrow and trouble. My memory is as the memory
of other men, but other men have not this choice. Yes,
I close the bargain. Yes! I WILL forget my sorrow,
wrong, and trouble!"

"Say," said the Spectre, "is it done?"

"It is!"

"IT IS. And take this with you, man whom I here renounce! The gift that I have given, you shall give again,
go where you will. Without recovering yourself the
power that you have yielded up, you shall henceforth
destroy its like in all whom you approach. Your wisdom
has discovered that the memory of sorrow, wrong, and
trouble is the lot of all mankind, and that mankind
would be the happier, in its other memories, without it.
Go! Be its benefactor! Freed from such remembrance,
from this hour, carry involuntarily the blessing of such
freedom with you. Its diffusion is inseparable and
inalienable from you. Go! Be happy in the good you
have won, and in the good you do!"

The Phantom, which had held its bloodless hand
above him while it spoke, as if in some unholy invoca-
tion, or some ban; and which had gradually advanced
its eyes so close to his, that he could see how they did
not participate in the terrible smile upon its face, but
were a fixed, unalterable, steady horror; melted from
before him, and was gone.

As he stood rooted to the spot, possessed by fear and
wonder, and imagining he heard repeated in melancholy
echoes, dying away fainter and fainter, the words, "Destroy its like in all whom you approach!" a shrill cry
reached his ears. It came, not from the passages beyond
the door, but from another part of the old building, and
sounded like the cry of some one in the dark who had
lost the way.

He looked confusedly upon his hands and limbs, as if to be assured of his identity, and then shouted in reply, loudly and wildly; for there was a strangeness and terror upon him, as if he too were lost.

The cry responding, and being nearer, he caught up the lamp, and raised a heavy curtain in the wall, by which he was accustomed to pass into and out of the theatre where he lectured,—which adjoined his room. Associated with youth and animation, and a high amphitheatre of faces which his entrance charmed to interest in a moment, it was a ghostly place when all this life was faded out of it, and stared upon him like an emblem of Death.

"Hollo!" he cried. "Hollo! This way! Come to the light!" When, as he held the curtain with one hand, and with the other raised the lamp and tried to pierce the gloom that filled the place, something rushed past him into the room like a wild-cat, and crouched down in a corner.

"What is it?" he said hastily.

He might have asked, "What is it?" even had he seen it well, as presently he did when he stood looking at it gathered up in its corner.

A bundle of tatters, held together by a hand, in size and form almost an infant's, but, in its greedy, desperate little clutch, a bad old man's. A face rounded and smoothed by some half dozen years, but pinched and twisted by the experiences of a life. Bright eyes, but not youthful. Naked feet, beautiful in their childish delicacy,—ugly in the blood and dirt that cracked upon them. A baby savage, a young monster, a child who had never been a child, a creature who might live to take the outward form of man, but who, within, would live and perish a mere beast.

Used, already, to be worried and hunted like a beast,

the boy crouched down as he was looked at, and looked back again, and interposed his arm to ward off the expected blow.

"I'll bite," he said, "if you hit me!"

The time had been, and not many minutes since, when such a sight as this would have wrung the Chemist's heart. He looked upon it now, coldly; but, with a heavy effort to remember something—he did not know what—he asked the boy what he did there, and whence he came.

"Where's the woman?" he replied. "I want to find the woman."

"Who?"

"The woman. Her that brought me here, and set me by the large fire. She was so long gone, that I went to look for her, and lost myself. I don't want you. I want the woman."

He made a spring, so suddenly, to get away, that the dull sound of his naked feet upon the floor was near the curtain, when Redlaw caught him by his rags.

"Come! you let me go!" muttered the boy, struggling, and clinching his teeth. "I've done nothing to you. Let me go, will you, to the woman!"

"That is not the way. There is a nearer one," said Redlaw, detaining him, in the same blank effort to remember some association that ought of right, to bear upon this monstrous object. "What is your name?"

"Got none."

"Where do you live?"

"Live! What's that?"

The boy shook his hair from his eyes to look at him for a moment, and then, twisting round his legs and wrestling with him, broke again into his repetition of "You let me go, will you? I want to find the woman."

The Chemist led him to the door. "This way," he

said, looking at him still confusedly, but with repugnance and avoidance, growing out of his coldness. "I'll take you to her."

The sharp eyes in the child's head, wandering round the room, lighted on the table where the remnants of the dinner were.

"Give me some of that!" he said, covetously.

"Has she not fed you?"

"I shall be hungry again to-morrow, sha'n't I? A'n't I hungry every day?"

Finding himself released, he bounded at the table like some small animal of prey, and hugging to his breast bread and meat, and his own rags, altogether, said:—

"There! Now take me to the woman!"

As the Chemist, with a new-born dislike to touch him, sternly motioned him to follow, and was going out of the door, he trembled and stopped.

"The gift that I have given, you shall give again, go where you will!"

The Phantom's words were blowing in the wind, and the wind blew chill upon him.

"I'll not go there, to-night," he murmured faintly.

"I'll go nowhere to-night. Boy! straight down this long-arched passage, and past the great dark door into the yard,—you will see the fire shining on a window there."

"The woman's fire?" inquired the boy.

He nodded, and the naked feet had sprung away. He came back with his lamp, locked his door hastily, and sat down in his chair, covering his face like one who was frightened at himself.

For now he was, indeed, alone. Alone, alone.

CHAPTER II

The Gift Diffused

A small man sat in a small parlor, partitioned off from a small shop by a small screen, pasted all over with small scraps of newspapers. In company with the small man, was almost any amount of small children you may please to name—at least, it seemed so; they made, in that very limited sphere of action, such an imposing effect, in point of numbers.

Of these small fry, two had, by some strong machinery, been got into bed in a corner, where they might have reposed snugly enough in the sleep of innocence, but for a constitutional propensity to keep awake, and also to scuffle in and out of bed. The immediate occasion of these predatory dashes at the waking world, was the construction of an oyster-shell wall in a corner, by two other youths of tender age; on which fortification the two in bed made harassing descents (like those accursed Picts and Scots who beleaguer the early historical studies of most young Britons), and then withdrew to their own territory.

In addition to the stir attendant on these inroads, and the retorts of the invaded, who pursued hotly, and made lunges at the bedclothes, under which the marauders took refuge, another little boy, in another little bed, contributed his mite of confusion to the family stock, by casting his boots upon the waters; in other words, by launching these and several small objects, inoffensive in themselves, though of a hard substance considered as missiles, at the disturbers of his repose,—who were not slow to return these compliments.

Besides which, another little boy—the biggest there, but still little—was tottering to and fro, bent on one side, and considerably affected in his knees by the weight of a large baby, which he was supposed, by a fiction that obtains sometimes in sanguine families, to be hushing to sleep. But oh! the inexhaustible regions of contemplation and watchfulness into which this baby's eyes were then only beginning to compose themselves to stare, over his unconscious shoulder!

It was a very Moloch of a baby, on whose insatiate altar the whole existence of this particular young brother was offered up a daily sacrifice. Its personality may be said to have consisted in its never being quiet, in any one place, for five consecutive minutes, and never going to sleep when required. "Tetterby's baby" was as well known in the neighborhood as the postman or the potboy. It roved from door-step to door-step, in the arms of little Johnny Tetterby, and lagged heavily at the rear of troops of juveniles who followed the Tumblers or the Monkey, and came up, all on one side, a little too late for everything that was attractive, from Monday morning until Saturday night. Wherever childhood congregated to play, there was little Moloch making Johnny fag and toil. Wherever Johnny desired to stay, little Moloch became fractious, and would not remain. Whenever Johnny wanted to go out, Moloch was asleep, and must be watched. Whenever Johnny wanted to stay at home, Moloch was awake, and must be taken out. Yet Johnny was verily persuaded that it was a faultless baby, without its peer in the realm of England; and was quite content to catch meek glimpses of things in general from behind its skirts, or over its limp flapping bonnet, and to go staggering about with it like a very little porter with a very large parcel, which was not directed to anybody, and could never be delivered anywhere.

The small man who sat in the small parlor, making

fruitless attempts to read his newspaper peaceably in the midst of this disturbance, was the father of the family, and the chief of the firm described in the inscription over the little shop front, by the name and title of A. TETTERBY AND CO., NEWSMEN. Indeed, strictly speaking, he was the only personage answering to that designation; as Co. was a mere poetical abstraction, altogether baseless and impersonal.

Tetterby's was the corner shop in Jerusalem Buildings. There was a good show of literature, in the window, chiefly consisting of picture-newspapers out of date, and serial pirates, and footpads. Walking-sticks, likewise, and marbles, were included in the stock in trade. It had once extended into the light confectionery line; but it would seem that those elegancies of life were not in demand about Jerusalem Buildings, for nothing connected with that branch of commerce remained in the window, except a sort of small glass lantern containing a languishing mass of bull's-eyes, which had melted in the summer and congealed in the winter until all hope of ever getting them out, or of eating them without eating the lantern too, was gone forever. Tetterby's had tried its hand at several things. It had once made a feeble little dart at the toy business; for, in another lantern, there was a heap of minute wax dolls, all sticking together upside down, in the direst confusion, with their feet on one another's heads, and a precipitate of broken arms and legs at the bottom. It had made a move in the millinery direction, which a few dry, wiry bonnet-shapes remained in a corner of the window to attest. It had fancied that a living might lie hidden in the tobacco trade, and had stuck up a representation of a native of each of the three integral portions of the British empire, in the act of consuming that fragrant weed; with a poetic legend attached, importing that united in one cause they sat and joked, one chewed tobacco, one took snuff, one smoked: but nothing seemed to have come of it—except flies. Time had been when it had put a forlorn trust in imitative jewelry, for in one pane of glass there was a card of cheap seals, and another of pencil-cases, and a mysterious black amulet of inscrutable intention labelled ninepence. But, to that hour, Jerusalem Buildings had bought none of them. In short, Tetterby's had tried so hard to get a livelihood out of Jerusalem Buildings in one way or other, and appeared to have done so indifferently in all, that the best position in the firm was too evidently Co.'s; Co., as a bodiless creation, being untroubled with the vulgar inconveniences of hunger and thirst, being chargeable neither to the poor's-rates nor the assessed taxes, and having no young family to provide for.

Tetterby himself, however, in his little parlor, as already mentioned, having the presence of a young family impressed upon his mind in a manner too clamorous to be disregarded, or to comport with the quiet perusal of a newspaper, laid down his paper, wheeled in his distraction, a few times round the parlor, like an undecided carrier-pigeon, made an ineffectual rush at one or two flying little figures in bed-gowns that skimmed past him, and then, bearing suddenly down upon the only unoffending member of the family, boxed the ears of little Moloch's nurse.

"You bad boy!" said Mr. Tetterby. "Haven't you any feeling for your poor father after the fatigues and anxieties of a hard winter's day, since five o'clock in the morning, but must you wither his rest, and corrode his latest intelligence, with *your* vicious tricks? Isn't it enough, sir, that your brother 'Dolphus is toiling and moiling in the fog and cold, and you rolling in the lap of luxury with a—with a baby, and everythink you can wish for," said Mr. Tetterby, heaping this up as a great climax of blessings, "but must you make a wilderness of home, and maniacs of your parents? Must you, Johnny? Hey?" At each interrogation, Mr. Tetterby made a feint of boxing his ears again, but thought better of it, and held his hand.

"Oh, father!" whimpered Johnny, "when I wasn't doing anything, I'm sure, but taking such care of Sally, and getting her to sleep. Oh, father!"

"I wish my little woman would come home!" said Mr. Tetterby, relenting and repenting, "I only wish my little woman would come home! I a'n't fit to deal with 'em. They make my head go round, and get the better of me. Oh, Johnny! Isn't it enough that your dear mother has provided you with that sweet sister?" indicating Moloch; "isn't it enough that you were seven boys before, without a ray of gal, and that your dear mother went through what she *did* go through, on purpose that you might all of you have a little sister, but must you so behave yourself as to make my head swim?"

Softening more and more, as his own tender feelings and those of his injured son were worked on, Mr. Tetterby concluded by embracing him, and immediately breaking away to catch one of the real delinquents. A reasonably good start occurring, he succeeded, after a short but smart run, and some rather severe cross-country work under and over the bedsteads, and in and out among the intricacies of the chairs, in capturing this infant, whom he condignly punished, and bore to bed. This example had a powerful, and apparently, mesmeric influence on him of the boots, who instantly fell into a deep sleep, though he had been, but a moment before, broad awake, and in the highest possible feather. Nor was it lost upon the two young architects, who retired to bed, in an adjoining closet, with great privacy and speed. The comrade of the Intercepted One also shrinking into his nest with similar discretion, Mr. Tetterby, when he paused for breath, found himself unexpectedly in a scene of peace.

"My little woman herself," said Mr. Tetterby, wiping his flushed face, "could hardly have done it better! I only wish my little woman had had it to do, I do indeed!"

Mr. Tetterby sought upon his screen for a passage appropriate to be impressed upon his children's minds on the occasion, and read the following.

" 'It is an undoubted fact that all remarkable men have had remarkable mothers, and have respected them in after-life as their best friends.' Think of your own remarkable mother, my boys," said Mr. Tetterby, "and know her value while she is still among you!"

He sat down again in his chair by the fire, and composed himself, cross-legged, over his newspaper.

"Let anybody, I don't care who it is, get out of bed again," said Tetterby, as a general proclamation, delivered in a very soft-hearted manner, "and astonishment will be the portion of that respected contemporary!"— which expression Mr. Tetterby selected from his screen. "Johnny, my child, take care of your only sister, Sally; for she's the brightest gem that ever sparkled on your early brow."

Johnny sat down on a little stool, and devotedly crushed himself beneath the weight of Moloch.

"Ah, what a gift that baby is to you, Johnny!" said his father, "and how thankful you ought to be! 'It is not generally known,' Johnny," he was now referring to the screen again, " 'but it is a fact ascertained, by accurate calculations, that the following immense percentage of babies never attain to two years old; that is to say' "—

"Oh, don't, father, please!" cried Johnny. "I can't bear it, when I think of Sally."

Mr. Tetterby desisting, Johnny, with a profounder sense of his trust, wiped his eyes, and hushed his sister.

"Your brother 'Dolphus," said his father, poking the fire, "is late to-night, Johnny, and will come home like a lump of ice. What's got your precious mother?"

"Here's mother, and 'Dolphus too, father!" exclaimed Johnny. "I think."

"You're right!" returned his father, listening. "Yes, that's the footstep of my little woman."

The process of induction, by which Mr. Tetterby had come to the conclusion that his wife was a little woman, was his own secret. She would have made two editions of himself, very easily. Considered as an individual, she was rather remarkable for being robust and portly; but considered with reference to her husband, her dimensions became magnificent. Nor did they assume a less imposing proportion, when studied with reference to the size of her seven sons, who were but diminutive. In the case of Sally, however, Mrs. Tetterby had asserted herself, at last; as nobody knew better than the victim Johnny, who weighed and measured that exacting idol every hour in the day.

Mrs. Tetterby, who had been marketing, and carried a basket, threw back her bonnet and shawl, and sitting down, fatigued, commanded Johnny to bring his sweet charge to her straightway, for a kiss. Johnny having complied, and gone back to his stool, and again crushed himself, Master Adolphus Tetterby, who had by this time unwound his torso out of a prismatic comforter, apparently interminable, requested the same favor. Johnny having again complied, and again gone back to his stool, and again crushed himself, Mr. Tetterby, struck by a sudden thought, preferred the same claim on his own parental part. The satisfaction of this third desire completely exhausted the sacrifice, who had hardly breath enough left to get back to his stool, crush himself again, and pant at his relations.

"Whatever you do, Johnny," said Mrs. Tetterby, shaking her head, "take care of her, or never look your mother in the face again."

"Nor your brother," said Adolphus.

"Nor your father, Johnny," added Mr. Tetterby.

Johnny, much affected by this conditional renunciation of him, looked down at Moloch's eyes to see that they were all right, so far, and skillfully patted her back (which was uppermost), and rocked her with his foot.

"Are you wet, 'Dolphus, my boy?" said his father. "Come and take my chair, and dry yourself."

"No, father, thankee," said Adolphus, smoothing himself down with his hands. "I a'n't very wet, I don't think. Does my face shine much, father?"

"Well it *does* look waxy, my boy," returned Mr. Tetterby.

"It's the weather, father," said Adolphus, polishing his cheeks on the worn sleeve of his jacket. "What with rain, and sleet, and wind, and snow, and fog, my face gets quite brought out into a rash sometimes. And shines, it does—oh, don't it, though!"

Master Adolphus was also in the newspaper line of life, being employed, by a more thriving firm than his father and Co., to vend newspapers at a railway station, where his chubby little person, like a shabbily disguised Cupid, and his shrill little voice (he was not much more than ten years old), were as well known as the hoarse panting of the locomotives, running in and out. His juvenility might have been at some loss for a harmless outlet, in this early application to traffic, but for a fortunate discovery he made of a means of entertaining himself, and of dividing the long day into stages of interest, without neglecting business. This ingenious invention, remarkable, like many great discoveries, for its simplicity, consisted in varying the first vowel in the word "paper," and substituting in its stead, at different periods of the day, all the other vowels in grammatical succession. Thus, before daylight in the winter-time, he went to and fro, in his little oilskin cap and cape, and his big comforter, piercing the heavy air with his cry of "Morn-ing Pa-per!" which, about an hour before noon, changed to "Morn-ing Pep-per!" which, at about two, changed to "Morn-ing Pip-per!" which, in a couple of hours, changed to "Morn-ing Pop-per!" and so declined with the sun into "Eve-ning Pup-per!" to the great relief and comfort of this young gentleman's spirits.

Mrs. Tetterby, his lady-mother, who had been sitting with her bonnet and shawl thrown back, as aforesaid, thoughtfully turning her wedding-ring round and round upon her finger, now rose, and divesting herself of her out-of-door attire, began to lay the cloth for supper.

"Ah, dear me, dear me, dear me!" said Mrs. Tetterby. "That's the way the world goes!"

"Which is the way the world goes, my dear?" asked Mr. Tetterby, looking round.

"Oh, nothing," said Mrs. Tetterby.

Mr. Tetterby elevated his eyebrows, folded his newspaper afresh, and carried his eyes up it, and down it, and across it, but was wandering in his attention, and not reading it.

Mrs. Tetterby, at the same time, laid the cloth, but rather as if she were punishing the table than preparing the family supper; hitting it unnecessarily hard with the knives and forks, slapping it with the plates, dinting it with the salt-cellar, and coming heavily down upon it with the loaf.

"Ah, dear me, dear me, dear me!" said Mrs. Tetterby. "That's the way the world goes!"

"My duck," returned her husband, looking round again, "you said that before. Which is the way the world goes?"

"Oh, nothing," said Mrs. Tetterby.

"Sophia!" remonstrated her husband, "you said *that* before, too."

"Well, I'll say it again if you like," returned Mrs. Tetterby. "Oh nothing—there! And again if you like, oh nothing—there! And again if you like, oh nothing—now then!"

Mr. Tetterby brought his eye to bear upon the partner of his bosom, and said, in mild astonishment,—

"My little woman, what has put you out?"

"I'm sure *I* don't know," she retorted. "Don't ask me. Who said I was put out at all? *I* never did."

Mr. Tetterby gave up the perusal of his newspaper as a bad job, and, taking a slow walk across the room, with his hands behind him, and his shoulders raised—his gait according perfectly with the resignation of his manner—addressed himself to his two eldest offspring.

"Your supper will be ready in a minute, 'Dolphus," said Mr. Tetterby. "Your mother has been out in the wet, to the cook's shop, to buy it. It was very good of your mother so to do. *You* shall get some supper, too, very soon, Johnny. Your mother's pleased with you, my man, for being so attentive to your precious sister."

Mrs. Tetterby, without any remark, but with a decided subsidence of her animosity towards the table, finished her preparations, and took, from her ample basket, a substantial slab of hot pease-pudding wrapped in paper, and a basin covered with a saucer, which, on being un-

covered, sent forth an odor so agreeable, that the three
pair of eyes in the two beds opened wide and fixed
themselves upon the banquet. Mr. Tetterby, without regarding this tacit invitation to be seated, stood repeating
slowly, "Yes, yes, your supper will be ready in a minute, 'Dolphus,—your mother went out in the wet, to the
cook's shop, to buy it. It was very good of your mother
so to do"—until Mrs. Tetterby, who had been exhibiting
sundry tokens of contrition behind him, caught him
round the neck, and wept.

"Oh, 'Dolphus!" said Mrs. Tetterby, "how could I go
and behave so!"

This reconciliation affected Adolphus the younger
and Johnny to that degree, that they both, as with one
accord, raised a dismal cry, which had the effect of immediately shutting up the round eyes in the beds, and
utterly routing the two remaining little Tetterbys, just
then stealing in from the adjoining closet to see what
was going on in the eating way.

"I am sure, 'Dolphus," sobbed Mrs. Tetterby, "coming home, I had no more idea than a child unborn"—

Mr. Tetterby seemed to dislike this figure of speech,
and observed, "Say than the baby, my dear."

"Had no more idea than the baby," said Mrs. Tetterby.—"Johnny, don't look at me, but look at her, or
she'll fall out of your lap and be killed, and then you'll
die in agonies of a broken heart, and serve you right.—
No more idea I hadn't than that darling, of being cross
when I came home; but somehow, 'Dolphus"—Mrs.
Tetterby paused, and again turned her wedding-ring
round and round upon her finger.

"I see!" said Mr. Tetterby. "I understand! My little
woman was put out. Hard times, and hard weather, and
hard work, make it trying now and then. I see, bless
your soul! No wonder! 'Dolf, my man," continued Mr.

Tetterby, exploring the basin with a fork, "here's your mother been and bought, at the cook's shop, besides pease-pudding, a whole knuckle of a lovely roast leg of pork, with lots of crackling left upon it, and with seasoning gravy and mustard quite unlimited. Hand in your plate, my boy, and begin while it's simmering."

Master Adolphus, needing no second summons, received his portion with eyes rendered moist by appetite and withdrawing to his particular stool, fell upon his supper tooth and nail. Johnny was not forgotten, but received his rations on bread, lest he should, in a flush of gravy, trickle any on the baby. He was required, for similar reasons, to keep his pudding, when not on active service, in his pocket.

There might have been more pork on the knuckle-bone,—which knuckle-bone the carver at the cook's shop had assuredly not forgotten in carving for previous customers,—but there was no stint of seasoning, and that is an accessory dreamily suggesting pork, and pleasantly cheating the sense of taste. The pease-pudding, too, the gravy and mustard, like the Eastern rose in respect of the nightingale, if they were not absolutely pork, had lived near it; so, upon the whole, there was the flavor of a middle-sized pig. It was irresistible to the Tetterbys in bed, who, though professing to slumber peacefully, crawled out when unseen by their parents, and silently appealed to their brothers for any gastronomic token of fraternal affection. They, not hard of heart, presenting scraps in return, it resulted that a party of light skirmishers in night-gowns were careering about the parlor all through supper, which harassed Mr. Tetterby exceedingly, and once or twice imposed upon him the necessity of a charge, before which these guerilla troops retired in all directions and in great confusion.

Mrs. Tetterby did not enjoy her supper. There seemed to be something on Mrs. Tetterby's mind. At one time she laughed without reason, and at another time she cried without reason, and at last she laughed and cried together in a manner so very unreasonable that her husband was confounded.

"My little woman," said Mr. Tetterby, "if the world goes that way, it appears to go the wrong way, and to choke you."

"Give me a drop of water," said Mrs. Tetterby, struggling with herself, "and don't speak to me for the present, or take any notice of me. Don't do it!"

Mr. Tetterby having administered the water, turned suddenly on the unlucky Johnny (who was full of sympathy), and demanded why he was wallowing there, in gluttony and idleness, instead of coming forward with the baby, that the sight of her might revive his mother. Johnny immediately approached, borne-down by its weight; but Mrs. Tetterby holding out her hand to signify that she was not in a condition to bear that trying appeal to her feelings, he was interdicted from advancing another inch, on pain of perpetual hatred from all his dearest connections; and accordingly retired to his stool again, and crushed himself as before.

After a pause, Mrs. Tetterby said she was better now, and began to laugh.

"My little woman," said her husband, dubiously, "are you quite sure you're better? Or are you, Sophia, about to break out in a fresh direction?"

"No, 'Dolphus, no," replied his wife. "I'm quite myself." With that, settling her hair, and pressing the palms of her hands upon her eyes, she laughed again.

"What a wicked fool I was, to think so for a moment!" said Mrs. Tetterby. "Come nearer, 'Dolphus, and let me ease my mind, and tell you what I mean. Let me tell you all about it."

Mr. Tetterby bringing his chair closer, Mrs. Tetterby laughed again, gave him a hug, and wiped her eyes.

"You know, 'Dolphus, my dear," said Mrs. Tetterby, "that when I was single, I might have given myself away in several directions. At one time, four after me at once; two of them were sons of Mars."

"We're all sons of Ma's, my dear," said Mr. Tetterby, "jointly with Pa's."

"I don't mean that," replied his wife, "I mean soldiers—sergeants."

"Oh!" said Mr. Tetterby.

"Well, 'Dolphus, I'm sure I never think of such things now, to regret them; and I'm sure I've got as good a husband, and would do as much to prove that I was fond of him, as"—

"As any little woman in the world," said Mr. Tetterby. "Very good. *Very* good."

If Mr. Tetterby had been ten feet high, he could not have expressed a gentler consideration for Mrs. Tetterby's fairy-like stature; and if Mrs. Tetterby had been two feet high, she could not have felt it more appropriately her due.

"But you see, 'Dolphus," said Mrs. Tetterby, "this being Christmastime, when all people who can, make holiday, and when all people who have got money, like to spend some, I did, somehow, get a little out of sorts when I was in the streets just now. There were so many things to be sold—such delicious things to eat, such fine things to look at, such delightful things to have—and there was so much calculating and calculating necessary, before I durst lay out a six-pence for the commonest thing; and the basket was so large, and wanted so much in it; and my stock of money was so small, and would go such a little way;—you hate me, don't you, 'Dolphus?"

"Not quite," said Mr. Tetterby, "as yet."

"Well! I'll tell you the whole truth," pursued his wife, penitently, "and then perhaps you will. I felt all this, so much, when I was trudging about in the cold, and when I saw a lot of other calculating faces and large baskets trudging about, too, that I began to think whether I mightn't have done better, and been happier, if—I—hadn't"—the wedding-ring went round again, and Mrs. Tetterby shook her downcast head as she turned it.

"I see," said her husband quietly; "if you hadn't married at all, or if you had married somebody else?"

"Yes," sobbed Mrs. Tetterby. "That's really what I thought. Do you hate me now, 'Dolphus?"

"Why no," said Mr. Tetterby, "I don't find that I do as yet."

Mrs. Tetterby gave him a thankful kiss, and went on,—

"I begin to hope you won't, now, 'Dolphus, though I am afraid I haven't told you the worst. I can't think what came over me. I don't know whether I was ill, or mad, or what I was, but I couldn't call up anything that seemed to bind us to each other, or to reconcile me to my fortune. All the pleasures and enjoyments we had ever had—*they* seemed so poor and insignificant, I hated them. I could have trodden on them. And I could think of nothing else except our being poor, and the number of mouths there were at home."

"Well, well, my dear," said Mr. Tetterby, shaking her hand encouragingly, "that's truth, after all. We *are* poor, and there *are* a number of mouths at home here."

"Ah! but, 'Dolf, 'Dolf!" cried his wife, laying her hands upon his neck, "my good, kind, patient fellow, when I had been at home a very little while—how different! Oh, 'Dolf, dear, how different it was! I felt as if there was a rush of recollection on me, all at once, that softened my hard heart, and filled it up till it was bursting. All our struggles for a livelihood, all our cares and wants since we have been married, all the times of sickness, all the hours of watching, we have ever had, by one another, or by the children, seemed to speak to me, and say that they had made us one, and that I never might have been, or could have been, or would have been, any other than the wife and mother I am. Then, the cheap enjoyments that I could have trodden on so cruelly, got to be so precious to me—Oh so priceless, and dear!—that I couldn't bear to think how much I had wronged them; and I said, and say again a hundred times, how could I ever behave so, 'Dolphus, how could I ever have the heart to do it!"

The good woman, quite carried away by her honest tenderness and remorse, was weeping with all her heart, when she started up with a scream, and ran behind her husband. Her cry was so terrified, that the children started from their sleep and from their beds, and clung about her. Nor did her gaze belie her voice, as she pointed to a pale man in a black cloak who had come into the room.

"Look at that man! Look there! What does he want?"

"My dear," returned her husband, "I'll ask him if you'll let me go. What's the matter? How you shake!"

"I saw him in the street when I was out just now. He looked at me, and stood near me. I am afraid of him."

"Afraid of him! Why?"

"I don't know why—I—stop! husband!" for he was going towards the stranger.

She had one hand pressed upon her forehead, and one upon her breast; and there was a peculiar fluttering all over her, and a hurried unsteady motion of her eyes, as if she had lost something.

"Are you ill, my dear?"

"What is it that is going from me again?" she muttered, in a low voice. "What *is* this that is going away?"

Then she abruptly answered: "Ill? No, I am quite well," and stood looking vacantly at the floor.

Her husband, who had not been altogether free from the infection of her fear at first, and whom the present strangeness of her manner did not tend to reassure, addressed himself to the pale visitor in the black cloak, who stood still, and whose eyes were bent upon the ground.

"What may be your pleasure, sir," he asked, "with us?"

"I fear that my coming in unperceived," returned the visitor, "has alarmed you; but you were talking and did not hear me."

"My little woman says—perhaps you heard her say it," returned Mr. Tetterby, "that it's not the first time you have alarmed her to-night."

"I am sorry for it. I remember to have observed her, for a few moments only, in the street. I had no intention of frightening her."

As he raised his eyes in speaking, she raised hers. It was extraordinary to see what dread she had of him, and with what dread he observed it—and yet how narrowly and closely.

"My name," he said, "is Redlaw. I come from the old college hard by. A young gentleman who is a student there lodges in your house, does he not?"

"Mr. Denham?" said Tetterby.

"Yes."

It was a natural action, and so slight as to be hardly noticeable; but the little man, before speaking again, passed his hand across his forehead, and looked quickly round the room, as though he were sensible of some change in its atmosphere. The Chemist, instantly transferring to him the look of dread he had directed towards the wife, stepped back, and his face turned paler.

"The gentleman's room," said Tetterby, "is up-stairs, sir. There's a more convenient private entrance; but as you have come in here, it will save your going out into the cold, if you'll take this little staircase," showing one communicating directly with the parlor, "and go up to him that way, if you wish to see him."

"Yes, I wish to see him," said the Chemist. "Can you spare a light?"

The watchfulness of his haggard look, and the inexplicable distrust that darkened it, seemed to trouble Mr. Tetterby. He paused; and looking fixedly at him in return, stood for a minute or so, like a man stupefied, or fascinated.

At length he said, "I'll light you, sir, if you'll follow me."

"No," replied the Chemist, "I don't wish to be attended, or announced to him. He does not expect me. I would rather go alone. Please to give me the light, if you can spare it, and I'll find the way."

In the quickness of his expression of this desire, and in taking the candle from the newsman, he touched him on the breast. Withdrawing his hand hastily, almost as though he had wounded him by accident (for he did not know in what part of himself his new power resided, or how it was communicated, or how the manner of its reception varied in different persons), he turned and ascended the stair.

But when he reached the top, he stopped and looked down. The wife was standing in the same place, twisting her ring round and round upon her finger. The husband, with his head bent forward on his breast, was musing heavily and sullenly. The children, still clustering about the mother, gazed timidly after the visitor, and nestled together when they saw him looking down.

"Come!" said the father, roughly. "There's enough of this. Get to bed here!"

"The place is inconvenient and small enough," the mother added, "without you. Get to bed!"

The whole brood, scared and sad, crept away; little Johnny and the baby lagging last. The mother, glancing contemptuously round the sordid room, and tossing from her the fragments of their meal, stopped on the threshold of her task of clearing the table, and sat down, pondering idly and dejectedly. The father betook himself to the chimney-corner, and impatiently raking the small fire together, bent over it as if he would monopolize it all. They did not interchange a word.

The Chemist, paler than before, stole upward like a thief; looking back upon the change below, and dreading equally to go on or return.

"What have I done!" he said, confusedly. "What am I going to do!"

"To be the benefactor of mankind," he thought he heard a voice reply.

He looked round, but there was nothing there; and a passage now shutting out the little parlor from his view, he went on, directing his eyes before him at the way he went.

"It is only since last night," he muttered gloomily, "that I have remained shut up, and yet all things are strange to me. I am strange to myself. I am here, as in a dream. What interest have I in this place, or in any place that I can bring to my remembrance? My mind is going blind!"

There was a door before him, and he knocked at it. Being invited, by a voice within, to enter, he complied.

"Is that my kind nurse?" said the voice. "But I need not ask her. There is no one else to come here."

It spoke cheerfully, though in a languid tone, and attracted his attention to a young man, lying on a couch, drawn before the chimney-piece, with the back towards the door. A meagre scanty stove, pinched and hollowed like a sick man's cheeks, and bricked into the centre of a hearth that it could scarcely warm, contained the fire, to which his face was turned. Being so near the windy house-top, it wasted quickly, and with a busy sound, and the burning ashes dropped down fast.

"They chink when they shoot out here," said the student, smiling, "so, according to the gossips, they are not coffins, but purses. I shall be well and rich yet, some day, if it please God, and shall live perhaps to love a daughter Milly, in remembrance of the kindest nature and the gentlest heart in the world."

He put up his hand as if expecting her to take it, but, being weakened, he lay still, with his face resting on his other hand, and did not turn round.

The Chemist glanced about the room;—at the student's books and papers, piled upon a table in a corner, where they, and his extinguished reading-lamp, now prohibited and put away, told of the attentive hours that had gone before this illness, and perhaps caused it;—at such signs of his old health and freedom, as the out-of-door attire that hung idle on the wall;—at those remembrances of other and less solitary scenes, the little miniatures upon the chimney-piece, and the drawing of home;—at that token of his emulation, perhaps, in some sort, of his personal attachment too, the framed engraving of himself, the looker-on. The time had been, only yesterday, when not one of these objects, in its remotest association of interest with the living figure before him, would have been lost on Redlaw. Now, they were but objects; or, if any gleam of such connection shot upon him, it perplexed, and not enlightened him, as he stood looking round with a dull wonder.

The student recalling the thin hand which had remained so long untouched, raised himself on the couch, and turned his head.

"Mr. Redlaw!" he exclaimed, and started up.

Redlaw put out his arm.

"Don't come near to me. I will sit here. Remain you where you are!"

He sat down on a chair near the door, and having glanced at the young man standing leaning with his hand upon the couch, spoke with his eyes averted towards the ground.

"I heard, by an accident, by what accident is no matter, that one of my class was ill and solitary. I received no other description of him, than that he lived in this street. Beginning my inquiries at the first house in it, I have found him."

"I have been ill, sir," returned the student, not merely with a modest hesitation, but with a kind of awe of him, "but am greatly better. An attack of fever—of the brain, I believe—has weakened me, but I am much better. I cannot say I have been solitary in my illness, or I should forget the ministering hand that has been near me."

"You are speaking of the keeper's wife," said Redlaw.

"Yes." The student bent his head, as if he rendered her some silent homage.

The Chemist, in whom there was a cold, monotonous apathy, which rendered him more like a marble image on the tomb of the man who had started from his dinner yesterday at the first mention of this student's case, than the breathing man himself, glanced again at the student leaning with his hand upon the couch, and looked upon the ground, and in the air, as if for light for his blinded mind.

"I remembered your name," he said, "when it was mentioned to me down-stairs, just now; and I recollect your face. We have held but very little personal communication together?"

"Very little."

"You have retired and withdrawn from me, more than any of the rest, I think?"

The student signified assent.

"And why?" said the Chemist; not with the least expression of interest, but with a moody, wayward kind of curiosity. "Why? How comes it that you have sought to keep especially from me, the knowledge of your remaining here, at this season, when all the rest have dispersed, and of your being ill? I want to know why this is."

The young man, who had heard him with increasing agitation, raised his downcast eyes to his face, and clasping his hands together, cried with sudden earnestness, and with trembling lips:—

"Mr. Redlaw! You have discovered me. You know my secret!"

"Secret?" said the Chemist, harshly. "*I* know?"

"Yes! Your manner, so different from the interest and sympathy which endear you to so many hearts, your altered voice, the constraint there is in everything you say, and in your looks," replied the student, "warn me that you know me. That you would conceal it, even now, is but a proof to me (God knows I need none!) of your natural kindness, and of the bar there is between us."

A vacant and contemptuous laugh, was all his answer.

"But, Mr. Redlaw," said the student, "as a just man, and a good man, think how innocent I am, except in name and descent, of participation in any wrong inflicted on you, or in any sorrow you have borne."

"Sorrow!" said Redlaw, laughing. "Wrong! What are these to me?"

"For Heaven's sake," entreated the shrinking student, "do not let the mere interchange of a few words with me change you like this, sir! Let me pass again from your knowledge and notice. Let me occupy my old reserved and distant place among those whom you instruct. Know me only by the name I have assumed, and not by that of Longford"—

"Longford!" exclaimed the other.

He clasped his head with both his hands, and for a moment turned upon the young man his own intelligent and thoughtful face. But the light passed from it, like the sunbeam of an instant, and it clouded as before.

"The name my mother bears, sir," faltered the young man, "the name she took, when she might, perhaps, have taken one more honored. Mr. Redlaw," hesitating, "I believe I know that history. Where my information halts, my guesses at what is wanting may supply something not remote from the truth. I am the child of a marriage that has not proved itself a well assorted or a happy one. From infancy, I have heard you spoken of with honor and respect—with something that was almost reverence. I have heard of such devotion, of such fortitude and tenderness, of such rising up against the obstacles which press men down, that my fancy, since I learnt my little lesson from my mother, has shed a lustre on your name. At last, a poor student myself, from whom could I learn but you?"

Redlaw, unmoved, unchanged, and looking at him with a staring frown, answered by no word or sign.

"I cannot say," pursued the other, "I should try in vain to say, how much it has impressed me, and affected me, to find the gracious traces of the past, in that certain power of winning gratitude and confidence which is associated among us students (among the humblest of us, most) with Mr. Redlaw's generous name. Our ages and positions are so different, sir, and I am so accustomed to regard you from a distance, that I wonder at my own presumption when I touch, however lightly, on that theme. But to one who—I may say, who felt no common interest in my mother once—it may be something to hear, now that is all past, with what indescribable feelings of affection I have, in my obscurity, regarded him; with what pain and reluctance I have kept aloof from his encouragement, when a word of it would have made me rich; yet how I have felt it fit that I should hold my course, content to know him, and to be unknown. Mr. Redlaw," said the student, faintly, "what I would have said, I have said ill, for my strength is strange to me as yet; but for anything unworthy in this fraud of mine, forgive me, and for all the rest forget me!"

The staring frown remained on Redlaw's face, and yielded to no other expression until the student, with these words, advanced towards him, as if to touch his hand, when he drew back and cried to him:—

"Don't come nearer to me!"

The young man stopped, shocked by the eagerness of his recoil, and by the sternness of his repulsion; and he passed his hand, thoughtfully, across his forehead.

"The past is past," said the Chemist. "It dies like the brutes. Who talks to me of its traces in my life? He raves or lies! What have I to do with your distempered dreams? If you want money, here it is. I came to offer it; and that is all I came for. There can be nothing else that brings me here," he muttered, holding his head again, with both his hands. "There *can* be nothing else, and yet"—

He had tossed his purse upon the table. As he fell into this dim cogitation with himself, the student took it up, and held it out to him.

"Take it back, sir," he said proudly, though not angrily. "I wish you could take from me, with it, the remembrance of your words and offer."

"You do?" he retorted, with a wild light in his eyes. "You do?"

"I do!"

The Chemist went close to him, for the first time, and took the purse, and turned him by the arm, and looked him in the face.

"There is sorrow and trouble in sickness, is there not?" he demanded, with a laugh.

The wondering student answered, "Yes."

"In its unrest, in its anxiety, in its suspense, in all its train of physical and mental miseries?" said the Chemist, with a wild, unearthly exultation. "All best forgotten, are they not?"

The student did not answer, but again passed his hand, confusedly, across his forehead. Redlaw still held him by the sleeve, when Milly's voice was heard outside.

"I can see very well now," she said, "thank you, 'Dolf. Don't cry, dear. Father and mother will be comfortable again, to-morrow, and home will be comfortable too. A gentleman with him, is there!"

Redlaw released his hold, as he listened.

"I have feared, from the first moment," he murmured to himself, "to meet her. There is a steady quality of goodness in her, that I dread to influence. I may be the murderer of what is tenderest and best within her bosom."

She was knocking at the door.

"Shall I dismiss it as an idle foreboding, or still avoid her?" he muttered, looking uneasily around.

She was knocking at the door again.

"Of all the visitors who could come here," he said, in a hoarse alarmed voice, turning to his companion, "this is the one I should desire most to avoid. Hide me!"

The student opened a frail door in the wall, communicating, where the garret-roof began to slope towards the floor, with a small inner room. Redlaw passed in hastily, and shut it after him.

The student then resumed his place upon the couch, and called to her to enter.

"Dear Mr. Edmund," said Milly, looking round, "they told me there was a gentleman here."

"There is no one here but I."

"There has been some one?"

"Yes, yes, there has been some one."

She put her little basket on the table, and went up to the back of the couch, as if to take the extended hand—but it was not there. A little surprised, in her quiet way, she leaned over to look at his face, and gently touched him on the brow.

"Are you quite as well to-night? Your head is not so cool as in the afternoon."

"Tut!" said the student, petulantly, "very little ails me."

A little more surprise, but no reproach, was expressed in her face, as she withdrew to the other side of the table and took a small packet of needlework from her basket. But she laid it down again, on second thoughts, and going noiselessly about the room, set everything exactly in its place, and in the neatest order; even to the cushions on the couch, which she touched with so light a hand, that he hardly seemed to know it, as he lay looking at the fire. When all this was done, and she had swept the hearth, she sat down, in her modest little bonnet, to her work, and was quietly busy on it directly.

"It's the new muslin curtain for the window, Mr. Edmund," said Milly, stitching away as she talked. "It will look very clean and nice, though it costs very little, and will save your eyes, too, from the light. My William says the room should not be too light just now, when you are recovering so well, or the glare might make you giddy."

He said nothing; but there was something so fretful and impatient in his change of position, that her quick fingers stopped, and she looked at him anxiously.

"The pillows are not comfortable," she said, laying down her work and rising. "I will soon put them right."

"They are very well," he answered. "Leave them alone, pray. You make so much of everything."

He raised his head to say this, and looked at her so thanklessly, that, after he had thrown himself down again, she stood timidly pausing. However, she resumed her seat, and her needle, without having directed even a murmuring look towards him, and was soon as busy as before.

"I have been thinking, Mr. Edmund, that *you* have been often thinking of late, when I have been sitting by, how true the saying is, that adversity is a good teacher. Health will be more precious to you, after this illness, than it has ever been. And years hence, when this time of year comes round, and you remember the days when you lay here sick, alone, that the knowledge of your illness might not afflict those who are dearest to you, your home will be doubly dear and doubly blest. Now, isn't that a good, true thing?"

She was too intent upon her work, and too earnest in what she said, and too composed and quiet altogether, to be on the watch for any look he might direct towards her in reply; so the shaft of his ungrateful glance fell harmless, and did not wound her.

"Ah!" said Milly, with her pretty head inclining thoughtfully on one side, as she looked down, following her busy fingers with her eyes. "Even on me—and I am very different from you, Mr. Edmund, for I have no learning, and don't know how to think properly—this view of such things has made a great impression, since you have been lying ill. When I have seen you so touched by the kindness and attention of the poor people downstairs, I have felt that you thought even that experience some repayment for the loss of health, and I have read in your face, as plain as if it was a book, that but for some trouble and sorrow we should never know half the good there is about us."

His getting up from the couch interrupted her, or she was going on to say more.

"We needn't magnify the merit, Mrs. William," he rejoined slightingly. "The people down-stairs will be paid in good time I dare say, for any little extra service they may have rendered me; and perhaps they anticipate no less. I am much obliged to you, too."

Her fingers stopped, and she looked at him.

"I can't be made to feel the more obliged by your exaggerating the case," he said. "I am sensible that you have been interested in me, and I say I am much obliged to you. What more would you have?"

Her work fell on her lap, as she still looked at him walking to and fro with an intolerant air, and stopping now and then.

"I say again, I am much obliged to you. Why weaken my sense of what is your due in obligation by preferring enormous claims upon me? Trouble, sorrow, affliction, adversity! One might suppose I had been dying a score of deaths here!"

"Do you believe, Mr. Edmund," she asked, rising and going nearer to him, "that I spoke of the poor people of the house, with any reference to myself? To me?" laying her hand upon her bosom with a simple and innocent smile of astonishment.

"Oh! I think nothing about it, my good creature," he returned. "I have had an indisposition, which your solicitude—observe! I say solicitude—makes a great deal more of, than it merits; and it's over, and we can't perpetuate it."

He coldly took a book, and sat down at the table.

She watched him for a little while, until her smile was quite gone, and then, returning to where her basket was, said gently:—

"Mr. Edmund, would you rather be alone?"

"There is no reason why I should detain you here," he replied.

"Except"—said Milly, hesitating, and showing her work.

"Oh! the curtain," he answered, with a supercilious laugh. "That's not worth staying for."

She made up the little packet again, and put it in her basket. Then, standing before him with such an air of patient entreaty that he could not choose but look at her, she said:—

"If you should want me, I will come back willingly. When you did want me, I was quite happy to come; there was no merit in it. I think you must be afraid, that, now you are getting well, I may be troublesome to you; but I should not have been, indeed. I should have come no longer than your weakness and confinement lasted. You owe me nothing; but it is right that you should deal as justly by me as if I was a lady—even the very lady that you love; and if you suspect me of meanly making much of the little I have tried to do to comfort your sick room, you do yourself more wrong than ever you can do me. That is why I am sorry. That is why I am very sorry."

If she had been as passionate as she was quiet, as indignant as she was calm, as angry in her look as she was gentle, as loud of tone as she was low and clear, she might have left no sense of her departure in the room, compared with that which fell upon the lonely student when she went away.

He was gazing drearily upon the place where she had been, when Redlaw came out of his concealment, and came to the door.

"When sickness lays its hand on you again," he said, looking fiercely back at him,—"may it be soon!—Die here! Rot here!"

"What have you done?" returned the other, catching at his cloak. "What change have you wrought in me? What curse have you brought upon me? Give me back myself!"

"Give me back *my*self!" exclaimed Redlaw like a madman. "I am infected! I am infectious. I am charged with poison for my own mind, and the minds of all mankind. Where I felt interest, compassion, sympathy, I am turning into stone. Selfishness and ingratitude spring up in my blighting footsteps. I am only so much less base than the wretches whom I make so, that in the moment of their transformation I can hate them."

As he spoke—the young man still holding to his cloak—he cast him off, and struck him: then, wildly hurried out into the night air where the wind was blowing, the snow falling, the cloud-drift sweeping on, the moon dimly shining; and where, blowing in the wind, falling with the snow, drifting with the clouds, shining in the moonlight, and heavily looming in the darkness, were the Phantom's words, "The gift that I have given, you shall give again, go where you will!"

Whither he went, he neither knew nor cared, so that he avoided company. The change he felt within him made the busy streets a desert, and himself a desert, and the multitude around him, in their manifold endurances and ways of life, a mighty waste of sand, which the winds tossed into unintelligible heaps and made a ruinous confusion of. Those traces in his breast which the Phantom had told him would "die out soon," were not, as yet, so far upon their way to death, but that he understood enough of what he was, and what he made of others, to desire to be alone.

This put it in his mind—he suddenly bethought himself, as he was going along, of the boy who had rushed into his room. And then he recollected, that of those with whom he had communicated since the Phantom's disappearance, that boy alone had shown no sign of being changed.

Monstrous and odious as the wild thing was to him, he determined to seek it out, and prove if this were really so; and also to seek it with another intention, which came into his thoughts at the same time.

So, resolving with some difficulty where he was, he directed his steps back to the old college, and to that part of it where the general porch was, and where, alone, the pavement was worn by the tread of the students' feet.

The keeper's house stood just within the iron gates, forming a part of the chief quadrangle. There was a little cloister outside, and from that sheltered place he knew he could look in at the window of their ordinary room, and see who was within. The iron gates were shut, but his hand was familiar with the fastening, and drawing it back by thrusting in his wrist between the bars, he passed through softly, shut it again and crept up to the window, crumbling the thin crust of snow with his feet.

The fire, to which he had directed the boy last night, shining brightly through the glass, made an illuminated place upon the ground. Instinctively avoiding this, and going round it, he looked in at the window. At first, he thought that there was no one there, and that the blaze was reddening only the old beams in the ceiling and the dark walls; but peering in more narrowly, he saw the object of his search coiled asleep before it on the floor. He passed quickly to the door, opened it, and went in.

The creature lay in such a fiery heat, that, as the Chemist stooped to rouse him, it scorched his head. So soon as he was touched, the boy, not half awake, clutched his rags together with the instinct of flight upon him, half rolled and half ran into a distant corner of the room, where, heaped upon the ground, he struck his foot out to defend himself.

"Get up!" said the Chemist. "You have not forgotten me?"

"You let me alone!" returned the boy. "This is the woman's house—not yours."

The Chemist's steady eye controlled him somewhat, or inspired him with enough submission to be raised upon his feet, and looked at.

"Who washed them, and put those bandages where they were bruised and cracked?" asked the Chemist, pointing to their altered state.

"The woman did."

"And is it she who has made you cleaner in the face, too?"

"Yes, the woman."

Redlaw asked these questions to attract his eyes towards himself, and with the same intent now held him by the chin, and threw his wild hair back, though he loathed to touch him. The boy watched his eyes keenly, as if he thought it needful to his own defense, not knowing what he might do next; and Redlaw could see well, that no change came over him.

"Where are they?" he inquired.

"The woman's out."

"I know she is. Where is the old man with the white hair, and his son?"

"The woman's husband, d'ye mean?" inquired the boy.

"Ay. Where are those two?"

"Out. Something's the matter, somewhere. They were fetched out in a hurry, and told me to stop here."

"Come with me," said the Chemist, "and I'll give you money."

"Come where? and how much will you give?"

"I'll give you more shillings than you ever saw, and bring you back soon. Do you know your way to where you came from?"

"You let me go," returned the boy, suddenly twisting out of his grasp. "I'm not a-going to take you there. Let me be, or I'll heave some fire at you!"

He was down before it, and ready, with his savage little hand, to pluck the burning coals out.

What the Chemist had felt, in observing the effect of his charmed influence stealing over those with whom he came in contact, was not nearly equal to the cold vague terror with which he saw this baby-monster put it at defiance. It chilled his blood to look on the immovable impenetrable thing, in the likeness of a child, with its sharp malignant face turned up to his, and its almost infant hand, ready at the bars.

"Listen, boy!" he said. "You shall take me where you please, so that you take me where the people are very miserable or very wicked. I want to do them good, and not to harm them. You shall have money, as I have told you, and I will bring you back. Get up! Come quickly!" He made a hasty step towards the door, afraid of her returning.

"Will you let me walk by myself, and never hold me, nor yet touch me?" said the boy, slowly withdrawing the hand with which he threatened, and beginning to get up.

"I will!"

"And let me go before, behind, or anyways I like?"

"I will!"

"Give me some money first, then, and I'll go."

The Chemist laid a few shillings, one by one, in his extended hand. To count them was beyond the boy's knowledge, but he said "one," every time, and avariciously looked at each as it was given, and at the donor. He had nowhere to put them, out of his hand, but in his mouth; and he put them there.

Redlaw then wrote with his pencil on a leaf of his pocket-book, that the boy was with him; and laying it on the table, signed to him to follow. Keeping his rags together, as usual, the boy complied, and went out with his bare head and his naked feet into the winter night.

Preferring not to depart by the iron gate by which he had entered, where they were in danger of meeting her whom he so anxiously avoided, the Chemist led the way through some of those passages among which the boy had lost himself, and by that portion of the building where he lived, to a small door of which he had the key. When they got into the street, he stopped to ask his guide—who instantly retreated from him—if he knew where they were.

The savage thing looked here and there, and at length, nodding his head, pointed in the direction he designed to take. Redlaw going on at once, he followed, somewhat less suspiciously; shifting his money from his mouth into his hand, and back again into his mouth, and stealthily rubbing it bright upon his shreds of dress, as he went along.

Three times, in their progress, they were side by side. Three times they stopped, being side by side. Three times the Chemist glanced down at his face, and shuddered as it forced upon him one reflection.

The first occasion was when they were crossing an old church-yard, and Redlaw stopped among the graves, utterly at a loss how to connect them with any tender, softening, or consolatory thought.

The second was, when the breaking forth of the moon induced him to look up at the Heavens, where he saw her in her glory, surrounded by a host of stars he still knew by the names and histories which human science has appended to them; but where he saw nothing else he had been wont to see, felt nothing he had been wont to feel, in looking up there, on a bright night.

The third was when he stopped to listen to a plaintive strain of music, but could only hear a tune, made manifest to him by the dry mechanism of the instruments and his own ears, with no address to any mystery within him, without a whisper in it of the past, or of the future, powerless upon him as the sound of last year's running water, or the rushing of last year's wind.

At each of these three times, he saw with horror that in spite of the vast intellectual distance between them, and their being unlike each other in all physical respects, the expression on the boy's face was the expression on his own.

They journeyed on for some time—now through such crowded places, that he often looked over his shoulder, thinking he had lost his guide, but generally finding him within his shadow on his other side; now by ways so quiet, that he could have counted his short, quick, naked footsteps coming on behind—until they arrived at a ruinous collection of houses, and the boy touched him and stopped.

"In there!" he said, pointing out one house where there were scattered lights in the windows, and a dim lantern in the door-way, with "Lodgings for Travellers" painted on it.

Redlaw looked about him; from the houses, to the waste piece of ground on which the houses stood, or rather did not altogether tumble down, unfenced, undrained, unlighted, and bordered by a sluggish ditch; from that, to the sloping line of arches, part of some neighboring viaduct or bridge with which it was surrounded, and which lessened gradually, towards them, until the last but one was a mere kennel for a dog, the last a plundered little heap of bricks; from that, to the child, close to him, cowering and trembling with the cold, and limping on one little foot, while he coiled the other round his leg to warm it, yet staring at all these things with that frightful likeness of expression so apparent in his face, that Redlaw started from him.

"In there!" said the boy, pointing out the house again. "I'll wait."

"Will they let me in?" asked Redlaw.

"Say you're a doctor," he answered with a nod. "There's plenty ill here."

Looking back on his way to the house-door, Redlaw saw him trail himself upon the dust and crawl within the shelter of the smallest arch, as if he were a rat. He had no pity for the thing, but he was afraid of it; and when it looked out of its den at him, he hurried to the house as a retreat.

"Sorrow, wrong, and trouble," said the Chemist, with a painful effort at some more distinct remembrance, "at least haunt this place, darkly. He can do no harm, who brings forgetfulness of such things here!"

With these words, he pushed the yielding door, and went in.

There was a woman sitting on the stairs, either asleep or forlorn, whose head was bent down on her hands and knees. As it was not easy to pass without treading on her, and as she was perfectly regardless of his near approach, he stopped, and touched her on the shoulder. Looking up, she showed him quite a young face, but one whose bloom and promise were all swept away, as if the haggard winter should unnaturally kill the spring.

With little or no show of concern on his account, she moved nearer to the wall to leave him a wider passage.

"What are you?" said Redlaw, pausing, with his hand upon the broken stair-rail.

"What do you think I am?" she answered, showing him her face again.

He looked upon the ruined temple of God, so lately made, so soon disfigured; and something, which was not compassion—for the springs in which a true compassion for such miseries has its rise, were dried up in his breast—but which was nearer to it, for the moment, than any feeling that had lately struggled into the darkening, but not yet wholly darkened, night of his mind— mingled a touch of softness with his next words.

"I am come here to give relief, if I can," he said. "Are you thinking of any wrong?"

She frowned at him, and then laughed; and then her

laugh prolonged itself into a shivering sigh, as she dropped her head again, and hid her fingers in her hair.

"Are you thinking of a wrong?" he asked, once more.

"I am thinking of my life," she said, with a momentary look at him.

He had a perception that she was one of many, and that he saw the type of thousands when he saw her, drooping at his feet.

"What are your parents?" he demanded.

"I had a good home once. My father was a gardener, far away, in the country."

"Is he dead?"

"He's dead to me. All such things are dead to me. You a gentleman, and not know that!" She raised her eyes again, and laughed at him.

"Girl!" said Redlaw sternly, "before this death, of all such things, was brought about, was there no wrong done to you? In spite of all that you can do, does no remembrance of wrong cleave to you? Are there not times upon times when it is misery to you?"

So little of what was womanly was left in her appearance, that now, when she burst into tears, he stood amazed. But he was more amazed, and much disquieted, to note that in her awakened recollection of this wrong, the first trace of her old humanity and frozen tenderness appeared to show itself.

He drew a little off, and in doing so, observed that her arms were black, her face cut, and her bosom bruised.

"What brutal hand has hurt you so?" he asked.

"My own. I did it myself!" she answered quickly.

"It is impossible."

"I'll swear I did! He didn't touch me. I did it to myself in a passion, and threw myself down here. He wasn't near me. He never laid a hand upon me!"

In the white determination of her face, confronting him with this untruth, he saw enough of the last perversion and distortion of good surviving in that miserable breast, to be stricken with remorse that he had ever come near her.

"Sorrow, wrong, and trouble!" he muttered, turning his fearful gaze away. "All that connects her with the state from which she has fallen, has those roots! In the name of God, let me go by!"

Afraid to look at her again, afraid to touch her, afraid to think of having sundered the last thread by which she held upon the mercy of Heaven, he gathered his cloak about him, and glided swiftly up the stairs.

Opposite to him, on the landing, was a door, which stood partly open, and which, as he ascended, a man with a candle in his hand, came forward from within to shut. But this man, on seeing him, drew back, with much emotion in his manner, and, as if by a sudden impulse, mentioned his name aloud.

In the surprise of such a recognition there, he stopped, endeavoring to recollect the wan and startled face. He had no time to consider it, for, to his yet greater amazement, old Philip came out of the room, and took him by the hand.

"Mr. Redlaw," said the old man, "this is like you, this is like you, sir! You have heard of it, and have come after us to render any help you can. Ah, too late, too late!"

Redlaw, with a bewildered look, submitted to be led into the room. A man lay there, on a truckle-bed, and William Swidger stood at the bedside.

"Too late!" murmured the old man, looking wistfully into the Chemist's face; and the tears stole down his cheeks.

"That's what I say, father," interposed his son in a

low voice. "That's where it is, exactly. To keep as quiet as ever we can while he's a-dozing, is the only thing to do. You're right, father!"

Redlaw paused at the bedside, and looked down on the figure that was stretched upon the mattress. It was that of a man, who should have been in the vigor of his life, but on whom it was not likely that the sun would ever shine again. The vices of his forty or fifty years' career had so branded him, that, in comparison with their effects upon his face, the heavy hand of time upon the old man's face who watched him had been merciful and beautifying.

"Who is this?" asked the Chemist, looking round.

"My son George, Mr. Redlaw," said the old man, wringing his hands. "My eldest son, George, who was more his mother's pride than all the rest!"

Redlaw's eyes wandered from the old man's gray head, as he laid it down upon the bed, to the person who had recognized him, and who had kept aloof, in the remotest corner of the room. He seemed to be about his own age; and although he knew no such hopeless decay and broken man as he appeared to be, there was something in the turn of his figure, as he stood with his back towards him, and now went out at the door, that made him pass his hand uneasily across his brow.

"William," he said in a gloomy whisper, "who is that man?"

"Why you see, sir," returned Mr. William, "that's what I say myself. Why should a man ever go and gamble, and the like of that, and let himself down inch by inch till he can't let himself down any lower!"

"Has *he* done so?" asked Redlaw, glancing after him with the same uneasy action as before.

"Just exactly that, sir," returned William Swidger, "as I'm told. He knows a little about medicine, sir, it seems;

and having been wayfaring towards London with my unhappy brother that you see here," Mr. William passed his coat-sleeve across his eyes, "and being lodging upstairs for the night—what I say, you see, is that strange companions come together here sometimes—he looked in to attend upon him, and came for us at his request. What a mournful spectacle, sir! But that's where it is. It's enough to kill my father!"

Redlaw looked up, at these words, and recalling where he was and with whom, and the spell he carried with him—which his surprise had obscured—retired a little, hurriedly, debating with himself whether to shun the house that moment, or remain.

Yielding to a certain sullen doggedness, which it seemed to be part of his condition to struggle with, he argued for remaining.

"Was it only yesterday," he said, "when I observed the memory of this old man to be a tissue of sorrow and trouble, and shall I be afraid, to-night, to shake it? Are such remembrances as I can drive away, so precious to this dying man that I need fear for *him*? No, I'll stay here."

But he stayed, in fear and trembling none the less for these words; and, shrouded in his black cloak with his face turned from them, stood away from the bedside, listening to what they said, as if he felt himself a demon in the place.

"Father!" murmured the sick man, rallying a little from his stupor.

"My boy! My son George!" said old Philip.

"You spoke, just now, of my being mother's favorite, long ago. It's a dreadful thing to think now, of long ago!"

"No, no, no," returned the old man. "Think of it. Don't say it's dreadful. It's not dreadful to me, my son."

"It cuts you to the heart, father." For the old man's tears were falling on him.

"Yes, yes," said Philip, "so it does; but it does me good. It's a heavy sorrow to think of that time, but it does me good, George. Oh, think of it too, think of it too, and your heart will be softened more and more! Where's my son William? William, my boy, your mother loved him dearly to the last, and with her latest breath said, 'Tell him I forgave him, blessed him, and prayed for him.' Those were her words to me. I have never forgotten them, and I'm eighty-seven!"

"Father!" said the man upon the bed, "I am dying, I know. I am so far gone, that I can hardly speak, even of what my mind most runs on. Is there any hope for me beyond this bed?"

"There is hope," returned the old man, "for all who are softened and penitent. There is hope for all such. Oh!" he exclaimed, clasping his hands and looking up, "I was thankful, only yesterday, that I could remember this unhappy son when he was an innocent child. But what a comfort is it, now, to think that even God himself has that remembrance of him!"

Redlaw spread his hands upon his face, and shrunk like a murderer.

"Ah!" feebly moaned the man upon the bed. "The waste since then, the waste of life, since then!"

"But he was a child once," said the old man. "He played with children. Before he lay down on his bed at night, and fell into his guiltless rest, he said his prayers at his poor mother's knee. I have seen him do it, many a time; and seen her lay his head upon her breast, and kiss him. Sorrowful as it was to her, and to me, to think of this, when he went so wrong, and when our hopes and plans for him were all broken, this gave him still a hold upon us, that nothing else could have given. Oh, Father, so much better than the fathers upon earth! Oh, Father, so much more afflicted by the errors of thy children! Take this wanderer back! Not as he is, but as he was then, let him cry to thee, as he has so often seemed to cry to us!"

As the old man lifted up his trembling hands, the son, for whom he made the supplication, laid his sinking head against him for support and comfort, as if he were indeed the child of whom he spoke.

When did man ever tremble, as Redlaw trembled, in the silence that ensued! He knew it must come upon them, knew that it was coming fast.

"My time is very short, my breath is shorter," said the sick man, supporting himself on one arm, and with the other groping in the air, "and I remember there is something on my mind concerning the man who was here just now. Father and William—wait!—is there really anything in black, out there?"

"Yes, yes, it is real," said his aged father.

"Is it a man?"

"What I say myself, George," interposed his brother, bending kindly over him. "It's Mr. Redlaw."

"I thought I had dreamed of him. Ask him to come here."

The Chemist, whiter than the dying man, appeared before him. Obedient to the motion of his hand, he sat upon the bed.

"It has been so ripped up to-night, sir," said the sick man, laying his hand upon his heart, with a look in which the mute, imploring agony of his condition was concentrated, "by the sight of my poor old father, and the thought of all the trouble I have been the cause of, and all the wrong and sorrow lying at my door, that"—

Was it the extremity to which he had come, or was it the drawing of another change, that made him stop?

—"that what I *can* do right, with my mind running on so much, so fast, I'll try to do. There was another man here. Did you see him?"

Redlaw could not reply by any word; for when he saw that fatal sign he knew so well now, of the wandering hand upon the forehead, his voice died at his lips. But he made some indication of assent.

"He is penniless, hungry, and destitute. He is completely beaten down, and has no resource at all. Look after him! Lose no time! I know he has it in his mind to kill himself."

It was working. It was on his face. His face was changing, hardening, deepening in all its shades, and losing all its sorrow.

"Don't you remember! Don't you know him?" he pursued.

He shut his face out for a moment, with the hand that again wandered over his forehead, and then it lowered on Redlaw, reckless, ruffianly, and callous.

"Why, d—n you!" he said, scowling round, "what have you been doing to me here! I have lived bold, and I mean to die bold. To the Devil with you!"

And so lay down upon his bed, and put his arms up, over his head and ears, as resolute from that time to keep out all access, and to die in his indifference.

If Redlaw had been struck by lightning, it could not have struck him from the bedside with a more tremendous shock. But the old man, who had left the bed while his son was speaking to him, now returning, avoided it quickly likewise, and with abhorrence.

"Where's my boy William?" said the old man hurriedly. "William, come away from here. We'll go home."

"Home, father!" returned William. "Are you going to leave your own son?"

"Where's my own son?" replied the old man.

"Where? why, there!"

"That's no son of mine," said Philip, trembling with resentment. "No such wretch as that, has any claim on me. My children are pleasant to look at, and they wait upon me, and get my meat and drink ready, and are useful to me, I've a right to it! I'm eighty-seven!"

"You're old enough to be no older," muttered William, looking at him grudgingly, with his hands in his pockets. "I don't know what good you are, myself. We could have a deal more pleasure without you."

"*My* son, Mr. Redlaw!" said the old man. "*My* son, too! The boy talking to me of *my* son! Why, what has he ever done to give me any pleasure, I should like to know?"

"I don't know what you have ever done to give *me* any pleasure," said William, sulkily.

"Let me think," said the old man. "For how many Christmas times running, have I sat in my warm place, and never had to come out in the cold night air; and have made good cheer, without being disturbed by any such uncomfortable, wretched sight as him there? Is it twenty, William?"

"Nigher forty, it seems," he muttered. "Why, when I look at my father, sir, and come to think of it," addressing Redlaw, with an impatience and irritation that were quite new, "I'm whipped if I can see anything in him, but a calendar of ever so many years of eating, and drinking, and making himself comfortable over and over again."

"I—I'm eighty-seven," said the old man, rambling on, childishly, and weakly, "and I don't know as I ever was much put out by anything. I'm not a-going to begin now, because of what he calls my son. He's not my son. I've had a power of pleasant times. I recollect once—no

I don't—no, it's broken off. It was something about a game of cricket and a friend of mine, but it's somehow broken off. I wonder who he was—I suppose I liked him? And I wonder what became of him—I suppose he died? But I don't know. And I don't care, neither; I don't care a bit."

In his drowsy chuckling, and the shaking of his head, he put his hands into his waistcoat pockets. In one of them he found a bit of holly (left there, probably last night), which he now took out, and looked at.

"Berries, eh?" said the old man. "Ah! It's a pity they're not good to eat. I recollect when I was a little chap about as high as that, and out a-walking with—let me see—who was I out a-walking with?—no, I don't remember how that was. I don't remember as I ever walked with any one particular, or cared for any one, or any one for me. Berries, eh? There's good cheer when there's berries. Well, I ought to have my share of it, and to be waited on, and kept warm and comfortable; for I'm eighty-seven, and a poor old man. I'm eigh-ty-seven. Eigh-ty-seven!"

The drivelling, pitiable manner in which, as he repeated this, he nibbled at the leaves, and spat the morsels out; the cold, uninterested eye with which his youngest son (so changed) regarded him; the determined apathy with which his eldest son lay hardened in his sin;—impressed themselves no more on Redlaw's observation; for he broke his way from the spot to which his feet seemed to have been fixed, and ran out of the house.

His guide came crawling forth from his place of refuge, and was ready for him before he reached the arches.

"Back to the woman's?" he inquired.

"Back, quickly!" answered Redlaw. "Stop nowhere on the way!"

For a short distance the boy went on before; but their return was more like a flight than a walk, and it was as much as his bare feet could do, to keep pace with the Chemist's rapid strides. Shrinking from all who passed, shrouded in his cloak, and keeping it drawn closely about him, as though there were mortal contagion in any fluttering touch of his garments, he made no pause until they reached the door by which they had come out. He unlocked it with his key, went in, accompanied by the boy, and hastened through the dark passages to his own chamber.

The boy watched him as he made the door fast, and withdrew behind the table when he looked round.

"Come!" he said. "Don't you touch me! You've not brought me here to take my money away."

Redlaw threw some more upon the ground. He flung his body on it immediately, as if to hide it from him, lest the sight of it should tempt him to reclaim it; and not until he saw him seated by his lamp, with his face hidden in his hands, began furtively to pick it up. When he had done so, he crept near the fire, and sitting down in a great chair before it, took from his breast some broken scraps of food, and fell to munching, and to staring at the blaze, and now and then to glancing at his shillings, which he kept clinched up in a bunch, in one hand.

"And this," said Redlaw, gazing on him with increasing repugnance and fear, "is the only one companion I have left on earth!"

How long it was before he was aroused from his contemplation of this creature whom he dreaded so—whether half an hour, or half the night—he knew not. But the stillness of the room was broken by the boy (whom he had seen listening) starting up, and running towards the door.

"Here's the woman coming!" he exclaimed.

The Chemist stopped him on his way, at the moment when she knocked.

"Let me go to her, will you?" said the boy.

"Not now," returned the Chemist. "Stay here. Nobody must pass in or out of the room, now. Who's that?"

"It's I, sir," cried Milly. "Pray, sir, let me in."

"No! not for the world!" he said.

"Mr. Redlaw, Mr. Redlaw, pray, sir, let me in."

"What is the matter?" he said, holding the boy.

"The miserable man you saw, is worse, and nothing I can say will wake him from his terrible infatuation. William's father has turned childish in a moment. William himself is changed. The shock has been too sudden for him; I cannot understand him; he is not like himself. Oh, Mr. Redlaw, pray advise me, help me!"

"No! No! No!" he answered.

"Mr. Redlaw! Dear, sir! George has been muttering in his doze, about the man you saw there, who, he fears, will kill himself."

"Better he should do it, than come near me!"

"He says, in his wandering, that you know him; that he was your friend once, long ago; that he is the ruined father of a student here—my mind misgives me, of the young gentleman who has been ill. What is to be done? How is he to be followed? How is he to be saved? Mr. Redlaw, pray, oh, pray advise me! Help me!"

All this time he held the boy, who was half-mad to pass him, and let her in.

"Phantoms! Punishers of impious thoughts!" cried Redlaw, gazing round in anguish, "Look upon me! From the darkness of my mind, let the glimmering of contrition that I know is there, shine up, and show my misery! In the material world, as I have long taught, nothing can be spared; no step or atom in the wondrous structure could be lost, without a blank being made in the great universe. I know, now, that it is the same with good and evil, happiness and sorrow, in the memories of men. Pity me! Relieve me!"

There was no response, but her "Help me, help me, let me in!" and the boy's struggling to get to her.

"Shadow of myself! Spirit of my darker hours!" cried Redlaw, in distraction, "Come back, and haunt me day and night, but take this gift away! Or, if it must still rest with me, deprive me of the dreadful power of giving it to others. Undo what I have done. Leave me benighted, but restore the day to those whom I have cursed. As I have spared this woman from the first, and as I never will go forth again, but will die here, with no hand to tend me, save this creature's who is proof against me,— hear me!"

The only reply still was, the boy struggling to get to her, while he held him back; and the cry increasing in its energy, "Help! let me in. He was your friend once, how shall he be followed, how shall he be saved? They are all changed, there is no one else to help me, pray, pray, let me in!"

CHAPTER III

THE GIFT REVERSED

Night was still heavy in the sky. On open plains, from hill-tops, and from the decks of solitary ships at sea, a distant low-lying line, that promised by and by to change to light, was visible in the dim horizon; but its promise was remote and doubtful, and the moon was striving with the night-clouds busily.

The shadows upon Redlaw's mind succeeded thick and fast to one another, and obscured its light as the night-clouds hovered between the moon and earth, and kept the latter veiled in darkness. Fitful and uncertain as the shadows which the night-clouds cast, were their concealments from him, and imperfect revelations to him; and, like the night-clouds still, if the clear light broke forth for a moment, it was only that they might sweep over it, and make the darkness deeper than before.

Without, there was a profound and solemn hush upon the ancient pile of building, and its buttresses and angles made dark shapes of mystery upon the ground, which now seemed to retire into the smooth white snow and now seemed to come out of it, as the moon's path was more or less beset. Within, the Chemist's room was indistinct and murky, by the light of the expiring lamp; a ghostly silence had succeeded to the knocking and the voice outside; nothing was audible but, now and then, a low sound among the whitened ashes of the fire, as of its yielding up its last breath. Before it on the ground the boy lay fast asleep. In his chair, the Chemist sat, as he had sat there since the calling at his door had ceased—like a man turned to stone.

At such a time, the Christmas music he had heard before began to play. He listened to it at first, as he had listened in the church-yard; but presently—it playing still, and being borne towards him on the night-air, in a low, sweet, melancholy strain—he rose, and stood stretching his hands about him, as if there were some friend approaching within his reach, on whom his desolate touch might rest, yet do no harm. As he did this, his face became less fixed and wondering; a gentle trembling came upon him; and at last his eyes filled with tears and he put his hands before them, and bowed down his head.

His memory of sorrow, wrong, and trouble had not come back to him; he knew that it was not restored; he had no passing belief or hope that it was. But some dumb stir within him made him capable, again, of being moved by what was hidden, afar off, in the music. If it were only that it told him sorrowfully the value of what he had lost, he thanked Heaven for it, with a fervent gratitude.

As the last chord died upon his ear, he raised his head to listen to its lingering vibration. Beyond the boy, so that his sleeping figure lay at its feet, the Phantom stood, immovable and silent, with its eyes upon him.

Ghastly it was, as it had ever been, but not so cruel and relentless in its aspect—or he thought or hoped so, as he looked upon it, trembling. It was not alone, but in its shadowy hand it held another hand.

And whose was that? Was the form that stood beside it indeed Milly's, or but her shade and picture? The quiet head was bent a little, as her manner was, and her eyes were looking down, as if in pity, on the sleeping child. A radiant light fell on her face, but did not touch the Phantom; for, though close beside her, it was dark and colorless as ever.

"Spectre!" said the Chemist, newly troubled as he looked, "I have not been stubborn or presumptuous in respect of her. Oh, do not bring her here. Spare me that!"

"This is but a shadow," said the Phantom; "when the morning shines, seek out the reality whose image I present before you."

"Is it my inexorable doom to do so?" cried the Chemist.

"It is," replied the Phantom.

"To destroy her peace, her goodness; to make her what I am myself, and what I have made of others!"

"I have said 'seek her out,' " returned the Phantom. "I have said no more."

"Oh, tell me," exclaimed Redlaw, catching at the hope which he fancied might lie hidden in the words. "Can I undo what I have done?"

"No," returned the Phantom.

"I do not ask for restoration to myself," said Redlaw. "What I abandoned, I abandoned of my own will, and have justly lost. But for those to whom I have transferred the fatal gift; who never sought it; who unknowingly received a curse of which they had no warning, and which they had no power to shun; can I do nothing?"

"Nothing," said the Phantom.

"If I cannot, can any one?"

The Phantom, standing like a statue, kept its gaze upon him for a while; then turned its head suddenly and looked upon the shadow at its side.

"Ah! Can she?" cried Redlaw, still looking upon the shade.

The Phantom released the hand it had retained till now, and softly raised its own with a gesture of dismissal. Upon that, her shadow, still preserving the same attitude, began to move or melt away.

"Stay," cried Redlaw, with an earnestness to which he could not give enough expression. "For a moment! As an act of mercy! I know that some change fell upon me, when those sounds were in the air just now. Tell me, have I lost the power of harming her? May I go near her without dread? Oh, let her give me any sign of hope!"

The Phantom looked upon the shade as he did—not at him—and gave no answer.

"At least, say this—has she, henceforth, the consciousness of any power to set right what I have done?"

"She has not," the Phantom answered.

"Has she the power bestowed on her without the consciousness?"

The Phantom answered: "Seek her out." And her shadow slowly vanished.

They were face to face again, and looking on each other, as intently and awfully as at the time of the bestowal of the gift, across the boy who still lay on the ground between them, at the Phantom's feet.

"Terrible instructor," said the Chemist, sinking on his knee before it, in an attitude of supplication, "by whom I was renounced, but by whom I am revisited (in which, and in whose milder aspect, I would fain believe I have a gleam of hope), I will obey without inquiry, praying that the cry I have sent up in the anguish of my soul has been, or will be heard, in behalf of those whom I have injured beyond human reparation. But there is one thing"—

"You speak to me of what is lying here," the Phantom interposed, and pointed with its finger to the boy.

"I do," returned the Chemist. "You know what I would ask. Why has this child alone been proof against my influence, and why, why, have I detected in its thoughts a terrible companionship with mine?"

"This," said the Phantom, pointing to the boy, "is the last, completest illustration of a human creature, utterly bereft of such remembrances as you have yielded up. No softening memory of sorrow, wrong, or trouble enters here, because this wretched mortal from his birth has been abandoned to a worse condition than the beasts, and has, within his knowledge, no one contrast, no humanizing touch, to make a grain of such a memory spring up in his hardened breast. All within this desolate creature is barren wilderness. All within the man bereft of what you have resigned, is the same barren wilderness. Woe to such a man! Woe, tenfold, to the nation that shall count its monsters such as this, lying here by hundreds and by thousands!"

Redlaw shrunk, appalled, from what he heard.

"There is not," said the Phantom, "one of these—not one—but sows a harvest that mankind MUST reap. From every seed of evil in this boy, a field of ruin is grown that shall be gathered in, and garnered up, and sown again in many places in the world, until regions are overspread with wickedness enough to raise the waters of another Deluge. Open and unpunished murder in a city's streets would be less guilty in its daily toleration, than one such spectacle as this."

It seemed to look down upon the boy in his sleep. Redlaw, too, looked down upon him with a new emotion.

"There is not a father," said the Phantom, "by whose side in his daily or his nightly walk, these creatures pass; there is not a mother among all the ranks of loving mothers in this land; there is no one risen from the state of childhood, but shall be responsible in his or her degree for this enormity. There is not a country throughout the earth on which it would not bring a curse. There is no religion upon earth that it would not deny; there is no people upon earth it would not put to shame."

The Chemist clasped his hands, and looked, with trembling fear and pity, from the sleeping boy to the Phantom, standing above him with its finger pointing down.

"Behold, I say," pursued the Spectre, "the perfect type of what it was your choice to be. Your influence is powerless here, because from this child's bosom you can banish nothing. His thoughts have been in 'terrible companionship' with yours, because you have gone down to his unnatural level. He is the growth of man's indifference; you are the growth of man's presumption. The beneficent design of Heaven is, in each case, overthrown, and from the two poles of the immaterial world you come together."

The Chemist stooped upon the ground beside the boy, and with the same kind of compassion for him that he now felt for himself, covered him as he slept, and no longer shrunk from him with abhorrence or indifference.

Soon, now, the distant line on the horizon brightened, the darkness faded, the sun rose red and glorious, and the chimney stacks and gables of the ancient building gleamed in the clear air, which turned the smoke and vapor of the city into a cloud of gold. The very sun-dial in his shady corner, where the wind was used to spin with such un-windy constancy, shook off the finer particles of snow that had accumulated on his dull old face in the night, and looked out at the little white wreaths eddying round and round him. Doubtless some blind groping of the morning made its way down into the forgotten crypt so cold and earthy, where the Norman arches were half buried in the ground, and stirred the dull sap in the lazy vegetation hanging to the walls, and quickened the slow principle of life within the little world of wonderful and delicate creation which existed there, with some faint knowledge that the sun was up.

The Tetterbys were up, and doing. Mr. Tetterby took down the shutters of the shop, and, strip by strip, revealed the treasures of the window to the eyes, so proof against their seductions, of Jerusalem Buildings. Adolphus had been out so long already, that he was half-way on to Morning Pepper. Five small Tetterbys, whose ten round eyes were much inflamed by soap and friction, were in the tortures of a cool wash in the back kitchen; Mrs. Tetterby presiding. Johnny, who was pushed and hustled through his toilet with great rapidity when Moloch chanced to be in an exacting frame of mind (which was always the case), staggered up and down with his charge before the shop-door, under greater difficulties than usual; the weight of Moloch being much increased by a complication of defenses against the cold, composed of knitted worsted-work, and forming a complete suit of chain-armor, with a head-piece and blue gaiters.

It was a peculiarity of this baby to be always cutting teeth. Whether they never came, or whether they came and went away again, is not in evidence; but it had certainly cut enough, on the showing of Mrs. Tetterby, to make a handsome dental provision for the sign of the Ball and Mouth. All sorts of objects were impressed for the rubbing of its gums, notwithstanding that it always carried, dangling at its waist (which was immediately under its chin), a bone ring, large enough to have represented the rosary of a young man. Knife-handles, umbrella-tops, the heads of walking-sticks selected from the stock, the fingers of the family in general, but especially of Johnny, nutmeg-graters, crusts, the handles of doors, and the cool knobs on the tops of pokers, were among the commonest instruments indiscriminately applied for this baby's relief. The amount of electricity that must have been rubbed out of it in a week, is not to be calculated. Still Mrs. Tetterby always said "it was coming through, and then the child would be herself;" and still it never did come through, and the child continued to be somebody else.

The tempers of the little Tetterbys had sadly changed with a few hours. Mr. and Mrs. Tetterby themselves were not more altered than their offspring. Usually they were an unselfish, good-natured, yielding little race, sharing short-commons when it happened (which was pretty often) contentedly and even generously, and taking a great deal of enjoyment out of a very little meat. But they were fighting now, not only for the soap and water, but even for the breakfast which was yet in perspective. The hand of every little Tetterby was against the other little Tetterbys; and even Johnny's hand—the patient, much-enduring, and devoted Johnny—rose against the baby! Yes. Mrs. Tetterby, going to the door by a mere accident, saw him viciously pick out a weak plate in the suit of armor, where a slap would tell, and slap that blessed child.

Mrs. Tetterby had him into the parlor, by the collar, in that same flash of time, and repaid him the assault with usury thereto.

"You brute, you murdering little boy," said Mrs. Tetterby. "Had you the heart to do it?"

"Why don't her teeth come through, then," retorted Johnny, in a loud rebellious voice, "instead of bothering me? How would you like it yourself?"

"Like it, sir!" said Mrs. Tetterby, relieving him of his dishonored load.

"Yes, like it," said Johnny. "How would you? Not at all. If you was me, you'd go for a soldier. I will, too. There a'n't no babies in the army."

Mr. Tetterby, who had arrived upon the scene of action, rubbed his chin thoughtfully, instead of correcting the rebel, and seemed rather struck by this view of a military life.

"I wish I was in the army myself, if the child's in the right," said Mrs. Tetterby, looking at her husband, "for I have no peace of my life here. I'm a slave—a Virginia slave;" some indistinct association with their weak descent on the tobacco trade perhaps suggested this aggravated expression to Mrs. Tetterby. "I never have a holiday, or any pleasure at all, from year's end to year's end! Why, Lord bless and save the child," said Mrs. Tetterby, shaking the baby with an irritability hardly suited to so pious an aspiration, "what's the matter with her now?"

Not being able to discover, and not rendering the subject much clearer by shaking it, Mrs. Tetterby put the baby away in a cradle, and, folding her arms, sat rocking it angrily with her foot.

"How you stand there, 'Dolphus," said Mrs. Tetterby to her husband. "Why don't you do something?"

"Because I don't care about doing anything," Mr. Tetterby replied.

"I'm sure I don't," said Mrs. Tetterby.

"I'll take my oath I don't," said Mr. Tetterby.

A diversion arose here among Johnny and his five younger brothers, who, in preparing the family breakfast table, had fallen to skirmishing for the temporary possession of the loaf, and were buffeting one another with great heartiness; the smallest boy of all, with precocious discretion, hovering outside the knot of combatants, and harassing their legs. Into the midst of this fray, Mr. and Mrs. Tetterby both precipitated themselves with great ardor, as if such ground were the only ground on which they could now agree; and having, with no visible remains of their late soft-heartedness, laid about them without any lenity, and done much execution, resumed their former relative positions.

"You had better read your paper than do nothing at all," said Mrs. Tetterby.

"What's there to read in a paper?" returned Mr. Tetterby, with excessive discontent.

"What?" said Mrs. Tetterby. "Police."

"It's nothing to me," said Tetterby. "What do I care what people do, or are done to."

"Suicides," suggested Mrs. Tetterby.

"No business of mine," replied her husband.

"Births, deaths, and marriages, are those nothing to you?" said Mrs. Tetterby.

"If the births were all over for good, and all to-day; and the deaths were all to begin to come off to-morrow; I don't see why it should interest me, till I thought it was a-coming to my turn," grumbled Tetterby. "As to marriages, I've done it myself. I know quite enough about *them*."

To judge from the dissatisfied expression of her face and manner, Mrs. Tetterby appeared to entertain the same opinions as her husband; but she opposed him, nevertheless, for the gratification of quarrelling with him.

"Oh, you're a consistent man," said Mrs. Tetterby, "a'n't' you? You, with the screen of your own making there, made of nothing else but bits of newspapers, which you sit and read to the children by the half hour together!"

"Say used to, if you please," returned her husband. "You won't find me doing so any more. I'm wiser now."

"Bah! wiser, indeed!" said Mrs. Tetterby. "Are you better?"

The question sounded some discordant note in Mr. Tetterby's breast. He ruminated dejectedly, and passed his hand across and across his forehead.

"Better!" murmured Mr. Tetterby. "I don't know as any of us are better, or happier either. Better, is it?"

He turned to the screen, and traced about it with his finger, until he found a certain paragraph of which he was in quest.

"This used to be one of the family favorites, I recollect," said Tetterby, in a forlorn and stupid way, "and used to draw tears from the children, and make 'em good, if there was any little bickering or discontent among 'em, next to the story of the robin redbreasts in the wood. 'Melancholy case of destitution. Yesterday a small man, with a baby in his arms, and surrounded by half a dozen ragged little ones, of various ages between ten and two, the whole of whom were evidently in a famishing condition, appeared before the worthy magistrate, and made the following recital:'—Ha! I don't understand it, I'm sure," said Tetterby; "I don't see what it has got to do with us."

"How old and shabby he looks," said Mrs. Tetterby, watching him. "I never saw such a change in a man. Ah! dear me, dear me, dear me, it was a sacrifice!"

"What was a sacrifice?" her husband sourly inquired.

Mrs. Tetterby shook her head; and without replying in words, raised a complete sea-storm about the baby, by her violent agitation of the cradle.

"If you mean your marriage was a sacrifice, my good woman"—said her husband.

"I *do* mean it," said his wife.

"Why, then I mean to say," pursued Mr. Tetterby, as sulkily and surlily as she, "that there are two sides to that affair: and that *I* was the sacrifice; and that I wish the sacrifice hadn't been accepted."

"I wish it hadn't, Tetterby, with all my heart and soul, I do assure you," said his wife. "You can't wish it more than I do, Tetterby."

"I don't know what I saw in her," muttered the newsman, "I'm sure;—certainly, if I saw anything, it's not there now. I was thinking so last night, after supper, by the fire. She's fat, she's aging, she won't bear comparison with most other women."

"He's common-looking, he has no air with him, he's small, he's beginning to stoop, and he's getting bald," muttered Mrs. Tetterby.

"I must have been half out of my mind when I did it," muttered Mr. Tetterby.

"My senses must have forsook me. That's the only way in which I can explain it to myself," said Mrs. Tetterby, with elaboration.

In this mood they sat down to breakfast. The little Tetterbys were not habituated to regard that meal in the light of a sedentary occupation, but discussed it as a dance or trot; rather resembling a savage ceremony, in the occasional shrill whoops, and brandishings of bread and butter, with which it was accompanied, as well as in the intricate filings off into the street and back again, and the hoppings up and down the door-steps, which were incidental to the performance. In the present instance, the contentions between these Tetterby children for the milk-and-water jug, common to all, which stood upon the table, presented so lamentable an instance of angry passions risen very high indeed, that it was an outrage on the memory of Dr. Watts. It was not until Mr. Tetterby had driven the whole herd out at the front door, that a moment's peace was secured; and even that was broken by the discovery that Johnny had surreptitiously come back, and was at that instant choking in the jug like a ventriloquist, in his indecent and rapacious haste.

"These children will be the death of me at last!" said Mrs. Tetterby, after banishing the culprit. "And the sooner the better, I think."

"Poor people," said Mr. Tetterby, "ought not to have children at all. They give *us* no pleasure."

He was at that moment taking up the cup which Mrs. Tetterby had rudely pushed towards him, and Mrs.

Tetterby was lifting her own cup to her lips, when they both stopped, as if they were transfixed.

"Here! Mother! Father!" cried Johnny, running into the room. "Here's Mrs. William coming down the street!"

And if ever, since the world began, a young boy took a baby from a cradle with the care of an old nurse, and hushed and soothed it tenderly, and trotted away with it cheerfully, Johnny was that boy, and Moloch was that baby, as they went out together.

Mr. Tetterby put down his cup; Mrs. Tetterby put down her cup. Mr. Tetterby rubbed his forehead; Mrs. Tetterby rubbed hers. Mr. Tetterby's face began to smooth and brighten; Mrs. Tetterby's began to smooth and brighten.

"Why, Lord forgive me," said Mr. Tetterby to himself, "what evil tempers have I been giving way to? What has been the matter here!"

"How could I ever treat him ill again, after all I said and felt last night!" sobbed Mrs. Tetterby, with her apron to her eyes.

"Am I a brute," said Mr. Tetterby, "or is there any good in me at all? Sophia! My little woman!"

" 'Dolphus dear," returned his wife.

"I—I've been in a state of mind," said Mr. Tetterby, "that I can't abear to think of, Sophy."

"Oh! It's nothing to what I've been in, Dolf," cried his wife in a great burst of grief.

"My Sophia," said Mr. Tetterby, "don't take on. I never shall forgive myself. I must have nearly broke your heart I know."

"No, Dolf, no. It was me! Me!" cried Mrs. Tetterby.

"My little woman," said her husband, "don't. You make me reproach myself dreadful, when you show such a noble spirit. Sophia, my dear, you don't know what

I thought. I showed it bad enough, no doubt, but what I thought, my little woman!"—

"Oh, dear Dolf, don't! Don't!" cried his wife.

"Sophia," said Mr. Tetterby, "I must reveal it. I couldn't rest in my conscience unless I mentioned it. My little woman"—

"Mrs. William's very nearly here!" screamed Johnny at the door.

"My little woman, I wondered how," gasped Mr. Tetterby, supporting himself by his chair, "I wondered how I had ever admired you—I forgot the precious children you have brought about me, and thought you didn't look as slim as I could wish. I—I never gave a recollection," said Mr. Tetterby, with severe self-accusation, "to the cares you've had as my wife, and along of me and mine, when you might have had hardly any with another man, who got on better and was luckier than me (anybody might have found such a man easily, I am sure); and I quarrelled with you for having aged a little in the rough years you've lightened for me. Can you believe it, my little woman? I hardly can myself."

Mrs. Tetterby, in a whirlwind of laughing and crying, caught his face within her hands, and held it there.

"Oh, Dolf!" she cried. "I am so happy that you thought so; I am so grateful that you thought so! For I thought that you were common-looking, Dolf; and so you are, my dear, and may you be the commonest of all sights in my eyes, till you close them with your own good hands. I thought that you were small; and so you are, and I'll make much of you because you are, and more of you because I love my husband. I thought that you began to stoop; and so you do, and you shall lean on me, and I'll do all I can to keep you up. I thought there was no air about you; but there is and it's the air of home, and that's the purest and the best there is, and GOD bless home once more, and all belonging to it, Dolf!"

"Hurrah! Here's Mrs. William!" cried Johnny.

So she was, and all the children with her; and as she came in, they kissed her, and kissed one another, and kissed the baby, and kissed their father and mother, and then ran back and flocked and danced about her, trooping on with her in triumph.

Mr. and Mrs. Tetterby were not a bit behindhand in the warmth of their reception. They were as much attracted to her as the children were; they ran towards her, kissed her hands, pressed round her, could not receive her ardently or enthusiastically enough. She came among them like the spirit of all goodness, affection, gentle consideration, love, and domesticity.

"What! are *you* all so glad to see me, too, this bright Christmas morning?" said Milly, clapping her hands in a pleasant wonder. "Oh dear, how delightful this is!"

More shouting from the children, more kissing, more trooping round her, more happiness, more love, more joy, more honor, on all sides, than she could bear.

"Oh dear!" said Milly, "what delicious tears you make me shed. How can I ever have deserved this! What have I done to be so loved!"

"Who can help it!" cried Mr. Tetterby.

"Who can help it!" cried Mrs. Tetterby.

"Who can help it!" echoed the children, in a joyful chorus. And they danced and trooped about her again, and clung to her, and laid their rosy faces against her dress, and kissed and fondled it, and could not fondle it, or her, enough.

"I never was so moved," said Milly, drying her eyes, "as I have been this morning. I must tell you, as soon as I can speak.—Mr. Redlaw came to me at sunrise, and with a tenderness in his manner, more as if I had been his darling daughter than myself, implored me to go with him to where William's brother George is lying ill. We went together, and all the way along he was so kind, and so subdued, and seemed to put such trust and hope in me, that I could not help crying with pleasure. When we got to the house, we met a woman at the door (somebody had bruised and hurt her, I am afraid) who caught me by the hand, and blessed me as I passed."

"She was right," said Mr. Tetterby. Mrs. Tetterby said she was right. All the children cried out she was right.

"Ah, but there's more than that," said Milly. "When we got up-stairs, into the room, the sick man who had lain for hours in a state from which no effort could rouse him, rose up in his bed, and, bursting into tears, stretched out his arms to me, and said that he had led a misspent life, but that he was truly repentant now, in his sorrow for the past, which was all as plain to him as a great prospect from which a dense black cloud had cleared away, and that he entreated me to ask his poor old father for his pardon and his blessing, and to say a prayer beside his bed. And when I did so, Mr. Redlaw joined in it so fervently, and then so thanked and thanked me, and thanked Heaven, that my heart quite overflowed, and I could have done nothing but sob and cry, if the sick man had not begged me to sit down by him,—which made me quiet of course. As I sat there, he held my hand in his until he sunk in a doze; and even then, when I withdrew my hand to leave him to come here (which Mr. Redlaw was very earnest indeed in wishing me to do), his hand felt for mine, so that some one else was obliged to take my place and make believe to give him my hand back. Oh dear, oh dear," said Milly, sobbing. "How thankful and how happy I should feel, and do feel, for all this!"

While she was speaking, Redlaw had come in, and, after pausing for a moment to observe the group of which she was the centre, had silently ascended the stairs. Upon those stairs he now appeared again; remaining there, while the young student passed him, and came running down.

"Kind nurse, gentlest, best of creatures," he said, falling on his knee to her, and catching at her hand, "forgive my cruel ingratitude!"

"Oh dear, oh dear!" cried Milly innocently, "here's another of them! Oh dear, here's somebody else who likes me. What shall I ever do!"

The guileless, simple way in which she said it, and in which she put her hands before her eyes and wept for very happiness, was as touching as it was delightful.

"I was not myself," he said. "I don't know what it was—it was some consequence of my disorder perhaps—I was mad. But I am so, no longer. Almost as I speak, I am restored. I heard the children crying out your name, and the shade passed from me at the very sound of it. Oh don't weep! Dear Milly, if you could read my heart, and only know with what affection and what grateful homage it is glowing, you would not let me see you weep. It is such deep reproach."

"No, no," said Milly, "it's not that. It's not, indeed. It's joy. It's wonder that you should think it necessary to ask me to forgive so little, and yet it's pleasure that you do."

"And will you come again? and will you finish the little curtain?"

"No," said Milly, drying her eyes, and shaking her head. "You won't care for *my* needle-work now."

"Is it forgiving me to say that?"

She beckoned him aside, and whispered in his ear.

"There is news from your home, Mr. Edmund."

"News? How?"

"Either your not writing when you were very ill, or the change in your handwriting when you began to be better, created some suspicion of the truth; however, that is—but you're sure you'll not be the worse for any news, if it's not bad news?"

"Sure."

"Then there's some one come!" said Milly.

"My mother?" asked the student, glancing round involuntarily towards Redlaw, who had come down from the stairs.

"Hush! No," said Milly.

"It can be no one else."

"Indeed?" said Milly. "Are you sure?"

"It is not"— Before he could say more, she put her hand upon his mouth.

"Yes it is!" said Milly. "The young lady (she is very like the miniature, Mr. Edmund, but she is prettier) was too unhappy to rest without satisfying her doubts, and came up, last night, with a little servant-maid. As you always dated your letters from the college, she came there; and before I saw Mr. Redlaw this morning, I saw her.—*She* likes me too!" said Milly. "Oh dear, that's another!"

"This morning! Where is she now?"

"Why, she is now," said Milly, advancing her lips to his ear, "in my little parlor in the Lodge, and waiting to see you."

He pressed her hand, and was darting off, but she detained him.

"Mr. Redlaw is much altered, and has told me this morning that his memory is impaired. Be very considerate to him, Mr. Edmund; he needs that from us all."

The young man assured her, by a look, that her caution was not ill-bestowed; and as he passed the Chemist on his way out, bent respectfully and with an obvious interest before him.

Redlaw returned the salutation courteously and even humbly, and looked after him as he passed on. He drooped his head upon his hand too, as trying to re-awaken something he had lost. But it was gone.

The abiding change that had come upon him since the influence of the music, and the Phantom's reappearance, was, that now he truly felt how much he had lost, and could compassionate his own condition, and contrast it, clearly, with the natural state of those who were around him. In this, an interest in those who were around him was revived, and a meek, submissive sense of his calamity was bred, resembling that which sometimes obtains in age, when its mental powers are weakened, without insensibility or sullenness being added to the list of its infirmities.

He was conscious, that, as he redeemed, through Milly, more and more of the evil he had done, and as he was more and more with her, this change ripened itself within him. Therefore, and because of the attachment she inspired him with (but without other hope), he felt that he was quite dependent on her, and that she was his staff in his affliction.

So, when she asked him whether they should go home now, to where the old man and her husband were, and he readily replied "yes"—being anxious in that regard—he put his arm through hers, and walked beside her; not as if he were the wise and learned man to whom the wonders of nature were an open book, and hers were the uninstructed mind, but as if their two positions were reversed, and he knew nothing, and she all.

He saw the children throng about her, and caress her, as he and she went away together thus, out of the house; he heard the ringing of their laughter, and their merry voices; he saw their bright faces, clustering round him like flowers; he witnessed the renewed contentment and affection of their parents; he breathed the simple air of their poor home, restored to its tranquillity; he thought of the unwholesome blight he had shed upon it, and might, but for her, have been diffusing then; and perhaps it is no wonder that he walked submissively beside her, and drew her gentle bosom nearer to his own.

When they arrived at the Lodge, the old man was sitting in his chair in the chimney-corner, with his eyes fixed on the ground, and his son was leaning against the opposite side of the fireplace, looking at him. As she came in at the door, both started and turned round towards her, and a radiant change came upon their faces.

"Oh, dear, dear, dear, they are pleased to see me like the rest!" cried Milly, clapping her hands in an ecstasy, and stopping short. "Here are two more!"

Pleased to see her! Pleasure was no word for it. She ran into her husband's arms, thrown wide open to receive her, and he would have been glad to have her there, with her head lying on his shoulder, through the short winter's day. But the old man couldn't spare her. He had arms for her too, and he locked her in them.

"Why, where has my quiet Mouse been all this time?" said the old man. "She has been a long while away. I find that it's impossible for me to get on without Mouse. I—where's my son William?—I fancy I have been dreaming, William."

"That's what I say myself, father," returned his son. "*I* have been in an ugly sort of dream, I think.—How are you, father? Are you pretty well?"

"Strong and brave, my boy," returned the old man.

It was quite a sight to see Mr. William shaking hands with his father, and patting him on the back, and rubbing him gently down with his hand, as if he could not possibly do enough to show an interest in him.

"What a wonderful man you are, father!—How are you, father? Are you really pretty hearty, though?" said William, shaking hands with him again, and patting him again, and rubbing him gently down again.

"I never was fresher or stouter in my life, my boy."

"What a wonderful man you are, father! But that's exactly where it is," said Mr. William, with enthusiasm. "When I think of all that my father's gone through, and all the chances and changes, and sorrows and troubles, that have happened to him in the course of his long life, and under which his head has grown gray, and years upon years have gathered on it, I feel as if we couldn't do enough to honor the old gentleman, and make his old age easy.—How are you, father? Are you really pretty well, though?"

Mr. William might never have left off repeating this inquiry and shaking hands with him again, and patting him again, and rubbing him down again, if the old man had not espied the Chemist, whom until now he had not seen.

"I ask your pardon, Mr. Redlaw," said Philip, "but didn't know you were here, sir, or should have made less free. It reminds me, Mr. Redlaw, seeing you here on a Christmas morning, of the time when you was a student yourself, and worked so hard that you was backwards and forwards in our library even at Christmas time. Ha! ha! I'm old enough to remember that; and I remember it right well, I do, though I am eighty-seven. It was after you left here that my poor wife died. You remember my poor wife, Mr. Redlaw?"

The Chemist answered yes.

"Yes," said the old man. "She was a dear creetur.—I recollect you come here one Christmas morning with a young lady—I ask your pardon, Mr. Redlaw, but I think it was a sister you was very much attached to?"

The Chemist looked at him, and shook his head. "I had a sister," he said vacantly. He knew no more.

"One Christmas morning," pursued the old man, "that you come here with her—and it began to snow, and my wife invited the young lady to walk in, and sit by the fire that is always a-burning on Christmas day in what used to be, before our ten poor gentlemen commuted, our great Dinner Hall. I was there; and I recollect, as I was stirring up the blaze for the young lady to warm her pretty feet by, she read the scroll out loud, that is underneath that picter. 'Lord keep my memory green!' She and my poor wife fell a-talking about it; and it's a strange thing to think of, now, that they both said (both being so unlike to die) that it was a good prayer, and that it was one they would put up very earnestly, if they were called away young, with reference to those who were dearest to them. 'My brother,' says the young lady—'My husband,' says my poor wife. 'Lord, keep his memory of me, green, and do not let me be forgotten!'"

Tears more painful, and more bitter than he had ever shed in all his life, coursed down Redlaw's face. Philip, fully occupied in recalling his story, had not observed him until now, nor Milly's anxiety that he should not proceed.

"Philip!" said Redlaw, laying his hand upon his arm. "I am a stricken man, on whom the hand of Providence has fallen heavily, although deservedly. You speak to me, my friend, of what I cannot follow; my memory is gone."

"Merciful Power!" cried the old man.

"I have lost my memory of sorrow, wrong, and trouble," said the Chemist; "and with that I have lost all man would remember!"

To see old Philip's pity for him, to see him wheel his own great chair for him to rest in, and look down upon him with a solemn sense of his bereavement, was to know in some degree, how precious to old age such recollections are.

The boy came running in, and ran to Milly.

"Here's the man," he said, "in the other room. I don't want *him*."

"What man does he mean?" asked Mr. William.

"Hush!" said Milly.

Obedient to a sign from her, he and his old father softly withdrew. As they went out, unnoticed, Redlaw beckoned to the boy to come to him.

"I like the woman best," he answered, holding to her skirts.

"You are right," said Redlaw, with a faint smile. "But you needn't fear to come to me. I am gentler than I was. Of all the world, to you, poor child!"

The boy still held back at first; but yielding little by little to her urging, he consented to approach, and even to sit down at his feet. As Redlaw laid his hand upon the shoulder of the child, looking on him with compassion and a fellow-feeling, he put out his other hand to Milly. She stooped down on that side of him, so that she could look into his face; and after silence, said,—

"Mr. Redlaw, may I speak to you?"

"Yes," he answered, fixing his eyes upon her. "Your voice and music are the same to me."

"May I ask you something?"

"What you will."

"Do you remember what I said, when I knocked at your door last night? About one who was your friend once, and who stood on the verge of destruction?"

"Yes, I remember," he said, with some hesitation.

"Do you understand it?"

He smoothed the boy's hair—looking at her fixedly the while, and shook his head.

"This person," said Milly, in her clear, soft voice, which her mild eyes, looking at him, made clearer and softer, "I found soon afterwards. I went back to the house, and, with Heaven's help, traced him. I was not too soon. A very little, and I should have been too late."

He took his hand from the boy, and laying it on the back of that hand of hers, whose timid and yet earnest touch addressed him no less appealingly than her voice and eyes, looked more intently on her.

"He *is* the father of Mr. Edmund, the young gentleman we saw just now. His real name is Longford.—You recollect the name?"

"I recollect the name."

"And the man?"

"No, not the man. Did he ever wrong me?"

"Yes!"

"Ah! Then it's hopeless—hopeless."

He shook his head, and softly beat upon the hand he held, as though mutely asking her commiseration.

"I did not go to Mr. Edmund last night," said Milly,—"You will listen to me just the same as if you did remember all?"

"To every syllable you say."

"Both, because I did not know, then, that this really was his father, and because I was fearful of the effect of such intelligence upon him, after his illness, if it should be. Since I have known who this person is, I have not gone either; but that is for another reason. He has long been separated from his wife and son—has been a stranger to his home almost from his son's infancy, I learn from him—and has abandoned and deserted what he should have held most dear. In all that time, he has been falling from the state of a gentleman, more and more, until"—she rose up, hastily, and going out for a moment, returned, accompanied by the wreck that Redlaw had beheld last night.

"Do you know me?" asked the Chemist.

"I should be glad," returned the other, "and that is an unwonted word for me to use, if I could answer no."

The Chemist looked at the man, standing in self-abasement and degradation before him, and would have looked longer, in an effectual struggle for enlightenment, but that Milly resumed her late position by his side, and attracted his attentive gaze to her own face.

"See how low he is sunk, how lost he is!" she whispered, stretching out her arm toward him, without looking from the Chemist's face. "If you could remember all that is connected with him, do you not think it would move your pity to reflect that one you ever loved (do not let us mind how long ago, or in what belief that he has forfeited), should come to this?"

"I hope it would," he answered. "I believe it would."

His eyes wandered to the figure standing near the door, but came back speedily to her, on whom he gazed intently, as if he strove to learn some lesson from every tone of her voice, and every beam of her eyes.

"I have no learning, and you have much," said Milly; "I am not used to think, and you are always thinking. May I tell you why it seems to me a good thing for us, to remember wrong that has been done us?"

"Yes."

"That we may forgive it."

"Pardon me, great Heaven!" said Redlaw, lifting up his eyes, "for having thrown away thine own high attribute!"

"And if," said Milly, "if your memory should one

day be restored, as we will hope and pray it may be, would it not be a blessing to you to recall at once a wrong and its forgiveness?"

He looked at the figure by the door, and fastened his attentive eyes on her again; a ray of clearer light appeared to him to shine into his mind, from her bright face.

"He cannot go to his abandoned home. He does not seek to go there. He knows that he could only carry shame and trouble to those he has so cruelly neglected; and that the best reparation he can make them now, is to avoid them. A very little money carefully bestowed, would remove him to some distant place, where he might live and do no wrong, and make such atonement as is left within his power for the wrong he has done. To the unfortunate lady who is his wife, and to his son, this would be the best and kindest boon that their best friend could give them—one too that they need never know of; and to him, shattered in reputation, mind, and body, it might be salvation."

He took her head between his hands, and kissed it, and said: "It shall be done. I trust to you to do it for me, now and secretly; and to tell him that I would forgive him, if I were so happy as to know for what."

As she rose, and turned her beaming face towards the fallen man, implying that her mediation had been successful, he advanced a step, and without raising his eyes, addressed himself to Redlaw.

"You are so generous," he said—"you ever were—that you will try to banish your rising sense of retribution in the spectacle that is before you. I do not try to banish it from myself, Redlaw. If you can, believe me."

The Chemist entreated Milly, by a gesture, to come nearer to him; and, as he listened, looked in her face, as if to find in it the clue to what he heard.

"I am too decayed a wretch to make professions; I recollect my own career too well, to array any such before you. But from the day on which I made my first step downward, in dealing falsely by you, I have gone down with a certain, steady, doomed progression. That, I say."

Redlaw, keeping her close at his side, turned his face towards the speaker, and there was sorrow in it. Something like mournful recognition too.

"I might have been another man, my life might have been another life, if I had avoided that first fatal step. I don't know that it would have been. I claim nothing for the possibility. Your sister is at rest, and better than she could have been with me, if I had continued even what you thought me: even what I once supposed myself to be."

Redlaw made a hasty motion with his hand, as if he would have put that subject on one side.

"I speak," the other went on, "like a man taken from the grave. I should have made my own grave, last night, had it not been for this blessed hand."

"Oh, dear, he likes me too!" sobbed Milly, under her breath. "That's another!"

"I could not have put myself in your way last night even for bread. But, to-day, my recollection of what has been between us is so strongly stirred, and is presented to me, I don't know how, so vividly, that I have dared to come at her suggestion, and to take your bounty and to thank you for it, and to beg you, Redlaw, in your dying hour, to be as merciful to me in your thoughts, as you are in your deeds."

He turned towards the door, and stopped a moment on his way forth.

"I hope my son may interest you, for his mother's sake. I hope he may deserve to do so. Unless my life should be preserved a long time, and I should know that I have not misused your aid, I shall never look upon him more."

Going out, he raised his eyes to Redlaw for the first time. Redlaw, whose steadfast gaze was fixed upon him, dreamily held out his hand. He returned and touched it—little more—with both his own—and bending down his head, went slowly out.

In the few moments that elapsed, while Milly silently took him to the gate, the Chemist dropped into his chair, and covered his face with his hands. Seeing him thus, when she came back, accompanied by her husband and his father (who were both greatly concerned for him), she avoided disturbing him, or permitting him to be disturbed; and kneeled down near the chair, to put some warm clothing on the boy.

"That's exactly where it is. That's what I always say, father!" exclaimed her admiring husband. "There's a motherly feeling in Mrs. William's breast that must and will have vent!"

"Ay, ay," said the old man; "you're right. My son William's right!"

"It happens all for the best, Milly dear, no doubt," said Mr. William, tenderly, "that we have no children of our own; and yet I sometimes wish you had one to love and cherish. Our little dead child that you built such hopes upon, and that never breathed the breath of life—it has made you quiet-like, Milly."

"I am very happy in the recollection of it, William dear," she answered. "I think of it every day."

"I was afraid you thought of it a good deal."

"Don't say afraid; it is a comfort to me; it speaks to me in so many ways. The innocent thing that never lived on earth, is like an angel to me, William."

"You are like an angel to father and me," said Mr. William, softly. "I know that."

"When I think of all those hopes I built upon it, and the many times I sat and pictured to myself the little smiling face upon my bosom that never lay there, and the sweet eyes turned up to mine that never opened to the light," said Milly, "I can feel a greater tenderness, I think, for all the disappointed hopes in which there is no harm. When I see a beautiful child in its fond mother's arms, I love it all the better, thinking that my child might have been like that, and might have made my heart as proud and happy."

Redlaw raised his head, and looked towards her.

"All through life, it seems by me," she continued, "to tell me something. For poor neglected children, my little child pleads as if it were alive, and had a voice I knew, with which to speak to me. When I hear of youth in suffering or shame, I think that my child might have come to that, perhaps, and that God took it from me in his mercy. Even in age and gray hair, such as father's, it is present: saying that it too might have lived to be old, long and long after you and I were gone, and to have needed the respect and love of younger people."

Her quiet voice was quieter than ever, as she took her husband's arm, and laid her head against it.

"Children love me so, that sometimes I half fancy—it's a silly fancy, William—they have some way I don't know of, of feeling for my little child, and me, and understanding why their love is precious to me. If I have been quiet since, I have been more happy, William, in a hundred ways. Not least happy, dear, in this—that even when my little child was born and dead but a few days, and I was weak and sorrowful, and could not help grieving a little, the thought arose, that if I tried to lead a good life, I should meet in Heaven a bright creature, who would call me Mother!"

Redlaw fell upon his knees, with a loud cry.

"O Thou," he said, "who, through the teaching of pure love, has graciously restored me to the memory which was the memory of Christ upon the cross, and of all the good who perished in His cause, receive my thanks, and bless her!"

Then he folded her to his heart; and Milly, sobbing more than ever, cried, as she laughed, "He is come back to himself! He likes me very much indeed, too? Oh, dear, dear, dear me, here's another!"

Then, the student entered, leading by the hand a lovely girl, who was afraid to come. And Redlaw so changed towards him, seeing in him, and in his youthful choice, the softened shadow of that chastening passage in his own life, to which, as to a shady tree, the dove so long imprisoned in his solitary ark might fly for rest and company, fell upon his neck, entreating them to be his children.

Then, as Christmas is a time in which, of all times in the year, the memory of every remediable sorrow, wrong, and trouble in the world around us, should be active with us, not less than our own experiences, for all good, he laid his hand upon the boy, and, silently calling Him to witness who laid His hand on children in old time, rebuking, in the majesty of his prophetic knowledge, those who kept them from him, vowed to protect him, teach him, and reclaim him.

Then, he gave his right hand cheerily to Philip, and said that they would that day hold a Christmas dinner in what used to be, before the ten poor gentlemen commuted, their great Dinner Hall; and that they would bid to it as many of that Swidger family, who, his son had told him, were so numerous that they might join hands and make a ring round England, as could be brought together on so short a notice.

And it was that day done. There were so many Swidgers there, grown up and children, that an attempt to state them in round numbers might engender doubts, in the distrustful, of the veracity of this history. Therefore the attempt shall not be made. But there they were, by dozens and scores—and there was good news and good hope there, ready for them, of George, who had been visited again by his father and brother, and by Milly, and again left in a quiet sleep. There, present at the dinner, too, were the Tetterbys, including young Adolphus, who arrived in his prismatic comforter, in good time for the beef. Johnny and the baby were too late, of course, and came in all on one side, the one exhausted, the other in a supposed state of double-tooth; but that was customary, and not alarming.

It was sad to see the child who had no name or lineage, watching the other children as they played, not knowing how to talk with them, or sport with them, and more strange to the ways of childhood than a rough dog. It was sad, though in a different way, to see what an instinctive knowledge the youngest children there, had of his being different from all the rest, and how they made timid approaches to him with soft words and touches, and with little presents, that he might not be unhappy. But he kept by Milly, and began to love her— that was another, as she said!—and, as they all liked her dearly, they were glad of that, and when they saw him peeping at them from behind her chair, they were pleased that he was so close to it.

All this, the Chemist, sitting with the student and his bride that was to be, and Philip, and the rest, saw.

Some people have said since, that he only thought what has been herein set down; others, that he read it in the fire, one winter night about the twilight time; others, that the Ghost was but the representation of his gloomy thoughts, and Milly the embodiment of his better wisdom. *I* say nothing.

—Except this. That as they were assembled in the old Hall, by no other light than that of a great fire (having dined early), the shadows once more stole out of their hiding-places, and danced about the room, showing the children marvellous shapes and faces on the walls, and gradually changing what was real and familiar there, to what was wild and magical. But that there was one thing in the Hall, to which the eyes of Redlaw, and of Milly and her husband, and of the old man, and of the student, and his bride that was to be, were often turned, which the shadows did not obscure or change. Deepened in its gravity by the firelight, and gazing from the darkness of the panelled wall like life, the sedate face in the portrait, with the beard and ruff, looked down at them from under its verdant wreath of holly, as they looked up at it; and, clear and plain below, as if a voice had uttered them, were the words:

Lord Keep My Memory Green

A Christmas parody—one man's success
is another man's excess.

THE HAUNTED MAN:
A CHRISTMAS STORY
BY CH-R-S D-C-K-N-S

Bret Harte

THE FIRST PHANTOM

Don't tell me that it wasn't a knocker. I had seen it
often enough, and I ought to know. So ought the
three o'clock beer, in dirty highlows, swinging himself over the railing, or executing a demoniacal jig upon
the doorstep; so ought the butcher, although butchers as
a general thing are scornful of such trifles; so ought the
postman, to whom knockers of the most extravagant description were merely human weaknesses, that were to
be pitied and used. And so ought, for the matter of that,
etc., etc., etc.

But then it was *such* a knocker. A wild, extravagant,
and utterly incomprehensible knocker. A knocker so
mysterious and suspicious that Policeman X 37, first
coming upon it, felt inclined to take it instantly in custody, but compromised with his professional instincts by

sharply and sternly noting it with an eye that admitted of no nonsense, but confidently expected to detect its secret yet. An ugly knocker; a knocker with a hard, human face, that was a type of the harder human face within. A human face that held between its teeth a brazen rod. So hereafter in the mysterious future should be held, etc., etc.

But if the knocker had a fierce human aspect in the glare of day, you should have seen it at night, when it peered out of the gathering shadows and suggested an ambushed figure; when the light of the street lamps fell upon it, and wrought a play of sinister expression in its hard outlines; when it seemed to wink meaningly at a shrouded figure who, as the night fell darkly, crept up the steps and passed into the mysterious house; when the swinging door disclosed a black passage into which the figure seemed to lose itself and become a part of the mysterious gloom; when the night grew boisterous and the fierce wind made furious charges at the knocker, as if to wrench it off and carry it away in triumph. Such a night as this.

It was a wild and pitiless wind. A wind that had commenced life as a gentle country zephyr, but wandering through manufacturing towns had become demoralised, and reaching the city had plunged into extravagant dissipation and wild excesses. A roystering wind that indulged in Bacchanalian shouts on the street corners, that knocked off the hats from the heads of helpless passengers, and then fulfilled its duties by speeding away, like all young prodigals—to sea.

He sat alone in a gloomy library listening to the wind that roared in the chimney. Around him novels and story-books were strewn thickly; in his lap he held one with its pages freshly cut, and turned the leaves wearily until his eyes rested upon a portrait in its frontispiece.

And as the wind howled the more fiercely, and the darkness without fell blacker, a strange and fateful likeness to that portrait appeared above his chair and leaned upon his shoulder. The Haunted Man gazed at the portrait and sighed. The figure gazed at the portrait and sighed too.

'Here again?' said the Haunted Man.

'Here again,' it repeated in a low voice.

'Another novel?'

'Another novel.'

'The old story?'

'The old story.'

'I see a child,' said the Haunted Man, gazing from the pages of the book into the fire—'a most unnatural child, a model infant. It is prematurely old and philosophic. It dies in poverty to slow music. It dies surrounded by luxury to slow music. It dies with an accompaniment of golden water and rattling carts to slow music. Previous to its decease it makes a will; it repeats the Lord's Prayer, it kisses the "boofer lady." That child—'

'Is mine,' said the phantom.

'I see a good woman, undersized. I see several charming women, but they are all undersized. They are more or less imbecile and idiotic, but always fascinating and undersized. They wear coquettish caps and aprons. I observe that feminine virtue is invariably below the medium height, and that it is always babyish and infantine. These women—'

'Are mine.'

'I see a haughty, proud, and wicked lady. She is tall and queenly. I remark that all proud and wicked women are tall and queenly. That woman—'

'Is mine,' said the phantom, wringing his hands.

'I see several things continually impending. I observe

that whenever an accident, a murder, or death is about to happen, there is something in the furniture, in the locality, in the atmosphere that foreshadows and suggests it years in advance. I cannot say that in real life I have noticed it—the perception of this surprising fact belongs—'

'To me!' said the phantom. The Haunted Man continued, in a despairing tone:

'I see the influence of this in the magazines and daily papers: I see weak imitators rise up and enfeeble the world with senseless formula. I am getting tired of it. It won't do, Charles! It won't do!' and the Haunted Man buried his head in his hands and groaned. The figure looked down upon him sternly: the portrait in the frontispiece frowned as he gazed.

'Wretched man,' said the phantom, 'and how have these things affected you?'

'Once I laughed and cried, but then I was younger. Now, I would forget them if I could.'

'Have then your wish. And take this with you, man whom I renounce. From this day henceforth you shall live with those whom I displace. Without forgetting me, 'twill be your lot to walk through life as if we had not met. But first you shall survey these scenes that henceforth must be yours. At one tonight, prepare to meet the phantom I have raised. Farewell!'

The sound of its voice seemed to fade away with the dying wind, and the Haunted Man was alone. But the firelight flickered gaily, and the light danced on the walls, making grotesque figures of the furniture.

'Ha, ha!' said the Haunted Man, rubbing his hands gleefully; 'now for a whiskey punch and a cigar.'

The Second Phantom

One! The stroke of the far-off bell had hardly died before the front door closed with a reverberating clang. Steps were heard along the passage; the library door swung open of itself, and the Knocker—yes, the Knocker—slowly strode into the room. The Haunted Man rubbed his eyes—no! there could be no mistake about it—it was the Knocker's face, mounted on a misty, almost imperceptible body. The brazen rod was transferred from its mouth to its right hand, where it was held like a ghostly truncheon.

'It's a cold evening,' said the Haunted Man.

'It is,' said the Goblin, in a hard metallic voice.

'It must be pretty cold out there,' said the Haunted Man, with vague politeness. 'Do you ever—will you—take some hot water and brandy?'

'No,' said the Goblin.

'Perhaps you'd like it cold, by way of change?' continued the Haunted Man, correcting himself, as he remembered the peculiar temperature with which the Goblin was probably familiar.

'Time flies,' said the Goblin coldly. 'We have no leisure for idle talk. Come!' He moved his ghostly truncheon toward the window, and laid his hand upon the other's arm. At his touch the body of the Haunted Man seemed to become as thin and incorporeal as that of the Goblin himself, and together they glided out of the window into the black and blowy night.

In the rapidity of their flight the senses of the Haunted Man seemed to leave him. At length they stopped suddenly.

'What do you see?' asked the Goblin.

'I see a battlemented medieval castle. Gallant men in mail ride over the drawbridge, and kiss their gauntleted fingers to fair ladies, who wave their lily hands in return. I see fight and fray and tournament. I hear roaring heralds bawling the charms of delicate women, and shamelessly proclaiming their lovers. Stay. I see a Jewess about to leap from a battlement. I see knightly deeds, violence, rapine, and a god deal of blood. I've seen pretty much the same at Astley's.'

'Look again.'

'I see purple moors, glens, masculine women, bare-legged men, priggish bookworms, more violence, physical excellence, and blood. Always blood—and the superiority of physical attainments.'

'And how do you feel now?' said the Goblin.

The Haunted Man shrugged his shoulders.

'None the better for being carried back and asked to sympathise with a barbarous age.'

The Goblin smiled and clutched his arm; they again sped rapidly through the black night, and again halted.

'What do you see?' said the Goblin.

'I see a barrack room, with a mess table, and a group of intoxicated Celtic officers telling funny stories, and giving challenges to duel. I see a young Irish gentleman capable of performing prodigies of valour. I learn incidentally that the acme of all heroism is the cornetcy of a dragoon regiment. I hear a good deal of French! No, thank you,' said the Haunted Man hurriedly, as he stayed the waving hand of the Goblin, 'I would rather *not* go to the Peninsula, and don't care to have a private interview with Napoleon.'

Again the Goblin flew away with the unfortunate man, and from a strange roaring below them, he judged they were above the ocean. A ship hove in sight, and the Goblin stayed its flight. 'Look,' he said, squeezing his companion's arm.

The Haunted Man yawned. 'Don't you think, Charles,

you're rather running this thing into the ground? Of course, it's very moral and instructive, and all that. But ain't there a little too much pantomime about it? Come now!'

'Look!' repeated the Goblin, pinching his arm malevolently. The Haunted Man groaned.

'Oh, of course, I see Her Majesty's ship *Arethusa*. Of course I am familiar with her stern First Lieutenant, her eccentric Captain, her one fascinating and several mischievous midshipmen. Of course, I know it's a splendid thing to see all this, and not to be sea-sick. Oh, there the young gentlemen are going to play a trick on the purser. For God's sake, let us go,' and the unhappy man absolutely dragged the Goblin away with him.

When they next halted, it was at the edge of a broad and boundless prairie, in the middle of an oak opening.

'I see,' said the Haunted Man, without waiting for his cue, but mechanically, and as if he were repeating a lesson which the Goblin had taught him—'I see the Noble Savage. He is very fine to look at! But I observe under his war paint, feathers, and picturesque blanket—dirt, disease, and an unsymmetrical contour. I observe beneath his inflated rhetoric deceit and hypocrisy. Beneath his physical hardihood, cruelty, malice, and revenge. The Noble Savage is a humbug. I remarked the same to Mr. Catlin.'

'Come,' said the phantom.

The Haunted Man sighed, and took out his watch. 'Couldn't we do the rest of this another time?'

'My hour is almost spent, irreverent being, but there is yet a chance for your reformation. Come!'

Again they sped through the night, and again they halted. The sound of delicious but melancholy music fell upon their ears.

'I see,' said the Haunted Man, with something of interest in his manner, 'I see an old moss-covered manse beside a sluggish, flowing river. I see weird shapes: witches, Puritans, clergymen, little children, judges, mesmerised maidens, moving to the sound of melody that thrills me with its sweetness and purity.

'But, although carried along its calm and evenly-flowing current, the shapes are strange and frightful: an eating lichen gnaws at the heart of each; not only the clergymen, but witch, maiden, judge, and Puritan, all wear Scarlet Letters of some kind burned upon their hearts. I am fascinated and thrilled, but I feel a morbid sensitiveness creeping over me. I—I beg your pardon.' The Goblin was yawning frightfully. 'Well, perhaps we had better go.'

'One more, and the last,' said the Goblin. They were moving home. Streaks of red were beginning to appear in the eastern sky. Along the banks of the blackly flowing river, by moorland and stagnant fens, by low houses, clustering close to the water's edge, like strange mollusks, crawled upon the beach to dry; by misty black barges, the more misty and indistinct seen through its mysterious veil, the river fog was slowly rising. So rolled away and rose from the heart of the Haunted Man, etc., etc.

They stopped before a quaint mansion of red brick. The Goblin waved his hand without speaking.

'I see,' said the Haunted Man, 'a gay drawing-room. I see my old friends of the club, of the college, of society, even as they lived and moved. I see the gallant and unselfish men whom I have loved, and the snobs whom I have hated. I see strangely mingling with them, and now and then blending with their forms, our old friends Dick Steele, Addison, and Congreve. I observe, though, that these gentlemen have a habit of getting too much in the way. The royal standard of Queen Anne, not in itself a beautiful ornament, is rather too prominent in the picture. The long galleries of black oak, the formal furniture, the old portraits, are picturesque, but depressing. The house is damp. I enjoy myself better here on the lawn, where they are getting up a Vanity Fair. See, the bell rings, the curtain is rising, the puppets are brought out for a new play. Let me see.'

The Haunted Man was pressing forward in his eagerness, but the hand of the Goblin stayed him, and pointing to his feet, he saw between him and the rising curtain, a new-made grave. And bending above the grave in passionate grief, the Haunted Man beheld the phantom of the previous night.

The Haunted Man started, and—woke. The bright sunshine streamed into the room. The air was sparkling with frost. He ran joyously to the window and opened it. A small boy saluted him with 'Merry Christmas.' The Haunted Man instantly gave him a Bank of England note. 'How much like Tiny Tim, Tom, and Bobby that boy looked—bless my soul, what a genius this Dickens has!'

A knock at the door, and Boots entered.

'Consider your salary doubled instantly. Have you read *David Copperfield*?'

'Yezzur.'

'Your salary is quadrupled. What do you think of *The Old Curiosity Shop*?'

The man instantly burst into a torrent of tears, and then into a roar of laughter.

'Enough! Here are five thousand pounds. Open a porterhouse, and call it, "Our Mutual Friend." Huzza! I feel so happy!' And the Haunted Man danced about the room.

And so, bathed in the light of that blessed sun, and yet glowing with the warmth of a good action, the Haunted Man, haunted no longer, save by those shapes which make the dreams of children beautiful, re-seated himself in his chair, and finished *Our Mutual Friend*.

The world is turned upside down—a spectre is haunting Christmas.

THE CONFESSIONS OF EBENEZER SCROOGE

James Morrow

Charity is the grin of slavery.
—JOHN CALVIN BATCHELOR

It was shaping up to be another of those confounded metaphysical Christmases, or so I surmised from the shimmering and diaphanous form standing in the doorway to my bedchamber.

"Begone!" I instructed my former partner's shade.

"Fish a herring, Ebenezer," replied Marley's spectral self.

"You're but the product of my wayward stomach," I said accusingly. "You're a dream made of rancid cheese. An illusion spawned by spoiled ham. A figment born of rotten figs."

"No more now than when last we met." The Spirit

lumbered toward my bed, dragging his preposterous chain behind him, the concomitant ledgers, cash boxes, keys, and padlocks clanking along my oaken floor as if to herald the incipient New Year.

Fear grew within me like hoarfrost on a windowpane. I'd never get used to these ambulatory corpses, never. "Am I not a new man, Jacob?" I pleaded. "Don't I contribute to every worthy cause in Christendom?" My goosebumps were as big as warts. "You should see the turkey Cratchit's getting this year. A veritable walrus. Why are you here?"

Remaining mute, Marley extended his arms and moved them spastically, like a clockwork maestro conducting an orchestra.

"Speak to me, Jacob!"

Although I'd latched the casement, a sharp wind came spiraling toward me like the Devil's own sneeze. Caught in the updraft, my candlesticks took to the air like twigs. The mirror above my dresser jerked free of its nail and, striking the floor, became a million glassy daggers. My bed pitched and rolled as if riding the lip of a maelstrom, its canopy snapping and fluttering, and suddenly I was off the mattress, hurtling across the room on a collision course with the door.

"From now on," I heard Marley say before the infernal jamb blew out my lights, "turkeys won't turn the trick."

I awoke—of all things—upright. My knees trembled, my legs shimmied, yet I stood erect. A moor spread before me, bathed in icy yellow moonlight and dotted with patches of fog. Twenty yards away, the mist congealed into a single seamless mass that slithered across the ground, rolled over a low stone wall, and lapped against a mountainous mansion like surf caressing a rocky shore.

"They're expecting you," said Marley, materializing suddenly atop the porch.

Crooked cupolas, tilted shutters, shattered windows: but the house's queerest aspect, surely, was the grim perversion of Yuletide its owners kept. On the muddy lawn the stark white skeletons of eight reindeer, their bones threaded with baling wire, pulled a sleigh jammed with ashes, coal, and decaying cornhusk dolls. Through the parlor window I glimpsed a pine tree, its needles brown and dead as shorn whiskers, its branches hung with stubby candles and moldly spheres of popcorn.

Knee-deep in fog, I approached the front steps. Marley pulled back the door and, seizing my frigid hands, guided me down a candlelit hallway to an immense dining room decorated in a singularly voluptuous baroque. The curtains were heavy, luminous, and fiery red, like molten earth spilling from a volcano. The rug boasted the thick emerald splendor of a peat moss roof. In one corner, a grandfather clock, bug-infested as a rotten log, tolled the midnight hour through a succession of hoarse, tubercular bongs. Opposite, a Christmas Eve fire seethed in a cavernous hearth, the tips of the flames narrowing into alphabet characters that spelled out an evanescent *NOEL.*

Laden with food—meats, breads, legumes, wines, desserts—the linen-swathed banquet table hosted a half-dozen of the most outré creatures I'd ever beheld. Living cadavers they seemed, deathly pale, their eyes dark and sunken as cliffside rookeries, their clothing ratty and torn like manuscripts at the mercy of book lice. Around his scrawny neck, each guest wore a small marble gravestone suspended on rusty chains like a particularly cumbersome pendant.

"Three years ago we operated wholly in the indicative mood—to wit, Christmas Past, Christmas Present, Christmas Future," Marley explained. "But reality is more complicated than that, don't you agree, Ebenezer?"

"If I were you, I'd attend carefully to what I'm about to hear," the Ghost of Christmas Subjunctive—so ran the inscription on his stone—asserted as he stabbed his fork into a soft ruddy potato and lifted the prize to his mouth. He was foppishly dressed, all velvet ribbons and lace filigree, an immaculate white handkerchief emerging from his waistcoat pocket like a puff of smoke.

The Ghost of Christmas Present Perfect sipped her claret and said, "We have traveled a long, hard road to bring you this message." For the price of her black silk dress, Cratchit's family could have fed itself for a year. An aristocrat, surely, as flawless in face, carriage, and wardrobe as her epithet implied.

The Ghost of Christmas Future Perfect was likewise female, likewise comely, but I could not for the life of me identify the silvery material enveloping her full, topographically varied form. "Before the evening is out," she said, sweeping her glossily gloved hand across the steaming heaps of plentitude, "your worldview will have undergone yet another revolution."

Quel banquet! Not one stuffed goose but two, big as albatrosses, their plucked flesh turned brown with immolation. A roast suckling pig, its mouth plugged with a plump red apple. A mound of aspic molded to resemble an angel. A knoll of spaghetti piled up like the brain of some preternatural whale.

"Observe this cloth," demanded the Ghost of Christmas Imperative, pulling the handkerchief from the pocket of the Ghost of Christmas Subjunctive. When alive, evidently, Christmas Imperative had been a military man, an officer. Epaulettes clung to his greatcoat like gold jellyfish. A wide leather belt bearing scabbard and sword constrained his overfed belly. "Note the sturdy, robust threads," he said, presenting me with the kerchief. "Tell me what material it is."

"Cotton?" I hazarded.

"Quite so. Finest flower of the Mississippi Delta. Now name the price."

"I have no idea," I replied, truthfully. "I run a counting house, not a textile factory."

"This afternoon you could buy a bale off the Bristol docks for six pounds," said the Ghost of Christmas Conditional. She'd made no effort to camouflage her profession. Rash-red cheeks, scraggly hair dyed a lurid crimson, low-cut dress displaying cleavage like a furrow in a cornfield. "If persistent, you could dicker them down to five."

"But permit us to tell you the *real* price," said the Ghost of Christmas Imperative, stroking the tanned flanks of the nearest goose.

The Ghost of Christmas Past Perfect—and a thing of the perfect past he was indeed, his body swathed in a toga, his head ringed by a crown of laurel—clapped his hands, whereupon the recently fondled goose split its seams and, like a bitch birthing some absurdly proliferous litter, spewed out a score of dark homunculi, each no higher than a pepper shaker. Dressed only in tattered trousers, the little men exuded pinpoints of perspiration as they trekked across the linen toward a porcelain bowl brimming with sugar cubes.

"To wit, the real price of cotton is the blood and misery of a million Negro slaves," said Marley as he seized a strand of spaghetti and handed it to the Ghost of Christmas Imperative.

"How grotesque!" I gasped.

"We had hoped to avoid frightening you," said the Ghost of Christmas Past Perfect, adjusting his laurel crown.

In the hearth, the flames spelled out *THE REAL PRICE.*

"Lift those bales!" With a merciless flick of the wrist, Christmas Imperative brought the spaghetti down hard against the Negroes' glistery, coal-black shoulders. Their flesh jumped spasmodically under the blow, their lungs unleashed high, steam-whistle shrieks. "Hurry! Now!" Like ants trapped in some insectile hell, the slaves hefted sugar cubes onto their backs and, staggering beneath the dense crystalline burdens, started toward the teapot.

"Nor does the price of cotton end here," said Marley.

As the slaves dumped their loads into the tea, a haggard child with dull grey eyes and tangled yellow hair wandered into the dining room gripping a hank of cotton yard. He was as transparent as water, insubstantial as grass. Face locked in a wince, he extended his free hand and plucked the apple from the roast piglet's jaw.

"See who must spin and wind the yarn," Christmas Imperative continued, gripping the handle of his sword. "Spin and wind, spin and wind, spin and wind—sixteen hours a day, seven days a week, fifty-two weeks a year!"

In a sudden burst of frenzy, the boy began twisting the yarn around the apple as if it were a bobbin.

"By his thirteenth birthday, he will have spent three-fourths of his waking hours within the walls of a brutish and stinking mill," asserted Christmas Future Perfect, rubbing a santiny glove against her metallic sleeve.

"He had hoped to save enough money to buy his

mother a silver locket for her fortieth birthday," noted
Christmas Past Perfect.

"She died first," said Marley.

The yarn was lacerating the boy's hands now. Gouts
of blood dribbled from his mangled flesh.

"What do you require of me?" I asked, tears of remorse flooding my eyes. "Shall I send the boy a thousand pounds? Fine! Reward any overseer who spares
the lash? Done! Believe me, Spirits, I'm the very soul
of Christmas. I'll give every slave a turkey."

"Philanthropy is a marvelous impulse," said Marley,
slicing off a serving of pork.

"This time out, however, we would prefer to teach
you a different truth." Christmas Conditional lifted a
small silver flask to her painted lips and gulped down
half the contents.

Slowly, like a snowman standing before a furnace,
the boy and his yarn vaporized, leaving the apple to
hover momentarily in the air. Now it began to move,
flying across the dining room and entering the piglet's
mouth like a musket ball burrowing into a rampart.

Marley swallowed a succulent chunk of pork. "You
see, Ebenezer, charity always begs a crucial question.
How did the bestower attain the lofty position from
which he now exercises his largesse?" My dead colleague cleaned his teeth with one of his many appended
keys. "Through imagination and merit? Or through inherited privilege and ruthless exploitation?" With a
quick, foxlike grin, he opened a cash box and drew out
a pamphlet labeled "*Manifest der Kommunisten* der
Friedrich Engels and Karl Marx," handing it to the
Ghost of Christmas Present Perfect. "The first copy
rolled off the presses last night in Brussels."

"By noon tomorrow, they will have printed ten thousand," noted the Ghost of Christmas Future Perfect.

"Given the capital, they would happily print ten thousand more," the Ghost of Christmas Conditional elaborated, swilling gin.

"Get to work!" screeched the Ghost of Christmas Imperative, scourging the tiny slaves and sending them pell-mell back to the sugar bowl.

"A new idea has entered the world." Christmas Present Perfect removed a fan from her bosom and, spreading it open, evaporated the sweat from her upper lip. "It has christened itself not philanthropy but justice." She turned back the cover of the pamphlet and placed her red fingernail atop the first sentence. *"A spectre is haunting Europe,"* she read, *"the spectre of communism."*

The hearth flames spelled out *COMMUNISM.*

Marley ate pork. "To wit, heaven will never come to earth simply because slaveholders exhibit flashes of mercy or children get grants from anonymous benefactors. Certain evils dwell in society's bedrock, and must be blasted out. You can't throw turkeys at every problem."

"Of course," I said. "Naturally. I understand. Give me Herr Engels's address, and I shall send him sufficient funds to buy his own printing press."

Marley unlocked another cash box, procuring a copy of my favorite story of all time—my own true biography, *A Christmas Carol.*

"Were I to affix an alternative title," said Christmas Subjunctive, "I'd call it *A Christmas Swindle.*" He pulled out his snuffbox and, like an artilleryman loading a cannon, rammed a pinch of sot-weed into his left nostril. "Thanks to this trickster Dickens, millions now regard greed as but the personality defect of a few isolated skinflints like yourself, when in fact it's inherent in the system."

The flames spelled out *THE SYSTEM*.

Marley lurched away from the volume, as if it were exuding an objectionable odor. "To wit, the thing's a pile of horse manure."

I blenched, my face becoming almost as bloodless as my partner's. "Such vulgarity, Jacob. Please . . ."

"Do you truly believe the spiritually deformed can be made to acknowledge their sins?" demanded Marley, filling his cup with freshly sugared tea. "Do you think Nero ever knew a single moment of guilt? Did the Borgias beg heaven for forgiveness? Did Bonaparte repent on his deathbed?"

"I don't know about Nero. I only know that three years ago you and the Spirits suffused my shadowed existence with the light of kindness and generosity."

"Yes, and if we had it to do over again . . ." Christmas Subjunctive took another pinch of snuff. "Ah, but we *do* have it to do over again, don't we?"

"Ebenezer, you must destroy the myth of the redeemable master," said Marley. "Among humankind's numerous and dearly held delusions, none is a greater impediment to utopia. Three years ago you mended your ways—and now you must unmend them."

"I wish you people would make up your minds," I said, my voice jagged with irritation.

"Eat!" said the Ghost of Christmas Imperative.

Thanks to my backsliding, Marley and his ectoplasmic crowd are at peace now, and so am I. Indeed, as I lie tonight beneath my silken sheets, making ready to join the Spirits on the sunless side of the grave, I realize that I've never felt better. I'm my old self again, my true self, contented and fulfilled.

Three days after the Spirits came, I abruptly revoked my contributions to the Asylum Fund, the Orphan

Drive, and Saint Christopher's Hospital for Indigents and Debtors. Epiphany found me lowering Cratchit's salary to its 1843 level and reducing his coal quota to one lump per day. The following week I contrived for my nephew's wife to learn of his various trysts. Of the whole wretched lot, only the runt prospered. Somehow he managed to conquer his infirmities, trading crutch for rifle. His twenty years' service to Queen and country climaxed in the Transvaal when, on his forty-fourth birthday, a Zulu spear entered his left eye and punctured his brain clear to the back of the cranium.

Marley, in his foresight, anticipated the fruits of my relapse. He knew I'd become exactly what the reformers, dreamers, uplifters, and socialists needed. A symbol. A rallying point. Scrooge the system. Thanks to the Spirits and me, a new world is coming, I'm sure of it.

God bless us, every one.

A child is attracted to a disreputable
shopping-mall Santa.

O COME LITTLE
CHILDREN . . .

―――

Chet Williamson

"It even *smells* like Christmas," the boy told his
mother, as they strolled down the narrow aisles of
the farmer's market. That it looked and sounded like
the happiest of holidays went without saying. Carols
blared everywhere, from the tiniest of the stand-holder's
transistor radios to the brass choir booming from the
market's PA system. Meat cases were farmed with
strings of lights, a myriad of small trees adorned a myriad of counters across which bills the color of holly
were pushed and goods and coins returned, and red and
green predominated above all other hues. But it was
that odors that entranced: the pungency of gingerbread,
the sweet olfactory sting of fresh Christmas cookies.
There were mince pies and pumpkin pudding, and a
concoction of cranberry sauce and dried fruit in syrup
whose aroma made the boy pucker and salivate as
though a fresh lemon had brushed his tongue. The

owner of the sandwich stand was selling small, one-dollar, Styrofoam plates of turkey and stuffing to those too rabid to wait until Christmas, three long days away. The smell was intoxicating, and the line was long.

The boy's mother, smiling and full of the spirit, bought many things that would find their way to their own Christmas table, and the sights and sounds and smells kept the boy from being bored, as he usually was at the Great Tri-County Farmer's and Flea Market.

It was on the way out, as he and his mother walked through the large passage that divided the freshness of the food and produce stands from the dusty tawdriness of the flea market, that the boy saw the man dressed as Santa Claus. At first glance he did not seem a very *good* Santa Claus. He was too thin, and instead of a full, white, cottony, fake beard, his own wispy mass of facial hair had been halfheartedly lightened, as though he'd dipped a comb in white shoe polish and given it a few quick strokes. "There," the boy's mother remarked, "is one of Santa's *lesser* helpers."

The boy was way past the point where every Santa was the *real* Santa. In truth, he was just short of total disbelief. TV, comic books, and the remarks of older friends had all taken their toll, and he now thought that although the existence of the great man was conceivable, it was not likely, and to imagine that any of these kindly, red-suited men who smiled wearily in every department store and shopping mall was the genuine article was quite impossible.

Even if he had believed fully, he doubted if anyone under two would have accepted the legitimacy of the Santa he saw before him. Aside from the thinness of both beard and frame, the man's suit was threadbare in spots, the black vinyl boots scuffed and dull, and the white ruffs at collar and cuffs had yellowed to the color of old piano keys. His lap was empty. The only person nearby was a cowboy-hatted man sitting on a folding chair identical to that on which the Santa sat. A Polaroid Pronto hung from his neck, and next to him a card on an easel read YOUR PICTURE WITH SANTA— $3.00. The $3.00 part was printed much smaller than the words. The boy and his mother were nearly by the men when the one in the red suit looked at them.

The boy stopped. "Mom," he said, loud enough for only his mother to hear. "May I sit on his lap?"

She gave an impatient sigh. "Oh, Alan . . ."

"Please?"

"Honey, do you really *want* your picture taken with . . . ?"

"I don't want a picture. I just want to sit on his lap."

"No, sweetie," she said, looking at the man looking at the boy. "I don't think so."

They were in the parking lot by the time she looked at her son once more. To her amazement, huge tears were running down his face. "What's wrong, honey?"

"I wanted to sit on his *lap*," the boy choked out.

"Oh, Alan, he's not Santa, he's just a helper. And not a very good one either."

"Can't I? Please? Just for a minute . . ."

She sighed and smiled, thinking that it would do no harm, and that she was in no hurry. "All right. But no picture."

The boy shook his head, and they went back inside. The man in the red suit smiled as he saw the boy approach without hesitation, and patted his thigh in an unspoken invitation for the boy to sit. The man in the cowboy hat stood up, but before he could bring the camera to eye level, the boy said, "No picture, please," and the man, with a look of irritation directed at the boy's mother, sat down again.

The boy remained on the man's lap for less than a minute, talking so quietly that his mother could not hear. When he started to slide off, he stopped suddenly, as though caught, and his mother saw that the metal buckle of the boy's loose-hanging coat belt had become entangled in the white plush of the man's left cuff. The man tried unsuccessfully to extricate it with the fingers of his gloved right hand, then put the glove in his mouth and yanked his hand free. With his long, thin fingers he freed the boy, who hopped smiling onto the floor and waved a hand enclosed in his own varicolored mittens. When he rejoined his mother, he was surprised to find her scowling. "What's wrong?"

"Nothing," she answered. "Let's go."

But he knew something was wrong and found out later at dinner. "*I* think he must have been *on* something."

"Oh, come on," his father said, taking a second baked potato. "Why?"

His mother went on as though he were not there. "He just *looked* it. He had these real hollow eyes, like he hadn't slept in days. Really thin. The suit just hung on him. And, uh . . ." She looked at the boy, who pretended to be interested in pushing an unmelted piece of margarine around on his peas.

"What?"

"His hand. He took off his glove and his hand was all bruised, like he'd been shooting into it or something."

"Shooting what?" the boy asked.

"Drugs," his father said, before his mother could make something up.

"What's that? Like what?"

His mother smiled sardonically at his father. "Go ahead, Mr. Rogers. Explain."

"Well . . . *drugs*. Like your baby aspirin, only a lot stronger. People take some drugs just to make them feel good, but then later they feel real bad, so you shouldn't ever take them at all."

"What's the shooting part?"

"Like a shot, when the doctor gives you a shot."

"Like Mommy's diabetes."

"Yeah, like that. Only people who take too many *bad* drugs have their veins . . ." He saw the question on the boy's face. ". . . their little blood hoses inside their skin collapse on them. So they might stick the needles in their legs, or in the veins in the backs of their hands, or even their feet or the inside of their mouth, or . . ."

"That's fine, thank you," his mother said sharply. "I think we've learned enough tonight."

"He wouldn't do *that*," the boy said. "He was too *nice*."

His father shook his head. "Aw, honey, you never know. Nice people can have problems too." And then his mother changed the subject.

The next day the boy told his mother that he wished he could see Santa Claus again. "Santa Claus?" she asked.

"At the market. *You* know."

"Oh, Alan, *him*? Honey, you saw him yesterday. You told him what you wanted then, didn't you?"

"I don't want to tell him what I want. I just want to see him because he's *nice*. I *liked* him."

After the boy was in bed, his father and mother sat in the living room, neither of them paying attention to the movie on cable. "He say anything to you about Santa today?" he asked her.

She nodded. "Couple of times. You?"

"Yeah. He really went for this guy, huh?"

"I don't know why."

"Oh, Alan can be so compassionate—probably felt sorry for the guy."

She shook her head. "No, it wasn't like that. He really seemed drawn by him, almost as though . . ." She paused.

"As though he really thought the guy was Santa Claus?" her husband finished.

"I don't know," she answered, looking at the car crash on the TV screen but not really seeing it. "Maybe."

She turned off the movie with no complaints from her husband, and began to go over the final list of ingredients for their Christmas dinner. "Uh-oh," she murmured, and went out to the kitchen. In a minute she returned, frowning lovingly at her husband. "Well, it's not that I don't appreciate your making dinner tonight, but I just realized your oyster stew used the oysters for the Christmas casserole."

"You're kidding."

"Nope." She was amused to see that there was actually panic in his face.

"What'll we *do*?"

"Do without."

"But . . . but oyster casserole's a tradition."

"Some tradition—just because we had it last year."

"I liked it."

"And where are we going to find oysters on a Sunday?"

"It's not the day, it's the month. And December has an *R* in it."

"Sure. But Sunday doesn't have *oysters* in it. The IGA's closed, Acme, Weis . . ."

His face brightened. "The farmer's market! They

have a fish stand, and they're open tomorrow. You could run out and . . ."

"Me? I didn't cook the oyster stew."

"You ate it."

She put her left hand over his head and pounded it gently with her right. "Sometimes you are a real sleazoid."

"Now, Mrs. Scrooge," he said, pulling her onto his lap, "where's that Christmas spirit, that charity?"

"Good King Wenceslas I ain't."

"How about if I vacuum while you're gone so my mother doesn't realize what a slob you are?"

"How many pounds of oysters do you want?"

It started to snow heavily just before midnight and stopped at dawn. The snow was light and powdery, easy for the early morning trucks to push from the roads. The family went to church, then came home for a simple lunch, as if afraid to ingest even a jot too much on the day before the great Christmas feast. "Well," the boy's mother said after they'd finished cleaning up the dishes, "I'm off for oysters. Anyone want to come?"

"To the farm market?" asked the boy. His mother nodded. "Can I see Santa?"

His father and mother exchanged looks. "I don't think so," she replied. "Do you want to go anyway?"

He thought for a moment. "Okay."

The parking lot was still covered with snow, although the cars had mashed most of it down to a dirty gray film. Only the far end of the parking lot, where a small, gray trailer sat attached to an old, nondescript sedan, was pristine with whiteness. It was typical, the boy's mother thought, of the management not to pay to have the lot plowed—anyone who'd hire a bargain basement Santa like that one and then charge three bucks for a thirty-five cent picture with him.

The seafood stand was out of oysters, but its owner said that the small grocery shop at the market's other end might still have some. "Could I see Santa?" the boy asked as they walked.

"Alan, I told you no. Besides, he's probably gone by now. He's got a busy night tonight." She knew it sounded absurd even as she said it. If *that* Santa was going to be busy, it wouldn't be delivering toys—it would probably be looking for a fix. Repulsion crossed her face as she thought again of those hollow eyes, that pale skin, the telltale bruises on his bare hand, and she wondered what her son could possibly see in that haggard countenance.

She thought she would ask him, but when she looked down, he was gone. In a sharp, reflexive motion, she looked to the other side, then behind her, but the boy was not there. She strained to see him through the forest of people, then turned and retraced her steps, as her heart beat faster and beads of cold sweat touched her face. "Alan!" she called, softly but high, to pierce the low, murmuring din around her. "Alan!"

It took some time for the idea to occur that her son had disobeyed her and had set out to find the market's Santa Claus on his own. She had not thought him capable of such a thing, for he knew and understood the dangers that could face a small child alone in a public place, especially a place like a flea market that had more than its share of transients and lowlifes. She told herself that he would be all right, that nothing could happen to a little boy the day before Christmas, that someone she knew would see him and stop him and take care of him until she could find him, or that he would be there on Santa Claus's lap, smiling sheepishly and guiltily when he spotted her.

She was running now, jostling shoppers, their arms

loaded with last-minute thoughts. Within a minute, she entered the large open area between the markets. The chairs and the sign were there, the Santa and his photographer were not. Neither was her son.

For a long moment she stood, wondering what to do next, and finally decided to find the manager and ask him to make an announcement on the PA system. But first she called her husband, for she could no longer bear to be alone.

By the time he met her in the manager's office, the announcement had been made four times without a response. The boy's father held his mother who was by this time crying quietly, very much afraid. "Where was he going?" the manager, a short, elderly man with a cigarette in one hand and a can of soda in the other, asked.

"I thought it was to see Santa, but he wasn't there when I got there."

The manager nodded. "Yeah, he quit at noon. I wanted him to work through five, but he wouldn't. Said he hadda meet somebody."

The boy's father looked at the manager intently over his wife's head. "Who is this guy?"

"Santa? Don't know his name. Just breezed in about a week ago and asked if I wanted a Santa cheap."

"What do you mean you don't know his name? You *pay* him, don't you?"

"Cash. Off the books. You'll keep that quiet now. And Riley, my helper, he got a Polaroid, so we made enough to pay him outta the pictures."

The boy's father took his arms from around his wife. "Where is this guy?"

"He's got a trailer the other side of the lot."

"All right," the father nodded. "We're going to talk

to him. And if he can't give us any answers, we're calling the police."

The manager started to protest, but the couple walked out of the office and down the aisles, trying hard not to run and so admit their panic to themselves. "It'll be all right," the boy's father kept saying. "We'll find him. It'll be all right."

And they did. When they walked into the open area where Santa had been, their son was standing beside the gold aluminum Christmas tree. He smiled when he saw them, and waved.

They ran to him, and his mother scooped him up and hugged him, crying. His father placed a hand on his head as if to be certain he was really there, then tousled his hair, swallowing heavily to rid his throat of the cold lump that had been there since his wife's call.

"Where *were* you?" the boy's mother said, holding him ferociously. "Where did you *go*?"

"I wanted to see him," he said, as if that were all the explanation necessary.

"But I told you *no*. You know better, Alan. Anything could've happened. We were worried sick."

"I'm sorry, Mom. I just *had* to see him."

"But you didn't," his father said. "So where *were* you? Why didn't you answer the announcements?"

"Oh, I saw him, Dad. I was *with* him."

"You . . . *where*?"

"He was here. He said he was waiting for me, that he'd been hoping I'd come again. He looked really different, he didn't have on his red suit or anything."

His mother shook her head. "But . . . I *looked* here."

"Oh, I *found* him here okay. But then we went to his place."

"What?" they both asked at once.

"His trailer. It's sort of like the one Grandpa and Grandma have."

"Why . . . did you go out there?" his mother asked, remembering the trailer and the car at the end of the lot.

"He asked me to."

"Alan," his father said, "I've told you never, *never* to go with anyone for *any* reason."

"But it was all right with him, Dad. I knew I'd be safe with *him*. He told me when we were walking. Out to his trailer."

"Told you *what*?"

"How he always looks for somebody."

"Oh, my God. . . ."

"What's the matter, Mom?"

"Nothing. Nothing. What else did this . . . man say?"

"He just said he always comes back this time of year, just to see if people still believe in him. He said lots of people *say* they do, but they don't, not really. He said they just say so because they want their *kids* to believe in him. But if he finds one person who really believes, and knows who he really is, then it's all gonna be okay. 'Til next Christmas. He said it's almost always kids, like me, but that that's okay. As long as there's somebody who believes in him and trusts him enough to go with him."

The boy's father knelt beside him and put his big hands on the boy's thin shoulders. "Alan. Did he touch you? Touch you anywhere at all?"

"Just here." He held up his mitten-covered hands. "My hands."

"Alan, this man played a mean joke on you. He let you think that he's somebody that he really isn't."

"Oh no, Dad, you're wrong."

"Now listen. This man was *not* Santa Claus, Alan."

The boy laughed. "*I* know *that*! I haven't believed in Santa Claus for almost a whole *month*!"

His mother barely got the words out. "Then who . . . ?"

"And you were wrong too, Mom. He didn't have any little needle holes in his hands. Just the big ones. Straight through. Just like he's supposed to."

Her eyes widened, and she put her fist to her mouth to hold in a scream. Her husband leaped to his feet, his face even paler than before. "Where's this trailer?" he asked in a voice whose coldness frightened the boy.

They strode out the door together into the late afternoon darkness. Street lights illuminated every part of the parking lot. "It . . . was there," she said, staring across at white emptiness.

"The *bastard*. Got out while the getting was good. He . . ." The father paused. "There?" he said, pointing.

"Yes. It was right over there." The boy nodded in agreement with his mother.

"It couldn't've been." He started to walk toward the open space, and his family followed. "There are no tracks. It hasn't snowed. And there's no wind." He looked at the unbroken plain of powdered snow.

"Hey! Hey, you folks!" They turned and saw the manager laboring toward them, puffs of condensation roaring from his mouth. "That your kid? He okay?"

The boy's father nodded. "Yeah. He seems to be. We were trying to find that man. Your Santa Claus. But he's . . . gone."

"Huh! You believe that? And I still owe him fourteen bucks." He turned back toward the warmth of the market, shaking his head. "Left without his money. Some people . . ."

"Never mind," his wife said. "He's all right. Let him believe." She touched her husband's shoulder.

"Maybe we should all believe. It's almost easier that way."

When they got home, the boy took off his mittens, and his father and mother saw the pale red marks, one in each palm, where he said the man's fingers had touched him. They were suffused with a rosy glow, as if the blood pulsed more strongly there. "They'll go away," the boy's father said. "In time, they'll go away."

But they did not.

—For Laurie

Some holiday ghosts require a
hard-boiled detective, okay?

But Do You Recall . . . ?

Greg Cox

Her name was Carrie Robbins, and I could tell by the
shadows under her eyes that she was haunted.

"It all started on the twenty-fifth," she explained,
"and it's been going on ever since, past New Year's.
Shaking furniture. Bumps in the night. This strange sort
of clattering sound on the roof. . . ."

"Kind of like the prancing and pawing of tiny
hooves?"

"Yeah! Exactly."

Damn, I thought, another reindeer. Just what I didn't
need.

At least she'd come to the right place. I sat behind
my desk and watched my new client pace nervously
about the small office. From outside, the lettering on
my door read TWINKLE LANE EXORCISMS (YULE
GHOULS OUR SPECIALTY). It hurt my neck to look up at
her. "Sit down," I said.

Even seated, she was taller than me. Probably five-foot-five. In her late twenties, with straight blond hair that stopped just short of her shoulders. Her smile kept trying to slide, sheepishly, off her face, giving me periodic glimpses of gum in the upper left-hand corner of her mouth. Just enough to keep my gaze focused on her lips. Like most of my clients, she seemed embarrassed to be in my office at all.

"Well, Mr. Tymn, what do you think?"

"Sounds to me like you've got one of the sleigh-deers."

"Slay?" she said anxiously.

"This is serious bad news. We're talking about holiday spirits of the upper echelons, just one tier below Old Nick himself."

"But you can't be sure of that, can you?"

"You tell me more about the manifestations, and I'll tell you how sure I am."

"Well . . ." Another nervous smile, another flash of gum. "It was probably just my imagination, but the other night I thought I saw something outside my window. Which is ridiculous because I live on the top floor of an eight-story housing project."

"Never mind that. What did you see?"

"A light. A glow. This single, blood-red ball of fire—like a huge, burning eye!"

"Nose," I corrected her, as my bad leg started to throb. Just my luck, it had to be Rudy. That, I knew, was one mean and bitter buck. Foggy night or no, he'd never quite forgotten being excluded from those stupid reindeer games.

Give Ms. Robbins points for being perceptive. Despite my best attempt at a poker face, she picked up on some of my anxiety. "I don't understand," she said. "I thought holidays were supposed to be fun!"

"They can be—when taken in moderation. Too many people get carried away with all the holiday craziness, though, and then find that the spirits they've raised won't go away just because the celebration's over. Halloween keeps most of my fellow exorcists busy all year, and there are always a few leprechauns left over after Saint Paddy's Day. Christmas, though, that's the worst."

"You sound angry. Something personal?"

Like I said, a perceptive lady. "I used to work at Macy's," I told her, which, if not the whole story, was at least part of the truth. "Where they start playing the Christmas Muzak the day after Thanksgiving. Do you know what it's like to listen to 'The Little Drummer Boy' ten times a day for four weeks?"

"Even the Bing Crosby–David Bowie version?"

"Especially that one!"

Neither of us said anything for a few moments after that. Perhaps she'd caught a note of evasion in my story and was wondering what I'd left out. Me, I felt bad about coming down so hard on a client, especially when that client was as attractive as Ms. Carrie Robbins. A cold January wind rattled the window frame, making me think of roaring fireplaces and other sources of warmth.

It was Carrie who broke the silence. "Tell me the truth, Mr. Tymn. Can you help me?"

Frankly, I didn't feel like taking on the Big R, but I'd been hooked by her haunted eyes and those peekaboo gums.

"Give me your address."

I spent the next morning down at City Hall, poring through various real estate records for reasons I hoped it wouldn't be necessary to divulge. Shortly before nightfall, I limped over to Carrie's place: a relatively new apartment complex on the Lower East Side. Not exactly luxurious, but clean and fairly safe. I remembered that Carrie said she worked as a nurse's aide.

She met me at the door of her apartment, wearing jeans, a woolen sweater, and a pair of bunny slippers. I shook the snow off my trench coat and stepped inside. "You know, you don't have to stay for this," I said nobly. "Maybe you ought to go stay with a friend tonight."

Carrie shook her head. "It's my apartment. I'm going to see this out."

She had guts. Either that or she liked my company. Or maybe she was just afraid I'd rip her off. Ah, the dizzying complexities of modern life.

I looked around the three-room apartment. The furnishings were Spartan: a couch, a television, two low end tables. The place had been recently cleaned, but I spotted telltale signs of a dangerous enthusiasm for the holidays. A smattering of pine needles in one corner of the living room. Traces of multicolored confetti. A half-empty bag of "100% Real Plastic Snow." (As opposed to what, I wondered.) No mistletoe, however. Damn.

"Care for a candy cane?" Carrie asked, pointing to a glass jar atop the TV.

"I'm allergic to peppermint."

"Figures."

Time to get down to business. I pushed the TV set and the couch against opposite walls, clearing a space more than big enough for Carrie and me. Harpo-style, I reached into the interior pockets of my trench coat and brought out a flask of eggnog, a string of silver sleigh bells, and a Ziploc bag of leftover sugar cookies. As always, it felt odd to be fighting Christmas with Christmas. Oh, well, no exorcist ever keeps his soul totally clean.

I smashed the cookies between my fingers and spread the crumbs around us, forming a protective circle. Then—and only then—I jingled the bells and uncapped the flask. Just to get Rudy's attention.

"Oh, come, all ye reindeer, unwelcome and unwanted," I sang, being careful not to sing quite the right words. A musky odor filled the room, like fur and yellow snow combined. Something scraped at the ceiling above, softly at first but with increasing fury. I almost expected a silvery hoof to come tearing through the plaster at any moment. Beside me, Carrie held onto my arm but not too tightly. So far, of course, this was nothing new to her. If anything, the raucous din overhead was far too familiar.

"God rest ye, red-nosed poltergeist, and rest ye far away. . . ."

The clattering stopped, only to resume directly in front of us, just beyond the circle of cookie crumbs. The hanging lamp that provided all the illumination in Carrie's living room dimmed and then went out entirely. In the darkness, I heard Carrie gasp, "This has never happened before!"

Both my legs—even the good one—felt like overcooked spaghetti. I tried to keep from shaking. "Don't go for the switch. Stay in the circle."

It didn't stay dark for long. A bright red spark flared into existence several feet above the floor, expanding rapidly until it cast an eerie crimson radiance over the entire scene. I felt trapped in a darkroom from Hell.

The glowing red solidified into a bulbous, incandescent sphere about the size of an average man's fist. (Mine are somewhat smaller.) Guessing what was coming next, I whispered an urgent "Hold on! Don't panic." Carrie probably thought I was talking to her.

Like an oversized Cheshire cat with antlers, Rudy materialized behind his nose.

It was an impressive sight. Animated Christmas specials notwithstanding, reindeer are *big*. Maybe Rudy was a bit of a runt, but he still took up most of the living room and part of the attached kitchenette. The jagged tines of his antlers grazed the ceiling, occasionally passing through the plaster without leaving any hole or tear behind. He snorted and stomped around us, passing over, around, and through the furniture.

Carrie's eyes widened in either fear or confusion. "But . . . but he's a ghost!"

"Of course. You don't think he's been alive all these years? What do you think the life span of a reindeer is?"

Actually, I had no idea. All I knew was that Santa's coursers hadn't been flesh-and-fur for some time.

Rudy glared at me with baleful yellow eyes. It was hard to tell what color his hairy coat was. Gray maybe, or brown. In the unholy light of that mutant nose, everything seemed splashed in blood.

The anti-carols having failed, I began my exorcism in earnest: "Unto Frosty and Kringle and into the keeping of the elves of the polar north, I consign thee, Rudolph. By the power of all calendars and the sprinkling of this eggnog, I banish thee until after the Thanksgiving Day Parade."

I spilled the thick, creamy eggnog onto Carrie's carpeted floor. Rudy reared up on his hind legs, spearing the ceiling with both antlers, and roared at me. His hot breath, redolent of roasting chestnuts, made me want to puke. The demonic strains of *The Nutcracker*, robustly performed by an unseen orchestra, assailed my eardrums, and I had to shout to make my final incantation heard: "To the top of the porch, to the top of the wall, now dash away, dash away, *dash away, all!*"

Nothing happened. I collapsed against Carrie, my lungs and vocal cords still burning from the fervor of my spell of banishment, and there was Rudy, as shaggy and malign as ever. I didn't understand. The ritual should have worked. Unless. . . .

I turned on Carrie. "You left him milk and carrots, didn't you?"

"Only on Christmas Eve," she protested. To her credit, I think she was blushing (or maybe it was only Rudy's nose). "It seemed a cute thing to do at the time."

Some people shouldn't be allowed to mess with holidays. I sighed loudly, realizing there was only one thing left to do. Dropping the useless jingle bells to the floor, I reached again into my coat pocket and brought out a membership card for a certain controversial political organization. "Listen, Rudy," I said, "I'll have you know this is a federally funded public housing project, partially supported by the local, state and municipal governments. Your presence here, as a manifestation of a major religious holiday, directly violates the separation of church and state. Thus, as a card-carrying member of the ACLU, I hereby declare you unconstitutional!"

Poof! Faster than eagles, Rudy vanished, leaving behind only the slightest whiff of reindeer musk, as well as, admittedly, a soggy mess of eggnog and cookie crumbs on the floor. So much, I thought, for my chance at the Republican nomination.

Still, perhaps there were some compensations. I put my arm around Carrie in a semiprofessional manner and said, "Don't look now, Ms. Robbins, but I think your reindeer problems are over with. For this year, at least."

"Forever!" she insisted. "I've learned my lesson. No more holidays for me."

"Well, I wouldn't go that far. In moderation, remember?" I hesitated for a moment before continuing. "Just for example, say, are you free on Valentine's Day?"

For once, her smile didn't try to sneak off her face. "Why, I think I am, Mr. Tymn."

"Call me Tiny."

A wandering ghost at Christmas
goes back a long way.

A HANDFUL OF SILVER

———

Mary Elizabeth Counselman

It was Christmas Eve and snowing hard when I
dropped into Joe's Bar and Grill after deadline time
and found a stool at the counter. Joe, bald and smiling
his gold-toothed smile, tipped me a nod.

"Evening, Mary. The usual glass of port?"

"No, make it a hot rum punch tonight, Joe. Whoo,
boy, what weather!"

I grinned back at him, shivering and beating my
numb hands together. My packages, in a leaning tower
on the floor beside me, tilted suddenly and collapsed
against the leg of the customer on the next stool.

"Sorry," I said.

I righted them with an apologetic smile at the man
hunched beside me—shabby, bearded, gaunt, and
wracked by a cough. He bent to retrieve one package
that had bounced from my grasp, and I caught a
glimpse of piercing black eyes deep-sunk in shadowed

sockets. The mouth half-hidden in the black beard was both severe and sensual. His narrow hooked nose caught my attention, as well as his marked accent. Italian? Lebanese? I could not place it.

But something about the slumped shoulders, the toneless despair in the stranger's voice, prompted me to add, impulsively, "Merry Christmas!"

He turned toward me with startling abruptness, recoiling as though I had struck him. Such misery burned from those dark eyes, I caught my breath audibly, as one might at sight of an open wound. He did not reply to my pleasantry, but merely stared for a moment, then turned back to his half-empty glass. Finishing his drink with a gulp, he moved to a nearby, recently vacated booth, with a manner less of rebuff than of humility.

He sat down wearily, gestured for another drink, and presently pulled out a small, dirty leather pouch with a draw-string. Opening it, he dumped its contents—a handful of small silver coins—on the tabletop and began to count them. In the sudden silence as the jukebox ended its chant of "Silver Bells," I overheard him mumble.

"Shanee, sh'leeshee, rve'e, chameeshee. . . ."

Hebraic, I noted idly. Some miserly old pawn-shop proprietor counting out his day's receipts. Incuriously, I glanced at the hoard, and my interest quickened.

I had not been a numismatist for years without learning to recognize a rare coin when I saw one. And these, all sixteen or seventeen of them, were both rare and extremely old. They were all alike. Their shape was roughly oval, their polished silver marred either by a dark reddish-brown stain or some sort of alloy in the metal. Peering at them more intently, I made out the likeness of a chalice on one; on another, the reverse side, that of a flowering lily. They were shekels, struck perhaps in the reign of Herod.

Burning eyes glanced up from the little pile and caught my stare. I looked away, embarrassed. Then, still with a friendly impulse born of the Christmas season, I turned to him again.

"You a coin collector?" I asked. "Nice hobby. I have a pretty fair collection myself—mostly half-dimes and Liberty nickels. If you'd like to see it sometime—I mean," I nodded at Joe, watching us laconically, as he polished a shot glass. "You a regular customer? I drop in every evening. Live around here?"

"No. No, I . . . travel," the bearded man murmured rather nervously. With one skeletal hand he raked the coins back into their pouch without offering to show them.

But one rolled off the tabletop and came to rest at my feet. I picked it up and handed it back. As our fingers touched, I noticed that the stranger's hand was colder than mine—a hard, unyielding cold, like steel, or the hand of a corpse. Involuntarily I drew back—and saw, from the expression in those hollow dark eyes, that the stranger had not missed my reaction. The thin, unnaturally red lips curled slightly in a tired smile, almost as though he had expected my revulsion.

Then his eyes softened. They traveled from my ringless left hand to my obviously pregnant waistline. Gently, without embarrassment, he murmured, "You're not in need, are you?—in trouble?"

"Me?" A smile touched my lips.

Joe, less tactful, burst out laughing. "Mary, an unwed mother? That's a hot one!" He guffawed. "Wait'll I tell Johnny!"

"Joe, knock it off!" I smiled at the bearded man. "No, I'm just another working wife. Newspaper gal.

Working as long as I dare, that is—to get the car and
the TV set paid for, before the launching! My husband's
a sports writer on the same paper. We've been married
only a year. My rings," I added, "are in hock so we
could buy an antique crib!" I turned to Joe. "Has my
lord and master been in here tonight? And *did* you tell
him to pick up that turkey we won in the raffle?"

Joe nodded. "Sure thing, Mary. He's got it and gone
home. Prob'ly has it in the oven by now if he—*Hey,
Bub*!" He broke off, smile vanishing. "You forgot to
pay for that last drink!"

The bearded man had started for the snowy street,
head down once more, shoulders slumped in a posture
of dull defeat. Seen from the rear, his neck revealed an
odd-looking red scar. Joe, noticing it also, punched me.

"Looka *that*!" he whispered. "Looks like our pal was
guest-of-honor at a lynchin' party!"

"Yeah," I gasped. "Rope-burn?"

"Sorry. I forgot." The man turned back to clink a
fifty-cent piece on the counter. Then, with a wry smile
at me—friendly, if it had not been so bitterly ironic—he
started for the street door again.

It burst open before he could reach for the knob, and
a "blind" beggar blew in with a gust of snowy wind.
His pencils and tin cup were clutched in an expensively
gloved hand, and the eyes faintly visible behind the
dark glasses sized up the sentimental atmosphere of the
place with an expert glance.

"Help the blind! Help the blind!" he intoned mechanically.

The bearded man halted. With a peculiar, hurried eagerness he pulled out the leather pouch and dropped
several of those rare, certainly valuable oval coins into
the beggar's cup with a musical clink of metal on metal.
A burning look of hope flared in the black eyes—to die

almost at once as the beggar fished out the coins, felt them, bit one, and then threw them contemptuously to the floor.

"Wise guy, huh?" he whined. "Try'n a palm off some worthless foreign money on a poor, handicapped fella. You got no shame at all, Mister?"

Light ebbed from the bearded man's eyes. With infinite weariness he stooped to retrieve his scorned donation. One coin lay half under a booth table, winking in the red and green Christmas lights like an evil eye. Perhaps it was only a trick of the light, but the dark stain seemed to have spread fractionally across its shiny surface. He returned them all to the pouch before getting heavily to his feet and heading again for the door.

Pity surged up in me for what had obviously been a fumbling attempt to do a kindness, first to me, then to the ungrateful beggar.

"Hey, Mister—wait a minute!" I called after him. Then, as he looked over his shoulder, startled, I added, "I wonder if you'd sell me one of those coins. If I'm not mistaken, they're museum pieces—first-century shekels? Probably struck in Jerusalem, maybe two thousand years ago or earlier?"

The piercing eyes met mine with a force like a physical shock. Some deep gnawing hunger in their depths made me step back involuntarily, almost fearful of their burning eagerness. I regretted my impulse, but went on:

"My husband and I are both coin collectors. If it isn't too expensive, could I buy one for him? Sort of an extra gift, to tie on to our Christmas tree. . . ?"

At mention of the season, the gaunt stranger winced visibly. Such a look of pain contorted his mouth and heavy eyebrows that I was taken aback. A faint groan issued from him, so very faint that it was just audible. The twisting lips compressed themselves in a tight line.

Eyes closed, the stranger seemed to fight for self-control. When he spoke, though, his voice was steady, but breathless with a peculiar tone of eagerness.

"These coins are not to be sold. But I will *give* you one! Gladly. *Please!* Take it. The . . . the stain will go away. . . ."

With desperate haste, he clawed out the leather pouch and extracted one of the silver pieces. He held it out to me with a trembling hand.

"Sorry, no." I laughed. "Give my husband an expensive antique that a strange man gave to me? You don't know my Johnny!" Then, as the hand proffering the coin sagged wearily: "But it would be a favor if you'd let me buy it. I know what a coin shop or museum would charge for such a rare piece. Ten dollars?" I fumbled with the catch of my handbag. "I know it's worth much more, but that's all I can afford."

The eager look had vanished from the black eyes. He shook his head dully. "You don't understand. These coins must be spent, used, given as a kindness, accepted with gratitude and without suspicion. A kindness without reward. . . ."

"I see." With a shrug I turned back to my hot rum punch.

Joe and I exchanged grimaces. Was the fellow some sort of cultist or religious crank? The big city is full of such, though their hidden motive is usually financial gain. I waited cynically for the stranger to boost his price. Instead, with an audible sigh, he moved again toward the street door.

A small boy of perhaps nine entered, brushing snow from a jacket too thin for the temperature outside. His face was red with cold, but he grinned at Joe as he thrust a wadded bill across the counter, revealing bruises like fingermarks on his thin wrist.

"Bourbon?" grunted Joe, like one repeating an old routine.

The boy nodded. Joe thrust the pint into a paper sack, rang up the sale, and went back to polishing glasses. The boy was gazing admiringly at the blinking Christmas lights and the small tree repeated in the bar mirror.

"Hey, it looks all right in here! Real *neat*!"

Joe smiled wryly. "You gonna get that camera for Christmas this year, Danny?—The one you been wantin', in the hockshop window?"

"Aw, I dunno." The boy laughed, shrugging cheerfully. "You know my ole man. 'Specially 'round Christmas and New Year's. Most of the time, though, he's okay," he added loyally. "Maybe he jist gets to missin' Mom."

"Sure." Joe nodded.

"He might even remember about the camera, though. He just might."

The boy started out, pulling up his jacket collar before facing the blizzard building up outside. Snow banked against the plate-glass window, making a dark mirror for the room. It reflected the bearded man's face as he hesitated at the door. Hope had flared once more in his haunted eyes.

"Boy?" He scrabbled hastily in the leather pouch and brought out a few of the oval coins. "Would you like a little money for yourself? Or for a present for your father?"

The urchin halted, eyeing the silver warily. "For doin' what?" he demanded, suspicious of the bearded man's over-eager expression. "Lissen—I ain't carrying no package for no *pusher*! Uh-*uh*, Mister. I ain't about to spend Christmas in no *juv court*!"

He brushed past the old man, almost rudely, and darted out into the snowy street, hugging his father's purchase. Again a look of bitter grief welled up in the old man's black eyes.

He leaned wearily against the door; a tear glistened in his dark beard. Then he started back as someone outside heaved at the portal blocked by his weight. It was flung angrily open, and a boozy blonde of middle age flounced in out of the cold.

"What's-a big idea? A gennelman would *open* the door for a lady." She glared at the bearded man, then changed her expression to one of kittenish charm as she turned to Joe. "Merry Christmas, you old whiskey-cutter! I just couldn't pass by without droppin' in."

Joe eyed her without cordiality. "No more hustlin' in here, Mae! I warned you last time. *Out!*" He jerked his thumb at the door through which she had entered. "You wanna get me closed down?"

"Well, I *never* been so insulted!" The blonde drew herself up, then winked. "All I want is a little drink. On the house, huh? One little teensy one? It's Christmas! Look, I brought you a present!" With a flourish, she laid a small hand-towel on the counter; it was baldly labeled "Central Hotel."

"Awright," Joe said. "One drink. Make it fast!"

"You're all heart, Joey boy. Here's mud in your eye."

The blonde backed toward the exit. The bearded man, with a gesture that held no mockery, opened the door for her. But as she shivered in the blast of wind from the street, his eyes shone once more with hope. Clawing out the pouch, he took out two coins and offered them.

"May I buy you a bottle? Or dinner, if you're hungry?" His voice shook like the bony hand holding out the silver.

Something about his blazing eyes repelled the blonde. Her kittenish smile vanished. She glared from the silver to the cavernous eyes. Abruptly she drew back, shaking her head.

"You got TB or something? Lissen—you can't buy no time with *me*—not for no lousy beer and maybe a hamburger. Let me *outa* here! I got a big date for later."

Chin up, she stalked out into the snowy night.

The bearded man, his hand still held out, slumped against the closing door. In the stillness, broken only by subdued traffic sounds and the monotonous jingle of a street-Santa's bell, I thought I heard him sob aloud. The old man stared at the oval coins on his palm with utter despair in his eyes—they were almost solid brown now, with little of the silver gleaming. His skeletal fingers closed over them, and his head fell back against the door, revealing again that raw, red scar circling his neck. His lips writhed; I could hear the words now. . . .

"Eloi, Eloi, lama sabachthani. . . ."

And with shocking clarity, I recalled their source. Another Man had spoken those words in His extremity—a prayer, a last cry of agony, by one dying, nailed to a wooden cross on a hill called Golgotha. . . .

With unwonted fellowship, Joe called out suddenly, "Hey, Bub—you care for another drink? On the house? You don't look so good."

The old man seemed not to have heard. Eyes tortured, he poured the rejected coins back into his pouch, counting soundlessly. Then, with a sigh like a chill wind through the branches of a bare tree, he flung open the street door and plunged into the night.

"Well, how about that?" Joe growled. "What a kook! Tryin' to give them foreign coins away one minute, and the next, refusin' to sell you one! And him with a whole sackful! How many of them things could he have been needin', now, for his own use?"

I sat silent for a moment, gulping the last of my hot

punch. A chill far more penetrating than the icy wind outside made me shiver; I longed for the comforting familiarity of the little flat my husband and I shared.

"How many? Oh, about thirty, I'd say, to buy what *he* needs." I thought of Biblical verses remembered from childhood: " '... *repented himself, and brought again the thirty pieces of silver to the chief priests and elders, saying: I have sinned in that I have betrayed the innocent. And they said: What is that to us? See thou to that. ...*' "

Joe came around the bar, concerned. "What're you talkin' about, Mary?"

" '*And he cast down the pieces of silver, and ... went and hanged himself ... !*' Even the grave rejected him, Joe. He's still walking the earth, trying to buy back his soul! Joe, *we've just met the Wandering Jew*!"

An old man's salvation is the ghost of love.

A MASQUERADE
OF VOICES

Susan Palwick

The first thing William Bernes knew after his long confusion was that his three-year-old great-granddaughter, from the vantage of her mother's arms, was snatching at the little doll that hung above his hospital bed. "No," he cried out suddenly, "don't hurt that—that's mine." These were the first words he'd spoken with a clear head since being loaded into the ambulance (how long ago? he must ask), but he saw from the averted gazes of his family that they thought he was still mired in the confusion; he had, indeed, spoken a great deal during the confusion, but none of it with a clear head.

"The toy," he told them now, terribly alarmed because it was swinging back and forth, "the little Christmas doll that Nancy put there—it saved my life."

The child, whose mother had stepped back a foot or so to remove the toy from reach, wrinkled her nose and began the series of hiccups which meant she was preparing to cry. William looked for Nancy but found only the baby's parents and his son-in-law, Nancy's husband, who stood at the foot of the bed, watching him gravely.

"How, Will? How did it save your life?"

"When everything was all confused and I didn't know where I was—why, I spotted that thing and it snapped me right out of it. Like it talked to me, said, 'You're in the hospital now, lying here in bed.' Nancy put it there. Where's Nancy?"

"Are you confused now? Tell me about being confused."

"No, no, I'm not confused now—well, except about what happened when I still was. How I got here, when. . . ."

"It's been four days, Will. You fell. Do you remember that? Falling?"

"Oh boy . . . yes, a little bit; I guess I do." He blinked, terribly weak from the effort of talking this much, of dealing with all these people, although he recognized now that they had been there through much of the confusion, too, standing above his bed looking frightened. He remembered snatches of visits, snatches of the television being on—there had been some show of little boys singing Christmas carols in an Arizona mission, which someone had put on for him because his wife, Marilyn, was in Arizona now, paralyzed by a stroke, unable to fly out to be with the family at Christmas.

"Go," she had managed to tell him, talking with half her face, and because they had been together for sixty years, he understood the rest she didn't say: silly for you not to be with the children just because I'm tied to this bed, to attendants and tubes and linen changes.

So he had hired people to care for her while he was

gone, and had flown East, been given a bedroom in
Nancy and David's house, a lovely room except that it
wasn't his own, didn't have Marilyn next door, and had
defeated him when he had to get up in the middle of the
night—furniture emerging from the darkness to bewil-
der him where no furniture should have been, so that he
had fallen with a cry which woke the household.

By the time he was loaded into the ambulance, he no
longer had any coherent idea of what was being done to
him. His perception of time had become unhinged with
an excruciating jolt when he fell, leaving him to grasp
at moments which had no sequence: a dizzying stretcher
journey down the stairs to the living room; Nancy
kneeling next to him wearing a bathrobe and her nurse's
stethoscope; someone in huge brown boots (too close to
his face), saying, "I don't like the way that leg is lying," and wrenching him, with gentle hands and kind
words which did nothing for the pain, onto a stretcher.

They had all been staying in the house: Nancy and
David's girl, her husband and the baby—everyone except Marilyn. As he was taken out of the house into a
chaos of blinking lights, swaddled in blankets, even his
head covered with a towel, they came forward and
kissed him, murmuring. Nancy rode in the ambulance
with him and held his hand, telling him she loved him,
and then he was wheeled into a desolation of white
where all the words and caresses faded into a pulsing
haze.

Dave and the children floated by with pale faces;
Nancy hung a bright red toy above his bed, "for Christmas," and millions of young girls in pink wound
through the corridors singing about bells. Later, the girls
in pink turned into little boys in white who sang in
Spanish, who bled out of the television into the white
room until they fluttered like angels above his head, and

the cold New Jersey light from the windows became the golden light he had left behind, the light which flowed through the canyons.

He had no idea where he was, then, and in his terror it was the toy which saved him. His eyes fell on that bright spot of color, the white-bearded little doll with its cheerful black button eyes and red stocking cap, all wrapped up in a red papoose with white polka dots—wrapped up like a baby, except that it was an old man, clearly; and then it told him, very distinctly, You're in the hospital, Will, all trussed up in bandages. In a hospital. That's why everything's white; and in a rush of gratitude he remembered that he, an old man like the little doll, had been wrapped up like it was now, on the stretcher going into the ambulance. He remembered the fall then, and regained what in the confusion he had lost: himself.

"Yes," he told David now, "yes, I remember falling. It's been four days? Four days since then?"

"You broke your hip, Will. It was a bad break; they had to operate. They had to put a pin in. And after the operation you were running a fever, Will, you were all doped up—for the fever and for the pain. That's why you were confused."

"My hip?" he repeated, with a sharp stab of fear. "Broken?"

"A bad break," David said gently.

"But I have to walk! I can't take care of Marilyn if I can't walk—Marilyn! Does she know? David, how long until I can walk?"

"I don't know, Will. You'll have to ask the doctor. It will probably be a while, but you'll be fine. Don't worry."

"Marilyn," he said, aghast, imagining her stuck with attendants, strangers who wouldn't even understand her because half her face was frozen. He pictured her lying there, sick with fear for him as he was for her, and unable to talk to anyone.

"Marilyn," he said again. "I have to tell Marilyn I'll be all right. That I'll be walking again as soon as I can, that I'll come back to her. I have to call her—just so she'll be able to hear my voice. Where's a telephone?" He glanced at the bedside table. "Don't I have a telephone?"

"You'll get one soon. Something's wrong with the wiring in the jack. They have to fix it."

"Well, tell Nancy to tell her, then. Where's Nancy? Why isn't she here?"

"She had some things to do, Will—errands that came up. She'll be here tomorrow, as soon as she can."

There was a small silence in which the baby whimpered, and her mother said, "We've got to be going now, Gramps. We have to get back to Boston. Get better. . . ." There was a flurry of kisses and reassurance, people bending over him because he was too weak with pain and worry to raise himself, and then they were all gone, leaving him in the cheerless room.

He looked the place over after they'd left, seeing things from the confusion which he now knew were real, and not madness: one of those plants with the bright red leaves, some presents—he vaguely recalled opening brightly wrapped boxes—a framed photograph of the baby, wearing antlers and a pout, labeled "Maura in the Pre-School Xmas Pageant." He lifted his head to peer at it a moment, puzzling over the thing, and then sank back onto his pillow with a sigh, his hip throbbing.

The toy Santa dangled merrily above the bed, laughing at him with its button eyes, and he looked away, chagrined at having thought that a bit of cloth could talk. He remembered a crib toy he and Marilyn had bought when

Nancy was born, a yellow Humpty-Dumpty with a manic grin. Nancy had grasped and gurgled at it as Maura had at this one—had in fact treasured it until she was four—but William was old, as old as the doll was made to appear, and no child to talk to toys. He hoped they wouldn't tell Marilyn how he'd behaved over a little doll; it would only make her more afraid for him.

No fear, the toy seemed to say as he was falling asleep, there's no need for fear, Will. Don't be afraid.

But that was falling asleep, when everyone heard voices.

He was afraid, very afraid, when the doctor came to see him the next day. From the confusion, like the smell from a sump which is blown downwind, wafted foul snatches of pain and bewilderment associated with this man who wore such a deadpan expression, who shut the curtain around the bed as if William were a potential embarrassment.

William had prepared himself for this interview since awakening that morning. "Never let doctors intimidate you," Marilyn had always told him, and she never had, not even after the stroke when she had been so completely at the mercy of doctors who knew so much and said so little. The doctors had said "Nursing home" with one breath, and Marilyn with half her face frozen had said "No," steadfastly. She and William had beaten them, proven that he and the visiting nurse could care for her as well as any nursing home, even with the back-breaking work, the lost sleep and fouled sheets—better, because he loved her and understood not only what she said, but what she couldn't say.

Now he spoke for both of them, as if Marilyn were here with him, drawing strength from her imagined presence to tell the doctor that he absolutely had to be home and on his feet as soon as possible, sooner than possible, because his wife needed him.

The doctor, clearing his throat and frowning down at his hands, answered, "Mr. Bernes, you have to be patient—with yourself, with brittle bones which will take a long time to heal—"

"I don't have a long time! My wife doesn't!"

"After you've gotten some strength back," the doctor continued quietly, "you may be able to use the walker, a little bit, hopping on one leg. That will depend on your balance and on how well the good leg holds up, and on your determination. You won't be able to put full weight on the injured leg for at least six months."

"Six months?"

"At least. In a few days we'll start physical therapy; you'll get a wheelchair and a walker—"

"Can I change my wife's bed from a wheelchair? Can I bathe her balancing on a walker? Tell me that, will you?"

"I'm afraid not."

"Well then, find a way I can! And stop looking at me as if you feel sorry for me. You'll have old bones too, soon enough, and you won't want pity then either!"

"Six months, Mr. Bernes. I'm sorry. I'm sure you can find good home care for your wife; rest now."

"I can't," William cried, clutching at the doctor's sleeve. "I can't rest! How can anyone expect me to *rest*? Tell me when I can go home!"

"That depends on how quickly the incision heals," the doctor said, and escaped.

Nancy came after lunch, alone, looking exhausted. "I'm sorry I wasn't here yesterday, Dad."

"No, no sorries. Nancy, the doctor says I can't walk for six months. That can't be right, can it? When David broke his ankle last year—"

"That wasn't a bad break, Dad. And he's younger."

"But six months! How will I take care of your mother?"

Nancy grimaced and sighed, covering her face with her hands. "The aides, Dad, the people you hired; they're good. They'll take care of her."

"Not like I could. Never like I could."

"Well, of course not, but it happened! You fell! You can't undo it!" She turned away then and mumbled, "I'm sorry"—Nancy who always apologized whether she needed to or not.

"For what?" Will asked gently. "For my falling? Because I was in your house, didn't know where things were? That's ridiculous."

"For yelling!" she said, nearly yelling again. "It's not fair to you, going through so much—you just can't undo it, that's all. Just . . . just give it time, do what the therapists tell you, listen to the doctors."

"Doctors!"

"Doctors," she repeated flatly. "Just don't let it defeat you, that's all."

"Well, I'm not. How could I, after your mother, the stroke—I'd be ashamed if I let a broken bone stop me. Nancy, what does she say? Does she know? She must know, because I wouldn't have gone so long without calling. Nancy, why haven't they fixed the jack yet?"

"I asked them. It's taking longer because of the holidays. It's all right, Dad; she knows. We called her."

"It's not all right! What did she say? How did she react?"

"Dad, I can't tell you much! No one can understand her on the phone, you know that, and the attendants can't understand her as well as you can, anyway. She was upset, of course. She's worried about you, she misses you, she hopes you aren't in much pain."

Too vague, too vague. Marilyn was never vague. "What did she say about the walker, about my not being able to take care of her?"

"She says you have to get well as soon as you can, that you have to get stronger—on your own account, not hers."

William nodded, even though Nancy was using her nurse's voice and he sensed she was inventing likely messages. That was what Marilyn would say, what he knew she'd say, but so far away from his wife that he feared losing touch even with his knowledge of her, he needed to hear it from someone else.

"She says," Nancy went on, "that you mustn't feel guilty about not being able to be with her, that she'll be all right."

"But she's alone! With just the attendants!"

"I know," Nancy said, and then the tightness of her face eased, the haggardness of it, as if she'd just solved a problem. "Dad, look, David and I will fly out there for a day or two. Would that make you feel better?"

"Yes, of course. But the expense—"

"No trouble," Nancy answered quickly. "We can get a flight tonight, stay there tomorrow, and fly back the next morning. Only we won't be able to visit you tomorrow, you understand?"

"I'm not daft. Go. Tell her—you know what. And call me to tell me how she is, Nancy, please; I want to hear it from you, not the aides. Isn't there another phone I can use now? In the hall, in another room?"

She answered as nurse, not daughter. "You need to sleep now. Don't worry. I'll take care of everything, I promise."

"I'll have the phone tomorrow, won't I?"

"I hope so, Dad. I'll remind the nurses about it when

I leave." William wondered what it was that made him
think she was lying.

The doll, the little toy he'd forgotten to thank Nancy
for, spoke to him a great deal that night, twirling gently
above him.

In a few more days it will be New Year's Eve, Will.
Your leg will be better by this time next year; you'll be
back in Arizona, with the canyons and the lovely light,
where everything shimmers in the heat and you can see
snow on the winter peaks.

"Oh boy," William murmured aloud, "you're quite
the prophet. What's all this for?"

Because there's no one to keep you company, the doll
laughed, and he said, "Better they should keep Marilyn
company."

Marilyn, the doll mused, who counted the rainbows
at Niagara Falls on your honeymoon—that's all the water God would have put into floods, she said, but He
keeps a promise—Marilyn who began planning a nursery the night Nancy was conceived, knowing it already, Marilyn who helped you build the house you still
live in, who was handier than you by far with a hammer
or saw, although she never much cared for sewing and
preferred your cooking to her own.

"Talkative, aren't you?" Will said, cursing the home-
sickness that put these voiceless words in his head, but
the bit about cooking reminded him of the time Marilyn
had somehow substituted baking soda for sugar in a
cake recipe, so that the batter came oozing out of its
pan. He'd been in the yard when he heard her howl of
laughter and cry of "Oh, Will, it's a monster!" Some
strange insect, he'd thought, and rushed indoors to find
her doubled over at the sight of the batter creeping, as
if it were alive, through the edges of the oven door.

He laughed aloud, inadvertently summoning a nurse who frowned at him and took his temperature, no doubt believing him in the confusion again. But he had no fever and warded off the proffered sleeping pill by explaining that he'd woken from a funny dream to which he'd gladly return, once she was kind enough to let him do so.

When the nurse left, he eyed the little doll again, with its papoose and stitched smile, wondering if he were senile, to be hearing voices and remembering all those things that had happened so long ago. "You my imagination?" he asked, frowning. "You an old man's fancy? What else would you be?"

That's enough, if it's comfort.

He grunted assent, growing tired, and held off sleep by asking, "Why a doll, then? why not just me talking to myself, and knowing it so?"

Because I was something bright, to pull you out of the confusion—something for your eyes to fall on when they wandered. And because I'm old like you and all trussed up like you are, unable to move. But cheerful—so there's hope, then, Will. See?

He nodded. Nancy had given him the toy, Nancy with her nurse's training and her clever heart, who had inherited her mother's wisdom. When Nancy, six or seven years old, was miserable with the measles, Marilyn had unearthed the manic yellow Humpty-Dumpty from some closet and hung it above the child's bed.

"When people are sick," she told the girl, "they act younger for a little while, because the part of your mind that's growing and learning new things has to stop doing that to help the medicine heal your sick body. That happens to everybody, so it's all right to have a baby toy now. I had the chicken pox when I was twelve, and I kept my teddy bear with me the whole time."

That reassured Nancy, to whom twelve had seemed ancient; William wondered if she'd remembered the incident when she bought the Santa doll. He'd have to ask her about it.

Best not, the doll counseled him. At least don't let on about voices. She'd be scared.

"Afraid of death," William suggested drowsily, and in the light from the hospital corridor the Santa seemed to wink at him from its papoose.

Maybe. Rest now.

"What would have rescued me if Nancy hadn't hung you there, I wonder? The plant? The picture of little Maura?"

Maura has her own voice, or will; plants have none people understand. Toys and animals are most likely to speak in the absence of people—but toys are better, Will, because people make them to begin with, and so the masquerade is honest.

That part puzzled him, deviating enough from sense so that he feared the return of the confusion, but he was already falling asleep, a healthy sleep with no fever or dreams that he remembered.

He didn't get his telephone the next day. Someone came early and deposited a walker in his room, its chilly angularity just out of reach, but there was no one to show him how to use it. He sat in bed and fretted, watching the stream of visitors and overworked staff in the hallways, becoming more frustrated with each jangle of a telephone in another room or at the nursing station. Nurses brushed him off with hurried explanations about holiday shortages of maintenance personnel. Finally, in desperation at his enforced solitude, he addressed the doll.

"You still there? Hey, intuition, whatever you are—say something."

Talk to the poinsettia, Will. It will help it grow.

"It doesn't talk back."

No, the doll agreed. But sometimes when you're frightened, it's best to do something useful.

"Like helping Marilyn," he replied bitterly, remembering how his devotion to her had been, in the early days after the stroke, as much a distraction from his terror as an expression of love. "If I could do that, I wouldn't be here! Six months of being useless to my wife!"

If you spend the time getting stronger, you won't be useless to anyone. The people who love you know that. You're already strong enough not to need voices anymore.

"You going away?"

Yes, and soon.

"Where? Back into my head?"

If you keep me there, that's where I'll be—with the light in the canyons and that monster cake. Talk to the poinsettia, Will, and Nancy, and Maura; talk to growing things. That's always best.

"I want to talk to Marilyn again! I want to go home!"

The aide entering the room with his lunch tray said wearily, "Everybody here wants to go home, Mr. Bernes. If it were up to us, you'd all heal up in a twinkle and be home with a click of your heels, like Dorothy, and so would we. This place is never nice, but it's ten times worse during the holidays."

As if to accentuate the point, she managed to spill a cup of soup on the bed. By the time the mess was cleaned up and the linen changed, William no longer felt like eating anything or talking to anyone. The repairman never came and the doll remained mute. Finally, unable to bear the silence and his immobility, he turned on the television set and numbed himself with news and old movies until dinner came, and long after that the blessed sleeping pill.

The doctor examined him after breakfast the next morning, probing the incision with gentle fingers. "This is coming along fine, Mr. Bernes. How's the pain? Better? Good—then you can start using the walker tomorrow. I'll notify the therapists."

"When will you know if it will be sooner than six months?"

The doctor gave him a sharp glance. "That depends on how quickly the bone knits."

William nodded, unable to contest this. "All right. Your terms, then. But is there any reason why I can't have the therapy at home?"

"None at all," the doctor said quietly. "In fact that's what we recommend, once the acute-care phase is over."

"Good. Now: when am I getting my phone? My daughter told me the jack should have been fixed yesterday, but it wasn't. The holidays, the nurses said. I need a phone."

"Of course," the doctor murmured, and William had that sense of evasion again, the one he'd gotten from Nancy before she went to Arizona. He frowned, knowing how Marilyn felt about such things. Never let hospitals intimidate you.

"I have to call my wife. Isn't there another phone I can use?"

"Your daughter and her husband are waiting outside to see you," the doctor said quickly, as if that explained something. "I'll send them in."

Oh God, William thought, his gorge rising, something's wrong, something's happened in Arizona, and that's why I've been getting the runaround—I never should have left her, never! Not for the holidays, not for anything!

He lay on the bed, marooned by his injury, trembling; after an age Nancy and David came in, their faces worn with fatigue. "Marilyn," he demanded.

"Dad," Nancy began, with evident effort, "the night you fell—"

"Marilyn?"

"She went into a coma," Nancy said, the words coming in a rush now. "We wanted to tell you, we did, but it wouldn't have made sense so soon after the operation. You were so weak."

The room was quiet, too quiet, Nancy staring at David's hands where they held her own, noises from the hall becoming distinct in the sudden silence. William drew a ragged breath, dizzy with dread and terrible certainty. "Gone, then. Or you wouldn't be telling me now."

"She died two days ago," Nancy went on. "That's why I didn't visit that day. Dad, the funeral was yesterday . . . you know she never wanted a wake—you couldn't have gone, we didn't know if you were strong enough to hear it then!" Her voice had risen; she met his gaze now, pleading. "So I told you we were going to see her, when you were so worried. To explain why we'd be gone. I'm sorry. I'm sorry!"

"Marilyn," William said, and wondered if she had felt like this after the stroke, as if half of her heart had been torn away without explanation or excuse. David, in the background, stuttered on apologies.

"She was what made you want to get well—we didn't want to pull all of that away at once, didn't want you to call and get suspicious, so we told them

not to give you a phone. Will, you must hate us for
it."

"No," William said, "I don't hate you." He stared at
the silent doll, aching, trying to find something concrete
to cling to as Nancy rattled on about the doctor having
said he seemed to be doing better now. "Give me times,
Nancy—the coma, the death, the funeral. Dates . . .
times."

Nancy swallowed. "She went into the coma the same
night you fell. Within an hour, I think. Almost like—"

"Yes. Go on."

"She died two days ago, at about four . . . five,
maybe. The funeral—it was yesterday. At ten."

"Arizona time? Noon here, then."

"Will," David said gently, "the aides did the best they
could, the hospital did—it wasn't anyone's fault, least
of all yours. You mustn't feel guilty for not being with
her. You couldn't have changed it."

"No," William answered, "I know that." It formed a
pattern now: the coma when he fell, the death the same
day the doll summoned him back from delirium, the funeral yesterday, at just the time the voice went away.
Marilyn had come to him when he needed her, in the
only way she could, and in her fashion, had tricked him
into believing the source of the voice to be himself, so
that he would accept the strengths it suggested as his
own and still have them when she had left for good—
and be comforted, thinking back on words which now
took on new meanings.

If you keep me there, that's where I'll be, the voice
had told him, and perhaps it was true; perhaps he was
more complete than he thought, even now when he felt
as though the sky had collapsed and smothered him and
he would never find his way out from under it.

He looked up at the toy, which was nothing but cloth

and yarn. "Nancy, the little doll; will you send it to Maura for me? She liked it."

Nancy and David stared at him, uncomprehending, and to reassure them and the voice which might be within him even now and perhaps himself, he turned to face the ugly aluminum walker, hating it, and said, "I still have to use this thing, don't I?"

A Christmas chiller, of a man alone and
stranded on Christmas Eve.

THE BREAKDOWN

Marjorie Bowen

The local line had broken down, as it not infrequently did, and the little group of people who had stepped out of the London express, and hurried across the platform to make the connection were left stranded, the half-dozen villages along the Somerset Marshland that were served by the tiny railway were completely cut off; the stationmaster had no consolation or even advice to offer, and it was a forlorn little group that stood irresolute under the glare of the gas-lamp.

John Murdoch left the others and asked the way to Mutchley Towers—only three miles along the high road, and he had an electric torch. The young man at once decided to walk, and leaving his baggage at the station, he struck out into the dark as the scanty conveyances of the village were being mustered for the benefit of his fellow-travellers.

When you are young, robust, contented, and just off

for your holidays after a very prosperous year, it is not such a bad thing to step out briskly on a frosty country road with the crystal facets of stars sparkling overhead and a crisp north wind whipping the blood to your face and emphasizing the warmth and comfort of a good overcoat.

It was Christmas Eve, and Murdoch was visiting an old college friend whom, though he had not seen him for some time, he had been very intimate with in his youth. Both the young men had been lucky; Murdoch was a remarkably successful lawyer, and Blanchard had succeeded to an ancient estate that had belonged to a distant kinsman; it was to view this new kingdom that this Christmas gathering had been got together, and Murdoch was looking forward to a really pleasant time in rather novel surroundings, for the busy city man had little time for any but the most conventional of holidays.

As he strode out along the hard road, leaving the lights of the village behind him, he recalled, as he had often recalled during his journey, the very charming association that he had with Blanchard. It was only a portrait, a delicate pencil drawing, touched with color, of a girl's head with black curls and a lace scarf with "Marie Blanchard" written beneath; Murdoch's youthful fancy had been strangely enthralled by this sketch—so much so that he had always been too self-conscious to ask Blanchard who it was, but the style of the drawing had led him to infer that it must be at least a hundred years old, and that Marie Blanchard had long since been dust. This, however, had not prevented the peculiar haunting loveliness of the pictured countenance from shining fitfully through his secret dreams.

And it was with an instant recollection of his visionary fancy that Murdoch had accepted this invitation.

And now, as he trudged through the star-spangled dark, he was thinking, with a delightful thrill, that he might see again that enchanting drawing or even another portrait or some delightful memorial of the vanished lady.

It was very cold; the deep mid-winter chill began to penetrate even Murdoch's fleecy coat. When he snapped on his torch the acrid sweep of electric light showed only the frozen ridges of the road and the bleak hedges, dry, hard, and lifeless as a bone.

Murdoch began to wonder how much further Mutchley Towers was and how he should find it; as his quick walking brought him no nearer any sign of human habitation. As the wild clouds began to roll over the stars he regretted his impulse to walk and flashed the torch about to discover any place or person where he could ask his way. None such appeared, and when the stars were completely obscured and a bitter sleet was cast in his face by the rising wind, the young man lost his cheerful confidence, and thought with some sharpness of yearning of the car, waiting for him at the station where he would never arrive, and the dinner preparing that would very likely be spoiled before he could sit down in comfort before it; he had not reckoned on the country being so desolate, and surely the porter's two or three miles was five or six.

As he thought thus with some impatience an upward flash of his torch clove the sleet and showed him, strangely close, a square white house, with a sign hanging in front on which was written in bold characters: THE WISHING INN.

Murdoch was almost startled to find that he had almost stumbled into a house without being aware of it, but pleased, too, and he went up to the flat home-painted door and knocked.

It was an old-fashioned inn, but rather dreary than picturesque; fluted pilasters relieved the drab front, blinds were drawn in the upper windows, and the only light was a faint glimmer behind the curtains of what was obviously the bar-parlor; the hedge came either side, right up to the house and the rough road directly to the one step. Murdoch was mentally commenting on the cold and inhospitable look of the place when the door was abruptly opened and a repulsive-looking man appeared dimly outlined against a dark passage.

"Can you tell me the way to Mutchley Towers?" asked Murdoch briskly.

"No," replied the man sullenly, "it is a long weary road from here, and no stranger could find it in the dark."

"But I must get there tonight," said Murdoch vexed. "Have you any conveyance or even someone to guide me?"

"Neither one nor the other," replied the innkeeper.

"You've no telephone? Where is the nearest? There must be somewhere a post office—a farm where I could get a trap, something—"

Murdoch looked at the forbidding inn, and then at the forlorn night.

The north wind was mounting higher with every blast, the sleet was changing to icy flakes of snow, every star was now concealed behind the oncoming storm-clouds. The young man considered that he might walk on till he dropped with fatigue and never find his way; it was quite likely that the information given at the station was wrong, or even that he had taken the wrong direction; in either case, to continue to press aimlessly through the darkness seemed foolish; better to trust till daylight to the uninviting hospitality of "The Wishing Inn."

"Can you give me some food and a bed?" he asked dubiously.

"Come inside," was the man's noncommittal reply.

Murdoch stepped across the dingy threshold, glad to be out of the blast, yet reluctant to enter the musty dusk of the passage.

"You have not many travellers here?" he suggested, "nor much custom, perhaps? You seem to be a long way from the village."

"The place is lonely," was the reply. "Will you wait in the parlor while your room is got ready for you?"

Murdoch followed him into the front room, where the light had glimmered between the folds of the drab curtains; this proved to be a lamp set on the center of a large table covered in dark green cloth that deadened the already feeble illumination; the walls were dark and dirty, a few obscure oiled prints and a case of lead-colored fish hung amongst this background, a meagre fire burnt on the open hearth; there were a few horse-hair chairs and a dull, locked cabinet.

"Good Lord," thought Murdoch, "who could have dreamt to find such an out-of-the-way place—so near the railway?"

"Are you the landlord?" he asked aloud.

"Yes," replied the queer-looking individual who had opened the door, "the place is mine."

Murdoch looked at him intently; he wore a soiled flowered dressing-gown tied tightly round his lean figure, and carpet slippers that caused him to shuffle; his head was bald, his face yellow and pinched, his look both dejected and repellent.

Murdoch glanced round, not without a shudder.

"You have a curious name," he said. "The Wishing Inn."

"There are old stories about the place," replied the

landlord with a shifty glance. "It is said that those who pass Christmas Eve here are allowed the fulfilment of one wish."

"Curious that this should be Christmas Eve!" exclaimed Murdoch. "Well, can you bring me some supper, when perhaps I can think of a wish?"

The man shuffled to the door, paused there, and glanced back.

"There are other travellers here I must consider," he grumbled gruffly, "a lady—a young lady—she must come down and warm herself here. There is no fire in her bedroom."

Murdoch's curiosity was fully roused, a woman that this man called a "young lady," staying in this wretched place on Christmas Eve!

"She is not alone?" he asked.

"She is alone, but she is waiting for someone," replied the man. "That is her wish, that he may come quickly—"

Jarred by the leer in the man's sullen tones, Murdoch turned aside, and, pulling off his dogskin gloves, busied himself warming his hands before the thin blaze.

"Bring what you have to eat at once, please," he said, knowing that it was hopeless to ask for any definite fare.

The door closed, and Murdoch tried to trim the lamp, and then with a squeaking pair of bellows to urge the pale fire; both his efforts were in vain, a cold dimness persisted in the dreary room, and neither fire nor lamp seemed to give either warmth or light!

Murdoch turned up his coat collar and sat shivering on one of the shiny horse-hair chairs. He wondered if the "young lady" upstairs was coming down to warm herself, as the dismal landlord had suggested, and whatever kind of romance it could be that chose such a place and time for its setting! Where was the tardy "he" coming from, and where did he intend to take the girl on such a night?

Christmas Eve, too, when all travel and conveniences would be suspended. The morrow was one of the most impossible days in the year for any kind of action, when the busiest cease their turmoil, and the most wretched have some shelter and peace.

So complete was the silence in which the inn was wrapped that Murdoch began to think that the landlord's tale was a mere fiction. Who would linger mute in such an icy, bleak bedroom as this place afforded?

Murdoch began to feel drowsy. He had lost the keen appetite that had urged him on the road, and regarded his ordered meal with repugnance. Huddled in the worn horse-hair chair, his mind went idly over the possible tale of the woman lurking upstairs, and then he dwelt, dreamily, on the tale of the wish—the wish on Christmas Eve—Wishing Inn!

"Now what could my wish be?" thought Murdoch, drowsily. "Supposing I was to think of something quite fantastical and foolish? Supposing I was to wish to see, to win, to love, Marie Blanchard!"

As he whispered the name, it seemed to him that a deeper chill took possession of the room that the dreary fire could not warm or the dreary lamp light; he turned round sharply, as if in apprehension.

The door was opened, though he had heard no sound, and a figure stood on the threshold.

The breath of icy air was more penetrating now and Murdoch shivered as he rose.

"Won't you come to the fire?" he said, "though I am afraid it does not give out any heat."

The figure advanced from the shadows of the passage and came to the hearth; it was Marie Blanchard as he

had seen her in the delicate sketch that had haunted his
secret fancy.

Here was every feature on which his boy's caprice
had so fondly dwelt, the straight nose, the level brows,
the dark liquid eyes, the fine black ringlets loosely confined with a silver ribbon, the slender neck and shoulders, the lace scarf and the clinging gown of fine
floating muslin; despite the attire and the bitterness of
the season she looked as fresh and blooming as if she
wandered in a shadowed summer garden.

She looked at him with the petulant, wilful yet be-
seeching expression that so well became her type of
loveliness and that in her portrait had so long haunted
Murdoch.

"He has not come," she said, "he has not come—but
you will, sir, help me to find him?"

She bent towards him, clasping her hands, and a
queer perfume, like the last breath of dying flowers,
was wafted to the young man.

"Who am I to find?" he stammered. "Are you not
Marie Blanchard?"

"Yes, I am that unfortunate woman. And I am here to
meet my lover. If he does not come they will take me
back—"

"They call this 'The Wishing Inn,' " said Murdoch.
"I wished to see you and you came."

She turned on him her sad, limpid gaze and Murdoch
shuddered.

"I used to worship a little picture of you," he continued.

Unheeding she turned towards the door.

"Oh, come, will you not help me find my lover?"
she entreated.

Murdoch, as if against her entreaties, he had not the
full use and power of his faculties, followed her to the

door, out into the black passage and then into the road, she gliding before him like a glimmer of white. Snow and wind had alike ceased and the night was one of close darkness through which faintly gleamed the dull light of two carriage lamps.

"See, my carriage is waiting!" cried Marie Blanchard. "Will you not enter and help me find my lover?"

Murdoch, as his eyes became accustomed to the encompassing gloom, discerned the dim outlines of a carriage.

"Perhaps you can put me on my way to Mutchley Towers," he said as he stepped after the slight figure of Marie Blanchard into the cavernous interior of the lumbering old-fashioned barouche, "for I," he added, vaguely, "am going to see your brother—is he not your brother—young Blanchard?"

The carriage was swinging forward now into the pitchy night; no ray of light penetrated the darkness where Murdoch sat on the chill seat, and where his companion was there was only the faintest blur of light where her white garments showed through the inky blackness.

"Help me to find my lover!" came her voice in continued anguish. "Ah, make haste to find him before it is too late!"

"Who is he, and how can I help you?" answered Murdoch, wildly, "and how can we find him? And where are you driving in this haste?"

For the carriage was bumping and jolting over what appeared to be rough heath strewn with boulders.

Murdoch pressed his face against the glass, and could just visualize whitish objects picked out for a fleeting second by the ghastly chill light of the carriage lamps.

"Where are we?" he cried. "Where are we going?"

And then he was overmastered by an overpowering desire to see his companion, and, like a lightning inspiration from another world, he thought of the electric torch lying in his overcoat pocket.

"Marie Blanchard!" he cried, as he fumbled with it, "Marie Blanchard!" as he snapped on the powerful ray of light.

The moan, "Oh help me find my lover!" faded in his ear and the torch showed an empty carriage; he saw frayed leather, worn velvet, weather-stained glass, but nothing else; he was alone in the ancient barouche.

With a feeling akin to panic he beat at the door, the crazy fastenings gave way and he was precipitated violently into the darkness.

Again before him flitted the figure of Marie Blanchard; by a kind of bluish glow that appeared to encircle her he could see her plainly; she was moving rapidly and the sound of her lamentations fell sadly on his ear as he followed her wildly, stumbling over hillocks and falling against stones.

"See, I have found him," she cried, and stopped; Murdoch was almost beside her; he could see her standing, smiling archly as in the portrait sketch, fresh and merry and gay. "Through here," she added and struck on what seemed a door. "Come, will you not see him, my dear delight?"

Murdoch hastened eagerly forward; the torch was still grasped in his hand, and without knowing it he pressed the button. A flood of white light spread in front of him, there was no woman, no door; only a heavy stone with a railing round it and frail snow outlining the inscription:

MARIE BLANCHARD
and
TOBIAS GRIEVE
1823

Murdoch wildly flashed the torch around the hillocks and graves, the stones were graves; he was in a large churchyard and the snow was falling noiselessly into the dark and silence.

With a shudder of deep and intense horror, Murdoch, keeping his torch lit, fumbled his way towards the church; as he reached the porch he saw a light, heard voices, and from a chaos of movement and darkness he heard a friend speak his name.

"You were pretty well done," grinned young Blanchard the next morning as Murdoch lingered over a late Christmas breakfast. "Why, you crept into the church like a ghost."

"I felt like one," replied Murdoch briefly. "If you hadn't been there—"

"Well, it is just the one night in the year you would have found anyone, and then it was only because we were late with decorations—but I say, old chap, how did you get so far out of your way, and why were you in such a state?"

"Oh, I don't know," replied Murdoch sheepishly. "I've been overworking lately—the dark and the cold and no food—I say," he added abruptly, "is there a place here called 'The Wishing Inn'?"

"Used to be—pulled down about a hundred years ago. Why?"

"Oh, I heard someone in the train mention it," said Murdoch. "Any story?"

"Yes. An ancestress of mine, Marie Blanchard, ran away on Christmas Eve to that inn to meet her lover— she chose that spot because a wish uttered there on that evening was supposed to come true! You know the usual tale."

"Well?"

"The poor lady wished that she might never be sep-arated from her lover—but he was found by her broth-ers on his way to the rendezvous and killed in a scuffle. He was a certain Tobias Grieve, a farmer, much beneath her, the good old days! She did the proper thing and died of a broken heart and then they relented enough to put her in his grave, so her wish came true after all."

Murdoch did not answer; he was looking intently out of the window.

"She isn't altogether a legend," continued Blanchard, "for you can still see the grave with the two names on it—and there is a sketch of her by Cosway; I liked it so I used to have it in my rooms. Do you remember? But as for 'The Wishing Inn'—"

The door opened and a girl stood on the threshold, the exact counterpart of Murdoch's vision of the night, except that she was dressed in furs and a plumed hat.

"You haven't met my sister, Marie? The same name as the lady of the adventure and rather like her, too—"

Murdoch thought of his last night's wish and his heart thrilled as he looked into the fair girl's eyes—"To meet—to—love—to—win—Marie Blanchard!"

A tale of ghostly adventure in an exotic land at
Christmas.

THE PECULIAR DEMESNE

Russell Kirk

The imagination of man's heart is evil from his youth.
—GEN. VIII:21

Two black torch-bearers preceding us and two following, Mr. Thomas Whiston and I walked
through twilight alleys of Haggat toward Manfred
Arcane's huge house, on Christmas Eve. Big flashlights
would have done as well as torches, and there were
some few streetlamps even in the lanes of the ancient
dyers' quarter, where Arcane, disdaining modernity,
chose to live; but Arcane, with his baroque conceits and
crotchets, had insisted upon sending his linkmen for us.

The gesture pleased burly Tom Whiston, executive
vice-president for African imports of Cosmopolitan–
Anarch Oil Corporation. Whiston had not been in Haggat before, or anywhere in Hamnegri. Considerably to
his vexation, he had not been granted an audience with

Achmet ben Ali, Hereditary President of Hamnegri and
Sultan in Kalidu. With a sellers' market in petroleum,
sultans may be so haughty as they please, and Achmet
the Pious disliked men of commerce.

Yet His Excellency Manfred Arcane, Minister without Portfolio in the Sultan's cabinet, had sent to
Whiston and to me holograph invitations to his Christmas Eve party—an event of a sort infrequent in the
Moslem city of Haggat, ever since most of the French
had departed during the civil wars. I had assured
Whiston that Arcane was urbane and amusing, and that
under the Sultan Achmet, no one was more powerful
than Manfred Arcane. So this invitation consoled Tom
Whiston considerably.

"If this Arcane is more or less European," Whiston
asked me, "how can he be a kind of grand vizier in a
country like this? Is the contract really up to him, Mr.
Yawby?"

"Why," I said, "Arcane can be what he likes: when
he wants to be taken for a native of Haggat, he can look
it. The Hereditary President and Sultan couldn't manage
without him. Arcane commands the mercenaries, and
for all practical purposes he directs foreign relations—
including the oil contracts. In Hamnegri, he's what
Glubb Pasha was in Jordan once, and more. I was consul here at Haggat for six years, and was made consul
general three years ago, so I know Arcane as well as
any foreigner knows him. Age does not stale, nor custom wither, this Manfred Arcane."

Now we stood at the massive carved wooden doors
of Arcane's house, which had been built in the seven-
teenth century by some purse-proud Kalidu slave trader.
Two black porters with curved swords at their belts
bowed to us and swung the doors wide. Whiston hesitated just a moment before entering, not to my surprise;

there was a kind of magnificent grimness about the place which might give one a grue.

From somewhere inside that vast hulking old house, a soprano voice, sweet and strong, drifted to us. "There'll be women at this party?" Whiston wanted to know.

"That must be Melchiora singing—Madame Arcane. She's Sicilian, and looks like a *femme fatale*." I lowered my voice. "For that matter, she *is* a *femme fatale*. During the insurrection four years ago, she shot a half dozen rebels with her own rifle. Yes, there will be a few ladies: not a harem. Arcane's a Christian of sorts. I expect our party will be pretty much *en famille*—which is to say, more or less British, Arcane having been educated in England long ago. This house is managed by a kind of chatelaine, a very old Englishwoman, Lady Grizel Fergusson. You'll meet some officers of the IPV—the Interracial Peace Volunteers, the mercenaries who keep your oil flowing—and three or four French couples, and perhaps Mohammed ben Ibrahim, who's the Internal-Security Minister nowadays, and quite civilized. I believe there's an Ethiopian noble, an exile, staying with Arcane. And of course there's Arcane's usual *ménage*, a lively household. There should be English-style games and stories. The Minister without Portfolio is a raconteur."

"From what I hear about him," Tom Whiston remarked *sotto voce*, "he should have plenty of stories to tell. They say he knows where the bodies are buried, and gets a two percent royalty on every barrel of oil."

I put my finger on my lips. "Phrases more or less figurative in America," I suggested, "are taken literally in Hamnegri, Mr. Whiston—because things are done literally here. You'll find that Mr. Arcane's manners are perfect: somewhat English, somewhat Austrian, somewhat

African grandee, but perfect. His Excellency has been a
soldier and a diplomat, and he is subtle. The common
people in this town call him 'the Father of Shadows.'
So to speak of bodies. . . ."

We had been led by a manservant in a scarlet robe up
broad stairs and along a corridor hung with carpets—
some of them splendid old Persians, other from the
cruder looms of the Sultanate of Kalidu. Now a rotund
black man with a golden chain about his neck, a kind of
majordomo, bowed us into an immense room with a
fountain playing in the middle of it. In tolerable English, the majordomo called out, after I had whispered
to him, "Mr. Thomas Whiston, from Texas, America;
and Mr. Harry Yawby, Consul General of the United
States!"

There swept toward us Melchiora, Arcane's young
wife, or rather consort: the splendid Melchiora, sibylline
and haughty, her mass of black hair piled high upon her
head, her black eyes gleaming in the lamplight. She extended her slim hand for Tom Whiston to kiss; he was
uncertain how to do that.

"Do come over to the divan by the fountain," she
said in flawless English, "and I'll bring my husband to
you." A fair number of people were talking and sipping
punch in that high-ceilinged vaulted hall—once the harem of the palace—but they seemed few and lonely in
its shadowy vastness. A string quartet, apparently
French, were playing; black servingmen in ankle-length
green gowns were carrying about brass trays of refresh-
ments. Madame Arcane presented Whiston to some of
the guests I knew already: "Colonel Fuentes . . . Major
MacIlwraith, the Volunteers' executive officer . . . Mon-
sieur and Madame Courtemanche. . . ." We progressed
slowly toward the divan. "His Excellency Mohammed

ben Ibrahim, Minister for Internal Security. . . . And a new friend, the Fitaurari Wolde Mariam, from Gondar.''

The Fitaurari was a grizzle-headed veteran with aquiline features who had been great in the Abyssinian struggle against Italy, but now was lucky to have fled out of his country, through Gallabat, before the military junta could snare him. He seemed uncomfortable in so eccentrically cosmopolitan a gathering; his wide oval eyes, like those in an Ethiopian fresco, looked anxiously about for someone to rescue him from the voluble attentions of a middle-aged French lady; so Melchiora swept him along with us toward the divan.

Ancient, ancient Lady Grizel Fergusson, who had spent most of her many decades in India and Africa, and whose husband had been tortured to death in Kenya, was serving punch from a barbaric, capacious silver bowl beside the divan. "Ah, Mr. Whiston? You've come for our petrol, I understand. Isn't it shockingly dear? But I'm obstructing your way. Now where has His Excellency got to? Oh, the Spanish consul has his ear; we'll extricate him in a moment. Did you hear Madame Arcane singing as you came in? Don't you love her voice?"

"Yes, but I didn't understand the words," Tom Whiston said. "Does she know 'Rudolph the Red-Nosed Reindeer'?"

"Actually, I rather doubt—Ah, there she has dragged His Excellency away from the Spaniard, clever girl. Your Excellency, may I present Mr. Whiston—from Texas, I believe?"

Manfred Arcane, who among other accomplishments had won the civil war for the Sultan through his astounding victory at the Fords of Krokul, came cordially toward us, his erect figure brisk and elegant. Two little wolfish black men, more barbaric foster sons than servants, made way for him among the guests, bowing, smiling with their long teeth, begging pardon in their incomprehensible dialect. These two had saved Arcane's life at the Fords, where he had taken a traitor's bullet in the back; but Arcane seemed wholly recovered from that injury now.

Manfred Arcane nodded familiarly to me and took Whiston's hand. "It's kind of you to join our pathetic little assembly here; and good of you to bring him, Yawby. I see you've been given some punch; it's my own formula. I'm told that you and I, Mr. Whiston, are to have, tête-à-tête and candidly, a base commercial conversation on Tuesday. Tonight we play, Mr. Whiston. Do you fancy snapdragon, that fiery old Christmas sport? Don't know it? It's virtually forgotten in England now, I understand, but once upon a time before the deluge, when I was at Wellington School, I became the nimblest boy for it. They insist that I preside over the revels tonight. Do you mind having your fingers well burnt?"

His was public-school English, and Arcane was fluent in a dozen other languages. Tom Whiston, accustomed enough to Arab sheikhs and African pomposities, looked startled at this bouncing handsome white-haired old man. Energy seemed to start from Arcane's fingertips; his swarthy face—inherited, report said, from a Montenegrin gypsy mother—was mobile, nearly unlined, at once jolly and faintly sinister. Arcane's underlying antique grandeur was veiled by ease and openness of manners. I knew how deceptive those manners could be. But for him, the "emergent" Commonwealth of Hamnegri would have fallen to bits.

Motioning Whiston and me to French chairs, Arcane clapped his hands. Two of the servingmen hurried up with a vast brass tray, elaborately worked, and set it upon a low stand; one of them scattered handfuls of raisins upon the tray, and over these the other poured a flagon of warmed brandy.

The guests, with their spectrum of complexions, gathered in a circle round the tray. An olive-skinned European boy—"the son," I murmured to Whiston—solemnly came forward with a long lighted match, which he presented to Arcane. Servants turned out the lamps, so that the old harem was pitch-black except for Arcane's tiny flame.

"Now we join reverently in the ancient and honorable pastime of snapdragon," Arcane's voice came, with mock portentousness. In the matchflame, one could make out only his short white beard. "Whosoever snatches and devours the most flaming raisins shall be awarded the handsome tray on which they are scattered, the creation of the finest worker in brass in Haggat. Friends, I offer you a foretaste of Hell! Hey presto!"

He set his long match to the brandy, at three points, and blue flames sprang up. In a moment they were ranging over the whole surface of the tray. "At them, brave companions!" Few present knowing the game, most held back. Arcane himself thrust a hand into the flames, plucked out a handful of raisins, and flung them burning into his mouth, shrieking in simulated agony. "Ah! Ahhh! I burn, I burn! What torment!"

Lady Fergusson tottered forward to emulate His Excellency; and I snatched my raisins, too, knowing that it is well to share in the play of those who sit in the seats of the mighty. Melchiora joined us, and the boy, and the Spanish consul, and the voluble French lady, and others. When the flames lagged, Arcane shifted the big tray slightly, to keep up the blaze.

"Mr. Whiston, are you craven?" he called. "Some of you ladies, drag our American guest to the torment!"

Poor Whiston was thrust forward, grabbed awkwardly at the raisins—and upset the tray. It rang upon the tiled floor, the flames went out, and the women's screams echoed in total darkness.

"So!" Arcane declared, laughing. The servants lit the lamps. "Rodríguez," he told the Spanish consul, "you've proved the greatest glutton tonight, and the tray is yours, after it has been washed. Why, Mr. Texas Whiston, I took you for a Machiavelli of oil contracts, but the booby prize is yours. Here, I bestow it upon you." There appeared magically in his hand a tiny gold candlesnuffer, and he presented it to Whiston.

Seeing Whiston red-faced and rather angry, Arcane smoothed his plumage, an art at which he was accomplished. With a few minutes' flattering talk, he had his Texas guest jovial. The quartet had struck up a waltz; many of the guests were dancing on the tiles; it was a successful party.

"Your Excellency," Grizel Fergusson was saying in her shrill old voice, "are we to have our Christmas ghost story?" Melchiora and the boy, Guido, joined in her entreaty.

"That depends on whether our American guest has a relish for such yarn-spinning," Arcane told them. "What's dreamt of in your philosophy, Mr. Whiston?"

In the shadows about the fountain, I nudged Whiston discreetly: Arcane liked an appreciative audience, and he was a tale-teller worth hearing.

"Well, I never saw any ghosts myself," Whiston ventured, reluctantly, "but maybe it's different in Africa. I've heard about conjure men and voodoo and witch doctors. . . ."

Arcane gave him a curious smile. "Wolde Mariam here—he and I were much together in the years when I served the Negus Negusti, rest his soul—could tell you more than a little of that. Those Gondar people are eldritch folk, and I suspect that Wolde Mariam himself could sow dragon's teeth."

The Abyssinian probably could not catch the classical allusion, but he smiled ominously in his lean way with his sharp teeth. "Let us hear him, then," Melchiora demanded. "it needn't be precisely a ghost story."

"And Manfred—Your Excellency—do tell us again about Archvicar Gerontion," Lady Fergusson put in. "Really, you tell that adventure best of all."

Arcane's subtle smile vanished for a moment, and Melchiora raised a hand as if to dissuade him; but he sighed slightly, smiled again, and motioned toward a doorway in line with the fountain. "I'd prefer being toasted as a snapdragon raisin to enduring that experience afresh," he said, "but so long as Wolde Mariam doesn't resurrect the Archvicar, I'll try to please you. Our dancing friends seem happy; why affright them? Here, come into Whitebeard's Closet, and Wolde Mariam and I will chill you." He led the way toward that door in the thick wall, and down a little corridor into a small whitewashed room deep within the old house.

There were seven of us: Melchiora, Guido, Lady Fergusson, Whiston, Wolde Mariam, Arcane, and myself. The room's only ornament was one of those terrible agonized Spanish Christ-figures, hung high upon a wall. There were no European chairs, but a divan and several leather stools or cushions. An oil lamp suspended from the ceiling supplied the only light. We squatted or crouched or lounged about the Minister without Portfolio and Wolde Mariam. Tom Whiston looked embarrassed. Melchiora rang a little bell, and a servant brought tea and sweet cakes.

"Old friend," Arcane told Wolde Mariam, "it is an English custom, Lord knows why, to tell uncanny tales at Christmas, and Grizel Fergusson must be pleased, and Mr. Whiston impressed. Tell us something of your Gondar conjurers and shape-shifters."

I suspect that Whiston did not like this soiree in the least, but he knew better than to offend Arcane, upon whose good humor so many barrels of oil depended. "Sure, we'd like to hear about them," he offered, if feebly.

By some unnoticed trick or other, Arcane caused the flame in the lamp overhead to sink down almost to a vanishing point. We could see dimly the face of the tormented Christ upon the wall, but little else. As the light had diminished, Melchiora had taken Arcane's hand in hers. We seven at once in the heart of Africa, and yet out of it—out of time, out of space. "Instruct us, old friend," said Arcane to Wolde Mariam. "We'll not laugh at you, and when you've done, I'll reinforce you."

Although the Ethiopian soldier's eyes and teeth were dramatic in the dim lamplight, he was no skilled narrator in English. Now and then he groped for an English word, could not find it, and used Amharic or Italian. He told of deacons who worked magic, and could set papers afire though they sat many feet away from them; of spells that made men's eyes bleed continuously, until they submitted to what the conjurers demanded of them; of Falasha who could transform themselves into hyenas, and Galla women who commanded spirits. Because I collect folktales of East Africa, all this was very interesting to me. But Tom Whiston did not understand half of what Wolde Mariam said, and grew bored, not believing the other half; I had to nudge him twice to keep him from snoring. Wolde Mariam himself was diffident, no doubt fearing that he, who had been a power in

Gondar, would be taken for a superstitious fool. He finished lamely: "So some people believe."

But Melchiora, who came from sinister Agrigento in Sicily, had listened closely, and so had the boy. Now Manfred Arcane, sitting directly under the lamp, softly ended the awkward pause.

"Some of you have heard all this before," Arcane commenced, "but you protest that it does not bore you. It alarms me still: so many frightening questions are raised by what occurred two years ago. The Archvicar Gerontion—how harmoniously perfect in his evil, his 'unblemished turpitude'—was as smoothly foul a being as one might hope to meet. Yet who am I to sit in judgment? Where Gerontion slew his few victims, I slew my myriads."

"Oh, come, Your Excellency," Grizel Fergusson broke in, "your killing was done in fair fight, and honorable."

The old adventurer bowed his handsome head to her. "Honorable—with a few exceptions—in a rude *condottiere*, perhaps. However that may be, our damned Archvicar may have been sent to give this old evildoer a foretaste of the Inferno—through a devilish game of snapdragon, with raisins, brandy, and all. What a dragon Gerontion was, and what a peculiar dragon-land he fetched me into!" He sipped his tea before resuming.

"Mr. Whiston, I doubt whether you gave full credence to the Fitaurari's narration. Let me tell you that in my own Abyssinian years I saw with these eyes of mine some of the phenomena he described; that these eyes of mine, indeed, have bled as he told, from a sorcerer's curse in Kaffa. O ye of little faith! But though hideous wonders are worked in Gondar and Kaffa and other Ethiopian lands, the Indian enchanters are greater than the African. This Archvicar Gerontion—he was a curiously well-read scoundrel, and took his alias from Eliot's poem, I do believe—combined the craft of India with the craft of Africa."

This story was new to me, but I had heard that name "Gerontion" somewhere, two or three years earlier. "Your Excellency, wasn't somebody of that name a pharmacist here in Haggat?" I ventured.

Arcane nodded. "And a marvelous chemist he was, too. He used his chemistry on me, and something more. Now look here, Yawby: if my memory serves me, Aquinas holds that a soul must have a body to inhabit, and that has been my doctrine. Yet it is an arcane doctrine"—here he smiled, knowing that we thought of his own name or alias—"and requires much interpretation. Now was I out of my body, or in it, there within the Archvicar's peculiar demesne? I'll be damned if I know—and if I don't, probably. But how I run on, senile creature that I am! Let me try to put some order into this garrulity."

Whiston had sat up straight and was paying sharp attention. There was electricity in Arcane's voice, as in his body.

"You may be unaware, Mr. Whiston," Manfred Arcane told him, "that throughout Hamnegri, in addition to my military and diplomatic responsibilities, I exercise certain judicial functions. To put it simply, I constitute in my person a court of appeal for Europeans who have been accused under Hamnegrian law. Such special tribunals once were common enough in Africa; one survives here, chiefly for diplomatic reasons. The laws of Hamnegri are somewhat harsh, perhaps, and so I am authorized by the Hereditary President and Sultan to administer a kind of *jus gentium* when European foreigners—and Americans, too—are brought to book. Otherwise European technicians and merchants might leave Hamnegri, and we might become involved in diplomatic controversies with certain humanitarian European and American governments.

"So! Two years ago there was appealed to me, in this capacity of mine, the case of a certain T. M. A. Gerontion, who styled himself Archvicar in the Church of the Divine Mystery—a quasi-Christian sect with a small following in Madras and South Africa, I believe. This Archvicar Gerontion, who previously had passed under the name of Omanwallah and other aliases, was a chemist with a shop in one of the more obscure lanes of Haggat. He had been found guilty of unlicensed trafficking in narcotics and of homicides resulting from such traffic. He had been tried by the Administrative Tribunal of Post and Customs. You may perceive, Mr. Whiston, that in Hamnegri we have a juridical structure unfamiliar to you; there are reasons for that—among them the political influence of the Postmaster-General, Gabriel M'Rundu. At any rate, jurisdiction over the narcotics traffic is enjoyed by that tribunal, which may impose capital punishment—and did impose a death sentence upon Gerontion.

"The Archvicar, a very clever man, contrived to smuggle an appeal to me, on the ground that he was a British subject, or rather a citizen of the British Commonwealth. 'To Caesar thou must go.' He presented a *prima facie* case for this claim of citizenship; whether or not it was a true claim, I never succeeded in ascertaining to my satisfaction; the man's whole life had been a labyrinth of deceptions. I believe that Gerontion was the son of a Parsee father, and born in Bombay. But with his very personal identity in question—he was so old, and had lived in so many lands, under so many aliases and false papers, and with so many inconsistencies in police records—why, how might one accurately ascertain his mere nationality? Repeatedly he had changed his name, his residence, his occupation, seemingly his very shape."

"He was fat and squat as a toad," Melchiora said, squeezing the minister's hand.

"Yes, indeed," Arcane assented, "an ugly-looking customer—though about my own height, really, Best Beloved—and a worse-behaved customer. Nevertheless, I accepted his appeal, and took him out of the custody of the Postmaster-General before sentence could be put into execution. M'Rundu, who fears me more than he loves me, was extremely vexed at this; he had expected to extract some curious information, and a large sum of money, from the Archvicar—though he would have put him to death in the end. But I grow indiscreet; all this is *entre nous*, friends.

"I accepted the Archvicar's appeal because the complexities of his case interested me. As some of you know, often I am bored, and this appeal came to me in one of my idle periods. Clearly the condemned man was a remarkable person, accomplished in all manner of mischief: a paragon of vice. For decades he had slipped almost scatheless through the hands of the police of a score of countries, though repeatedly indicted—and acquitted. He seemed to play a deadly criminal game for the game's sake, and to profit substantially by it, even if he threw away most of his gains at the gaming tables. I obtained from Interpol and other sources a mass of information about this appellant.

"Gerontion, or Omanwallah, or the person masquerading under yet other names, seemed to have come off free, though accused of capital crimes, chiefly because of the prosecutors' difficulty in establishing that the prisoner in the dock actually was the person whose name had appeared on the warrants of arrest. I myself have been artful in disguises and pseudonyms. Yet this Gerontion, or whoever he was, far excelled me. At different periods of his career, police descriptions of the offender deviated radically from earlier descriptions; it seemed as if he must be three men in one; most surprising, certain sets of fingerprints I obtained from five or six countries in Asia and Africa, purporting to be those of the condemned chemist of Haggat, did not match one another. What an eel! I suspected him of astute bribery of record-custodians, policemen, and even judges; he could afford it.

"He had been tried for necromancy in the Shan States, charged with having raised a little child from the grave and making the thing do his bidding; tried also for poisoning two widows in Madras; for a colossal criminal fraud in Johannesburg; for kidnapping a young woman—never found—in Ceylon; repeatedly, for manufacturing and selling dangerous narcotic preparations. The catalogue of accusations ran on and on. And yet, except for brief periods, this Archvicar Gerontion had remained at a licentious liberty all those decades."

Guido, an informed ten years of age, apparently had not been permitted to hear this strange narration before; he had crept close to Arcane's knees. "Father, what had he done here in Haggat?"

"Much, Guido. Will you find me a cigar?" This being produced from a sandalwood box, Arcane lit his Burma cheroot and puffed as he went on.

"I've already stated the indictment and conviction by the Tribunal of Post and Customs. It is possible for vendors to sell hashish and certain other narcotics, lawfully, here in Hamnegri—supposing that the dealer has paid a tidy license fee and obtained a license which subjects him to regulation and inspection. Although Gerontion had ample capital, he had not secured such documents.

Why not? In part, I suppose, because of his intense pleasure in running risks; for one type of criminal, evasion of the law is a joyous pursuit in its own right. But chiefly his motive must have been that he dared not invite official scrutiny of his operations. The local sale of narcotics was a small item for him; he was an exporter on a large scale, and Hamnegri has subscribed to treaties against that. More, he was not simply marketing drugs but manufacturing them from secret formulas—and experimenting with his products upon the bodies of such as he might entice to take his privy doses.

"Three beggars, of the sort that would do anything for the sake of a few coppers, were Gerontion's undoing. One was found dead in an alley, the other two lying in their hovels outside the Gate of the Heads. The reported hallucinations of the dying pair were of a complex and fantastic character—something I was to understand better at a later time. One beggar recovered enough reason before expiring to drop the Archvicar's name; and so M'Rundu's people caught Gerontion. Apparently Gerontion had kept the three beggars confined in his house, but there must have been a blunder, and somehow in their delirium the three had contrived to get into the streets. Two other wretched mendicants were found by the Post Office Police locked, comatose, into the Archvicar's cellar. They also died later.

"M'Rundu, while he had the chemist in charge, kept the whole business quiet; and so did I, when I had Gerontion in this house later. I take it that some rumor of the affair came to your keen ears, Yawby. Our reason for secrecy was that Gerontion appeared to have connections with some sort of international ring or clique or sect, and we hoped to snare confederates. Eventually I found that the scent led to Scotland; but that's another story."

Wolde Mariam raised a hand, almost like a child at school. "Ras Arcane, you say that this poisoner was a Christian? Or was he a Parsee?"

The Minister without Portfolio seemed gratified by his newly conferred Abyssinian title. "Would that the Negus had thought so well of me as you do, old comrade! Why, I suppose I have become a kind of *ras* here in Hamnegri, but I like your mountains better than this barren shore. As for Gerontion's profession of faith, his Church of the Divine Mystery was an instrument for deception and extortion, working principally upon silly old women, yet unquestionably he did believe fervently in a supernatural realm. His creed seemed to have been a debauched Manichaeism—that perennial heresy. I don't suppose you follow me, Wolde Mariam; you may not even know that you're a heretic yourself, you Abyssinian Monophysite: no offense intended, old friend. Well, then, the many Manichees believe that the world is divided between the forces of light and of darkness; and Gerontion had chosen to side with the darkness. Don't stir so impatiently, little Guido, for I don't mean to give you a lecture on theology."

I feared, nevertheless, that Arcane might launch into precisely that, he being given to long and rather learned, if interesting, digression; and like the others, I was eager for the puzzling Gerontion to stride upon the stage in all his outer and inner hideousness. So I said, "Did Your Excellency actually keep this desperate Archvicar here in this house?"

"There was small risk in that, or so I fancied," Arcane answered. "When he was fetched from M'Rundu's prison, I found him in shabby condition. I never allowed to police or troops under my command such methods of interrogation as M'Rundu's people employ. One of the Archvicar's legs had been broken; he was startlingly sunken, like a pricked balloon; he had been denied medicines—but it would be distressing to go on. For all that, M'Rundu had got precious little information out of him; I obtained more, far more, through my beguiling kindliness. He could not have crawled out of this house, and of course I have guards at the doors and elsewhere.

"And do you know, I found that he and I were like peas in a pod—"

"No!" Melchiora interrupted passionately. "He didn't look in the least like you, and he was a murdering devil!"

"To every coin there are two sides, Best Beloved," Arcane instructed her. " 'The brave man does it with a sword, the coward with a kiss.' Not that Gerontion was a thorough coward; in some respects he was a hero of villainy, taking ghastly risks for the satisfaction of triumphing over law and morals. I mean this: he and I both had done much evil. Yet the evil that I had committed, I had worked for some seeming good—the more fool I—or in the fell clutch of circumstance; and I repented it all. 'I do the evil I'd eschew'—often the necessary evil committed by those who are made magistrates and commanders in the field.

"For his part, however, Gerontion had said in his heart, from the beginning, 'Evil, be thou my good.' I've always thought that Socrates spoke rubbish when he argued that all men seek the good, falling into vice only through ignorance. Socrates had his own *daimon*, but he did not know the Demon. Evil is pursued for its own sake by some men—though not, praise be, by most. There exist fallen natures which rejoice in pain, death, corruption, every manner of violence and fraud and treachery. Behind all these sins and crimes lies the monstrous ego."

The boy was listening to Arcane intently, and got his head patted, as reward, by the Minister without Portfolio. "These evil-adoring natures fascinate me morbidly," Arcane ran on, "for deep cries unto deep, and the evil in me peers lewdly at the evil in them. Well, Archvicar Gerontion's was a diabolic nature, in rebellion against all order here below. His nature charmed me as a dragon is said to charm. In time, or perhaps out of it, that dragon snapped, as you shall learn.

"Yes, pure evil, defeated evil, can be charming—supposing that it doesn't take one by the throat. Gerontion had manners—though something of a chichi accent—wit, cunning, breadth of bookish knowledge, a fund of ready allusion and quotation, penetration into human motives and types of character, immense sardonic experience of the world, even an impish malicious gaiety. Do you know anyone like that, Melchiora—your husband, perhaps?" The beauty compressed her lips.

"So am I quite wrong to say that he and I were like peas in a pod?" Arcane spread out his hands gracefully toward Melchiora. "There existed but one barrier between the Archvicar and myself, made up of my feeble good intentions on one side and of his strong malice on the other side; or, to put this in a different fashion, I was an unworthy servant of the light, and he was a worthy servant of the darkness." Arcane elegantly knocked the ash off his cigar.

"How long did this crazy fellow stay here with you?" Tom Whiston asked. He was genuinely interested in the yarn.

"Very nearly a fortnight, my Texan friend. Melchiora was away visiting people in Rome at the time; this city and this whole land were relatively free of contention and violence that month—a consummation much to be desired but rare in Hamnegri. Idle, I spent many hours in the Archvicar's reverend company. So far as he could navigate in a wheelchair, Gerontion had almost the run of the house. He was well fed, well lodged, well attended by a physician, civilly waited upon by the servants, almost cosseted. What did I have to fear from this infirm old scoundrel? His life depended upon mine; had he injured me, back he would have gone to the torments of M'Rundu's prison.

"So we grew almost intimates. The longer I kept him with me, the more I might learn of the Archvicar's international machinations and confederates. Of evenings, often we would sit together—no, not in this little cell, but in the great hall, where the Christmas party is in progress now. Perhaps from deep instinct, I did not like to be confined with him in a small space. We exchanged innumerable anecdotes of eventful lives.

"What he expected to gain from learning more about me, his dim future considered, I couldn't imagine. But he questioned me with a flattering assiduity about many episodes of my variegated career, my friends, my political responsibilities, my petty tastes and preferences. We found that we had all sorts of traits in common—an inordinate relish for figs and raisins, for instance. I told him much more about myself than I would have told any man with a chance of living long. Why not indulge the curiosity, idle though it might be, of a man under sentence of death?

"And for my part, I ferreted out of him, slyly, bits and pieces that eventually I fitted together after a fashion. I learnt enough, for one thing, to lead me later to his unpleasant confederates in Britain, and to break them. Couldn't he see that I was worming out of him information which might be used against others? Perhaps, or even probably, he did perceive that. Was he actually betraying his collaborators to me, deliberately enough, while pretending to be unaware of how much he gave away? Was this tacit implication of others meant to please me, and so curry favor with the magistrate who held his life in his hands—yet without anyone being able to say that he, Gerontion, had let the cat out of the bag? This subtle treachery would have accorded well with his whole life.

"What hadn't this charlatan done, at one time or another? He had been deep in tantric magic, for one thing, and other occult studies; he knew all the conjurers' craft of India and Africa, and had practiced it. He had high pharmaceutical learning, from which I was not prepared to profit much, though I listened to him attentively; he had invented or compounded recently a narcotic, previously unknown, to which he gave the name *kalanzi*; from his testing of that, the five beggars had perished—"a mere act of God, Your Excellency," he said. He had hoodwinked the great and obscure. And how entertainingly he could talk of it all, with seeming candor!

"On one subject alone was he reticent: his several identities, or masks and assumed names, He did not deny having played many parts; indeed, he smilingly gave me a cryptic quotation from Eliot: 'Let me also wear/Such deliberate disguises/Rat's coat, crowskin, crossed staves. . . .' When I put it to him that police descriptions of him varied absurdly, even as to fingerprints, he merely nodded complacently. I marveled at how old he must be—even older than the broken creature looked—for his anecdotes went back a generation before my time, and I am no young man. He spoke as if his life had known no beginning and would know no end—this man, under sentence of death! He seemed to entertain some quasi-Platonic doctrine of transmigration of souls; but, intent on the track of his confederates, I did not probe deeply into his peculiar theology.

"Yes, a fascinating man, wickedly wise! Yet this rather ghoulish entertainer of my idle hours, like all remarkable things, had to end. One evening, in a genteel way, he endeavored to bribe me. I was not insulted, for I awaited precisely that from such a one—what else? In exchange for his freedom—'After all, what were those five dead beggars to you or to me?'—he would give me a very large sum of money; he would have it brought to me before I should let him depart. This was almost touching: it showed that he trusted to my honor, he who had no stitch of honor himself. Of course he would not have made such an offer to M'Rundu, being aware that the Postmaster General would have kept both bribe and briber.

"I told him, civilly, that I was rich already, and always had preferred glory to wealth. He accepted that without argument, having come to understand me reasonably well. But I was surprised at how calmly he seemed to take the vanishing of his last forlorn hope of escape from execution.

"For he knew well enough by now that I must confirm the death sentence of the Administrative Tribunal of Post and Customs, denying his appeal. He was guilty, damnably guilty, as charged; he had no powerful friends anywhere in the world to win him a pardon through diplomatic channels; and even had there been any doubt of his wickedness in Haggat, I was aware of his unpunished crimes in other lands. Having caught such a creature, poisonous and malign, in conscience I could not set it free to ravage the world again.

"The next evening, then, I said—with a sentimental qualm, we two having had such lively talk together, over brandy and raisins, those past several days—that I could not overturn his condemnation. Yet I would not return him to M'Rundu's dungeon. As the best I might do for him, I would arrange a private execution, as painless as possible; in token of our mutual esteem and comparable characteristics, I would administer *le coup de grâce* with my own hand. This had best occur the next day; I would sit in formal judgment during the morning, and he would be dispatched in the afternoon. I expressed my regrets—which, in some degree, were sincere, for Gerontion had been one of the more amusing specimens in my collection of lost souls.

"I could not let him tarry with me longer. For even an experienced snake handler ought not toy overlong with his pet cobra, there still being venom in the fangs. This reflection I kept politely to myself. 'Then linger not in Attalus his garden. . . .'

" 'If you desire to draw up a will or to talk with a clergyman, I am prepared to arrange such matters for you in the morning, after endorsement of sentence, Archvicar,' I told him.

"At this, to my astonishment, old Gerontion seemed to choke with emotion; why, a tear or two strayed from his eyes. He had difficulty getting his words out, but he managed a quotation and even a pitiful smile of sorts: 'After such pleasures, that would be a dreadful thing to do.' I was the Walrus or the Carpenter, and he a hapless innocent oyster!

"What could he have hoped to get from me, at that hour? He scarcely could have expected, knowing how many lives I had on my vestigial conscience already, that I would have spared him for the sake of a tear, as if he had been a young girl arrested for her first traffic violation. I raised my eyebrows and asked him what possible alternative existed.

" 'Commutation to life imprisonment, Your Excellency,' he answered, pathetically.

"True, I had that power. But Gerontion must have known what Hamnegri's desert camps for perpetual imprisonment were like: in those hard places, the word 'perpetual' was a mockery. An old man in his condition could not have lasted out a month in such a camp, and a bullet would have been more merciful far.

"I told him as much. Still he implored me for commutation of his sentence: 'We both are old men, Your Excellency: live and let live!' He actually sniveled like a fag at school, this old terror! True, if he had in mind that question so often put by evangelicals—'Where will you spend eternity?'—why, his anxiety was readily understood.

"I remarked merely, 'You hope to escape, if sent to a prison camp. But that is foolish, your age and your body considered, unless you mean to do it by bribery. Against that, I would give orders that any guard who might let you flee would be shot summarily. And, as the Irish say, "What's all the world to a man when his wife's a widdy?" No, Archvicar, we must end it tomorrow.'

"He scowled intently at me; his whining and his tears ceased. 'Then let me thank Your Excellency for your kindnesses to me in my closing days,' he said, in a controlled voice. 'I thank you for the good talk, the good food, the good cognac. You have entertained me well in this demesne of yours, and when opportunity offers I hope to be privileged to entertain Your Excellency in my demesne.'

"*His* demesne! I suppose we all tend to think our own selves immortal. But this fatuous expectation of living, and even prospering, after the stern announcement I had made to him only moments before—why, could it be, after all, that this Archvicar was a lunatic merely? He had seemed so self-seekingly rational, at least within his own inverted deadly logic. No, this invitation must be irony, and so I replied in kind: 'I thank you, most reverend Archvicar, for your thoughtful invitation, and will accept it whenever room may be found for me.'

"He stared at me for a long moment, as a dragon in the legends paralyzes by its baleful eye. It was discomfiting, I assure you, the Archvicar's prolonged gaze, and I chafed under it; he seemed to be drawing the essence out of me. Then he asked, 'May I trouble Your Excellency with one importunity? These past few days, we have become friends almost; and then, if I may say so, there are ties and correspondences between us, are there not? I never met a gentleman more like myself, or whom I liked better—take that as a compliment, sir. We have learnt so much about each other; something of our acquaintance will endure long. Well'—the intensity of his stare diminished slightly—'I mentioned cognac the other moment, your good brandy. Might we have a cheering last drink together, this evening? Perhaps that really admirable Napoleon cognac we had on this table day before yesterday?'

" 'Of course.' I went over to the bellpull and summoned a servant, who brought the decanter of cognac and two glasses—and went away, after I had instructed him that we were not to be disturbed for two or three hours. I meant this to be the final opportunity to see whether a tipsy Archvicar might be induced to tell me still more about his confederates overseas.

"I poured the brandy. A bowl of raisins rested on the table between us, and the Archvicar took a handful, munching them between sips of cognac; so did I.

"The strong spirit enlivened him; his deep-set eyes

glowed piercingly; he spoke confidently again, almost as if he were master in the house.

" 'What is this phenomenon we call dying?' he inquired. 'You and I, when all's said, are only collections of electrical particles, positive and negative. These particles, which cannot be destroyed but may be induced to rearrange themselves, are linked temporarily by some force or power we do not understand—though some of us may be more ignorant of that power than others are. Illusion, illusion! Our bodies are feeble things, inhabited by ghosts—ghosts in a machine that functions imperfectly. When the machine collapses, or falls under the influence of chemicals, our ghosts seek other lodging. *Maya!* I sought the secret of all this. What were those five dead beggars for whose sake you would have me shot? Why, things of no consequence, those rascals. I do not dread their ghosts: they are gone to my demesne. Having done with a thing, I dispose of it—even Your Excellency.'

"Were his wits wandering? Abruptly the Archvicar sagged in his wheelchair; his eyelids began to close; but for a moment he recovered, and said with strong emphasis, 'Welcome to my demesne.' He gasped for breath, but contrived to whisper, 'I shall take your body.'

"I thought he was about to slide out of the wheelchair altogether; his face had gone death-pale, and his teeth were clenched. 'What is it, man?' I demanded. I started up to catch him.

"Or rather, I intended to rise. I found that I was too weak. My face also must be turning livid, and my brain was sunk in torpor suddenly; my eyelids were closing against my will. 'The ancient limb of Satan!' I thought in that last instant. 'He's poisoned the raisins with that infernal *kalanzi* powder of his, a final act of malice, and we're to die together!' After that maddening reflection I ceased to be conscious."

Mr. Tom Whiston drew a sighing breath: "But you're still with us." Melchiora had taken both of Arcane's hands now. Wolde Mariam was crossing himself.

"By the grace of God," said Manfred Arcane. The words were uttered slowly, and Arcane glanced at the Spanish crucifix on the wall as he spoke them. "But I've not finished, Mr. Whiston: the worst is to come. Melchiora, do let us have cognac."

She took a bottle from a little carved cupboard. Except Guido, everybody else in the room accepted brandy too.

"When consciousness returned," Arcane went on, "I was in a different place. I still do not know where or what that place was. My first speculation was that I had been kidnapped. For the moment, I was alone, cold, unarmed, in the dark.

"I found myself crouching on a rough stone pavement in a town—not an African town, I think. It was an ancient place, and desolate, and silent. It was a town that had been sacked—I have seen such towns—but sacked long ago.

"Do any of you know Stari Bar, near the Dalmatian coast, a few miles north of the Albanian frontier? No? I have visited that ruined city several times; my mother was born not far from there. Well, this cold and dark town, so thoroughly sacked, in which I found myself was somewhat like Stari Bar. It seemed a Mediterranean place, with mingled Gothic and Turkish—not Arabic— buildings, most of them unroofed. But you may be sure that I did not take time to study the architecture.

"I rose to my feet. It was a black night, with no moon or stars, but I could make out things tolerably well, somehow. There was no one about, no one at all. The doors were gone from most of the houses, and as for those which still had doors—why, I did not feel inclined to knock.

"Often I have been in tight corners. Without such previous trying experiences, I should have despaired in this strange clammy place. I did not know how I had come there, nor where to go. But I suppose the adrenaline began to rise in me—what are men and rats, those natural destroyers, without ready adrenaline?—and I took stock of my predicament.

"My immediate necessity was to explore the place. I felt giddy, and somewhat uneasy at the pit of my stomach, but I compelled myself to walk up that steep street, meaning to reach the highest point in this broken city and take a general view. I found no living soul.

"The place was walled all about. I made my way through what must have been the gateway of the citadel, high up, and ascended with some difficulty, by a crumbling stair, a precarious tower on the battlements. I seemed to be far above a plain, but it was too dark to make out much. There was no tolerable descent out of the town from this precipice; presumably I must return all the way back through those desolate streets and find the town gates.

"But just as I was about to descend, I perceived with a start a distant glimmer of light, away down there where the town must meet the plain. It may not have been a strong light, yet it had no competitor. It seemed to be moving erratically—and moving toward me, perhaps, though we were far, far apart. I would hurry down to meet it; anything would be better than this accursed solitude.

"Having scrambled back out of the citadel, I became confused in the complex of streets and alleys, which here and there were nearly choked with fallen stones. Once this town must have pullulated people, for it was close-built with high old houses of masonry; but it seemed perfectly empty now. Would I miss that flickering faint light, somewhere in this fell maze of ashlar and rubble? I dashed on, downward, barking my shins more than once. Yes, I felt strong physical sensations in that ravaged town, where everyone must have been slaughtered by remorseless enemies. 'The owl and bat their revel keep. . . .' It was only later that I became aware of the absence of either owl or bat. Just one animate thing showed itself: beside a building that seemed to have been a domed Turkish bathhouse, a thick nasty snake writhed away, as I ran past; but that may have been an illusion.

"Down I scuttled like a frightened hare, often leaping or dodging those tumbled building-stones, often slipping and stumbling, unable to fathom how I had got to this grisly place, but wildly eager to seek out some other human being.

"I trotted presently into a large piazza, one side of it occupied by a derelict vast church, perhaps Venetian Gothic, or some jumble of antique styles. It seemed to be still roofed, but I did not venture in then. Instead I scurried down a lane, steep-pitched, which ran beside the church; for that lane would lead me, I fancied, in the direction of the glimmering light.

"Behind the church, just off the lane, was a large open space, surrounded by a low wall that was broken at various points. Had I gone astray? Then, far down at the bottom of the steep lane which stretched before me, I saw the light again. It seemed to be moving up toward me. It was not a lantern of any sort, but rather a mass of glowing stuff, more phosphorescent than incandescent, and it seemed to be about the height of a man.

"We are all cowards—yes, Melchiora, your husband too. That strange light, if light it could be called, sent me quivering all over. I must not confront it directly until I should have some notion of what it was. So I dodged out of the lane, to my left, through one of the gaps in the low wall which paralleled the alley.

"Now I was among tombs. This open space was the graveyard behind that enormous church. Even the cemetery of this horrid town had been sacked. Monuments had been toppled, graves dug open and pillaged. I stumbled over a crumbling skull, and fell to earth in this open charnel house.

"That fall, it turned out, was all to the good. For while I lay prone, that light came opposite a gap in the enclosing wall, and hesitated there. I had a fair view of it from where I lay.

"Yes, it was a man's height, but an amorphous thing, an immense corpse-candle, or will-o'-the-wisp, so far as it may be described at all. It wavered and shrank and expanded again, lingering there, lambent.

"And out of this abominable corpse-candle, if I may call it that, came a voice. I suppose it may have been no more than a low murmur, but in that utter silence of the empty town it was tremendous. At first it gabbled and moaned, but then I made out words, and those words paralyzed me. They were these: 'I must have your body.'

"Had the thing set upon me at that moment, I should have been lost: I could stir no muscle. But after wobbling near the wall-gap, the corpse-candle shifted away and went uncertainly up the lane toward the church and the square. I could see the top of it glowing above the wall until it passed out of the lane at the top.

"I lay unmoving, though conscious. Where might I have run to? The thing was not just here now; it might be anywhere else, lurking. And it sent into me a dread more unnerving than ever I have felt from the menace of living men.

"Memory flooded upon me in that instant. In my mind's eye, I saw the great hall here in this house at Haggat, and the Archvicar and myself sitting at brandy and raisins, and his last words rang in my ears. Indeed, I had been transported, or rather translated, to the Archvicar's peculiar demesne, to which he consigned those wretches with whom he had finished.

"Was this ruined town a 'real' place? I cannot tell you. I am certain that I was not then experiencing a dream or vision, as we ordinarily employ those words. My circumstances were actual; my peril was genuine and acute. Whether such an object as that sacked city exists in stone somewhere in this world—I do not mean to seek it out—or whether it was an illusion conjured out of the Archvicar's imagination, or out of mine, I do not know. *Maya!* But I sensed powerfully that whatever the nature of this accursed place, this City of Dis, I might never get out of it—certainly not if the corpse-candle came upon me.

"For that corpse-candle must be in some way the Archvicar Gerontion, seeking whom he might devour. He had, after all, a way out of the body of this death: and that was to take my body. Had he done the thing before, twice or thrice before, in his long course of evil? Had he meant to do it with one of those beggars upon whom he had experimented, and been interrupted before his venture could be completed?

"It must be a most perilous chance, a desperate last recourse, for Gerontion was enfeebled and past the height of his powers. But his only alternative was the executioner's bullet. He meant to enter into me, to penetrate me utterly, to perpetuate his essence in my flesh;

and I would be left here—or the essence, the ghost of me, rather—in this place of desolation beyond time and space. The Archvicar, master of some Tantra, had fastened upon me for his prey because only I had lain within his reach on the eve of his execution. And also there were those correspondences between us, which would diminish the obstacles to the transmigration of Gerontion's malign essence from one mortal vessel to another: the obverse of the coin would make itself the reverse. Deep cried unto deep, evil unto evil.

"Lying there among dry bones in the plundered graveyard, I had no notion of how to save myself. This town, its secrets, its laws, were Gerontion's. Still—that corpse-candle form, gabbling and moaning as if in extremity, must be limited in its perceptions, or else it would have come through the wall-gap to take me a few minutes earlier. Was it like a hound on the scene, and did it have forever to track me down?

" 'Arcane! Arcane!' My name was mouthed hideously; the vocal *ignis fatuus* was crying from somewhere. I turned my head, quick as an owl. The loathsome glow now appeared behind the church, up the slope of the great graveyard; it was groping its way toward me.

"I leaped up. As if it sensed my movement, the sightless thing swayed and floated in my direction. I dodged among tall grotesque tombstones; the corpse-candle drifted more directly toward me. This was to be hide-and-seek, blindman's buff, with the end foreordained. 'Here we go round the prickly pear at five o'clock in the morning!'

"On the vague shape of phosphorescence came, with a hideous fluttering urgency; but by the time it got to the tall tombstones, I was a hundred yards distant, behind the wreck of a small mausoleum.

"I never have been hunted by tiger or polar bear, but I am sure that what I experienced in that boneyard was worse than the helpless terror of Indian villager or wounded Eskimo. To even the worst ruffian storming an outpost at the back of beyond, the loser may appeal for mercy with some faint hope of being spared. I knew that I could not surrender at discretion to this *ignis fatuus*, any more than to tiger or bear. It meant to devour me.

"Along the thing came, already halfway to the mausoleum. There loomed up a sort of pyramid-monument some distance to my right; I ran hard for it. At the lower end of the cemetery, which I now approached, the enclosing wall looked too high to scale. I gained the little stone pyramid, but the corpse-candle already had skirted the mausoleum and was making for me.

"What way to turn? Hardly knowing why, I ran upward, back toward the dark hulk of the church. I dared not glance over my shoulder—no tenth of a second to spare.

"This was no time to behave like Lot's wife. Frantically scrambling, I reached a side doorway of the church, and only there paused for a fraction of a second to see what was on my heels. The corpse-candle was some distance to the rear of me, drifting slowly, and I fancied that its glow had diminished. Yet I think I heard something moan the word 'body.' I dashed into the immensity of that church.

"Where might I possibly conceal myself from the faceless hunter? I blundered into a side-chapel, its floor strewn with fallen plaster. Over its battered altar, an icon of Christ the King still was fixed, though lance-thrusts had mutilated the face. I clambered upon the altar and clasped the picture.

"From where I clung, I could see the doorway by

which I had entered the church. The tall glow of corruption had got so far as that doorway, and now lingered upon the threshold. For a moment, as if by a final frantic effort, it shone brightly. Then the corpse-candle went out as if an extinguisher had been clapped over it. The damaged icon broke loose from the wall, and with it in my arms I fell from the altar."

I felt acute pain in my right arm: Whiston had been clutching it fiercely for some minutes, I suppose, but I had not noticed until now. Guido was crying hard from fright, his head in Melchiora's lap. No one said anything, until Arcane asked Grizel Fergusson, "Will you turn up the lamp a trifle? The play is played out; be comforted, little Guido."

"You returned, Ras Arcane," Wolde Mariam's deep voice said, quavering just noticeably. "What did you do with the bad priest?"

"It was unnecessary for me to do anything—not that I could have done it, being out of my head for the next week. They say I screamed a good deal during the nights. It was a month before I was well enough to walk. And even then, for another two or three months, I avoided dark corners."

"What about the Archvicar's health?" I ventured.

"About ten o'clock, Yawby, the servants had entered the old harem to tidy it, assuming that the Archvicar and I had returned. They had found that the Archvicar had fallen out of his wheelchair, and was stretched very dead on the floor. After a short search, they discovered me in this little room where I sit now. I was not conscious, and had suffered some cuts and bruises. Apparently I had crawled here in a daze, grasped the feet of Our Lord there"—nodding toward the Spanish Christ upon the wall—"and the crucifix had fallen upon me, as the icon had fallen in that desecrated church. These correspondences!"

Tom Whiston asked hoarsely, "How long had it been since you were left alone with the Archvicar?"

"Perhaps two hours and a half—nearly the length of time I seemed to spend in his damned ruined demesne."

"Only you, Manfred, could have had will strong enough to come back from that place," Melchiora told her husband. She murmured softly what I took for Sicilian endearments. Her fine eyes were wet, though she must have heard the fearful story many times before, and her hands trembled badly.

"Only a man sufficiently evil in his heart could have been snared there at all, my delight," Arcane responded. He glanced around our unnerved little circle. "Do you suppose, friends, that the Archvicar wanders there still, among the open graves, forlorn old ghoul, burning, burning, burning, a corpse-candle forever and a day?"

Even the Fitaurari was affected by this image. I wanted to know what had undone Gerontion.

"Why," Arcane suggested, "I suppose that what for me was an underdose of his *kalanzi* must have been an overdose for the poisoner himself: he had been given only a few seconds, while my back was turned, to fiddle with those raisins. What with his physical feebleness, the strain upon his nerves, and the haste with which he had to act, the odds must have run against the Archvicar. But I did not think so while I was in his demesne." Arcane was stroking the boy's averted head.

"I was in no condition to give his mortal envelope a funeral. But our trustworthy Mohammed ben Ibrahim, that unsmiling young statesman, knew something of the case; and in my absence, he took no chances. He had Gerontion's flaccid husk burnt that midnight, and stood by while the smoke and the stench went up. Tantric magic, or whatever occult skill Gerontion exercised upon me, lost a grand artist.

"Had the creature succeeded in such an undertaking before—twice perhaps, or even three times? I fancy so; but we have no witnesses surviving."

"Now I don't want to sound like an idiot, and I don't get half of this," Whiston stammered, "but suppose that the Archvicar could have brought the thing off. . . . He couldn't of course, but suppose he could have—what would he have done then?"

"Why, Mr. Whiston, if he had possessed himself of my rather battered body, and there had been signs of life remaining in that discarded body of his—though I doubt whether he had power or desire to shift the ghost called Manfred Arcane into his own old carcass—presumably he would have had the other thing shot the next day; after all, that body of his lay under sentence of death." Arcane finished his glass of cognac, and chuckled deeply.

"How our malicious Archvicar Gerontion would have exulted in the downfall of his host! How he would have enjoyed that magnificent irony! I almost regret having disobliged him. Then he would have assumed a new identity: that of Manfred Arcane, Minister without Portfolio. He had studied me most intensely, and his acting would have adorned any stage. So certainly he could have carried on the performance long enough to have flown abroad and hidden himself. Or conceivably he might have been so pleased with his new identity, and so letter-perfect at realizing it, that he merely could have stepped into my shoes and fulfilled my several duties. That role would have given him more power for mischief than ever he had known before. A piquant situation, friends?"

Out of the corner of my eye, I saw the splendid Melchiora shudder from top to toe.

"Then how do we know that he failed?" my charge Tom Whiston inquired facetiously, with an awkward laugh.

"Mr. Whiston!" Melchiora and Grizel Fergusson cried with simultaneous indignation.

Manfred Arcane, tough old charmer, smiled amicably. "On Tuesday morning, when we negotiate our new oil contract over brandy and raisins, my Doubting Thomas of Texas, you shall discover that, after all, Archvicar Gerontion succeeded. For you shall behold in me a snapdragon, Evil Incarnate." Yet before leading us out of that little room and back to the Christmas waltzers, Arcane genuflected before the crucified figure on the wall.

The dark fantastic Christmas of a boy is explained by the supernatural in later life.

ICICLE MUSIC

—

Michael Bishop

Chimes on the roof, like icicles being struck in sequence by a small silver mallet.

Wind whistled away the icicle shards, hurled them back together somewhere above Danny's bedroom, turned their disconcerting chimes into a hair-raising electronic drone, then boomed so fiercely over cottonwood grove and nearby river that he had to suppose he'd only imagined the eerie icicle music.

Or had he? It was Christmas Eve, 1957 (to be exact, very early Christmas morning), and maybe those unearthly chimes were coming from another Soviet spaceshot, a beep-beep-beeping sputnik passing over Van Luna, polluting Kansas's atmosphere with commie radiation and a sanity-sabotaging barrage of high-frequency sound pulses. Who could say?

Danny got up. Careful not to rouse his mother (who ordinarily commuted thirty-plus miles, round-trip, to her job in personnel at McConnell Air Force Base in Wichita), he crept barefooted into the boxy little house's living room. He let the Christmas tree in the corner— light-strings unplugged, foil tinsel agleam, fragile glass ornaments minutely rotating—emerge from the gloom.

Had Santa come yet? *Ha!* Danny wasn't misled. He was twelve, had been for more than a month. And even if he hadn't just had his birthday, he hadn't believed in Santa for three or four years. And he hadn't really bought the scam of Jolly Saint Nick's year-end gift-giving since the year Esther Jane Onions let him take her bubble gum in a "kiss exchange"—a double-dare-you bet with Freddie DeVore—in the bushes behind the grain elevator off Depot Street.

Danny'd been, yeah, nine that year. The kiss exchange—Esther Jane's breath smelling just like her last name—had made him feel really funny. He would never do *that* again. It had destroyed his faith in Freddie DeVore's friendship, the inevitability of girls, and, in fact, the reliability of nearly everyone. (Even Ike with that famous grin of his, for which his folks had voted in '56, was probably a cheat in some ways, fudging golf scores and "forgetting" to report on his taxes all the money he'd won.) Anyway, E.J.'s breath, Freddie's refusal to ante up the agreed-upon Eddie Yost baseball card, Ike's secret sins, and three more disappointing years had forever numbed the kid in him.

Nine. Ten. Eleven.

And—*wham!*—he was illusion-free, a twelve-year-old dreaming of his driver's license, his first legal beer, and the full assumption of Daddy Pitts's role as head of household and chief provider. The rotten skipout. In fact, Danny hoped his dad was in jail somewhere this Christmas, or in a cardboard box over a steam grate in K.C. or Topeka, or even—sucks to him, anyhow—in a

wooden one under a pile of gooey black Kansas dirt.
It'd served the bum right.

Actually, "Santa"—Milly, Danny's mom—had already come. His main present, unwrapped, lay on the
green flannel tree skirt under the scrawny pine he'd
chopped down on Mr. Arno's place. It glinted there like
the sword of a medieval Turk.

It was the shotgun he'd begged for, a gas-operated
"automatic" 12-gauge, the kind that absorbed some of
its recoil instead of kicking back like a colicky mule.
Even in the darkness, Danny could tell that it was beautiful. His mom must have set aside ten—no, *fifteen*—
bucks a month for the better part of this past year to
buy it for him. He approached the tree, lifted and cra-
dled the gun, and let his fingers roam it from red-
velvet-edged butt plate to the evil-looking shark-fin
notch of its front bead, dumbstruck by the deadly power
in his arms.

Two small packages, wrapped, lay beside the shot-
gun, and Danny guessed that they contained shells.
Kneeling and hefting one of the boxes, he confirmed his
guess. Now he could go dove hunting with Brad Selley.
Not *now*, of course—but in the morning, after he and
Mom had had their Christmas together.

His immediate problem was that morning, even if
Mom got up at six or so, was still a good four hours
away. The wall clock in the kitchen (designed to resemble the pilot's wheel on an old-fashioned clipper ship)
said so. Figuring himself safe for a time, Danny sat
down Buddha-style, the shotgun in his lap, and meticu-
lously removed the slick red paper from one of the
boxes of shells. Then, holding his breath, he loaded the
gun, aimed it at the cockeyed angel atop the tree, faked
pulling the trigger, and faked, too, the 12-gauge's rumbling discharge: *Ka-SHOOOOOOOM!* An imaginary

explosion sloshed back and forth in his mouth and throat.

Then, upon lowering the shotgun, Danny heard the wind die. He heard a faint, panicky pawing overhead and the same dreamy icicle music that had called him from sleep. Dad had built their place near Van Luna's riverside dump, on a muddy patch of land inherited from Mom's grandparents. It was two miles from the city limits, a mile from their nearest neighbors, and the boy began to wonder if a crook—or a couple of crooks, a whole *army* of them—had cased their house, decided it was an easy hit, and showed up tonight (Christmas morning) to break in, bag up all their silverware and presents, and then skedaddle, booty-laden, into Arkansas or Oklahoma.

Danny, holding the 12-gauge, got up and backed away to the door of his own bedroom. The popping icicle music continued, as did the agitated scrabbling on the rooftop shingles. Then both the chimes and the pawing ceased, and there was only a hushed curling of wind—and Danny's heartbeat, like acorns falling into a rusted gasoline drum—to suggest that God had ever created sound waves or that the universe had ever before experienced them.

The living room had a fireplace. Dad had built it (lopsidedly, Mom accused, and the cattywampus fireplace supported this gripe) of river stones and second-rate mortar. He'd put in no damper. When it rained, huge drops whistled down the flue, hit the inner hearth, and splattered the livingroom rug with inky soot. Disgusted, Mom had stopped trying to use it. In fact, she'd stuffed the throat of the chimney with wadded-up sheets of the *Wichita Beacon* to keep the oily rain from further staining the hearth rug.

Now, to Danny's dismay, a crinkled ball of newspaper fell out of the chimney into the firebox. A second sheet cascaded down, and a third, and a fourth.

Then, a pair of booted feet appeared in the firebox, dangling down uncertainly, both boots as worn as harness leather. *Whumpf!* The boots crashed through the crumpled newspaper to the hearth. A pair of skinny legs in mud-fouled khaki materialized in the shadows above them. With a grunt and a muttered curse, a man in a heavy red-plaid coat kicked away the papers, ducked out of the firebox, and hobbled over to the tree, carrying what looked like a grungy World War II duffel bag.

Santa Claus? wondered Danny. Father Christmas? Kris Kringle? Saint Nick? Or just a chimney-shinnying thief?

The man's duffel *looked* empty. It hung down his back like a collapsed parachute. His greasy white hair squeezed out from under the roll of his red woolen sailor's cap to tickle the frayed collar of his jacket. In spite of the darkness, Danny could see the man clearly, as if his unexpected arrival had triggered an explosion of ghostly amber light.

Then, turning, the intruder looked straight at him.

Danny ducked out of sight. A moment later, though, he peered back around and saw that Klepto Kris Kringle had a pale, stubbly beard and a pair of bleak, ever-moving eyes.

What if he weren't just a thief? What if he were a rapist or a murderer? What if he had his sights on the shotgun now in Danny's arms? Assuming, as seemed likely, that he'd staked out their house and watched Mom bring it home. . . .

Danny (Danny told himself), you've waited too long. You should *do* something. You've got the draw on him, don't you? Why are you being so wishy-washy?

"Hold it, mister!" Danny said, stepping out of the

doorway and leveling the twin barrels of his shotgun on the intruder. Santa—no, the lousy burglar—twisted an ornament off the tree and hurled it all the way across the room. It struck the lintel over Danny's head, showering pieces of feathery, mirrored plastic. A flashing, quicksilver rain of tiny knives.

Ducking, Danny thumbed the safety off and shot. The blast spat flames, a burst of orange and blue that knocked Danny backward into a pile of clothes in his bedroom.

Klepto Kris howled.

The Christmas tree toppled, like a bombed pagoda bringing down all the bamboo chimes, hammered-tin animals, and folded-paper fish hanging from its dozens of eaves. The noise was *loud*. The entire house shook. Had there been an earthquake?

Golly, Danny thought, struggling to his feet. My shotgun's a gas-powered job. It's not supposed to kick.

"Danny!" his mother shouted from her own bedroom. *"Danny, hon, are you all right?"* She sounded panicked, downright rattled. For a moment Danny regretted squeezing off a pellet pattern in reply to a desperately flung Christmas-tree ornament. But all he'd done was issue a command—a reasonable command, given the circumstances—and Klepto had tried to take his head off. If the 12-gauge had been in the other guy's hands, Danny knew, *he'd* be dead now. Gut-shot by a stinking burglar on Jesus's birthday.

He met his mom outside their bedroom doors, which were across the hall from each other. At first, Klepto seemed not to be there any longer, as if he'd simply vanished, but then Mom saw a rotting boot dangling down from the throat of the chimney. *"What's that?"* She grabbed Danny's shotgun, rushed to the tree, kicked its fallen branches aside, found a box of shells, expertly loaded the shotgun, and ran to the fireplace.

Danny was already there, reaching repeatedly for the toe of the visible boot, as if it were the persnickety beak of a cottonmouth. Each time he grabbed for it, it struck back. So Danny reached and pulled away, reached and pulled away.

Who wanted to get booted in the kisser? And why, now that he thought of it, had Mom taken his shotgun? He had more right to it than she did. After all, blood dripping into the wadded-up pages of the *Beacon* proved that he'd hit his target.

Then the boot withdrew, a storm of soot whirled from the smoke chamber above the missing damper, and both he and Mom were fitfully coughing, waving their hands and colliding with each other in their attempts to back away.

When the soot storm subsided, Mom knelt and pointed the barrels of Danny's shotgun up the angled flue.

"Come down here, you snake! Who do you think you are, stealing our Christmas?"

The burglar's soot-dislodging climb went on.

Mom, fiery-eyed, shouted, "Come down or I'll shoot!"

"Don't do it," Danny warned her. "You'll hit him in the butt, maybe, but most of the pellets'll come back on us."

That was good enough for Mom. Flicking on a light as she ran, she headed through the kitchen to the back door. Danny followed, still aching to get the shotgun back but no longer conscious of the biting cold. Mom hit the porch light, ran down the steps into the yard, gimped barefoot over the brown grass to a spot from which she and Danny could see the black jut of the chimney, and reached out a hand to halt Danny beside her.

Danny gaped.

No moon sailed the indigo velvet of the Sedgwick County sky, but every star visible from the northern hemisphere had winked into being up there. He was dazzled. It was hard to make out if the smear on the roof—the bundled silhouette of the man he'd shot—was a living thing or merely a phantom of starlight, wind, and jittery shadows. Danny saw this figure hoist itself out of their chimney, stumble over a lofty plain of shingles, and fall atop a four-legged shape with a white flag for a tail and two black branches of horn for headgear.

Unless he was imagining things, there was a *deer* on their roof, a buck with twelve to fifteen points. The guy who'd tried to steal their Christmas was mounting the jumpy creature. He encouraged it—*"Up, Blitzen, up!"*—to fly him to safety over both the riverside dump and the rooftops of their sleeping town.

"Stop!" Mom shouted. "Stop or I'll shoot!" She sounded just like a sheriff on a TV cowboy show.

"No, Milly!" the man on the roof pleaded. "Don't!"

"Clifton?" Mom murmured. Then, louder: *"Clifton?"*

The compact little buck (a courser, Danny thought, like in "The Night Before Christmas," which Mrs. French had read them on the day before their holidays) soared up from the house. It lifted like a dream creature, pawing the night air and defining both itself and its desperate, neck-clutching rider against a blowing purple scrim of stars. All Danny could do was marvel. There should have been seven other reindeer (if the words of that silly poem counted for anything), but one was about all Danny could handle.

The deer—the courser—drew an invisible circle over

their backyard. Mom and he looked up to see its glinting hooves and white belly. Then the thief sprawled across the deer took a shiny ball from the pocket of his coat and nearly unseated himself sidearming it with all his wounded strength at Mom and him.

"Here's something for you, Milly!" And the stolen ornament—a second one, Danny realized—shattered on Mom's forehead.

"Ouch!"

"Merry Christmas to both you and the brat, bitch! And to all a good ni—"

Mom brushed fragments from her hair, raised the shotgun, took aim at the departing courser, and fired. Rider and mount received the ripping impact of the pellets. A cry from the man. A brief, anguished bleating from the reindeer.

The man fell headlong into the yard. The animal veered toward the dump, legs flailing, but crashed onto the barbed-wire fence Mom had put up to keep rabbits and stray dogs out of their vegetable garden. Its body crumpled the rusty strands of the fence, slicing itself open on the barbs.

Meanwhile, Mom thrust the weapon into Danny's hands and ran to the shotgunned intruder.

Danny ran to see whatever he could see.

The intruder—the would-be reindeer pilot—was dead, his neck broken and his head tilted away from his coat as if it wanted nothing to do with the hobo corpse to which it still so obviously belonged.

"Clifton," Mom said. "You stupid fool."

At his mother's direction, Danny hauled the deer off the fence, gutted it, and spent the remainder of that unending Christmas dawn butchering the deer on the back porch. They could use the venison, Mom said, and if

1958 wasn't any better than 1957 had been, they'd need a *lot* of it.

Meanwhile, Mom dragged the dead man into the dump; planted him in the cottony guts of a hide-a-bed sofa; wrestled the sofa into a mountain of ancient tires, mushy cardboard boxes, splintered orange crates, and broken tool handles; doused the heap with lighter fluid from her Ronco and a gallon of gasoline siphoned from her pink-and-charcoal Rambler station wagon; and threw a burning Winston into all that jumbled trash to light it.

The pyre burned all night, a surrealistic flickering that Danny could see through the screened-in porch on which he was processing the carcass of the flying deer. Later, Mom helped him wrap all the different cuts of meat in smooth butcher paper—steaks, roasts, spareribs, reindeer burgers. Then they washed their hands, limped into the living room, and sat down cross-legged next to the toppled tree to hunt for their presents.

"Was that Dad?" Danny said, avoiding Mom's eyes.

"Yeah."

"It didn't look like him."

"He'd changed a lot."

"Why?"

"I don't know. You'd have to ask him. Which, I guess, isn't possible anymore."

"He called that deer Blitzen. It flew."

"Yeah, well, Papa didn't always tell the truth." Mom dug the boy's only gift to her out from under a waterfall of tinsel. "Ah, this is great. How did you know I wanted a handmade ashtray? The way the colors swirl together—pretty."

"Thanks," said Danny, rubbing his shoulder.

"I'll exchange the gun for one with less kick. You've

got my word on it. Please don't let it ruin your Christmas."

Mom leaned over and kissed Danny on the nose.

Then she handed him his other presents: a complete set of the plays of William Shakespeare and a book of poetry by somebody Mom called William Butler Yeets. Danny didn't think he'd get to them very soon.

"I am—I mean, I *was*—the boy in that story," Daniel Pitts told Philip, the worried young man sitting next to his bed in a hospital room in Denver. The blinds on the only window had been hoisted; the icicles on the exterior cornice hung down like the barrels of a glassblower's panpipe.

"You don't mean me to take it as true, do you?" said Philip.

Once upon a time, Daniel had known Philip's surname. Tonight—Christmas Eve, 1987—he couldn't recall it. His memory did better with events of a decade, two decades, even thirty-plus years ago. Ancient history.

"Why not?" There were tubes in Daniel's nose. The plastic bag of an IV drip hung over him like a disembodied lung.

"Your mother killed an intruder, then burned his corpse in the Van Luna dump?"

"Yes."

"Okay, Daniel, if you say so. What about 'Blitzen'?"

"See Moore, Clement Clarke. *I* didn't name the creature."

"The creature's name's a red herring." Philip grimaced. "What about its reality?"

"Specious, I guess. At least as a courser. Mom probably shot my dad as he was fleeing into the cottonwoods. She bagged the poor deer purely by accident."

"There *was* a deer?"

"I butchered it. I used a hacksaw, a hammer, a dozen different knives. We had venison for months."

"Not a talent we'd've ever attributed to you, Daniel." Philip meant the actors and aspiring playwrights in the theater projects that Daniel raised money for and directed.

"Meat processing?" Daniel said.

Philip gave him a faint smile. "Your mother wasn't prosecuted for the slaying?"

"It was self-defense. Or property-defense, call it. Besides, no one ever found out."

"Your dad's bones are still out there in the dump?"

"I guess. But even if his bones are still there, his surviving aura isn't. Not always, anyway."

Philip wanted an explanation. Or *pretended* to want one. He was trying to be kind. Daniel was grateful. At this crucial pass, he thought it important to narrate the fallout of what happened on that long-ago Christmas morning.

"My father—his ghost, anyway—appeared to me ten years later. To the day. Christmas, nineteen sixty-seven."

"In Van Luna?"

"No. I left there after graduating high school. I vowed never to go back, Philip. A vow I've kept."

"So where were you?"

"Cross-country skiing over a meadow of snow and ice-laden trees in the northwestern corner of Yellowstone Park. A scene out of *The Empire Strikes Back*, Philip. Unearthly. Alien. Some of the trees had gusted together, and then frozen, in architectures of special-effects weirdness. The sky looked nickel-plated, but with a light behind it like thousands of smeared-out coals."

"And your dad—the ghost?"

"Hold on, okay?" Daniel opened his eyes as fully as he could, given all the plastic tubing. "I had a hemispherical tent. On Christmas Eve, I pitched it near a fountain of spruces. I snuggled deep into my sleeping bag. I listened to the crazy-lady arias of the wind. A super feeling. Peaceful. Exhilarating."

"Yeah. Alone on Christmas. Thirty-five below."

"Toward morning, before dawn, icicle music woke me. If you've never heard it, I can't explain it. A guy in a red-plaid coat was quivering like geyser steam outside my tent."

"Klepto Kris?"

"A.k.a. Clifton Pitts. He—it—sort of modulated in and out of existence with the moaning of the wind. Then he retreated, backing away toward the mountains. I had to throw on my coat and boots and go after him."

"Just what I do when I see a ghost: I chase it."

Daniel, taking his time now, breathing as if invisible crystals of ice had interthreaded the air, told Philip (who, he remembered, almost always ran lights for him) that his pursuit of his father's aura had been successful: He had caught up with it.

The ghost had questioned him, wondering why Daniel was alone on Christmas day, what he'd done with his life, and how, at his young age, he'd escaped taking up an M-16 in the war against the Reds in Southeast Asia. A Pitts—a strapping kid like Danny—should have volunteered.

"Did you tell him how you'd 'escaped'?" Philip asked.

"I told him. And he—it—retreated, fading away into the wind so that I wasn't able to follow it any longer. A bit later, after eating, I began to think I'd hallucinated the haint's visit. The cold. The high, thin air. It wasn't unlikely, the possibility my mind had played tricks."

"Sounds good to me. Better than a visitation."

"Except—"

"Yeah?"

"Right after thinking I'd hallucinated my dad's visit, I looked around and saw my sleeping bag was gone. My father—his ghost—had taken it."

"An animal dragged it off, Daniel. Some other outdoorsy dude stole it while you were chasing your mirage.

"No. There'd've been signs. Tracks. Footprints. Something. And I hadn't been gone that long."

"What would a ghost want with your sleeping bag?"

"To kill me, Philip. As soon as I recollected that it had come on an anniversary—the tenth anniversary of Clifton Pitts's death—I knew why it had come. An eye for an eye, a tooth for a tooth. On Jesus's birthday."

"A sleeping bag?"

"Not just that. As soon as I'd realized what was happening, my tent blew away. It flipped back, beat against the trees, whirled off into the clouds. I was miles from the nearest town. Without my tent or sleeping bag, I was screwed."

"But you got out okay."

"I followed some elk tracks to a hay bale left out by a tenderhearted rancher. Pure luck."

"But you did get out."

"No thanks to Papa Pitts."

"Who's haunted you every Christmas?"

"No. Only on ten-year anniversaries of that reindeer shoot in Van Luna."

Philip cocked his head. "What happened last time?"

"In seventy-seven, he materialized in an intensive-care unit in Wichita. On which occasion he stole my mother."

"You saw it?"

"It began with icicle music—this time, though, from a hospital cart turning over in a hall. Test tubes shattering." Daniel shut his eyes. "Festively."

"You'd returned to Kansas to be at your mom's bedside?"

"Yes. Dad showed, too. It annoyed him, how well I was doing. Healthy-looking, hedonistic, contented. Mom's lung cancer was a nice counterbalance for him—proof that the woman who'd killed him wasn't immortal. And that her son—*his* son as well—might also be vulnerable. In fact, after taking Mom's soul, he assured me that my heyday was over. *Our* heyday."

Daniel remembered that he had received this news while staring perplexedly at his mother's waxen face. Then the ghost—an unseen mirage to all the medical folk traipsing in and out—had begun to fade, Milly's soul—the ghost had kissed her—fading with it. How did it feel to be swallowed by a mirage?

"He told you that?" Philip said. "Our heyday was over?"

Daniel blinked a yes.

"How do you suppose he knew?"

"Who can say? Maybe he guessed. Or maybe it was just redneck spleen. A cartoon of 'Rudolph the Red-Nosed Reindeer' on a TV in a seventh-floor waiting room rubbed him wrong; he wasn't happy about the way the war'd turned out; he didn't like the peanut farmer in Washington. Grievances, grievances."

Philip got up, walked around the sick man's bed to the window. He seemed agitated. "This is another ten-year anniversary. To the day, Daniel. He's due again."

"Right. Maybe you'd better split, Philip."

"I'll drop in again tomorrow. With Mario and Trent."

"Gary," Daniel said. "I want Gary to drop in."

"Gary was a sweet man, Daniel. But he's gone. We can't recall him to us. You know that."

"I know that."

"Hang on, okay? Just hang on." Philip leaned down, touched his lips to Daniel's brow, and murmured, "Good-bye." Then, finally, finally, he exited.

The radio at the nurses' station down the hall was broadcasting carols. An intern and a candy striper were dancing together just outside Daniel's room. Someone at the other end of the floor blew a raspberry on a noisemaker. The intern peeked in, sporting a cap with plastic reindeer antlers. Daniel waved feebly to let him know his getup was amusing. Satisfied, the intern backed out.

Fa-la-la-la-*la*, la-la-la-la.

Outside Daniel's window, faint icicle music. The glassblower's panpipe hanging from the cornice had begun to melt, releasing long-pent melodies.

"Come on," Daniel murmured. "Come on."

He couldn't wait. He wanted his father's bitter ghost to get a move on. If it materialized in the room and stole his soul, that would be a welcome violation: a theft and a benediction, the first Christmas present his daddy had given him in over thirty years.

Come quickly, Father. Come.

"This generous selection would be an asset to any collection and ought to be in every library."
—*The Magazine of Fantasy & Science Fiction*

The Ascent of Wonder:
The Evolution of Hard SF
edited by
David G. Hartwell

0-312-85062-X
$35.00/$49.95 Canada